RUDDLEMOOR

RUDDLEMOOR

E. V. Thompson

HEADLINE

First published in 1995
by HEADLINE BOOK PUBLISHING

10 9 8 7 6 5 4 3 2 1

British Library Cataloguing in Publication Data

Thompson, E. V.
Ruddlemoor
I. Title
823.914 [F]

ISBN 0-7472-1265-1

Typeset by
CBS, Felixstowe, Suffolk

Printed and bound in Great Britain by
Mackays of Chatham PLC, Chatham, Kent

HEADLINE BOOK PUBLISHING
A division of Hodder Headline PLC
338 Euston Road
London NW1 3BH

RUDDLEMOOR

BOOK ONE

1893

Chapter 1

In a cleared space in front of the office of the Sharptor copper mine, Josh Retallick finished speaking and reluctantly took up his pen. Miriam, his wife, was seated on his left and mine captain Malachi Sprittle on his right. Standing about them unsmiling was the whole of their workforce, men, women and children.

Slowly and deliberately, Josh made an entry in the large leatherbound ledger on the table before him. When it was done he picked up a rocker-style blotter and carefully dried the ink on the entry.

Not until he was fully satisfied did he put down the blotter and slowly close the ledger. The action caused a brief stir among the watching men and women, but still no one said anything.

Thin leather laces were glued into the binding of the ledger. Tying them together in a neat bow, Josh sat back in his chair. Only Miriam knew the depths of anguish he was feeling at this moment. In the darkness of the bedroom of their moorland home, Josh had spent much of the previous night agonising about the decision that he was having to take.

Visibly moved, it was some moments before he could gather enough composure to speak, and Miriam reached out a hand to squeeze his arm in an affectionate and supportive gesture.

Josh was in his late-sixties now. Tall and upright, he boasted that he was as fit as most men half his age, but at this moment he looked gaunt and strained. Resting a hand on the closed ledger, he looked slowly from face to face of those who stood about him.

When he finally spoke, his voice was charged with emotion.

'You've just witnessed the last entry in the ledger of the Sharptor mine. All debts are settled and everyone who works for me has been paid off. The working life of Sharptor has finally come to an end.'

His words released a sudden babble of sound. It was as though no one had dared speak whilst the last rites were being administered to the already deceased mine.

'It's a sad day, Josh – especially for you.' The sentiment was expressed hesitantly by Malachi Sprittle, whom fate had decreed would be the last captain of the Sharptor Mine.

'A day I hoped would never come to pass,' agreed Josh, aware of Miriam's hand on his arm and trying his best to control the emotion he

3

felt. 'But we've kept going for longer than most. No one knows better than you that the mine should have shut down years ago. We've been working at a loss for the past five years – and struggling to break even for many years before that.'

As those who had lost their livelihood on the mine began to drift away with undisguised reluctance, Josh looked out across the wide Tamar Valley. Beginning at the edge of the slope below Sharptor, it stretched for as far as a man could see, all the way from Bodmin Moor to its much larger sister moor, Dartmoor, no more than a faint upland mass on the far horizon.

Born on Sharptor, Josh's earliest memories were of the view before him now. He had no need to count the chimneys of the engine-houses that stood tall in the near-distance, rising above everything about them.

There were eleven in number. For very many years he had stood here on this spot, watching the smoke belching from those same chimneys. Weather vanes for the capricious wind, they had also been barometers of the fortunes of Cornwall's equally unpredictable mining industry.

Smoke rising from an engine-house chimney signalled a return on the investments made by the mining adventurers. It also indicated that money was going into some five thousand homes, providing food, clothing and warmth for the occupants and dignity for the man of the house.

Today there was no smoke. Washed clean by the previous night's rain, the sky between chimney and heaven was unblemished by God or man.

Josh surveyed the scene with great sadness. During his lifetime he had witnessed both the heyday and the passing of an industry that had been an integral part of Cornwall for some centuries.

'Do you still intend staying on at the house here?'

Miriam put the question to Malachi who had stood up and was standing silently beside him.

'If that's all right with you and Josh? Maggie and I are too old to move on now, Miriam. Our needs are small and I've got a bit of money put by. What with the garden and a pig or two, we'll manage comfortably enough.'

'You don't need to ask me if it will be all right, Malachi,' replied Josh, without shifting his gaze from the panoramic view before him.

He would no doubt be leaving Bodmin Moor soon and knew this was what he would miss most of all. It was something he did not want to think about too deeply.

He and Miriam had already spent many hours debating the matter. They had both accumulated sufficient years and money to retire if they so wished. However, Josh had made the decision to move to China clay country and continue to work. That way they could guarantee employment to those who had loyally served them for years and who would otherwise be left with little prospect of ever working again. The Sharptor mine had been one of only a handful still operating on Bodmin Moor.

Returning his thoughts to Malachi, Josh said, 'I've told you, the house is yours. It's a return for all the years of service you've given to the Sharptor mine. You'll not need to want for anything, either. Copper mining might have come to an end, but I have money coming in from my China clay shares. I've never regretted buying them. If I hadn't, the mine would have closed nigh on twenty years ago. As it is, clay will provide work for any of the Sharptor men who are prepared to move. For their families too.'

'The women will push their menfolk into moving, Josh,' said Miriam. 'They'll need to have money coming into the household – though they'll be as sad as anyone else to move from here.'

'I'm not so sure all the men will be able to make the change.' Malachi shook his head doubtfully. 'You can't tell a mole it's got to change its habits and live above ground like a mouse.'

'They've either got to change or leave Cornwall – leave England. Mining has always been my life and that of my father before me, but it's all but finished, Malachi, as all thinking men know.'

'It's not logic but emotion involved here, Josh. For most of us mining comes as natural as breathing, or eating. It's difficult for men to imagine life without a mine on their doorstep.'

Josh made a gesture of hopelessness. 'We've all got to learn that times have changed. Future generations are going to grow up without the clatter of a stamp in their ears. They'll never have heard the earth-shaking thud of a beam-engine. It's sad, Malachi, but that's the truth of the matter.'

As silence fell between the two men, Miriam looked up sharply. There was a sudden commotion among the crowd moving down the slope towards Henwood village. Suddenly men and women began turning back to the mine, following a young man who came up the hill at an unsteady run.

When he picked out Josh, he headed towards him, scrambling to his feet quickly when he slipped on a patch of mud.

'Mr Retallick . . .' standing splay-legged before Josh, the man gasped out his words, fighting for breath, 'the Notter mine . . . engine-house has collapsed . . . The beam's slid down the main shaft . . . carried tackle and ladders away. Men too. The cap'n says we haven't enough men above ground to set to and bring 'em out. We need help . . .'

A few moments before, Josh and the men with him had been feeling sorry for themselves because of the closure of the Sharptor mine. All such feelings disappeared immediately they heard the distraught man's words.

Josh knew the Notter mine well. Situated on a hill on the far side of

5

Henwood village it had experienced a decline similar to that which had hit Sharptor. However, unlike Sharptor, the mine had attempted to maintain production by economising on such things as maintenance. Their engineer had left the year before. Recently, Josh had heard rumours that the engine was 'running rough' and shaking the engine-house apart.

There would undoubtedly be miners hurt in the Notter mine disaster. Men whose need for work had forced them to keep to themselves any misgivings they might have had about safety on the mine.

'Malachi, take all the surface men to Notter with you right away. Seth –' he turned to his below-ground captain, 'collect as many shift-men as you can find. Miriam, can you and the women find bandages and anything else that might be used for injured men? Sam, bring a couple of wagons with tackle for lifting – spare horses too, for winching up. The Notter mine's been running down for a long time, they'll have little rescue equipment to hand.'

Miners who had been listening to Josh's instructions were running to various parts of Sharptor as he talked. They shouted to others still returning. Men and women ran to help, according to their capabilities.

Some headed off immediately for the Notter mine. Others, older or less able, helped to load the wagons that would carry rescue equipment to the scene of the accident.

Every man, woman and child worked to the limit of his or her strength. All had known mine tragedies in the area before and each had suffered some degree of loss.

Death was a notorious stealer of husbands and fathers. He stood constantly by the shoulder of a miner.

Suddenly, the troubles of the Sharptor mine were brought into perspective and set to one side. This was the dark side of mining that would never need to be experienced again by the Sharptor community.

Chapter 2

When Josh arrived at the Notter mine he was presented with a scene of chaos. A large part of the stone wall of the engine-house had collapsed. Rubble and broken beams from the house were strewn around the head of the shaft, immediately beneath the spot where the giant iron bob of the beam-engine had been. Spars from the pithead structure protruded from the shaft entrance. Many more would have fallen into the shaft.

Men were milling amidst the wreckage about the gaping shaft, but none appeared to be doing anything useful. Josh looked for injured men around the engine-house. To his surprise there were none to be seen.

When he met up with Malachi Sprittle, the ageing Sharptor mine captain, Josh learned the reason.

'We're having problems getting to the men underground, Josh. The bob carried the ladders away for at least ten fathoms when it fell. It's jammed, with the rest of the pithead gear, about forty or fifty fathoms down the shaft. I winched a man down there as soon as I arrived. He's just come to the surface and says it's a dangerous mess. We don't know what's holding the bob. It could break free again at any moment.'

'What about the adit? Haven't any of the underground men come out that way?'

The adit was a drainage tunnel, dug through the hillside to the main workings. It should have provided an escape route for any men trapped in the mine.

'This isn't the Sharptor, Josh. Things have been let go. All the lower levels are flooded because the adit tunnel collapsed and no one did anything about it.'

'How many men are underground?'

Malachi shook his head. 'No one knows for certain. Twelve at least. Possibly twice that number.'

'We've got to do something to bring them out. Where's the man who was winched down the shaft?'

A small crowd of Sharptor miners had gathered around them. Aware there were men below ground to be rescued, they looked to Josh and the Sharptor mine captain to give them orders. One of their number stepped forward now.

'I went down, Mr Retallick.'

Josh knew the man. He was an experienced miner. Any report he

7

gave would be accurate. He nodded his head in silent acknowledgement of the man's courage. A tangle of broken and dangerous pitwork still hung over the shaft opening. It could have fallen at any time.

'The adit's blocked. Our only chance of reaching the men underground is to clear the shaft. What's it like down there?'

The Sharptor man shook his head doubtfully. 'It's a mess, Mr Retallick. The end of the bob's poking up through a whole jumble of timbers, ladders and the like. I don't know what the other end's resting on, but there's a lot of weight in a bob. It could go at any time – and there's nigh a hundred fathoms of shaft down below the blockage.'

'There's no other way in. We can probably blast enough of the tangle away to get the men up, but they need to be warned first, otherwise some of them are likely to be trying to climb the shaft. We also need to place the charge *beneath* the wreckage. Do you think it's at all possible for anyone to get through?'

The miner shook his head, but with less certainty this time. 'There *are* spaces among the wreckage, but they're very small. To my mind the only thing likely to get through is one of they monkeys I've heard tell of.'

'So it isn't a solid mass blocking the shaft?' Josh clutched at the only faint glimmer of hope the man's report had given him.

'Well, I didn't stand on it for fear it'd give way under me, but I saw a gap or two. I didn't go close enough to see any more than that.'

'You can't ask a man to risk his life among the mess down there, Josh. It's likely to collapse at any time.'

'Can you think of any other way, Malachi?'

The Sharptor mine captain could not, but shook his head dubiously.

At that moment a young man, stoop-shouldered and thin to the point of emaciation, stepped from the crowd which had been listening to the conversation of the two men.

'Is there something I can do down there, Josh?'

The young man was Darley Shovell, a great-nephew of Josh's. His home was in St Austell, some twenty-five miles away, in clay country. With his sister, Lily, he had been sent to stay with Josh and Miriam on Bodmin Moor for a few days. His mother, Lottie, hoped the moorland air might improve his ailing health.

'You, Darley?' Josh looked at the slight young man and tried to keep the pity he felt for him from showing. 'It will take a team of men and lifting gear to make an impression on the tangle down there without risking more lives.'

'Uncle Josh is right.' A slim, bright-eyed young girl of about nine stepped forward and took Darley's hand. 'It's dangerous in the shaft. Ma would be angry if she knew you were even thinking about going down there.'

'I'm not talking of trying to shift anything, but if there's room to

8

squeeze through to the men who're trapped, I reckon I could manage better than anyone else.'

'You were sent to the moor to improve your health, Darley. Your ma . . .'

'Why do you and Lily keep bringing Ma into this? She's not here to say yes or no. Besides, one of the first stories I can remember being told was how, when Ma was a young girl, she was saved from a fire in the Sharptor mine by Pa. He squeezed through a narrow space in the roof to do it, I believe? The story's repeated every time more than two of the family get together. I would hope she'd understand, Josh. Especially as there are miners down there, some of them injured no doubt. They'll be relying upon someone up here to do something to save them.'

It should not have taken Josh by surprise that although Darley's body appeared weak, his resolve was not. Darley's mother, Lottie, was one of the strongest-minded women that Josh knew. His father too was a strong-willed man. He had organised a powerful Benevolent Association of clayworkers in the St Austell area of Cornwall, despite considerable opposition from the works' owners.

'Let *me* go down there,' said Lily, unexpectedly.

Despite the seriousness of the situation, Josh smiled. Lily certainly had the determination and grit required for the task, but she was probably no more than half her brother's weight.

'This is a man's job, Lily. Besides, you'd get yourself all tangled up in that dress.'

'I'd take it off,' she declared defiantly, the remark bringing more than one chuckle from the anxious miners who had been listening to the exchange.

'If we don't do something soon the men trapped underground will try to do something for themselves,' said Malachi, grimly. 'They're likely to bring the beam and everything else down on them.'

Josh knew he spoke the truth. The Notter miners would not be aware that the Sharptor men were above ground planning their rescue. They'd believe they could rely only upon the scant resources of a run-down mine.

'You're right, Malachi.' Josh arrived at a quick decision. 'Very well, Darley. I'll let you go down the shaft because you're our best hope to get through to the men down there. But you take care, you hear? I'll be in enough trouble when your ma finds out what I've let you do. If you hurt yourself my life won't be worth living.'

He walked away from the head of the shaft, the shrill voice of Lily, raised in protest, ringing in his ears.

The rope harness hurt Darley beneath his armpits as he was lowered slowly down the mine shaft on the end of a stout rope. Too excited to

9

worry very much about it, he wriggled inside the harness in a bid to make it more comfortable.

In his hand, Darley held a thinner cord, being paid out alongside the rope that supported him. With this he could signal to the men at the top of the shaft. One pull to stop lowering or drawing up. Two tugs to lower him. Three to pull him up.

Glancing up at the dwindling entrance to the shaft, Darley tried hard not to allow the fear that kept welling up inside him take over. For the first time in his life he was doing something important for others, instead of having them take care of him.

Darley was nineteen years of age now, but he looked much younger. It seemed to him he had been ill for most of his life. He could not remember a time when he had not suffered from fatigue, or a cough that frequently left him helpless. He was always being told he should not do this or that, at a time when the other members of his family seemed to be doing whatever they wanted. He had been forced to spend a great deal of time inside the home. Nevertheless, he had made use of this by learning all he could about everything contained in the many books his father acquired for him.

In spite of the situation in which he now found himself, Darley grinned nervously. His mother would be horrified if she knew what he was doing. She had always molly-coddled him to the point of embarrassment. Josh had been right, she would make his life unbearable if anything went wrong. Darley determined it would not.

He had almost reached the tangled wreckage that blocked the shaft now. Unhooking the paraffin-fed bull's-eye lantern that glimmered at his belt, he turned up the wick and directed the light downwards.

Protruding up through the tangle of wood, masonry and steel was one rounded end of the great iron bob that had brought down tons of masonry when it crashed from its axis in the engine-house. In reality the bob consisted of *two* giant beams, linked side by side, the whole weighing more than sixteen tons.

It lay at an angle, the lower end apparently snagged on something in the shaft. Even with much of it buried in the tangle of debris, the bob dwarfed Darley as he slowly descended beside it.

He gave a sharp tug on the cord as his feet landed on a wooden timber. The men above ground were slow to respond. The rope to which he was attached snaked over the wood beside his feet before jerking to a halt. He cursed at the tardiness of their reaction. Another time, his life might depend on the speed of their response.

Darley swung the lamp to and fro, assessing the situation. He could see no obvious place where he might gain access to the shaft below, but the thought came to him that he might prove small enough to squeeze through the space between the two linked beams.

It was a dangerous manoeuvre. He had no way of knowing what had

10

brought the beam to a halt in its plunge down the shaft. If it were precariously balanced, his weight might prove sufficient to cause it to break away. It would then continue its drop down the shaft, snapping the rope that supported Darley as easily as a strand of cotton, carrying him with it.

Squeezing through the gap between the two halves of the bob, he had to signal for more rope. When he had enough to go farther down he swiftly discovered there was wreckage beneath the bob too.

Carefully, Darley tested his weight on a piece of timber that must have been at least six inches thick. It seemed to be firm and he breathed a deep sigh of relief.

He was shining his lantern about him seeking a space where he might squeeze through when, without any warning, the timber gave way beneath him.

He went with it for perhaps six feet. The supporting rope brought him up with a jerk that expelled the breath from his thin body. It sent a sharp pain through his chest, as though his ribs had been crushed.

As he struggled with the pain, he could hear timbers bouncing off the sides of the tunnel. The sound grew fainter as they crashed towards the water, deep down in the heart of the mine.

Three jerks on the rope, followed immediately by a single signal brought him back up to the bob. He supported himself in the gap between the two halves for a few minutes, grateful to be able to take the weight from the harness about his aching ribs.

He had barely recovered his breath when he heard voices from the shaft beneath him. The sound made him forget his pain immediately.

'Hello! Can you hear me?' Darley shouted down the shaft, the sound loud in the confined space.

There was a cheer from somewhere a long way beneath him. Then a voice called, 'What's happening up there? Have you come to get us out? We can't climb any higher than the seventy-fathom level, the ladders have been torn away.'

'The engine-house has collapsed. I'm here above you, sitting on the bob. It's blocking the tunnel and will need to be blasted clear before we can get a kibble down to you. Is anyone seriously hurt?'

'Jack Hooper's got a smashed shoulder and he's bleeding a lot. Charlie Coombe's got a broken wrist. That's all.'

'How many of you down there?'

'Nine.'

Darley frowned. 'They thought, up top, there were more.'

There was silence for a few minutes before the same voice replied, 'Two men were working on the rods in the shaft when we came on shift. We thought . . . We hoped they'd gone to grass before the accident happened.'

Anyone working in the shaft when the engine-house collapsed would

11

have been swept away by the falling debris. Darley knew this and so did the men to whom he was speaking.

'I'll need to go up top now and tell them of the situation down here. Stay well back in the level where you are now until we've blasted the beam free. It's likely to take a while.'

'Will you be tackling it?'

Darley thought about it. 'I expect so. There's no one else skinny enough to squeeze through the tangle of wreckage here.'

There was some conversation between the trapped miners before their spokesman called up again. 'Who are you, friend? We don't recognise your voice. You're not a Notter man.'

'I'm Darley Shovell, from St Austell. I came to Notter with the Sharptor men.'

'Josh Retallick's up top? Is he in charge of the rescue work?'

'Yes.'

There was another cheer from the men below Darley and the unseen man called, 'Then we're going to be all right. Good luck to you, friend. We'll thank you properly when we set foot on grass once more.'

Chapter 3

At the top of the Notter mine shaft Darley sat on the ground, surreptitiously rubbing his chest whenever he thought Lily and the others were not looking. He did not want them to know just how much he ached as a result of his underground exertions.

'We'll need to try to blast the bob clear . . .' Josh was talking to Malachi Sprittle. 'How much powder do you think it will take?'

Malachi stroked his greying beard and shook his head dubiously. 'I wouldn't like to say, Josh. I'm not even sure it'll work. We'll be swinging the powder down among the wreckage with a fuse attached. What it really needs is to be set into a hole in the shaft wall, below the beam. That's the only certain way of doing the job.'

Josh rested a hand on Darley's aching shoulder. 'You're the only one who's seen it down there, Darley. Is there any chance that a man could squeeze through anywhere – and get back up again in a hurry?'

Darley thought of his tight squeeze through the bob and the wreckage tangled about it. He shook his head. 'Not unless there's anyone skinnier than me. I had a job to make it.'

'Then we'll have to try to lower the explosive into the wreckage and hope for the best . . .'

'It's all right. I'll go back down there and do it.'

Now the words were out, Darley almost regretted uttering them. Those limbs and muscles that did not actually hurt, ached almost as painfully. Besides, he had already performed a task that was more arduous than any he had ever before attempted.

Josh was aware of this. 'You've done more than your share already, Darley. Don't worry, our way *might* work.'

Carrying a mug of steaming tea that had been made for Darley by one of the mine women, Lily overheard the conversation. Indignantly, she said, 'Of course he's done enough!' Placing the mug carefully in her brother's shaking hands, she said more gently, 'Here, Darley. Drink this, it'll buck you up. It always does.'

'Thanks, Lily.' He took the cup, trying hard to control the trembling that threatened to spill the tea. 'I can do with this – but I've got to go down again.'

Looking up at his great-uncle, he said, 'I told the men down there I would, Josh. There's one of them with a smashed shoulder, and they

13

said he's bleeding badly. If there was anyone else could do it I'd be more than happy for them to go instead. But there isn't. If it's to work, the job needs to be done properly. That means boring a hole beneath the bob and trying to blow it clear – and I'm the only one who can get through the wreckage.'

Josh knew Darley spoke the truth, but he had grave doubts about sending the sick young man down the shaft yet again. 'Have you ever set a charge before?'

'No, but I've watched them doing it in the clay quarries. I know what needs to be done.'

'Darley, you mustn't. You shouldn't have gone down the first time . . .' Lily was close to tears.

He reached out a hand to her. 'I know you're worried, Lily, and I love you for caring, but I've *got* to do this. You understand.'

Despite her concern, Lily *did* understand. She understood her brother better than any other member of her family. She was aware of the pride and frustration that lived within his frail body. Reluctantly, she bit her lip and nodded her head.

'Are you certain, Darley?' Josh was less easy to convince than was Lily.

'Of course I am.' Handing the cup he held to Lily, Darley made a supreme effort and pushed himself up from the ground. 'Where do I get the powder, and the tools for boring?'

Dangling on the rope in the shaft, the bulk of the bob jammed precariously above him, Darley paused in his work to take a breather. The end of a spade-tipped drill protruded from a narrow hole in front of him. Another drill, secured by a rope, dangled at his belt. In his hand was a heavy, short-handled hammer, also secured to his belt by a rope.

Such precautions were necessary. Three times he had dropped the drill before it was far enough in the hole to be safe. He had lost count of the number of times the heavy hammer had slipped from his numb and aching fingers.

Darley was wearier than he had ever been in his life. The drill needed to be constantly turned in his fingers as it was hammered home into the hole. More than once his clumsy swing with the hammer missed altogether. It seemed to him he had been working for hours, yet the hole was still not deep enough to take the charge of gunpowder packaged up in a pouch slung over his shoulder.

Darley worked as hard as he could, but he needed to take frequent rests. He quickly lost all count of time, yet he was aware that the rest periods were occurring more often, each lasting longer than the last.

As he worked, the shadow of the giant iron bob was a threatening presence, looming ominously above his head. It provided a constant reminder of the task he had to perform – and of the danger he was in.

14

'How's it going up there?'

The voice from farther down the shaft called to him for perhaps the sixth or seventh time, checking on his progress.

'It's coming on slowly.' Darley resisted the urge to make an impatient reply. His task seemed to him to be taking a long time. It must seem even longer to the men waiting to be rescued. 'How's the man with the injured shoulder?'

'He's lost consciousness. I fear we might lose him.'

'I'll see if I can go any faster.' Darley swung the hammer and it struck sparks from the drill. Again and again he struck the bit, even though the hammer seemed now to be four times heavier than when he started.

Not until twenty more minutes had passed was Darley satisfied that the hole he was boring was deep enough to take the gunpowder he carried in the pouch slung on his back. Setting the fuse and tamping the charge home was the most critical part of the operation. By the time he had completed the task Darley was perspiring profusely.

Calling a warning to the men who were trapped in the shaft below, he fumbled with numb and aching fingers to strike a flame from the matches he held. Eventually he succeeded. Moments later the fuse spluttered into life. Jerking urgently on his line, he began to rise, away from the explosive.

Almost immediately, it seemed, Darley was tugging frantically on his cord once more. The drill dangling from his belt had caught up among the wreckage. As a result he was hanging only feet above the tangled mass, at a painfully acute angle.

He had spoken to the men on the winch about their earlier tardiness before being lowered down the shaft for the second time. They reacted immediately to his signal. He fell back on to the wreckage, hitting his head painfully against the iron beam.

Dazed, it was some moments before he recovered his senses sufficiently to bring the descent to a halt. Then, with increasing panic, he discovered he could not free the drill. In desperation he undid his belt and released it.

Signalling for the men to pull him up once more, he felt the movement on the rope – but instead of rising up the shaft, he was *pulled* down. The slack rope had snagged on a piece of the wreckage!

Desperate by now, Darley tugged on the rope again. Its movement ceased.

Darley realised that the men at the top of the shaft must be confused by the contradictory signals he was giving them. Their alarm was as nothing compared to the fear he was himself experiencing.

Beneath him the fuse was burning steadily towards the explosive charge set in the wall of the shaft – and he was tangled in the wreckage. At any moment an explosion was likely to blow the wreckage clear and send it crashing to the bottom of the deep shaft – carrying him with it!

Reaching down, he found where the rope had encircled a beam. After a few fraught moments he was able to pull it clear. Another tug on the rope and he was rising up the shaft once more. The men above ground realised he must have run into difficulties and they were hoisting him at a much greater speed than before. More than once he was obliged to kick himself clear when he banged against the rough side of the shaft.

He could see the opening of the shaft above him and had almost reached grass when there was a gigantic explosion far below. Enveloped in an upward rush of hot air, he was lifted faster than the winch-men could bring him up.

Desperately fighting for breath, he was pulled clear of the shaft. As he was dragged semi-conscious away from the shaft by two men, he was aware of Lily shrieking in fright somewhere nearby.

Then, still in possession of his senses, he was being lauded by the men about him. He recognised Josh's voice telling him how well he had done – and then he passed out.

Darley never knew how long he was lying unconscious. When he came to he was being held by his softly weeping young sister.

'It's all right . . . I'm all right, Lily. Truly I am.'

Her response was to hold him even tighter to her.

'I was praying for you, Darley. All the time I was holding you, I was praying for you.'

Her words made him realise just how worried she had been about him. Their father was a Methodist lay preacher but most of the arguments in the household stemmed from the fact that Lily would not accept his teachings without question. He could not remember an occasion when she had admitted to anyone that she turned to prayer in moments of desperation.

He struggled to sit up, embarrassed by her attentions.

'You were very brave, Darley – but they shouldn't have let you do it. They shouldn't!' There were tears on her cheeks as she repeated the words.

'No one else could have done it, Lily. But he *has* been brave. Very brave. It will never be forgotten by the men hereabouts.'

Darley felt embarrassed by Josh's praise – and even more embarrassed when it was echoed later by the Notter men, winched up in a kibble from the depths of the shaft.

After the seriously injured man had been carried away, the other miners crossed to where Darley sat, still recovering from his ordeal. Gravely, each man shook him by the hand and thanked him for what he had done for the trapped Notter miners.

When Darley Shovell was eventually led gently away from the ruined engine-house, with Lily clinging tightly to one hand, he was more weary than he had ever been before. His bowed, slight shoulders sagging towards his narrow chest served to emphasise his gaunt frame.

Yet, in spite of his obvious exhaustion, Darley was also happier than at any time in his life. There was a pride within him such as he had never known.

Deeply aware of this, Lily tried to make the knowledge override the deep concern she felt because her sick brother had seriously over-taxed himself.

Chapter 4

'The Ruddlemoor clay workings are good, Josh. Probably among the best in the whole St Austell area. Ten years ago it was three small separate pits, each barely scraping a living. Then Solomon Rosevear purchased them and brought them together. Trouble was, he spent more than he could afford on the purchase. It left him nothing spare to work them as one. He died a month since and his widow just wants Ruddlemoor taken off her hands.'

Jethro Shovell was talking to Josh as the two men walked together across the springy green turf of the moor, two days after the Notter mine disaster.

Jethro had walked to Sharptor from St Austell, but would be borrowing Josh's pony and shay to take Darley and Lily home.

While his son and daughter readied themselves for the journey, Jethro had suggested he and Josh should take a walk. He had something of importance to say to him.

Josh feared Jethro might want to complain about the part his sickly son had taken in the rescue of the Notter Tor miners. Jethro had been informed of the rescue and had told Darley how proud he was of him, but it was possible he would want to protest at Josh's part in the incident. However, he only wanted to speak of the Ruddlemoor China clay works. As they walked he gave Josh a detailed description of what was on offer.

When Jethro paused, Josh said, 'It's tempting. Very tempting indeed. Especially as I believe the future of Cornwall lies in clay country, not here in copper mining.'

Josh's gesture took in the wide sweep of the moorland about the rocky crag that was Sharptor. Heavy, dark grey clouds were scudding off the moor, overtaking higher, less angry clouds before spreading out across the wide Tamar valley.

There was an autumnal chill in the air. Josh thrust his hands deeper into the pockets of his coat and pondered the implications of throwing himself wholeheartedly into a new venture.

It would be hard to leave Bodmin Moor. He had been born here, on the slopes of Sharptor. Among the mines, in a mining community. Mining was in his blood. Even during the years he had spent in Africa as a younger man, he had been involved in a number of mining ventures.

But it was the moor itself he would miss most. Looking at it now he wondered whether, like Malachi Sprittle, he should forget the idea of taking on something entirely new. Perhaps he should remain here with Miriam, in comfortable retirement.

Josh was an old man by the standards of the nineteenth century. There was certainly no need for him to keep working. He and Miriam had all the money they needed for their old age. Their only son, Daniel, was a wealthy man in his own right in Matabeleland, in Africa.

From the place where he and Jethro were walking, Josh looked down upon the Sharptor mine. Behind the silent building was Henwood village, a handful of houses huddled together around the chapel. This was where most of the Sharptor miners lived.

On the road between mine and village was a family group comprised mainly of young children. Each carried a bag, loaded according to the strength of its bearer, borne on back or shoulder.

They were removing coal from the Sharptor mine. Several tons had been stock-piled before Josh took the decision to shut down. The coal had been donated to the villagers – his late employees.

Miners had a long tradition of independence, Cornish miners more than most. Despite this, Josh felt he bore a responsibility for them and for their families. It weighed heavily upon him. He knew the strengths and weaknesses of every man who worked in the mine. Had seen them married and could call each of their children by name. They were part of the Sharptor mining community. Part of Josh himself.

Suddenly, he reached a decision. He owed a future to these men, women and children. He would not let them down.

'When can we go and look at this clay works?'

'The sooner the better.' Jethro was surprised at the speed with which Josh had made up his mind, but he replied eagerly. 'We should do it before someone from up-country comes along and puts their money down.'

'I'll come along to your place tomorrow morning. We'll go and look at it some time in the afternoon. Miriam will probably come too. Hopefully, she'll take some of the sting out of your Lottie's attack on me. She's bound to be angry about the state in which Darley is returning home. She sent him up to the moor thinking he'd come back feeling better for breathing our moorland air! Instead, he's going home in a state of near exhaustion.'

Jethro smiled. Lottie's forthrightness was a legend among those who knew her. 'You needn't worry about her being angry for very long, Josh. I've just been talking to Darley. He's weak, yes, but Lottie and I have seen him weak before. What *is* wonderful is his state of mind. He's a man among men at last. Darley's proved himself before everyone.'

'He's certainly done that. He's a good, courageous lad.' Josh hesitated. 'Is there any chance he'll one day recover his health?'

19

Jethro's manner became more sombre. 'He's been seen by every doctor of note in Cornwall. They all say the same. Medicine can't help him. The last one suggested we should pray for him. I can assure you, Josh, Lottie and I have done a great deal of that on Darley's behalf.'

'We all have,' affirmed Josh. 'And after the way he behaved at Notter, I've no doubt the Lord will be hearing a few more petitions on Darley's behalf. Being a little more practical, is he capable of any form of work?'

'He has learning, certainly. Much more than me – and he's quick to pick things up. He'd like nothing more than to bring a wage into the house, but there are bad weeks when he's barely capable of standing up. Who'd employ a lad like that?'

'I would,' declared Josh, firmly. 'We'll look over this clay works tomorrow, Jethro. If I decide to buy it, I'll make a place in the office for Darley.'

The party which arrived to look over the Ruddlemoor China clay works the following day was larger than Josh had anticipated. Miriam accompanied her husband, and Jethro and Lottie had decided they would come too. Surprisingly, Darley appeared to have recovered well from his dramatic exertions at the Notter mine. When he heard of Josh's offer of work, he was eager to join the party. As was usual, where Darley went, Lily came too.

The arrival at the clay works of the carriage carrying the visitors caused a stir among the workers. Rumours had been rife that Widow Rosevear was keen to sell the works and they were apprehensive about their futures. They guessed, correctly, that Josh was a prospective buyer.

Abel Bolitho, Captain of the Ruddlemoor China clay works, did not share the anxieties of the men who worked under his supervision. An experienced clay captain, he boasted that he could find work on any one of a dozen workings in the St Austell area. Besides, he did not seriously believe Mrs Rosevear intended selling the works. Why should she when it was making a good profit for her?

When he came out of the office, taken by surprise by the arrival of the party, his chief emotion was anger – and it was aimed at Jethro.

'What are you doing in my works, Jethro Shovell? I have no Union men working at Ruddlemoor, as well you know. I'll not have you here talking to my workers and stirring up trouble.'

'I'm here with Josh Retallick to look around the workings, Cap'n Bolitho.'

'*I* say who'll walk around here – and you're not on my list.'

Josh decided it was time he put the Ruddlemoor works captain firmly in his place.

'I've not come to listen to you air any personal grievances you may have, Cap'n Bolitho. I'm here with Mrs Rosevear's blessing, as a prospective buyer. *I'll* say who accompanies me. If you have any objections I suggest you take them up with your employer. Now, shall I find someone else to show me around? If not perhaps you'll act as guide – to all of us?'

Josh was no longer a young man, but he was big enough to make anyone think twice before carrying an argument with him too far. He also carried an air of authority that was not lost on the Ruddlemoor captain.

'If Widow Rosevear has said you're to be shown over the workings I'll be the one to do it. But I'd like to remind you I'm employed here to produce clay at a profit – and without trouble.'

He looked at Darley and the women. 'It's not the easiest of places to walk around, especially when we get down to the pit. Perhaps the women and the boy would prefer to wait in the carriage . . .'

'We'll do no such thing, thank you,' declared Miriam, firmly. 'I've been in far worse places in my time. Off you go, Cap'n Bolitho, or the day will be over before we've seen anything.'

Captain Bolitho was not used to being ordered about by a woman but there was something in Miriam's voice that brooked no argument.

'What is it you want to see?' he asked Josh, grudgingly.

'Everything. We'll start in the pit and end up in the drying sheds.'

'Please yourself.' Brusque to the point of rudeness, Captain Bolitho shrugged his shoulders in resignation. 'I hope the boy and the women have got more stamina than it appears. There's a lot to see if you want to look at everything and still get home before dark.'

Chapter 5

Abel Bolitho had been unreasonably reluctant to take Josh and the others around the Ruddlemoor workings, but he had not exaggerated the rigours of such a tour.

The visitors were first taken to the deep quarries. Here the clay was prised from the high, steep sides and washed by a stream of water to the floor of the pit where it was drawn off and pumped away. When it had passed through numerous processes, some taking weeks, the clay ended its works life in a 'dry'. Finally it was transported to the small harbour at Charlestown, only a few miles away, to be shipped to the commercial world.

There were two such 'dries' in the Ruddlemoor workings. One was a modern building where the clay was dried by means of coal-fires. The other was a much older, air dried operation.

Darley kept up with the others until the air 'dry' was reached. Here he felt obliged to wave them on their way while he sat down and took a rest. By now the sun was low in the sky and there was a distinct chill in the air. Lily said she would return to the carriage to fetch the heavy coat Darley had left there.

A number of girls were at work nearby, under cover in the air 'dry'. Their task was to scrape sand from the base of blocks of dried clay, before stacking the end product for shipping.

Darley had been seated on a bench for some minutes, fighting to regain his breath after a prolonged bout of coughing, when one of the girls came to him, ignoring the cat-calls of her workmates. In her hand she carried a mug.

Handing it to him, she said, 'You look as though a drink of water might do you some good.'

'Thanks.' Darley took the mug gratefully and put it to his lips. After drinking half the water he was still gasping for breath, but the urge to cough had receded.

'Do you often have coughing attacks like that?' The girl asked the question sympathetically.

Darley nodded. 'Too often.'

'Then you chose the wrong day to have a look around the works. The wind's from the east and blowing dust off the spoil heap. It's not good for anyone with breathing problems.'

Darley looked to where the miniature mountain of China clay waste rose above the edge of the deep pit. As he watched he saw the wind raise a flurry of dust and deposit it in the depths of the pit whence it had been raised.

At the far end of the drying shed Darley's mother put in a momentary appearance. He could make out her anxious expression even at this distance. He raised an arm in what he hoped was a reassuring wave.

'Is Mr Retallick thinking of making an offer for the workings, or is he just looking around?' The girl seemed in no hurry to leave Darley and return to her work.

'Josh Retallick is here to buy the Ruddlemoor works. He's my great-uncle. He's offered me work in the office if he takes it, so I came along with the others to look around.'

'Are you strong enough to work?' The girl asked the question in a gentle manner that did not offend Darley. However, Lily, returning with his coat, overheard the question and leapt to her brother's defence immediately.

'Darley's a lot stronger than he looks. He went down a shaft on the Notter mine and rescued some men who'd been trapped there because of an accident.'

The girl's eyes widened. 'I've heard about that. Someone came to tell my ma last night. My uncle was one of those down the mine. He was brought up with a smashed shoulder. The man who came to our house said he'd have died if he'd been trapped down there any longer. He also said that the young man who went down showed a lot of courage.'

The girl looked again at Darley's thin, pinched face and frail body. 'Was that *really* you?'

'I've said it was!' Lily was indignant that her statement was being questioned. 'Darley can do anything anyone else can do – and do it better most of the time.'

'I don't doubt it.'

Touched by Lily's fierce defence of her brother, the girl smiled at her and made a mental note of Darley's name before taking the now empty mug from him. 'I hope your great-uncle buys the Ruddlemoor works. We need someone who knows what they're doing working in the office. They've had five or six different ones in there this last year. None of them could count farther than fingers and toes.'

'Working with Cap'n Bolitho probably made them nervous,' suggested Darley. 'He doesn't seem to have a lot of patience with anyone.'

'Oh, he's all right some of the time,' said the girl. 'You've caught him on one of his bad days.'

'You tell that to my pa! Cap'n Bolitho wanted to throw him off the workings. They must have met somewhere before, although I've never heard Pa mention him.'

'Who's your father?'

23

'Jethro Shovell.'

'The man who founded the Clay Workers' Benefit Association?' The girl seemed genuinely taken aback.

'That's right.' Darley smiled ruefully. 'I don't suppose there are many people in clay country who haven't heard of him.'

'No wonder they didn't get on together!'

The girl looked to where Captain Bolitho and the others had emerged from the far end of the coal-heated 'dry'. 'Captain Bolitho's daughter is a bal maiden here. She says he hates the Trades Unions and Associations. In the troubles of 1876 his father refused to join a Union with the others. The Union men waylaid him and gave him a very bad beating. He wasn't able to work again and died a year later, probably as a result of his injuries. No one was ever arrested for it, but there's never been a Union man working at Ruddlemoor since Captain Bolitho's been in charge.'

'No wonder they didn't get on. Pa gave his support and help to those who organised the '76 strike. I expect Cap'n Bolitho is aware of that.'

The Captain of Ruddlemoor and the party accompanying him emerged from the 'dry'. As they began walking towards them the girl said hurriedly, 'I'd better get back to work, or I'll be in trouble too.'

'Thanks for the water.' As an afterthought Darley called after her as she hurried away. 'What's your name?'

'Jo . . . It's short for Josephine.'

'Jo what?'

The girl had almost reached the bench piled high with blocks of China clay and he did not want to raise his voice too much for fear of bringing on another bout of coughing.

For a moment he thought she could not have heard. Then she looked back at him over her shoulder. 'Jo Bray. My father is the shift captain on afternoon duty this week.'

Darley was still digesting this piece of information when Josh and the others reached him. Much to Darley's surprise, Captain Bolitho stopped and, hands on hips, glowered down at him.

'What do you mean by interfering with the work of my bal maidens?'

For a moment Darley did not understand what the mine captain was talking about. Then he said, 'I didn't interfere with their working. I had a coughing bout. J— one of the girls brought me a mug of water. It was a very kind act, nothing more.'

'Bal maidens are here for clay working, not to act as serving girls for visitors.'

'If she hadn't brought it, I'd have gone off and got some for him,' Lily flared up angrily. 'Although if I had you'd no doubt have said I was trying to steal the mug!'

'I was talking to him, not to you, young lady – and you're old enough to have learned a few manners. Anyway, it doesn't matter a lot. I doubt

24

if we'll ever see either of you on the Ruddlemoor works after today so there's little fear of it happening again.'

'I wouldn't be too certain of that, Cap'n Bolitho.'

Josh had heard the exchange between Lily, Darley and the China clay captain. He had also see Lottie Shovell puffing up with anger at the way Captain Bolitho had spoken to her son. Josh thought, not for the first time that day, that it would be necessary to put the clay works captain in his place before too long.

'I've decided to buy the Ruddlemoor works. When I take over, young Darley will be coming to work in the office to keep the accounts.'

'A boy as sick as he is won't last a day out. Why don't you find a fit clerk? Men who can read and add up are two-a-penny these days.'

'There's no shortage of good clay captains either, Cap'n Bolitho. It might be as well to remember that. Darley will start work on the day the purchase goes through.'

Chapter 6

Widow Rosevear was anxious to sell up the Ruddlemoor works and leave England. She intended travelling to Missouri, in America, where she would live with her son and his young family who had emigrated there a few years before. She sold Josh not only the clay works, but her comfortable home in the nearby Gover Valley on the edge of the clay-working area.

On a dull Monday morning, only two-and-a-half weeks after viewing the Ruddlemoor works for the first time, Josh entered the office as its new owner. Darley was with him.

Captain Abel Bolitho was nowhere to be seen but shift captain Jim Bray was in the office. He told Josh that Bolitho was carrying out his usual daily routine of checking the works, adding, 'He set off for the quarry about twenty minutes ago.'

'Didn't he know I was coming?' Josh asked the question, although he knew what the answer must be. He had sent a messenger to the works three days before.

'I believe he did,' said the embarrassed shift captain, uncertain where his loyalties should lie. 'But I expect you're a bit earlier than he thought you'd be.'

'What time will he be back?'

'Hard to say. When he's checked out the quarry he'll have a look at the drags, the settling pits and the tanks. If there are no problems, he'll finish up at the "dry" close to eleven o'clock. That's his usual routine.'

'I'm pleased to know he's so conscientious, but he can break his routine this morning. Find him and tell him I want to see him here.'

The shift captain paled. '*Tell him?* It's not for a shift captain to *tell* Cap'n Bolitho to do anything.'

'Very well,' Josh said patiently. '*Ask* him, if it will make you feel better, but I want him here – and I want him here quickly. Off you go, Captain Bray.'

When Jim Bray had hurried off in search of the works captain, Josh went around the office opening drawers and checking inside the cupboards. One or two were locked, as was the heavy steel safe in a corner of the office.

'Is there anything I can be doing, Josh?' Darley felt slightly ill-at-ease. He believed there would be an angry confrontation between Josh and Bolitho when the works captain returned to the office.

'Yes. You can empty out that desk by the window.' Josh pointed to the desk at which the shift captain had been seated when they entered the office. 'You'll be able to work there without getting under Cap'n Bolitho's feet too much. What I want you to do first of all is take charge of all the books that Captain Bolitho keeps. Go through them thoroughly. Find out exactly how much clay the Ruddlemoor produced, week by week, last year. I want to know who we sold to, and the prices we obtained. I also want you to copy out a plan of the workings and make a map of this area, taking in adjacent workings.'

Observing Darley's fleeting expression of bewilderment, Josh smiled. 'I don't intend trying to run before I can walk, Darley, but I've had a financial interest in clay for some years. I know something about it. What's more, I've promised to find work for any of the Sharptor miners who are willing to come here and join me. In order to keep them employed, the Ruddlemoor works will need to expand. I want to know how it can best be done.'

The shift captain returned to the office within ten minutes, but it was half an hour before Abel Bolitho arrived. He offered no excuses for his tardiness and Josh said nothing.

Looking to where Darley was sorting out the papers removed from the shift captain's desk, Bolitho said, 'What's he doing?'

'He's cleared the desk – on my orders. That's where Darley will work. He'll also take over all your books. I want details of production, sales, customers, expenditure . . . everything to do with the works.'

'I gave all the figures to Mrs Rosevear.'

'I've seen the *figures*. Now I want the details. When I have them I'll decide the future of Ruddlemoor and those who work here. *All* who work here, Cap'n Bolitho, so let's have all drawers and the safe unlocked. We'll go through everything together before Darley takes them on.'

Captain Abel Bolitho did as he was told, but he did it with a bad grace, his resentment plain to see.

Examining the ledgers and documents held in the office took up a great deal of the morning. Abel Bolitho continued to protest as, one by one, they were handed over to Darley.

Josh's response was to inform the works captain that he had plans for expanding the Ruddlemoor pits. The captain would be kept too busy to bother himself with irksome paperwork.

Not until almost noon was Josh satisfied he had a reasonable grasp of what was happening in the works he had purchased. He was thoughtful as he made his way homeward to the Gover valley, and Miriam.

The Retallicks' move from Sharptor to the clay area had been hurried, but it was almost completed now. Nevertheless, Miriam complained that all in their new Gover Valley home was utter chaos. It was larger than the Sharptor house. She could not find many of the household essentials that had been brought with them and reminded Josh he had promised to spend the remainder of the day helping her.

Back at the Ruddlemoor works, Jim Bray, the shift captain, came to the office to join Abel Bolitho during the latter's lunchtime break. Abel was still smouldering with resentment at the manner in which the new Ruddlemoor owner had put him very firmly in his place.

Not wanting to sit and listen to Bolitho's thinly veiled criticisms of Josh, Darley took his pasty outside. He found a low wall on which to sit and eat his own lunch. It was quite pleasant out here, the sun trying hard to break through the clouds and it was not too cold.

He had not been there for very long when Jo Bray came towards him from the drying shed. He watched her approach, hoping she was coming to speak to him. Much to his disappointment, she passed him by and made her way to a nearby water butt.

As she returned with a jug of water, Darley said, 'When I saw you making your way over here I thought you were coming to speak to me.'

'Oh! And why should I do that?'

Her reply deflated him far more than it should have. Suddenly he was no longer a young man flirting with a girl, but had remembered he was a sickly, frail semi-invalid. 'There's no reason at all . . . I'm sorry.'

Jo guessed the reason for the sudden change in his attitude towards her. More kindly, she said, 'What would you say if I told you I only came to get some water so I would have an excuse to speak to you?'

'Why would you do that?'

Darley's surprise was genuine and Jo laughed. It was a very pleasant sound and brought about an amazing transformation in her. Jo's face had remained in his memory since her earlier kindness to him. Even so, he would not have said she was the most attractive girl he had ever seen – until he witnessed her smile. Now he made a rapid reassessment of her beauty.

'I was interested in knowing how you are now. Whether you'd fully recovered from the other day.'

'Yes, thanks. I'm used to my attacks by now. They don't usually last very long. Not unless I do something that really tires me out.'

'Like being lowered down a mine shaft to rescue trapped miners?'

Darley grimaced. 'I don't think I've ever been so exhausted before – or so scared. I doubt if I'll ever do anything like that again.'

'You would if you needed to.'

There were a few moments of silence between them until Jo said, 'There are lots of rumours going around the works. It's said Mr Retallick's going to bring some of the Sharptor miners here. That a lot of us will be out of work when he does.'

'I wouldn't take too much notice of such rumours. He's hoping to expand, certainly, but Josh Retallick looks after those who work for him. He always has . . .'

Jo's sudden change of expression caused Darley to break off. Turning his head, he saw Captain Bolitho advancing towards them from the office. It seemed his lunch had done nothing to improve his mood.

'What do you two think you're doing? Jo, get back to your place of work. You, of all people, should be setting an example to others. Go on, girl . . . now!'

For a moment Darley thought she was about to speak up for herself, but she did not. Turning away, she walked quickly and silently back to the other bal maidens, all of whom had overheard the works captain's admonition.

'She came to fetch water, Cap'n Bolitho, that's all. Our talk was of the future of Ruddlemoor now Josh Retallick has taken over.'

'I don't care *what* you were talking about. You're both paid to work here, not to talk. In future you can take your break inside the office, where I can keep an eye on what you're up to.'

Darley was about to retort that he would eat his meal where he pleased, but he held back. Getting into an argument with Captain Bolitho on his first day at work would help no one. He would tell him if and when the question arose again.

Folding the linen cloth that had contained his pasty, he went inside the office. Jim Bray was making a list of the men on duty and quietly smoking his pipe. Through the window Darley could see the works captain heading for another part of the works.

'Does Cap'n Bolitho hate everyone?'

The shift captain drew quietly on his pipe before answering, his words accompanied by a slow trickle of smoke.

'Not all the time. Mind you, he don't care for many folks. He's particularly against them who has anything to do with Unions or the like – and them who he thinks is likely to make eyes at his daughter. She's one of the bal maidens – and you seem to have made a hit with them.'

'I wasn't "making eyes" at anyone, and I've only ever spoken to Jo. She's a nice girl, Cap'n Bray. She brought me a drink of water the other day when I walked around with Josh Retallick and got over-tired. Cap'n Bolitho can't make anything of that, surely? As for Unions – they interest my pa, not me.'

'It's close enough for Cap'n Bolitho. If you have any regard for Jo and the other bal maidens, you won't give him any cause to get angry with them. Be especially carefully with young Tessa, his daughter. She's sixteen now, but that won't stop him taking his belt to her.'

29

'Giving her a beating? Surely not?' Darley looked at the shift captain in disbelief.

'I'm not paid to repeat gossip. I live next-door to Abel Bolitho. There are times when we don't see his wife for days on end. When she does put her nose out of doors there's likely to be more bruising than sunburn on her face, I'll tell you that. I've seen young Tessa come in to work looking as though she's spent the night in tears, too, and she tells the others what he does. Cap'n Bolitho guards her like an old hen with a single chick. Mind you, that girl's a wild one. She takes after her father, but I wouldn't tell him that. I'm sure the only reason she's working here is so he can keep an eye on her *all* the hours of the day and night. He's no need to send her out to work at all.'

Darley shook his head as he looked across the space between the office and the place where the bal maidens were laughing among themselves. 'It's hard to believe . . .'

'You believe it, young Shovell – and watch your own step in your dealings with Cap'n Bolitho. He's not a person to cross, as more than one good man's learned to his cost.'

Jim Bray rose to his feet and shrugged himself into a coat before going outside. 'I'm telling you all this out of sympathy for you. I had another daughter once, but lost her with your complaint. What's more, you've made a hit with young Jo – and she's as good a judge of character as anyone I know.'

Chapter 7

Josh called a meeting of the Ruddlemoor workers the following day. As it was raining he gathered them together at one end of the drying shed. It was warm and dry here and sheltered from the chill, easterly wind.

Standing on a stout table that had been carried in for the purpose, he gazed out at the faces of more than a hundred men and women. They were all strangers to him, yet he was aware that they were totally dependent upon him for their livelihood. Observing them he saw a mixture of resentment, curiosity and apprehension in their expressions.

Holding up a hand for silence, he said, 'I won't keep you long, but I thought it was time I introduced myself to you. As you probably already know, I'm Josh Retallick. I've bought the Ruddlemoor works from Widow Rosevear. I haven't had an opportunity to talk to each of you in person yet, although I intend doing something about that as quickly as I can. But I've called you together today because I believe there are rumours circulating. I'm told that some of you fear you are likely to lose your jobs here . . .'

Darley was standing beside the table on which Josh was standing. He had already located Jo Bray in the second row of those listening to Josh. He saw her turn her head to look at him. She knew the fears she had expressed to Darley had been passed on to the new works owner.

'I've called you together today to put your minds at rest. You have my promise that I have no plans whatsoever to dismiss any man or woman from the Ruddlemoor workforce. On the contrary. By next week I hope to have purchased a large piece of land to the north of our workings. When the sale's completed, I intend expanding. There'll be a new pit – and I'm having an engine-house built for pumping work there.'

When the buzz of interest his words had caused had died down, Josh continued, 'I'm doing this partly so that I can take on those Sharptor miners who are willing to come and work here. They are all men who have worked for me for many years. I hope they, and you, will continue to work for me for many more years to come. That's all I have to say to you today, but I'll be coming around the works during the coming weeks and meeting you all. We have a good works here at Ruddlemoor. I want it to be the best in the whole of the clay country – and the

31

happiest. I hope you'll always feel free to tell me of any concerns or suggestions you might have. That's all.'

As Josh walked back to the office accompanied by Captain Bolitho, there was a great upsurge of sound in the drying shed. Darley thought it was almost possible to feel the relief felt by the Ruddlemoor workers at Josh's words.

He did not hurry to follow Josh and before he left the drying shed, Jo had caught up with him. Tessa Bolitho was with her.

'Did you tell Mr Retallick what I said to you yesterday? Is that why he called the meeting?'

'I merely mentioned to him that some of you were worried about the future.'

'Mr Retallick doesn't waste time, does he?'

'Not where his employees are concerned. I've told you before, he's a good man to work for.'

Jo gave Darley one of her smiles. 'We're all grateful to you.'

At this point Tessa spoke for the first time. 'I'm not sure my pa would agree with you. He and Mr Retallick don't seem to be getting along too well at the moment.'

'It's not really surprising. From what I hear, Mr Rosevear rarely showed his face at the works. He let Cap'n Bolitho run things his way. Josh Retallick isn't that kind of owner. There's bound to be some resentment from your father. If he can see that for himself and come halfway to meet Josh, he'll have no more problems with him. Once Josh is satisfied the works are being run the way he wants them, he'll let your father get on with things without bothering him too much.'

Tessa shrugged. 'My pa's used to everything being done *his* way. He can be very stubborn sometimes . . .'

As she was speaking, they heard Captain Bolitho's raised voice approaching the drying shed from the direction of the office. Tessa abruptly broke off what she was saying and both girls hurried away.

Moments later, Captain Bolitho entered the shed. When he saw Darley, he frowned. 'You still here, Shovell? You should be in the office, searching out all the secrets of managing a clay works. Isn't that what Mr Retallick wants? If he intends carrying out all these grand schemes of his, he'll need to know a great deal more about the business than he does at the moment.'

Snorting derisively, Captain Bolitho added, 'You can feed him as many figures as you like. All the paper learning in the world can't turn a miner into a successful clay works owner.'

'That's why he has you and me working for him, Cap'n Bolitho. You to produce good quality clay, me to check that he's making more money selling it than is being spent producing it.'

'I don't need any scrawny, beardless boy to tell *me* whether or not I'm running my works efficiently,' said Abel Bolitho, angrily. 'A clay captain has years of experience, not a few months' schooling. I *know* it's making a profit.'

'So does Josh Retallick, otherwise he wouldn't have bought the Ruddlemoor works. But until he knows just how *much* profit you're making, he can't plan for future expansion. *That's* what I'm being paid for.'

Darley spoke patiently and respectfully. This was the longest conversation he had ever had with the works captain. He hoped that if he could justify his presence, the works captain might be more ready to accept him. It was uncomfortable working in the office in the face of the resentment Bolitho constantly showed to him.

The captain's next words left him disappointed.

'Mr Retallick did things his way up at Sharptor – and the mine failed. That's hardly a recommendation for his management skills. He should leave things well alone at Ruddlemoor. Let those who understand clay do the work. All he needs to do is sit back and take the profits I make for him. Most men would be more than happy to do that.'

Darley could have told Captain Bolitho that Josh Retallick did not do things that way. He could also have pointed out that the failure of the Sharptor mine – and almost every other copper mine in Cornwall – had nothing to do with the manner in which the mine was being run.

World-wide the price of copper had collapsed dramatically in recent years. Only in those countries where copper deposits were close to the surface and labour costs negligible, were mines able to survive. They produced copper cheaply, more often than not helped by the experience of expatriate Cornish copper miners. By so doing, the foreign workings were putting the deep mines of Cornwall out of business.

Captain Bolitho was talking again. 'I can't stay here talking nonsense to you. I have a works to run. It's pay-day tomorrow. You've already got the paying-out book. Work out how much money you're going to need and write a cheque. I'll sign it when I come back. You can go to St Austell first thing in the morning to fetch the money from the bank. Don't forget to deduct the money owed by some of the men to the works shop. If it's more than they've earned, deduct a third and let me know their names. I'll see they're given no more credit until they've settled up. More than one man's run up a bill he can't possibly pay and then run off leaving us to make good the loss.'

Chapter 8

Darley was ready to go to St Austell to fetch the men's pay early the following morning. However, he was startled to learn that no one would be accompanying him as an escort for the money. His only companion would be an elderly wagoner who would take him on the return trip in a light cart pulled by a single horse.

When Darley expressed his concern to Captain Bolitho, the works captain scoffed at him. 'How much are you collecting, five hundred pounds? It doesn't need more than one man or boy to carry that much. You're being paid to sit on your backside doing nothing for the time it takes to get to St Austell and back – make the most of it. Besides, you're in clay country now, we're honest men in these parts.'

'I don't doubt the honesty of the local men,' Darley persisted, 'but there are a great many others wandering around who are *not* from this area. You know that yourself. We've turned away at least a dozen every day this week. Men from shut-down mines, most of them with families to support and desperate for money.'

'You'd know best about what might be expected from mining men, but it's a busy road between St Austell and here. Wagons are on the road carrying clay to the dock at Charlestown all the time. You'll likely be in a line of forty or fifty all the way to town, with as many coming the other way. It's too busy for anyone to try anything.'

Darley was less confident than the works captain and was unhappy with the arrangements that had been made. However, his day improved when he received a smile and a wave from Jo as he left the office.

He found Lily waiting for him outside the works. 'Can I come for the ride with you? I've got nothing else to do today.'

'Shouldn't you be at school?'

'There's no school today. The teacher's sick.'

'Then you should be at home, helping Ma.'

'She's gone off to see Great-aunt Miriam for the day.'

'Didn't she leave you some work to do at home?' Darley looked at her suspiciously.

'I've done it all,' said Lily, airily. 'I'd have been sitting indoors all day with nothing to do if I hadn't come here to see you.'

Her replies were too glib. Darley was prepared to give her the benefit of the doubt about school. The teacher had not been well for some time and when she was ill the school had to be closed. Nevertheless, there was no way Lily could have completed the chores she had been given in such a short time. However, he always enjoyed her company. He decided to ask no more awkward questions.

Lily's cheerfulness was in direct contrast to the mood of the old man driving the wagon. After complaining about having Lily on the wagon, he uttered no more than a dozen words along the way – all directed at the patient, plodding horse. Darley tried on a number of occasions to draw him into conversation but gave up when he received only irritable grunts in reply. He chatted to Lily, instead.

St Austell was a small country town, its houses sprawled about a square-towered church. It possessed a single main shopping area, and this was extremely busy. Shoppers and street vendors who crowded the narrow road risked their lives every time they crossed from one side to the other. They needed to dodge between the cumbersome China clay wagons that constantly rumbled through the heart of the town.

Each of the huge wagons was pulled by as many as four horses, harnessed in line. The wagons themselves were as large as could be sensibly constructed. Here and there along the narrow road were places where wagoners could rein in to enable others to pass by, but most drivers were reluctant to make use of them.

There was occasional excitement in the town when a wagoner refused to give way to a wagon and horses owned by a rival clay company. When this happened the passage of vehicles along the road would come to a halt and there would be much shouting along the line. Unless the town constable was quick to intercede and order one of the men to back up his vehicle, a fight would ensue. This was to happen twice during the time Darley and Lily were in the town.

The old man driving the Ruddlemoor wagon parked on a piece of waste ground just outside the town. Many other wagons and small pony carts were already here. The wagoner grunted the information that he intended remaining with his horse and vehicle, while Darley went to the bank with Lily.

All the clay workings around St Austell paid their workers on the same day of the week. As a result the bank was very, very crowded. It did not help that service was slow and laborious. It was an hour before Darley handed over the Ruddlemoor cheque. In return he was given a pouch which contained banknotes to the value of five hundred pounds.

The pouch went inside Darley's shirt and he buttoned his coat tightly about it before leaving the bank and returning to the crowded street once more. He was glad he had taken such precautions when he saw the crowd of loafers lounging against the wall beside the bank doorway.

When he and Lily reached the waste ground the area was still busy. He eventually located the Ruddlemoor wagon but, to his surprise and

35

annoyance, the old wagoner was not with his vehicle.

It was exposed here, on the waste ground. After sitting on the wagon seat for some minutes, Darley climbed down and he and Lily walked about in a bid to keep warm.

It was half-an-hour before the wagoner returned, by which time Darley was shivering violently, despite all his efforts to stay warm.

It was immediately apparent how the Ruddlemoor wagoner had spent the time while Darley had been collecting the works' wages. He reeked of alcohol and his nose was as red and shiny as an apple.

'Where the hell have you been?' Darley was annoyed that the man could have been so irresponsible when he knew Darley had gone to collect a great deal of money. 'You were supposed to be here waiting for me.'

'It's all right for you.' The man's voice confirmed his state. 'It was cold stuck here.'

'Cold for *you*? Darley's been waiting here for half-an-hour.' Lily raised her voice in anger.

'Hush, Lily.' Talking to the driver, he said, 'I'm carrying wages for a hundred and fifty men and women here. I expected you to show at least a bit of responsibility.'

The Ruddlemoor wagoner shrugged. 'Well, I'm here now.'

'Yes, and I'll make certain it's the last time you bring me in on a wages day!'

While they argued, the wagoner removed the nose bag from the horse, displaying an awkwardness that suggested he had drunk far more than was good for him during his morning's drinking session.

As he returned to the wagon carrying the bag, a group of rowdy men made their way over from the nearby inn. Darley hurriedly helped Lily on to the wagon. Threading their way between the other vehicles, the men called out to the Ruddlemoor man. From their greetings, Darley learned that his driver's name was Alf.

The men also directed a number of ribald remarks at Lily that angered Darley. He had to remind himself of the money he was carrying and say nothing.

The men were not dressed as clay workers, and did not appear to be miners. Darley believed they were part of the army of vagabonds that gathered in Cornwall's towns at this time every year. Yet their presence in St Austell today made him uneasy.

When the men passed out of hearing, heading along the road the wagon would be taking out of St Austell, Darley questioned the surly old man about them. He was mindful of the money he was carrying.

'Who they are is none of your business. They're my friends.'

'Friends – or men who've spent the last hour and a half buying you drinks?'

When the old man failed to reply, Darley asked, 'Did you tell them

36

why we're in town? That I'd come here to collect the Ruddlemoor wages?'

'I might have done. There again, I might not. What difference does it make? Everyone knows clay men's wages are collected on a Friday.'

It was the longest speech Darley had heard the man make, but it did nothing to put his mind at ease. Looking about him, he made a snap decision. 'You go back to Ruddlemoor on your own. Lily and I will get a ride with someone else.'

The wagoner was startled into temporary sobriety. 'But the cap'n gave me orders . . .'

'Captain Bolitho didn't know you were going to spend an hour-and-a-half in a public house. You've probably told every villain within hearing that we're returning to Ruddlemoor with the week's wages. No doubt you also let them know there'd be just you, me and Lily on the wagon?'

The wagoner *had* made much of the fact that he was expected to act as a nursemaid to an unshaven boy without enough meat on him to feed a cat. But he was not going to admit this to Darley.

While the wagoner tried desperately hard to invent a plausible denial, Darley took one of the pick handles from the wagon. With Lily holding his other hand, he walked away from the Ruddlemoor vehicle and its drunken driver.

Among the wagons on the piece of waste ground he had seen one about to leave. It carried two passengers, both of whom had been in the bank at the same time as himself.

Intercepting the wagon as it was driven from the waste ground to the road, he called up: 'Are you going anywhere near the Ruddlemoor works?'

'Why?'

After eyeing up Darley and Lily, the reply came from the man who was quite evidently acting as escort for the money his companion carried in a satchel slung over his shoulder. A giant of a man, with a bushy black beard that hung halfway down his chest, he would have been a formidable deterrent to all but the most determined robber.

'I'm carrying the wages for the Ruddlemoor clay works and this is my young sister. I think our wagoner's let it be known to a crowd of vagrants that we're travelling without an escort. A lot of them have just made off along the road we'll be travelling. I believe they might be planning to rob me.'

'The driver's *drunk*,' Lily added scornfully.

'Are you with old Alf Tooze?' The question came from the wagoner accompanying the two men.

'His first name's certainly Alf. I haven't been told his surname. He's spent the last hour and a half in the pub over there.'

'That's Alf Tooze all right. You're wise to be concerned. The old

37

fool would tell anything to anyone willing to buy him a drink. I saw him leave the General Wolfe with a half-dozen villains. *I* wouldn't like to meet up with any of 'em on a dark night.'

'You'd better both come with us, son.' The man with the satchel spoke for the first time. 'It won't take us far out of our way to drop you off at the Ruddlemoor workings. Mind you, I doubt if Abel Bolitho will show any gratitude to the Varcoe clay works for doing him a favour.'

Chapter 9

Travelling in the wagon with the men from the Varcoe clay works, Darley learned that the man carrying the satchel was Jeremiah Rowe, the works captain.

The black-bearded giant was Lanyon Sweet. Darley's nod of greeting for him contained an almost awed respect. The big man was the champion wrestler of Cornwall and the West Country. His prowess and great strength were legendary. Fate could not have provided Darley and the Ruddlemoor wages with a more formidable escort.

Unfortunately, events were to show that Sweet's discipline and acumen did not match his wrestling skills.

The incident that uncovered Sweet's shortcomings occurred when the wagon was passing beneath a canopy of trees, only a short distance out of St Austell. Contrary to Captain Bolitho's assertion that the road would be crowded in both directions, there were only four wagons in sight. Two, heavily laden, were heading towards St Austell and the port of Charlestown beyond. The wagon on which Darley was a passenger was travelling in the opposite direction. A hundred yards behind them was the Ruddlemoor wagon with its driver, Alf.

Darley was telling Jeremiah Rowe about the change of ownership of the Ruddlemoor works and giving him details of Josh Retallick's background when they heard a loud shout of alarm.

Looking back, they saw the Ruddlemoor wagon surrounded by the vagrants with whom Alf had been drinking in the General Wolfe only a short while before. The mood of his erstwhile friends had undergone an ugly change.

Two of the vagrants were on the wagon, arguing heatedly with Alf. Others hacked at the leather harness straps securing the frightened horse to the wagon.

It seemed the vagrants had climbed on the wagon in the mistaken belief they would find Darley and the money he carried on board.

As he watched, one of the men struck Alf, knocking him backwards inside the body of the high-sided wagon. Then the vagrants gathered around the offside of the wagon. After a few practice heaves, they slowly lifted the side of the wagon high off the ground. To the watchers it seemed to balance on its side for a second or two, then it toppled right over and crashed down a steep wooden slope at the bottom of which was a fast-flowing stream.

Uttering an angry oath, Lanyon Sweet vaulted over the side of the wagon. Before Jeremiah Rowe could prevent him, the wrestler began a lumbering run along the road towards the scene of the fracas.

'Lanyon! Come back here. You're supposed to be protecting the Varcoe money . . .'

It was doubtful whether the giant wrestler even heard him. Bellowing like an angry bull, he ran towards the scene of the abortive robbery, shouting for the vagrants to come back and fight him.

The men he sought had disappeared from the road within seconds of sending the Ruddlemoor wagon tumbling down the slope – but they had not fled the scene altogether. While Lanyon Sweet pursued them in one direction, they were running through the undergrowth beside the road, heading towards the Varcoe wagon.

Hearing the sound of breaking branches, Darley turned in time to see one of the vagrants emerge from the undergrowth nearby. The man was followed by another . . . and a third. Behind them the remainder of the vagrant gang could be heard scrambling up the steep bank towards the road.

When Darley shouted a warning, the driver realised the danger they were in. He cracked his whip over the back of his startled horse – but he was already too late. A vagrant had taken a firm grip on the horse's bridle. The horse flung its head up, but could do no more.

A quick-thinking vagrant seized the thong of the whip and tried to tug it free from the driver's hand. The driver refused to release his grip but his adversary was a younger, stronger man. He gave a fierce tug and a moment later driver and whip were lying in the mud of the road.

Jeremiah Rowe shouted loudly for the errant escort to return. At the same time he kicked out at a vagrant who was climbing over the high side of the wagon.

While Jeremiah was off balance, a stave wielded by yet another of the would-be robbers knocked him to the floor of the wagon.

The vagrant succeeded in getting only one foot on the edge of the wagon. The pick handle, wielded in desperation by Darley, hit him across the face and knocked him off the wagon and to the ground.

The man picked himself up and staggered across the road. Shrieking in pain, he clutched at his face, as blood trickled between his fingers.

Darley had no time to observe the results of his handiwork. The man who had unseated the driver was climbing over the front of the wagon. Another desperate jab from the end of Darley's pick handle took him in the chest and sent him tumbling back again.

Lily was not idle. She stamped as hard as she could on the fingers of another man who was trying to climb on the wagon. At the same time she shrieked at the top of her shrill young voice. Momentarily, it seemed to have an unnerving effect on the attackers.

The Varcoe wagoner picked himself up off the ground in time to prevent another of the vagrants from climbing on to the wagon via one of the wheels.

The horse, frightened by what was going on, tried to pull away from the man holding its bridle. It failed in its efforts, but succeeded in dislodging two vagrants who were using the wheels as ladders to climb on board.

Meanwhile, the drivers of two approaching clay wagons had seen what was going on. Abandoning their own horses and wagons, they ran to join the battle.

Belatedly, the giant Lanyon Sweet realised the grave error of judgement he had made in deserting his post. Bellowing in anger, he ran to the rescue – and moments later the attack faded away.

Yet, even as the would-be robbers fled from the scene, one of them picked up a jagged piece of slate from the side of the road. In a final gesture of frustration, he hurled it at the defenders of the Varcoe wagon.

The stone caught Darley on the side of the face. A shout of pain escaped from him and he dropped to his knees, clutching the injured cheek.

When Lily went to his aid, her face paled in fright at the amount of blood she could see on her brother's face.

Pulling his hand away she cried, 'Let me look, Darley. Let me look!'

It was a very bad gash and bleeding profusely.

Peering over Lily's shoulder, Jeremiah Rowe pulled a clean handkerchief from his pocket and handed it to her.

Suddenly, it seemed, there were many people around the wagon. Three horsemen had appeared from somewhere and the two wagon drivers were talking with the Varcoe driver. All were muttering darkly about rogues and vagabonds.

Ignoring them all, Lily pressed Jeremiah Rowe's handkerchief against Darley's face, removing it frequently to check the wound, all the time anxiously asking her brother how he felt.

'I think he should see a doctor,' said one of the horsemen, peering at the wound from the saddle of his horse.

'I'm sure it will be all right.' Embarrassed by all the fuss, Darley was anxious to be on his way. 'I've got the Ruddlemoor wages to deliver. I'll have my face cleaned up when I get there.'

'Talking of seeing a doctor . . . Alf Tooze is lying in the woods back there. He's badly hurt,' said Lanyon Sweet. 'I reckon the wagon must have rolled over him.'

Looking back along the road, Darley saw a cluster of men about the spot where the Ruddlemoor wagon had been tipped off the road.

As he watched, four men carried the inert body of Alf Tooze from the woods and placed it inside an empty wagon. Amidst much gesticulating, information was shouted to the men on the Varcoe wagon that they would take Tooze to hospital in St Austell. One of the horsemen said he would gallop ahead to report the matter to the St Austell constable.

There was nothing to delay the Varcoe wagon any longer. It set off once more and all the way to the Ruddlemoor works Lily knelt beside her brother, holding Jeremiah Rowe's handkerchief to his injured face.

As they approached Ruddlemoor they met with a whole army of clay workers heading in the direction of St Austell. Most were from the Ruddlemoor works, although they seemed to have gathered other clay men along the way.

When they saw the wagon with Darley on board, they set up a resounding cheer and swarmed about it.

'Where are you men going?' The question was put to the clay workers by the Varcoe captain.

'We're going to flush out those murdering thieves from the Menacuddle Woods. They'll not lie in wait for any more of our wagons.'

'There's no need for that,' said Darley. 'They didn't get the wages. They're safe, here with me.'

'That's right,' said Jeremiah Rowe. 'Your lad saved the Ruddlemoor wages. The Varcoe money too. You'd best leave things to the St Austell constables now.'

'We're pleased to hear our money's safe, Cap'n Rowe,' said one of the Ruddlemoor men. 'But we're going to do this for Alf Tooze.'

'Tooze is in St Austell Hospital being taken care of by those who know how best to treat him. You'd do well to go back to work and make up his money until he's well enough to come home.'

'Alf's in no hospital,' said another of the men. 'He was dead when they got him there. He's on his way to the town morgue right now. A horseman came to Ruddlemoor up the back road from St Austell and told us.'

'It'll be the turn of they tinkers when we get our hands on 'em,' said the first spokesman. 'We'll beat 'em out of the woods like pheasants.'

'That's right. We'll bring a brace of 'em back for you.'

Shouting their intentions, the clay workers made their way along the road towards St Austell. Behind them Lily, Darley and the Varcoe men watched them until they passed from sight around a bend in the road.

'I can't say that I agree with the way they're going about things,' declared the Varcoe clay works captain. 'But one thing's certain: the road through Menacuddle will be a safer place after today.'

Chapter 10

When the wagon carrying Darley and the others reached Ruddlemoor, the only employees remaining at the clay workings were Abel Bolitho, his shift captain, and the bal maidens.

Darley still held the bloody handkerchief to his cheek, and blood streaked his face and stained his shirt. Nevertheless, the Ruddlemoor captain's first question was about the wages Darley had been sent to collect. 'What's happened to them? We heard they'd been stolen.'

'They're here,' replied Darley. Reaching inside his shirt, he extracted the pouch and threw it down to Bolitho.

'And only safe because this young man had the sense to ask if he might ride with me. If he hadn't, you'd have lost your money and be mourning *two* Ruddlemoor men. Your drunken wagoner fell victim to the men who'd got him in that state.'

There was controlled anger in Jeremiah Rowe's voice as he added, 'What's more, if it hadn't been for him, the Varcoe works would have lost its wages too.'

'Then I won't be having to thank you,' said Bolitho, ungraciously. 'I don't want to be beholden to a Varcoe man.'

While this exchange was taking place, Darley climbed down from the wagon, helping Lily down after him.

'The horse could do with some water before we go,' said the driver. 'I'll take it over to the trough.'

'We'll all go,' said Jeremiah Rowe. 'I had hoped time might have mellowed you, Abel Bolitho. Regrettably, it hasn't.'

Ordering his driver to take the horse and wagon to the trough, Jeremiah Rowe called to Darley as the wagon creaked away, 'You'd better get someone to look at that face, Darley. It's a nasty wound.'

'Let me have a look at it.'

Jo and the other bal maidens had drawn close to hear what was being said and now Jo stepped forward.

'This is none of your business, Jo. You're a bal maiden, not a nurse. Get back to your work.'

Jo stood her ground against the works captain. 'You heard what Captain Rowe said. Someone should look at Darley's face. You know very well there's no one better than me hereabouts.'

43

Her attitude was every bit as forceful as Abel Bolitho's. Unexpectedly, he did not pursue the argument.

Turning her attention to Darley, she reached out for the handkerchief. 'Let me have a look at it.'

Removing the handkerchief, she winced and there was a sharp intake of breath from the watching bal maidens.

'It *is* nasty.'

Calling to Captain Bolitho's daughter, Jo said, 'Tessa, go to the office and bring me the medicine box. Quickly now. I'll be over by the water tank.'

As she hurried away, Captain Bolitho glared at the remaining bal maidens. 'The rest of you can get back to work. The men might have marched off the works, but that doesn't mean you need do nothing for the remainder of the day.'

When she and Darley reached the water tank, Jo turned on the tap and washed much of the blood from the handkerchief before using it to clean up Darley's face.

She was watched anxiously by Lily who asked, 'Is it serious?'

Without stopping what she was doing, she replied, 'I'll clean it up as much I can, but Darley should really see a doctor.'

Tessa returned very quickly with the medicine chest, wincing anew at sight of the ugly cut on Darley's cheek. But her father was standing nearby, glaring at her, and she reluctantly hurried away to join the other bal maidens.

As Jo added iodine liquid to the wet handkerchief and began dabbing it on the ugly wound, she asked quietly, 'Have you always gone around playing the hero, Darley Shovell?'

'Not *me*, but you should have seen Lily! They'd have overwhelmed us for certain if she hadn't been there. She stamped on the fingers of one of them as he tried to climb on the wagon. She'd probably have fought them off single-handed had we not been there.'

Without pausing in what she was doing, Jo smiled at Lily. 'I don't doubt it. Especially if she believed you to be in danger. How many of them were there, Lily?'

'Seven – and Darley beat off three of them all on his own.'

Speaking to Darley once more, Jo said, 'Yet despite the excitement you're not nearly as exhausted as you were when you'd been walking around the works that first day I saw you.'

'Or like he was when he'd been down the mine shaft at Notter,' added Lily.

'Well! Perhaps you're getting better, Darley.'

Looking sadly sceptical, he said, 'I'd like to think I was.'

'It does happen, you know,' said Jo. 'I've heard folks say so. Tessa was telling me only the other day of someone who'd been curcd. She said he was worse than you.'

44

'Were you talking to her about me?'

Jo coloured up. 'I can't remember now.'

Suddenly, Darley put a hand to his face. 'Hey! What are you doing?'

Jo was wrapping a bandage over his head and down beneath his chin. After a couple of turns, she twisted it so it passed around his forehead too. 'I've put a dressing on the wound. This is the only way I know to keep it in place.'

When she was satisfied with her work, she said, 'You were lucky your cheekbone wasn't smashed or your sight affected. Anyway, how does it feel now?'

Working his jaw back and forth, Darley said, 'I feel silly – but I do appreciate what you've done, Jo. It's very kind of you.'

'I should think you *ought* to be grateful,' said Lily, unexpectedly taking Jo's side. 'She's made a good job of it. Where did you learn to do things like that?'

'One of my ma's aunts was a nurse in the Crimea, with Florence Nightingale. She taught me. I've always wanted to be a nurse too, but Pa is against it.'

'Would you teach me about bandaging and things, sometime?' Lily asked eagerly.

'Of course.'

From the door of the works office, Captain Bolitho was glaring at them but Jeremiah Rowe was returning with the wagon and the Ruddlemoor captain stayed where he was.

'I hope that face heals quickly,' said Rowe. 'At least you have a very pretty nurse to look after you. Thank you for your help in protecting the Varcoe wages. Without you and that young sister of yours there would be no pay for my men today.'

'I should be thanking you,' said Darley. He found speaking difficult because the bandage restricted the movement of his jaw. 'In fact, I feel guilty about it all. If it hadn't been for me, you wouldn't have been involved.'

'Not today, perhaps, but if they had got away with it there would have been another time. I doubt very much if there will be now.'

As the wagon was about to move on, Lanyon Sweet jumped to the ground and extended a hand to Darley. 'You have a great deal of courage, young man – and I admire courage. If you ever need a strong arm, call on Lanyon Sweet. It'll be yours.'

The big man caught Lily's eye as he turned away and he suddenly bent down and picked her up as easily as if she weighed nothing at all.

Holding her at arms' length, her face on a level with his, he said, 'You're going to have every young man in the district running after you when you're a few years older. If you ever want to break anything more than a heart or two, you come and find Lanyon. I'll do it for you.'

As the Varcoe clay works men left Ruddlemoor, Lily said, 'I'd better

45

be going now. Are you coming home, Darley?'

'No, you go. I've still got to pay out the men when they return – but leave me to tell Ma about what happened, do you hear?'

Lily was on her way to the works gate when Abel Bolitho made his way to where Jo stood with Darley.

'Now all the excitement's died down, perhaps we can get a little work done around here. Back to the office, Shovell. You get back to your work too, Jo – but clean yourself up first. We don't want to have the clay discoloured by blood.'

Calling across to the bal maidens, he said, 'Tessa, come and put this medicine box back where it came from.'

She returned the medicine box and was making her way back to the drying shed when her father fell in step beside her. 'I don't know what Ruddlemoor is coming to. It's the first time the men have walked out on me – for whatever reason. I suppose that's what comes of having a Union man working in the office.'

Glancing at his daughter, he added, 'You keep clear of Darley Shovell, you hear me, Tessa? That boy is trouble. Nothing but trouble.'

Chapter 11

Abel Bolitho was in favour of stopping a day's pay from all the men who had walked out of the works to scour the Menacuddle Woods in search of the would-be robbers. He made the suggestion to Josh when the Ruddlemoor owner next visited the works.

Josh thought otherwise. Standing in the captain's office, looking out of the window at all the activity outside, he said, 'I support the action they took. One of their own was killed and an attempt made to steal *their* pay. Acting together the way they did is what belonging to a community – any community – is all about. Whatever you say, Captain Bolitho, clay men and miners are not so very different from each other. They stick together. That's the way it should be.'

In truth, the miners' actions had not culminated in any great victory. All they had succeeded in doing was to flush out a number of men and women living rough in the woods, and destroy their dwellings. There had been no sign of the men who had murdered Alf Tooze.

'By the way,' Josh turned away from the window, 'which of the girls out there is Captain Bray's daughter? She made a good job of dressing that nasty gash on Darley's face. He'll carry a scar for the remainder of his life, but I think she's prevented it from becoming infected.'

Josh was in an amiable mood this morning. Things were beginning to assume some semblance of order in the new Retallick house. Just before he left home Miriam had admitted that she thought she might settle down in the Gover Valley very happily. The house was larger than she was used to, but it had a happy atmosphere.

'Darley's mother gave me the sharp edge of her tongue when I saw her yesterday evening. She blamed me because he was caught up in the attempted robbery. It's the second time recently he's played the hero on my behalf. She's insisted he takes today off in case he feels any after-effects.'

Abel Bolitho did not share Josh's feeling of *bonhomie*. 'It strikes me that trouble follows close on the heels of that young man. He takes after his father, no doubt.'

'You'll be well acquainted with Jethro Shovell then, Captain Bolitho?' There was sarcasm in Josh's question.

'I spoke to him for the first time when he came here with you. If that's the only time, I'll be the happier for it.'

'I *do* know him, Captain Bolitho. I've known him for nigh on thirty years, and I knew his father before him. I can assure you there's not a more honest, God-fearing, caring, family man in the whole of Cornwall.'

'My father was an honest, caring man too. He did his duty as he saw it and gave his loyalty to the man who paid his wages. His reward was to be attacked and beaten into an early grave by Shovell's thugs. I don't need to *know* Shovell to understand what he stands for. What's more, I've never taken on a Union man at the Ruddlemoor works. Because of that policy we've never had a day's trouble. If you've the stomach for it, you'll keep it that way.'

Having offered Josh this forceful suggestion, Captain Abel Bolitho shrugged on his heavy coat and left the office.

Watching his captain stride away towards the drying shed, head down and body held stiffly against the chill wind, Josh felt his feeling of well-being ebbing away.

He would have liked to point out to Abel Bolitho the subtle difference between Jethro's organisation, which was more in the nature of a Benevolent and Sick Fund – though perhaps one with more teeth – and a Trades Union, but he knew it would make no difference. Although it remained unsaid, it was apparent that Abel Bolitho thought no more highly of clay owners than he did of Union men. It would inevitably lead to a clash between them.

Not all the members of the Bolitho family shared the bitterness Abel felt towards the Shovells. On Sunday, the day after Josh's brief conversation with the clay captain, there was a knock on the door of the Shovells' St Austell home.

Lily answered the door and greeted the callers with wide-eyed, speechless surprise. Jo Bray was standing outside. With her was Tessa Bolitho and an older woman who bore such a striking resemblance to Tessa that Lily knew it must be her mother. All three were dressed in their Sunday best clothes.

'Who is it, Lily?' a voice called from somewhere at the back of the house.

'It's . . . it's Jo Bray, Tessa Bolitho and her ma . . . I think.'

'That's right, Lily.' Jo smiled. 'The Bolithos are neighbours. We're on our way home from St Austell church. I persuaded them we should call and see how Darley is.'

Lottie Shovell appeared in the passageway behind Lily. Unfastening her apron as she advanced towards the door, she said, 'Don't leave them outside in the cold, girl. Ask them in.'

'We can't stop, Mrs Shovell, it's a long walk home. But as we were in St Austell I thought we'd call in to inquire after Darley. That stone caused a nasty gash on his face and I was concerned when he didn't come to work yesterday.'

48

'He's all the better for your kindness to him, Miss Bray,' said Lottie as she ushered Jo and the others inside the house and along the passageway. 'He had a bad day yesterday. I'm happy to say he's much improved this morning. Do you know where he is right now, Lily?'

'Up in his room reading, I expect. That's how he spends most of his time.'

'Go and tell him to come down, please. Won't you all sit down for a while? When Darley joins us I'll make us all a nice cup of tea. It has the feel of winter outside today.'

'We really mustn't be too late getting home.' Doris Bolitho spoke for the first time, constantly clasping and unclasping her hands nervously.

'You'll have a cup of tea at least? It will warm you for the walk home. Churches are cold places on the best of days. Besides, I really do want to thank Miss Bray for the way she dressed the gash on Darley's face. You should be a nurse, Miss Bray – Jo, isn't it? You were kind to him the day we walked around the works too, I remember.'

'It was the least I could do for him on Friday. He saved our wages. He also saved the life of my uncle when he hurt his shoulder down the Notter mine. My aunt said that if he hadn't been brought up when he was, he would have bled to death.'

As she was speaking, Darley put in an appearance. He still wore a bandage, tied in the same fashion as before, but it was not as tidy as it had been when Jo put in on and looked far too loose to her critical eye.

Darley looked somewhat uncertainly from Jo to Tessa and her mother. 'This is a very nice surprise.'

Returning his rather shy smile, Jo said, 'We were so close it seemed foolish not to call and see how you are.'

'I'll go and make that tea,' said Lottie. 'Come with me, Mrs Bolitho, we can chat in the kitchen. Lily, you can come along and help.'

Lily would have preferred to remain in the front room, but she was ushered from the room ahead of her mother and Mrs Bolitho.

For a few minutes after the others had left the room, there was an awkward silence. It was broken by Darley.

'It really is nice of you to come calling on me.'

Tessa shrugged. 'It was Jo's idea, not mine.'

'I've been worried,' said Jo, hastily. 'You took a nasty blow. I didn't think your cheekbone was broken, but I couldn't be certain.'

'You did very well. Ma said so. She changed the dressing last night but didn't make as good a job of the bandaging as you.'

'I can see that, it's working loose. Well, as I'm here I might as well change it for you now. Come and sit on this chair so I can reach it.'

'Would you two like me to go out to the kitchen with the others and leave you alone?'

Tessa sounded petulant. It seemed to her Jo and Darley were excluding her from their conversation.

49

'Don't be silly. Come here and watch what I do. You might learn something.'

When Darley sat down, Jo peeled off the bandage. As she carefully rolled it, she asked, 'What were you reading when we arrived?'

'A book by Charles Dickens called *Great Expectations*. My Great-uncle Josh – Josh Retallick – found a few of his books when he and Miriam moved into their new house. He brought them here for me. Have you read any of them?'

'I've heard of Charles Dickens,' Jo said, 'but I've never read anything of his. We don't have many books in the house.'

Tessa said nothing. Abel Bolitho read only with difficulty and was scornful of books.

'I'll lend one to you,' said Darley, delighted to be able to do something for her. 'I'll lend you one as well, Tessa. You'll enjoy them . . . ouch!'

The exclamation of pain was forced from him as Jo made a tentative attempt to remove the dressing from the wound on his face.

'We'll need some hot water from the kitchen to soak this off,' she declared. 'Will you fetch some, Tessa?'

To Darley's disappointment, when Tessa returned to the room with a basin filled with hot water she was accompanied by her mother, and by Lily and his own mother too.

They all stood about Darley, making sympathetic sounds as Jo succeeded in removing the dressing with a minimal amount of pain.

All except Tessa's mother declared the wound was looking much better than when they had first seen it. Doris Bolitho turned away, confessing that the sight of blood 'turned her stomach'.

'It is a lot better,' agreed Jo. 'I've also noticed that Darley seems better in himself. Perhaps his lungs are healing too.'

'I'd like to think so,' said Darley, almost angrily. 'But I have good months and I have bad ones. This happens to be a better spell than I've had for a long time.'

As Jo replaced the bandage, Doris Bolitho said anxiously, 'We really must be going now, Tessa. Your father won't be pleased if he's home before us.'

'I'll go upstairs and get the books I promised,' said Darley. 'Then I'll walk to the edge of town with you.'

'I'll come too,' said Lily brightly. This time Lottie did nothing to prevent her from accompanying her brother.

Lily and Darley parted company with Jo and the others on the outskirts of the small town. As they walked back to the house, Lily said, 'I've never known you give books away before. Especially before you've finished reading them.'

'It's all right, I know I'll get them back – from Jo, at least.'

'You like her, don't you?'

50

'Yes.'

'Better than you like me?'

Darley put an arm about his young sister's shoulders. 'I'll never like anyone better than I like you, Lily. It's just . . . I don't know, I feel differently about her, that's all.'

'Do you think you'll marry her, one day?'

Darley pulled his arm away from his sister's shoulders. 'How can I ever marry *anyone*, Lily?'

'Why not?' She realised her idle chatter had upset the brother she adored and took his hand. 'You're much better now than you have been for a very long time. I've noticed it. So has Jo – and you've said so yourself.'

'All the same, I doubt if I'll ever be well enough to marry anyone. No, Lily, you and Ma are stuck with me.'

Lily gripped his hand more tightly, her thoughts those of a confused nine year old. She desperately wanted Darley to get better. She wanted it more than anything else in the world. But if he did she knew he would marry Jo – and it would break her heart if ever he left home.

Chapter 12

Early in 1894, Darley was at work in the Ruddlemoor works office when a young man of about seventeen rode up on a lathered pony.

Tethering the horse outside, the young man hurried inside. Seeing Jethro, he said, 'Are you Mr Retallick?'

'No, he's in the pit with Cap'n Bolitho. Who wants him?'

'Mrs Retallick, over at Gover Valley. I'm a baker's boy from St Austell. We were delivering to Mrs Retallick when Mr Potter, the baker, told me to take the pony and come over here. I was to tell Mr Retallick to get home quick. Something about a letter from America or Africa, somewhere like that. Anyway, it seems it's upset Mrs Retallick. It must be urgent, because Mr Potter ain't never let me go off on my own on his pony before.'

Darley knew that Daniel, Josh and Miriam's only son, was living in Africa with his wife and family. He had met them once when they came to England on a visit, many years before.

'I'll send someone to find Josh Retallick and bring him here. Then I'll send him off home straightaway.'

The baker's boy looked doubtful. He had been sent on an urgent mission. If he returned and told Mr Potter he had not given the message to Mr Retallick personally . . .

'It's all right,' Darley guessed the reason for the young man's hesitation. 'I'm Mr Retallick's great-nephew. He'll get the message, I promise you. He'll probably pass you on the road and be back at Gover Valley before you get there.'

Darley went outside and found Tessa filling a kettle to make tea for the other bal maidens. He sent her to find Josh.

Ten minutes later Josh hurried into the office. 'What is it, Darley? One of the bal maidens just found me in the pit and told me I had to hurry back here. What's happening?'

'Miriam sent a delivery boy here to find you. She's had a letter from Matabeleland and wants you at home urgently.'

Josh hesitated for a moment, wondering what news could have arrived that needed his urgent attention.

'The boy said Miriam was very upset.'

Josh prevaricated no longer. 'I'll go home right away. Tell Cap'n Bolitho I'll see him in the morning about extending the pit.'

52

Josh left Ruddlemoor in a great hurry. His ageing horse was not used to being urged on at such a pace, but it responded well. Josh reached the Gover Valley house no more than twenty minutes after the message had been delivered to Darley.

Miriam had been looking out of one of the windows for him. Now she left the house and ran down the path to meet him. Josh took one look at her tearful face and knew that something really serious had happened.

'Oh, Josh. Thank God you're here! Just thinking about it . . . I feel as though I'm being torn apart . . .'

She clung to him fiercely and he felt a tension in her that frightened him.

'I was told you've had a letter from Matabeleland. Is it from Daniel? Has something happened to one of the children?'

'The letter's from . . . from Elvira.'

Elvira was the Portuguese-born wife of Daniel, their son.

Speaking as though the words were being torn from her, Miriam wailed, 'Daniel's dead, Josh. He's been . . . killed. So has Wyatt.'

Josh felt as though an icy hand had suddenly closed its grip about him, squeezing his chest so tight he had difficulty in breathing. Daniel was their only child, Wyatt their eldest grandson.

'What happened? Some accident? Has Elvira said?' Josh held Miriam even more tightly as he felt her body shaking against him.

'They were killed . . . murdered in a tribal uprising . . . The letter's inside.'

As he guided Miriam towards the house, Josh asked, 'What of the others? Are any of them hurt?' He shook his head in agonised disbelief. 'I've always thought they got on so well with the Matabele tribesmen. Daniel was a friend of Lobengula, their king.'

'Lobengula's dead too. It sounds as though the whole country is in chaos.'

They were inside the house now. Suddenly Miriam turned. Clinging to Josh, she began to cry. She wept as he had not heard her cry since she was a young girl.

Holding her here, in these still unfamiliar surroundings, he thought back over all that had happened in the eventful intervening years.

As a young man, Josh had been wrongly convicted of illegal Trades Union activities. His sentence was transportation to Australia. Miriam had elected to go with him, taking Daniel their son, then only three years old, with them.

Shipwrecked on the Skeleton Coast of South West Africa, they had lived an adventurous existence among the tribesmen. Then, eighteen years later, Josh had been granted a pardon.

When they returned to England, Daniel had remained behind. He made his home in Matabeleland where the Matabele king, Lobengula, granted him a vast tract of land in the Insimo Valley. Even when Cecil Rhodes added Matabeleland to his vast and expanding Southern African empire, Daniel's tenure was secure.

Now he and his eldest son were dead, apparently killed by the very people he had served and loved for so many years.

Later that evening, Josh read Elvira's letter aloud to Jethro and Lottie Shovell while Lily listened wide-eyed. On his return home, Darley had told them what little he knew and the family had hurried to the Retallick house.

It was the fourth or fifth time Josh had read the letter, but it added very little to what Miriam had said when he first returned home. Daniel and Wyatt were dead. Elvira was left in the Insimo Valley with her three surviving sons, Nat, Adam and Ben, the eldest only thirteen.

Lottie had brought a meal for the others, knowing they would not feel like cooking. Miriam was convinced that in her grief any attempt to eat would choke her, but she ate a token meal.

'What do you think will happen now?' asked Lottie. 'Will Elvira and the boys return to England?'

'I wish it was as simple as that,' said Josh as Miriam put down her knife and fork and pushed the half-eaten meal from her. 'But Elvira wouldn't be at home here. She was born in Mozambique – Portuguese East Africa. The boys were born and bred in Matabeleland. They are all African.'

'They're so far away from us,' said Miriam, blinking back tears once more. 'When I think of Daniel and Wyatt dying out there . . . in Africa.'

'It was where they wanted to be,' said Josh, his own voice gruff with the emotion he felt. 'Daniel had made enough money to settle his family anywhere in the world they cared to go. But he loved Insimo. They all did.'

'Do you think they'll want to stay now this has happened?' The question came from Jethro.

'I don't know.' Josh shook his head. 'I just don't know what they'll do. Elvira's father is dead, so I doubt if she'll return to Mozambique.'

'You'll write and suggest they all come here, of course?' said Lottie.

'It takes a long time for letters to travel to and from Insimo. It could be years before anything's settled. Everything that Elvira mentions in her letter probably happened at least two months ago.'

'All the same, we must do something,' said Miriam, 'One of us should go out there and see if anything can be done to help the family.'

She looked across the table at Josh. 'Much as I feel I desperately want to go, I think it will have to be you, Josh. It's not a journey for a woman, especially if there's trouble with the tribesmen.'

'How can I go, Miriam? There's so much happening here at the moment. We're in a new home with a new venture on our hands and I'm halfway through purchasing that piece of land between Ruddlemoor and the Varcoe workings. Things couldn't be more complicated.'

'Complicated they may be, but not half as complicated as I'll find it if I have to travel to Matabeleland – and on my own. I could run a business, whether it's a clay works or anything else, but getting to the Insimo Valley is quite another matter.'

'You couldn't manage the Ruddlemoor works, Miriam, even if Captain Bolitho were to be co-operative – and he shows no sign of that.'

'If you give me full powers of authority over Ruddlemoor he'll either take orders – or go.'

Josh was thoughtful for a few minutes. He knew just what Miriam was capable of when she turned her mind to it, and she was right. The hazardous journey to Matabeleland was not one for a woman to undertake, especially if there were still serious troubles there.

'You'd help her out, Jethro, if something came up that was too much for Miriam to handle?'

'Of course I would.'

'And what do you think might happen that I couldn't handle on my own, Josh Retallick?'

He looked at her fondly. 'Nothing, Miriam. Nothing at all. All right. As you say, one of us needs to go to Insimo and I can't think of anyone more capable of managing things here. I'll set about making the travel arrangements first thing in the morning.'

Chapter 13

Three days after the letter from Elvira reached the Gover Valley, Josh set off from Cornwall, bound for far-off Matabeleland.

Miriam, accompanied by Jethro, Lottie and Lily, was torn between grief and anxiety as she watched the train carrying Josh steam laboriously out of St Austell station. This was only the first leg of an eight-thousand-mile journey.

Travel had become far more sophisticated since she and Josh had returned to England from Africa, almost thirty years before. Nevertheless, it was still an uncertain adventure and Matabeleland was a primitive land, peopled by volatile tribesmen. Few of them would remember Josh.

Lottie was watching Miriam closely. She thought she knew something of what she was thinking at this moment. Giving her aunt a hug, she said, 'Try not to worry about Josh, Miriam. Just think, he might return to England with your grandchildren. They'd liven the place up and no mistake!'

'He has to get there first. Matabeleland is an awful long way from here.'

'Josh will be all right, you'll see.'

'Of course he will.' Jethro added his assurances to those of his wife. With Lily, both had come to the station with Miriam. 'He'll sort things out and be back before you know it.'

Miriam appreciated the attempt by her niece and Jethro to reassure her. However, neither appreciated the many dangers involved in travelling through Africa during a time of tribal unrest.

She and Josh had experienced tribal warfare once before . . . although it all seemed so long ago now. Almost as though it had occurred during another lifetime. She tried to quell her fears by telling herself that times had changed a great deal since then. Colonisation of the country by Cecil Rhodes and his British South Africa Company meant there were forces on hand to deal with any threat to travellers.

Then her thoughts returned to the tragic reason for Josh's long journey. If ever a man should have been safe in Matabeleland, it was Daniel. He had lived, worked and fought beside the Matabele. He was regarded by them as a brother. Their king had given him a vast area of land in recognition of their special relationship.

Despite this, Daniel and his eldest son were now dead. Killed by those very same 'brothers'.

The pain of such thoughts welled up inside Miriam, threatening to overflow and embarrass her before her relatives.

Abruptly, she switched her mind to other matters. 'I'll no doubt be kept busy while Josh is away. The time until his return will pass before I know it. There's the purchase of the new pit to be completed. Then I'll need to get it working. There will be an engine-house to build. The miners from Sharptor must be brought here with their families and housed – not to mention the day-to-day running of the Ruddlemoor works.'

'That's the way to think about things,' said Jethro, approvingly. 'If you feel you need any help, you can call on me.'

'Me too,' said Lily with intense sincerity.

Miriam gave them a bleak smile. 'Now there's a thought! I wonder what Captain Bolitho would think of having Jethro Shovell advising me – and him, no doubt – on the running of the Ruddlemoor?'

Miriam's working relationship with the works captain began no more propitiously than had her husband's.

Abel Bolitho set the tone for the day when he arrived at the office minutes after Darley had arrived for work.

Noisily slapping a book down on the desk in front of Darley, he said, 'What do you mean by giving this to Tessa to read?'

Darley was taken aback. He had loaned three or four books to Jo since she, Tessa and Doris Bolitho had visited the Shovell house in St Austell. He had almost forgotten he had also loaned a Dickens novel to Tessa. It certainly contained nothing unsuitable for a young girl's reading.

'I thought she might like to read it. It's a very good book.'

'*I'll* decide what's good reading for my daughter, not you. I'll not have any Trades Union ideas put into her head by such rubbish.'

Darley looked at the mine captain in astonishment, 'Dickens had nothing to do with Trades Unions. He simply wrote a good story, that's all.'

'That's not what my father used to say. He swore it was men like this Dickens who were at the root of most of the troubles we still have in this country. Trying to persuade ignorant, impressionable folk they're the equal to their betters. "A recipe for insurrection", he called it. I can remember him saying it as though it were only yesterday. "A recipe for insurrection". I'll not have you putting any such ideas in my daughter's head. You'll keep your books to yourself – and stay away from Tessa. You hear me, Shovell?'

Darley said nothing. It was no use trying to argue with the bigoted works captain, especially when he was in one of these moods.

As he placed the book in a desk drawer and prepared for the day's work, he wondered what trouble there had been between them when Abel Bolitho took the book from Tessa.

An hour later Darley was paying out termination wages to two men who had been summarily dismissed by the works captain, their offence an apparent failure to check a waste wagon before it was hoisted up the steep side of the waste-tip, beside the pit.

The result was that the wagon's load had been deposited halfway up the slope, sending sand and stones tumbling back into the depths of the pit.

When the men left the office, pale and angry at the loss of their livelihood, Darley suggested to Captain Bolitho that dismissal was a harsh punishment. It was possible the accident had been attributable to a faulty securing pin, as one of the two men had suggested.

Abel Bolitho rounded on him immediately. 'They were paid to secure the wagons and make certain nothing was wrong. The load from the wagon might have derailed others and started an avalanche that could have swept the whole hoist away. Quite apart from the money it would have wasted, men might have been killed. Just keep your opinions to yourself on things you know nothing about, Shovell. If you don't you'll be putting a line through your own name on the Ruddlemoor pay-roll. You'll not have your uncle – or great-uncle, whatever he is – playing nursemaid to you during the next few months. A lot can happen in that time. Don't you forget it!'

Josh was temporarily absent from Ruddlemoor, but if Abel Bolitho thought he would have a free hand in managing the clay works during this time, he was to be sadly disillusioned.

The day after Josh departed for Matabeleland, Miriam arrived at Ruddlemoor driving herself in a small trap, pulled by a lively little grey pony.

Abel Bolitho was in the office with Jim Bray. He happened to be looking through the window when Miriam arrived. He hurriedly put down the mug of tea he was drinking and donned an outside coat in a bid to be out of the office before she came in.

He was not quite quick enough. They met in the office doorway.

'Ah, Captain Bolitho! You're just the man I want to talk to . . .'

'I'm sorry, Mrs Retallick. I'm exceptionally busy at the moment. I'm needed in the pit. If you're still here in an hour or so we'll speak then.'

With this, Abel pushed past her and hurried away in the direction of the pit.

Her expression inscrutable, Miriam watched him walking hurriedly away. Then she turned and walked inside the office.

Captain Bray had leaped to his feet the moment she arrived in the doorway and stood saying nothing, seemingly embarrassed. Whether it was on account of her unexpected arrival, or because of Abel Bolitho's abrupt exit, it was difficult to say.

Taking in the half-empty cup standing on the table where the works captain had left it, Miriam spoke to Jim Bray. 'There's no need to stand on ceremony. I'm Mrs Retallick. I don't think we've met before?'

'No, ma'am. I'm Jim Bray, one of the shift captains.'

'Well, Captain Bray, since there's some tea going, perhaps you'll pour me a cup.'

Looking across the office, she nodded to Darley. 'Aren't you having any?'

'I don't have tea with the captains.'

'Well, you will today. Pour another, Captain Bray. We've some work to do together.'

Beneath her arm Miriam carried a long cardboard tube wrapped in a piece of oil-cloth. Removing the waterproof covering, she handed the tube to Darley. 'There's a map inside. Spread it out somewhere – on the table over there will do. It shows the piece of land Josh had bought for the new pit. I signed the purchase only this morning and I want you both to have a look at the map, so you know exactly what is ours. Then we'll take it outside and mark the ground off. Parts of it are very close to the Varcoe workings, so we'll need to make certain our markers are accurate. We don't want any trouble with them while Josh is away.'

Darley spread the map on the table and all three pored over it as they drank their tea.

'Marking the ground off shouldn't be too difficult,' said Captain Bray, after a thorough inspection of the map. 'Much of the Varcoe ground is already fenced. If we put down our own markers a yard or two on our side of the fence, Captain Rowe won't give us any trouble.'

'I'm sure he won't,' said Darley, confidently. 'He's the man I was riding with when we were attacked in the Menacuddle Woods.'

'Good.' Miriam rolled up the map. 'How about the other boundaries? Do you anticipate any trouble marking them?'

'None at all,' said Captain Bray. 'There's a smallholding in one corner, they're well fenced. For the rest . . . the surrounding land is mostly waste.'

'Then let's go and mark it out. While we're at it we'll decide where the engine-house and the waste-heap are going to go – together with anything else we're likely to need.'

Jim Bray seemed suddenly uncertain of what was being asked of him. 'Shouldn't we wait until Captain Bolitho is free to come along and help with such decisions?'

'You heard what he said to me, Captain Bray. He's too busy. We'll do it without him – that's unless you don't feel confident enough to make such decisions?'

'I'm every bit as experienced as Captain Bolitho – or any other clay captain, Mrs Retallick. Making decisions doesn't bother me, but making *trouble* does, especially where Cap'n Bolitho is concerned.'

'There will be no trouble,' Miriam declared. 'You're simply obeying the orders of the owner. Shall we go?'

Chapter 14

As Miriam walked around the newly purchased land with Darley and the Ruddlemoor shift captain, she found herself increasingly impressed with Jim Bray. He was not afraid of taking decisions. He also offered considered and practical suggestions about the surveying work they were carrying out and the places where various buildings should be sited. His ideas were duly recorded on the map Darley carried.

At the end of the morning, when Miriam felt they had dealt with everything to her satisfaction, she was warm in her praise of the Ruddlemoor shift captain.

'You've been most helpful, Captain Bray. We have achieved far more than I hoped for today. We've mapped the area of the new pit, decided where the engine-house will go and agreed on the tunnelling that's needed. What will be the first task when work begins?'

'Removing the "overburden" – that's the topsoil covering the clay. Then we'll drive a shaft from the place where the engine will be to the centre of the pit, in order to pump out the clay. Do you intend having new settling tanks and dries here, or will you use those at the Ruddlemoor?'

Not certain what he was talking about, but unwilling to show her ignorance, Miriam replied, 'I haven't made up my mind yet. What would you suggest?'

Jim Bray removed his hat, disclosing a small bald patch. Scratching his head thoughtfully, he said, 'You've asked my opinion and I'll give it to you, though Cap'n Bolitho probably won't agree with me. You're having an engine brought in for the pumping. I go along with that. There's no water on the new ground. We could probably take enough from the Ruddlemoor to wash clay down to the bottom of the pit, but not enough to power a water wheel. So, if you're having an engine, you might as well have your own tanks and a "dry" too.

'There's another thing. The Varcoe works are talking of having a railway line brought in. With the amount of clay you'll be taking out of the two pits, you can either come to an arrangement with Cap'n Rowe of the Varcoe works or build your own line around them. It would make a lot more sense to share costs with the Varcoe and extend the line to take clay from here and from the Ruddlemoor.'

'What would Cap'n Bolitho think about working so closely with the

Varcoe mine?' Darley remembered Abel Bolitho's reaction to having Captain Rowe help out during the attempted robbery.

'He won't like it. Nevertheless, if the cost is worked out and it's proved to be cheaper, then he'll have to go along with it. After all, the works belongs to Mr and Mrs Retallick. Captain Bolitho takes their pay so he must accept their orders, same as the rest of us.'

'You're absolutely right, Captain Bray,' declared Miriam, firmly. 'Unfortunately, I feel Captain Bolitho needs occasional reminding of the situation.'

Miriam had decided she liked Jim Bray. She felt he was a man to rely on. He had none of Bolitho's bluster or churlishness and possessed a quiet confidence in himself. What was more, he obviously had a sound knowledge of the China clay industry.

'When Darley has finished putting our ideas on the map, I'd like you to have a couple of men mark out the ground. Then I'll come along here again and see for myself where everything is going.'

'When is work likely to begin on producing clay?'

'As soon as we're ready. Within the month certainly. This afternoon I'm going to inspect the new houses Josh has had built, just down the road. If they're ready I'll have the Sharptor men and their families move in right away. They'll take on the building of the engine house and any tunnelling that needs to be done. But we'll have another meeting about everything before then.'

Miriam welcomed the challenges presented by the tasks Josh had left for her. It helped deaden the heartache she felt whenever she thought of the death of Daniel – and she thought about it for much of each waking day.

'We'll need to cost out the new works carefully, Darley. Keep it separate from the Ruddlemoor accounts – initially, at any rate. Can you do that?'

'Yes, but I'll need help in the office. More than one person if we go ahead with a railway line. I'd like to turn much of the Ruddlemoor paperwork over to someone else for a while and concentrate on costing out the new pit. Mind you, Cap'n Bolitho isn't going to be happy about having another clerk in his office.'

'When we've been hard pushed in the past for someone to keep the books Cap'n Bolitho has brought his girl in, young Tessa, to help out,' said Jim Bray.

The idea did not appeal to Darley immediately. 'She has the learning, certainly – but so does your Jo.' He sounded a cautionary note. 'Anyway, I can't see Cap'n Bolitho allowing Tessa to work in the office with me. He gets angry if I so much as talk to her when we pass each other by.'

'We'll tackle that problem when we come to it,' said Miriam. 'First, we ought to see whether either Tessa or Jo would be willing to work in the office. Let's go back there now.'

Captain Bolitho was still absent from the office. Darley thought it was probably because the works captain was aware that Miriam was still around.

Tessa and Jo left their work in the drying shed to a chorus of ribaldry from their fellow bal maidens. The other girls were aware Jo was 'sweet on Mrs Retallick's great-nephew', while Tessa would 'look twice at anything wearing trousers'. They suggested the summons was to check whether either of the girls might suit Miriam Retallick's great-nephew.

Miriam's initial greeting did little to give either girl an immediate explanation for the summons.

Speaking to Jo first, she said, 'So you're the young lady I've heard so much about from Darley's mother? You seem to have made quite an impression on the Shovell family.'

Darley was unaware Miriam and his mother had ever discussed Jo. Concerned lest Miriam say something to embarrass him in front of Jo's father, he said hurriedly, 'Jo had a relative who nursed soldiers in the Crimean War. Jo learned some of her skills. She treats all those who hurt themselves while they're working at Ruddlemoor.'

'She does that,' observed Jim Bray, dryly. 'But I think she enjoys tending some more than others.'

Both Jo and Darley coloured up and Miriam came to their rescue, saving them from further embarrassment. 'It's comforting to know there's someone on the works with such skills. I hope you'll continue to use them, Jo, but that isn't why I've called you and Tessa in here. Captain Bray tells me that Tessa's helped out with clerical duties here in the past and Darley says you read and write well too.'

'I've worked in here sometimes,' Tessa admitted. 'But only to help out my father.'

'Do you both think you might enjoy doing such work on a more permanent basis?'

After a moment's hesitation while Jo tried to anticipate where such questioning was going, Tessa nodded her head, 'Yes. Yes, I do.'

Jo was less certain. 'Why do you ask?'

'We're expanding the works to bring in the land between Ruddlemoor and the Varcoe works. This will require much more detailed accounting and record-keeping. Darley will need help in the new office I intend having built. Your pay would be increased if you took on such work, of course.'

'I'd be working with Darley?' Suddenly much more enthusiastic, Jo's gaze shifted to the subject of her query.

Now it was Tessa's turn to be dubious about the offer. 'I doubt if my father would agree to that.'

'You leave that to me, young lady. If he's concerned for your reputation, I'll take on an elderly man from Sharptor to work in the

63

office too. I have someone in mind who's a well-known preacher.'

Jim Bray hid a smile from his employer. Tessa Bolitho was barely sixteen years of age, but she already had a certain notoriety among the bal maidens for her flirtatious nature.

'Speak to your father about it, Tessa, then you and Jo think about my offer – but don't leave it too long. I want the office built and working as soon as possible.'

When Jo and Tessa had returned to the drying shed, Miriam said, 'Darley, I'd like you and Captain Bray to decide where the new office should be sited. Remember, you'll be doing all the paperwork for both workings there. Captain Bray, can you bring in some men to start the work? They'll be helped by the Sharptor men when they arrive.'

'That's no problem at all, Mrs Retallick – and I have no objection to Jo working in the office.'

He hesitated. 'But shouldn't we discuss all this with Captain Bolitho before we make any firm decisions?'

'If Captain Bolitho had put himself out to be here he would have been included in the discussion. However, he's made it perfectly clear he finds the Ruddlemoor works as much as he can manage. In view of this I think the new works should be run separately from the Ruddlemoor – although I will expect the two to co-operate in every way possible. It means a captain must be appointed for the new works. I'd like you to take on the task, Captain Bray. If you agree, you can start recruiting men right away and supervise all the necessary building work.'

Smiling at the astonishment of the two men standing before her, she said, 'Splendid. Now that's decided I can go on my way and see to all the other matters that need my attention. Goodbye, Captain Bray. Goodbye, Darley. I am quite sure we are all going to work very well together.'

Chapter 15

Not ten minutes after Miriam had left the Ruddlemoor clay works, Abel Bolitho stormed into the office. Pointing a quivering finger at Darley, he shouted, 'You! What's all this nonsense Tessa's just told me about coming to work in the office with you? You're out of your mind if you think I'll ever allow such a thing.'

Darley's calm manner belied the inner turmoil that Bolitho's manner always provoked within him, but before he could reply, Jim Bray was speaking.

'Why, Abel? I've said I'll be pleased for my Jo to work in the office with Tessa. I can't see either of them coming to any harm.'

Abel Bolitho looked at the shift captain as though he had taken leave of his senses. 'You'd let Jo work in an office when she's likely to spend time alone . . . with him?'

'Why not? From all accounts the office is likely to be a busy place when the new workings are opened up.'

Captain Bolitho's angry expression changed to one of bemusement. 'What does that woman think she's doing? We don't need a man and two girls to keep the books. If she thinks I'm going to have them all crowded in here then she'd better think again.'

'We won't be in here, Cap'n Bolitho. Mrs Retallick's having a new office built so that all the paperwork and accounting for the two pits can be done in the one office.'

'*Two* pits? Will someone tell me exactly what's been going on behind my back this morning? Jim?'

'Mrs Retallick has finalised the purchase of the piece of land between us and the Varcoe pit. We've been out checking the boundaries this morning. She intends opening up the ground and having work begin on it within the month.'

'That's out of the question. The Ruddlemoor tanks and the "dry" can't cope with any more clay than we're producing ourselves at the moment.'

'She knows that. Everything that's needed will be built on the new ground. It will be virtually independent of the Ruddlemoor.'

Darley could see that Jim Bray was uneasy about telling Captain Bolitho of his own role in the new clay works – and the works captain was making it no easier for him.

'*She's* decided all this . . . opening up a new pit, planning production . . . All without consulting me?' Abel Bolitho was almost beside himself with rage once more.

'She came to the Ruddlemoor this morning to discuss it with you, Cap'n Bolitho, but you said you were too busy to speak to her.' Darley broke into the conversation once more. 'Miriam Retallick isn't a woman who lets anything put her off if there's something to be done. She's off now making arrangements for the Sharptor men to come over here.'

'Oh, is she? Well they'll find themselves kicking their heels when they get here. She's going to have to come and see me again, because I'm not taking on a new pit without proper consultation.'

'There'll be no extra work for you, Abel.' Jim Bray spoke quietly, appearing to be concentrating on packing tobacco into his pipe. 'Mrs Retallick intends operating the new pit independent of the Ruddlemoor. She's asked me if I'll take on the job of captain there. I've accepted.'

'You've WHAT?' Abel Bolitho seemed to swell with anger. '*This* is what it's all about, isn't it? The pair of you have been plotting behind my back so you can become a works captain. I'm surprised you stopped at the captaincy of the new works. Couldn't you quite bring yourself to ask if you could take over the Ruddlemoor as well?'

'It's not like that, Abel, either for me or for Mrs Retallick. She came here this morning to see you. When you said you were too busy she asked me to show her around the new ground. To be honest, you've brought this on yourself. She said that since the Ruddlemoor keeps you so busy, you couldn't possibly manage the new works in addition to this one.'

'She said *that*! Well, we'll soon see. Where is she now?' Furious at the events of the morning, Bolitho put the question to Darley.

'Mrs Retallick's gone to look at the houses that have been built just along the road for the men she's bringing from Sharptor,' said Darley. Hesitantly, he added. 'But . . . do you think it's wise to try to speak to her today? It might be better if you left it for some other time.'

'Don't you try to tell me what I should or shouldn't be doing. Not unless she's made you a captain over my head as well!'

Turning to Captain Bray once more, he said, 'Since you're so eager to take over a clay works you can look after the Ruddlemoor until I come back. I'm going to see Mrs Retallick and find out what she's playing at.'

When the works captain had stormed from the office, Darley grinned at Jim Bray. 'I'm glad we've got that behind us. I was afraid he might get angry.'

Captain Bray had been more apprehensive than Darley about Abel Bolitho's reaction. He lit his pipe now, trying to keep the hand holding the match from shaking. He was a quiet, unassuming man, unused to violence or altercation.

When the tobacco in his pipe was glowing and a cloud of blue smoke drifted about his head, he said, 'Don't you think you ought to try to find Mrs Retallick before Cap'n Bolitho? Warn her about him?'

Darley shook his head confidently. 'I think Captain Bolitho is about to get the surprise of his life. He might have little regard for women, but I doubt if he's met one quite like Great-aunt Miriam. She's cut bigger men than him down to size.'

The houses being built for the men from Sharptor were only a short distance along the road from the Ruddlemoor works. Abel hurried there on foot. His anger and impatience would not have allowed him to wait while a horse was brought from the Ruddlemoor stables and saddled for him.

It began to rain when he was halfway to the new houses and he arrived wet and still angry. It did nothing for his temper to see Miriam emerge from one of the houses accompanied by an unctuously smiling builder.

She was carrying an umbrella. She opened it when she saw the rain and raised it above her head before stepping from the doorway.

Abel met her halfway along the path and her greeting did nothing to improve his state of mind.

'Hello, Captain Bolitho. I'm surprised to see you here. I thought you were so very busy at Ruddlemoor. I do hope nothing has happened there.'

'You know damn' well why I'm here, so don't play foolish games with me.'

'You just mind your language when you're talking to Mrs Retallick, Bolitho, or you'll be taught some manners. You're not at your works talking to clay men now.'

The builder stepped to Miriam's side and glared at the works captain. He was a big, bearded man who appeared well able to back up any threat he made. In addition, there were some twenty of the builder's workmen all within hearing distance.

'Thank you for your concern, Mr Kent,' Miriam said to the builder. 'But I don't think I need fear Captain Bolitho.'

'You may be right, Mrs Retallick, perhaps 'tis only his own wife he's fond of knocking about. I've known him since we were boys in the same village. He had twice as much tongue as brain, even then. What Doris Hooper, as was, ever saw in him, I'll never know. She could have had the pick of the village . . .'

'All right, Mr Kent. You may go back inside now. I shall be quite safe.'

'If you say so, Mrs Retallick. But, remember, I shan't be far away should you need me.'

With a final belligerent glance at the unusually silent Abel Bolitho, the bearded builder went back inside the newly completed house.

When he had passed from hearing, Abel began, 'I've come looking for you because I have something to say . . .'

'Now you've found me *I* have something to say to you, Captain Bolitho. If you ever again talk to me the way you did just now you'll find yourself looking for work – and I'll make quite certain you never find it in clay country. Is that understood?'

'I came looking for you because . . .'

'I said, *is that understood*? I'm awaiting your reply.' Miriam fixed Bolitho with a look that had caused stronger men than the works captain to quail.

'I . . . I shouldn't have said what I did.' The mumbled words were spoken reluctantly.

'No, you shouldn't – and you never will again! Now, what is it you were in so much of a hurry to say to me?'

As works captain, Abel Bolitho controlled the destiny of the men and women who worked under his command at the Ruddlemoor works. For the same reason, he also had a considerable status within the community in which he lived. He was unused to being put firmly in his place by a woman. Yet he knew instinctively that Miriam Retallick was a woman who meant every word she said.

'I'm not happy with what you intend doing with the land next to the Ruddlemoor.'

'Oh? And what exactly is it that you don't like? Captain Bray being put in charge of the works?'

'No. Well . . . Not entirely.'

'Then what is it? You made it quite clear to me this morning you are too busy at Ruddlemoor to take on anything else. I took you at your word and placed Captain Bray in charge of the new works. Do you have objections to that?'

'I . . . Well, I feel I should have been consulted. I'm certain it's what Mr Retallick would have done . . .'

Abel Bolitho was floundering for words to express the way he felt. He had made a grave error of judgement in snubbing Miriam Retallick that morning. He realised it now, but could think of no way of recovering lost ground.

'You *should* have been consulted, I agree wholeheartedly. Indeed, I came to Ruddlemoor to consult you. However, you made it perfectly clear you were far too busy to speak with me, so there was no way I could discuss the new works with you. I did the only thing I could. I sorted it out for myself – with the help of Captain Bray. Now he will take over the new works, so everyone should be happy. As for Mr Retallick not agreeing . . . We discussed what we would do before he left. He left me with a letter of attorney, giving me full powers to do whatever I believe to be in his best interests. I have acted accordingly. Is there anything else?'

Rain was falling hard now and Abel Bolitho was getting very wet. He recognised he was staring defeat squarely in the face but tried once more to retrieve at least some of the ground he had lost through his own intransigence.

'We'll need to discuss the new arrangements. It will have an effect on the working of the Ruddlemoor.'

'Of course it will. It will make the works far more efficient when we have a railway link with the new pit – and with the Varcoe works.'

'A railway? The Varcoe works?' Abel realised his morning's error had provoked more far-reaching consequences than he had realised.

'That's right. Oh! There's another thing. I want your daughter to work in the office. Captain Bray's daughter will probably be working there too. I trust you have no objections?'

Abel Bolitho had a great many objections, but it would have taken a braver man than he to raise them with Miriam Retallick at this moment.

'She can work in the office . . . if that's what she wants.'

He justified his about-face by telling himself it would be useful to have someone close to him working in the office. Tessa would be able to let him know exactly what was going on in the new set up this woman had brought into being.

'Good, then I'll bid you good day, Captain Bolitho. If I were you I would hurry back to the Ruddlemoor and change those clothes. With all the things we have planned for the future we don't want you going off sick, do we?'

Chapter 16

Jo saw Captain Bolitho leave the Ruddlemoor office and hurry off. There was aggression in every line of his body. Both she and Tessa were concerned about what might have taken place in the office, but for different reasons.

Jo was concerned that Captain Bolitho might have taken out his anger on Darley. Tessa, less confident of Miriam Retallick's ability to withstand the wrath of her father, suffered an acute sense of despondency. She believed her father's anger was the direct result of the suggestion that she should become a clerk in the new works office.

By the time Captain Bray left the office some twenty minutes later, heading for the pit, the curiosity of both girls had reached fever pitch. Finally, Jo could contain it no longer.

'I'm going to the office for a few minutes,' she said to Tessa. 'I think there must have been an almighty row. I want to find out what it's all about. Try to warn me if you see your father returning.'

'Are you quite sure curiosity's the only reason you're going to the office? Or is it because Darley's in there on his own now?'

'Don't be so stupid!' said Jo with far more feeling than was wise. 'I've told you why I'm going. Anyway, what might have been going on is more important to you than it is to me.'

Once in the office, Jo asked Darley what had happened when Miriam's ideas had been put to the works captain. He tried to reassure her that nothing had changed. He suggested that much of Captain Bolitho's anger had been because his advice had not been asked about all that was being planned for the two works.

'All the same,' Jo persisted, 'if he's gone off to have a big row with Mrs Retallick he certainly won't agree to Tessa working in the new office. I wouldn't be surprised if he puts a stop to me working here too.'

'Does that mean you've made up your mind to take up her offer?'

'Not yet. I'd like to work here, I really would, but I'd have to use arithmetic, and I'm not very good at it. I never have been.'

'I'd help you.'

'That wouldn't be fair. Not to you, or to Tessa. But, as I've said, I'll think about it.'

'It'll all be all right, you'll see – and don't worry about what Captain Bolitho might do. He hasn't come up against Great-aunt Miriam

70

before. She's more than a match for the toughest man.'

'I hope so, Darley. I feel sorry for Mrs Retallick though. Having all this on top of the bad news about her son.' She hesitated. 'Perhaps, with two works here, she'll want a nurse.'

Her words caused Darley automatically to finger the livid red scar that crossed his cheekbone. 'It could be. If she did, Miriam would never regret taking you on, I'm quite certain of that.'

His declaration caused a brief moment of embarrassment between them before Jo asked, 'Who told Mrs Retallick about me being good at writing and reading? Was it my father?'

'No, it was me.'

'Why did you do that?'

'Miriam spoke of taking someone else on to work in the office and I thought of you.' Darley did not think it wise to tell her there were few moments in the day when she was out of his thoughts. 'I believe you could do the work and it's better than working outside in all weathers.'

'I'm very grateful to you, Darley, whether or not I take the job.'

They were still talking when they heard the sound of footsteps outside the door. Moments later Captain Bolitho entered the office and Jo paled.

Surprise and anger struggled for supremacy on Captain Bolitho's face as he looked from one to the other. When he spoke, it was to Jo. 'What are you doing here?'

'I wanted to speak to my father about working in the office. I thought he was here,' she lied desperately in the hope of placating the works captain.

'You can discuss that at home, in your own time. I've told you before, the same as I've told Tessa. We're only fathers when we're at home. When we're here I'm Captain Bolitho and he's Shift Captain Bray. Now get back to the drying shed. You're not working in the office yet.'

Jo left the office without another word, but she realised that Captain Bolitho had not said that she and Tessa were *not* to be allowed to work in the new office. Indeed, his words had been, 'You're not working in the office *yet*.' It must mean that whatever had occurred between Abel Bolitho and Mrs Retallick, her move to the office was not in jeopardy.

This knowledge did not prevent her from taking Tessa to task for not warning her of Captain Bolitho's return to Ruddlemoor.

'I couldn't help it,' Tessa declared defensively. 'I was taken short and had to go to the privy.'

'That's a pretty story!' retorted Winnie Gilbert.

The most senior of the bal maidens, Winnie's weather-worn face beneath the curved rim of her bonnet advertised her status. 'You might have dropped your drawers, but it had nothing to do with any privy. I saw you go into the boiler room back of the "dry" not a minute after that Tom Sparrow had gone in there. Talk about "When the cat's away, the mice'll play". I don't know what's the matter with you young girls these days. If Captain Bolitho wasn't around every minute of the day there'd be little work done here, and that's a fact.'

Jo looked accusingly at her friend.

Tessa glared at Winnie, then, only mildly penitent, shrugged nonchalantly at Jo. 'I wanted to see Tom – same as you wanted to speak to Darley.'

'The difference is that young Darley Shovell's a single man. Tom Sparrow's not,' Winnie Gilbert commented as she thumped a block of dried China clay down on the table in front of her.

'Who asked your opinion, Winnie Gilbert?' Tessa retorted angrily. 'You're just jealous because no man's ever cast an eye in your direction.'

Winnie Gilbert was a spinster who still lived with her very aged mother.

'I've turned away more young men in my time than you'll ever have running after you, Tessa Bolitho. That's how I know that no good'll come from sneaking to the boiler room with a married man. You might keep it a secret for a while, but once word gets out it spreads faster than a spring shower. Before you know it his wife will hear of it – and she's not a girl to cross, I'll tell you that for nothing. Tom Sparrow's married into a gipsy family. They don't take such things lightly.'

Tessa sniffed derisively, but Jo took the old woman's warning more seriously. Speaking quietly to her friend, she said, 'You ought to take notice of what Winnie's said. I've seen some of Tom's in-laws. They're a wild crowd.'

'Then I'll just have to be careful and hope my "friends" can keep their mouths shut.' Tessa threw down her metal scraper. 'Now I really do want to go to the privy. Do you want to come with me, Winnie, to make certain that's where I'm going?'

'You can go to hell for all I care, girl. Saying you should be careful of what you're doing is for your good, not for mine.'

When Tessa had gone beyond hearing, Winnie said, 'You watch that girl, Jo. She'll lead you into trouble. It's not as though she's madly in love with Tom Sparrow, or even very fond of him. It's just a bit of excitement for her, that's all. There'll be a high price to pay for it, you just mind my words.'

As she scraped the base of a block of clay, Jo wondered what Winnie would say if she knew how much *she* cared for Darley.

Then her thoughts returned to Tessa. Jo hoped Winnie would prove to be wrong about Tessa and the trouble she would find as a result of her association with Tom Sparrow. Tessa was hopelessly amoral, but she was not an unkind girl and Jo was fond of her.

Chapter 17

The trouble that Abel Bolitho had forecast Darley Shovell would bring to the mine captain's family, erupted in violence on an early spring Sunday in 1894.

But this time the new office had been completed, despite a delay caused by a heavy snowfall in January. It was erected on the boundary dividing the Ruddlemoor and the newly named Daniel pit. It was a name of which Miriam thought Josh would approve.

The newer of the two workings had not yet been brought into production, but it would not be long now. Most of the overburden had been removed, exposing a vast area of high quality China clay.

The engine-house that would provide the power for pumping out the clay was also nearing completion. The engine had been brought from Sharptor and installed by the ex-miners who would be working here.

In spite of Captain Bolitho's bitter opposition, a tramway was also under construction. It would link all the Retallick-owned workings with the Varcoe works and carry the final product of both to the busy port of Fowey.

The small, south coast harbour was rapidly establishing itself as the premier shipping port for the area's China clay, overtaking nearby Charlestown.

This Sunday had followed the course of recent weeks. Jo, Tessa and Doris Bolitho walked to St Austell to attend church there. It was a routine Jo had actively encouraged because on their return from church they would pay a call on the Shovell household.

They would stay only long enough to have a cup of tea and a chat. Then Darley would accompany them along the road to the edge of St Austell. Here he would leave them to make their way home, arriving in time for Doris to have lunch on the table when Abel returned from the Sawle's Arms public house.

The pattern of this day was broken by Abel. He returned from the public house an hour earlier than usual – and he was in a furious mood. Storming into the kitchen where his wife and Tessa were still preparing the meal, he greeted them with, 'And where do the two of you think you've been?'

Doris Bolitho was terrified of her husband when he was in one of these moods. Fumbling nervously with the ladle of pearl barley she was carrying to the pot, she dropped the lot on the floor.

'You know very well where we've been, Father. To church, in St Austell,' said Tessa.

'I'm glad one of you has something to say for yourself. Perhaps you'll also tell me who went to church with you?'

Now both women were genuinely puzzled. Once again, it was Tessa who replied, 'We've not been to church with anyone – except Jo Bray. Mind you, there were quite a few others at the service.'

'Darley Shovell was one of them, no doubt?'

'I don't think so. In fact, I'm certain he wasn't there.'

'Don't lie to me,' Abel shouted the words. 'You were seen walking through St Austell with him.'

'So? He *lives* in St Austell. We met him and he walked to the edge of town with us.'

'You met him? He didn't go to church with you? Don't you dare lie to me . . .'

'I'm telling you he did not go to church with us,' declared Tessa, equally heatedly. 'If you don't want to believe me then you can please yourself.'

Aware she was on reasonably strong ground with this argument, she was equally as indignant as her father. 'Not that it matters to anyone. If he wanted to go to church he'd go, even though his father is a staunch Methodist. I certainly wouldn't refuse to sit with him if he did.'

Realising he had probably jumped to the wrong conclusion, Abel began to calm down. 'Are you quite sure you didn't go to St Austell just to see young Shovell in church?'

'I've already said so, haven't I?'

'All right, but I've told you before, I don't want you seeing any more than you have to of that young lad. His family are a bad lot.'

Had Doris Bolitho not broken the silence she had judiciously maintained until that moment, all would have been well. Unfortunately, seeing her husband's anger subside, relief overrode her natural caution. 'I think you're being very hard on them, Abel. Darley's mother, in particular, is a very warm and caring sort of person.'

He seized upon her unguarded remark immediately. Rounding on her, he demanded, 'What do you know of Darley Shovell's mother?'

'I . . . well . . . She's a nice woman, that's all.'

Her reply did not satisfy Abel. 'When did you meet her? How . . .?'

Realising she had committed a grave error, Doris Bolitho became so flustered she could not gather her wits together.

'We went to see them, Abel. When the lad hurt his face. We were with Jo Bray when she called in to see how he was.'

'YOU DID WHAT?' Abel's fury seemed to cause him to swell before the eyes of his family. 'Knowing what he did to my father, YOU WENT TO SEE HIM AT HIS HOME?'

'There was no harm down, Abel. It was a Christian thing to do. He had been hurt protecting the Ruddlemoor Works pay . . .'

'You went to the home of Jethro Shovell? You were willing to make me a laughing stock before all those who know how I feel about him?'

Doris Bolitho was about to protest that she had no intention of doing anything to harm her husband's reputation, but she had left it too late. The back of Abel's hand cut the protest short.

It was delivered with all the force he could muster. Doris was knocked back against the wall. Dazed, she slid to the ground, staring stupidly at her husband, blood trickling from a cut at the corner of her mouth. Foolishly, she tried to rise to her feet immediately. This time it was Abel's fist that knocked her down once more.

'Father . . . stop it!' Tessa lunged forward in an attempt to prevent a third blow.

Without looking around, Abel swung his arm back and sent his daughter reeling across the room.

Looking down at his battered wife, Abel fumed, 'Jethro Shovell sent my father to an early grave. All these years I've fought hard to prevent the Union from getting a foothold at the Ruddlemoor works. Now you're destroying all those years of my work by visiting the Shovells at their home. Not only that, you have the gall to tell me they're "warm and caring" people. How I came to marry such a stupid woman I don't know. I ought to beat you to within an inch of your life.'

Bending over his wife, Abel matched word with deed, giving her a punch that caused her head to snap back and hit the wall behind her.

'Don't, Father. Stop it . . . please!'

Tessa caught hold of her father's arm, but he flung her from him once more. Leaning over his wife, he drew back his foot and kicked her in the stomach.

Doris Bolitho cried out in pain, but it had no effect on her enraged husband. He drew back his foot as she slumped sideways, and this time his heavy boot struck her in the face, just beneath her left eye.

Tessa was crouching on the floor where she had been flung. She saw her mother slump sideways to lie upon the floor, groaning in agony.

Her father drew back his foot and kicked his wife again . . . and again.

Tessa realised that if she did not do something quickly, her mother was likely to be kicked to death. There was a pile of logs at the side of the fireplace, placed here to fuel the kitchen range. Crawling to them, Tessa snatched up one of the heavy logs and rose to her feet.

As her father drew back his foot for yet another kick, Tessa struck out with the log, hitting him as hard as she could.

The blow caught Abel just behind his right ear. Off balance, as he was, he fell to the ground in front of his moaning wife.

For a moment, Tessa thought she had killed him. Then she heard him groan. Reaching down, she put an arm about her mother and tried to raise her from the ground. She was too heavy and Tessa said, 'Quick, Ma. Get up! We must get out of here before Father comes round or he'll kill us both.

'Oh . . . I can't, Tessa. I hurt so . . .'

'You *must*! Get up, Ma.'

Somehow, Tessa raised her mother to her feet. Despite the older woman's protestations, she managed to get her to the door and outside to the road.

Once here, Tessa half dragged, half carried her mother along the road. She did not know where they would go. She only knew that unless she got her mother away from their home, she would die at the hands of her father.

Chapter 18

The problem of where Tessa could take her mother to be safe was resolved when a Methodist preacher came upon the scene.

Seeing the two distressed women, one of whom was obviously in considerable pain, the minister brought his pony and trap to a halt alongside them. Explaining that he was on his way to preach in St Austell, he asked if he might be of any assistance.

'Yes, please. My mother's had ... an accident. Could you take us to St Austell?'

Doris climbed into the trap with some difficulty. The minister looked at her doubtfully as he flicked the long rein to set the pony in motion. 'She seems to be in a bad way. How did the accident happen?'

'She was in the kitchen,' Tessa replied vaguely. 'She'll be all right once we are in town.'

'Do you have friends in St Austell? Your mother looks as though she should be taken straight to the hospital.'

'No.' Tessa had not thought beyond getting her mother as far from the house as possible before her father regained consciousness. But she was thinking now.

'If you could take us ... to the Shovell house. I'll tell you where it is when we're closer. It shouldn't take you too far out of your way.'

Before this moment Tessa had not considered the Shovell house as a possible refuge. Her thinking now was that it was far enough away from Stenalees to be safe from her father. At least, for the immediate future.

'Do you mean *Jethro* Shovell's house?'

'That's right.'

'You've no need to tell me where *that* is. Jethro is one of my lay preachers.'

Much to Tessa's relief, the preacher talked of Jethro for the remainder of the journey. She did not really listen. She was more concerned with what she and her mother could do once they reached Darley and his family. After what had happened back at her own house, they dared not remain at the Shovell home for very long. In her father's present mood he might come looking for them there.

The problem was taken out of her hands when she and the preacher helped her mother inside the Shovell house. Miriam Retallick was visiting.

It was evident to Miriam that Tessa did not wish to speak in front of the Methodist minister. Once he had left she demanded to know what had happened.

'My father came home from the Sawle's Arms today. Someone had seen us walking with Darley after church. He demanded to know what was going on. Ma let it slip that she'd visited here . . .'

Tessa shrugged. 'This is the result. He hates the Shovell family . . . and he'd been drinking.'

'The man's an animal! When he goes into work tomorrow he can collect what's owed to him, and go. I'll not have a man working for me who does this to a woman.'

'Don't do that, Mrs Retallick . . . please! If you were to sack every man at Ruddlemoor who beats his wife you'd have no one left to work for you. He got carried away this time, that's all. Everyone knows how he feels about Jethro Shovell. He felt that by coming here behind his back we'd made him a laughing-stock. It was my fault. I should never have let Jo persuade us to come here in the first place.'

'You can't blame yourself for what's been done to your mother,' protested Miriam. 'Your father is the one who's responsible.'

'I *do* blame myself,' insisted Tessa. 'These past few months have been difficult for him. For years he's been given a free hand to run the Ruddlemoor workings – and he's run them well. Then you and Mr Retallick come along and he has to take orders again. It can't have been easy.'

'It's still no excuse for what he's done to your mother.'

'I'm not trying to make excuses for him. I'm only telling you why it's happened.'

'You're a better daughter than he deserves, Tessa Bolitho. But neither of you can go back home tonight, that's certain. Does he know you've come here?'

'No, but he's likely to think of it once he sobers up.' Hesitantly, Tessa told how she had struck her father with a piece of wood and left him barely conscious on the kitchen floor.

'Good for you!' was Miriam's cryptic comment. 'But, as you say, it will be best if you don't remain here. We'll go to my house and call in on a doctor along the way. When we get home I'll send someone to tell your father where you are. Otherwise he's likely to come here and make trouble. Mind you, I'll also send orders that he stays away from you. If he tries to see you I'll have the police on him.'

'By the time you reach your house, Cap'n Bolitho could be half-way here,' said Darley. 'The best thing would be for me to go and tell him.'

'You can't do that!' Lottie was horrified at the thought of her son facing up to the bullying Captain Bolitho. 'He's an angry man. Look what he did to his wife.'

78

'That was the drink,' said Darley. 'By the time I get there he'll have sobered up.'

'I'll come with you.' Lily was no less positive than her brother.

Darley was about to say no as an automatic reaction to her suggestion. Then he realised her offer made a great deal of sense. There would be no need for her to enter the house – even were he to be invited to go in – but she would be able to fetch help if the works captain became violent towards him.

'Fine. But we'd better set off right away. We won't be there and back much before dark as it is.'

'When you return, call at my house and let me know what happened. I'll send you home in the trap. Be sure to come there though, I'll be worrying until I've seen you both.'

When Darley and Lily reached the Bolitho house the sky had clouded over and the light was uncertain, but the house was in darkness.

Warily, not knowing what to expect, Darley knocked on the front door. There was no reply. Suddenly, he remembered that Tessa had hit her father on the head with a log. What if she had hit him too hard and he was still lying unconscious on the kitchen floor? What if he were dead?

'He's not in. Shall we go home now?' Lily made the suggestion hopefully, feeling very nervous.

'We've come too far to turn around and go home again after knocking only once at the door. Tessa said the trouble took place in the kitchen. We'll go around to the back door.'

Lily would much rather have returned straight home, but she swallowed her fear and loyally followed her brother as he went around the side of the house in search of a back door.

It was in darkness here too but, through a window, Darley thought he could just distinguish a faint red glow. It could have been the embers of a low-burning fire. Beside the window was another door and Darley knocked upon it. When there was no response from inside the house, he knocked again.

Suddenly, Lily put her hand in his, her courage deserting her. 'Let's go, Darley. I'm frightened.'

'There's nothing to be frightened of, Lily. I don't think anyone can be in, but we'll look into the kitchen, just in case . . .'

Pushing open the door before completing the sentence, Darley stepped inside carefully, hoping his foot would not come in contact with a still body.

'Who's that?' The voice was thick. The voice of a man who had been sitting alone for so long that his tongue had become tethered.

Nevertheless, there was no mistaking who was speaking. It was Captain Bolitho. Lily gripped Darley's hand so tightly it hurt.

'It's me, Cap'n Bolitho, Darley Shovell.'

'What do you want? Haven't you caused enough trouble in the Bolitho family already?'

The Ruddlemoor works captain sounded resentful but, to Darley's great relief, he seemed to be reasonably sober.

'I've been sent by Mrs Retallick to give you news of your wife and Tessa . . . Can we have some light in here? I can't even see where you are.'

'Mrs Retallick? What's she got to do with it? But you said you have news of Doris and Tessa. Where are they? By God, if they're in your house . . .'

Darley felt Lily's hand grip his fingers even tighter.

'They're at Gover Valley, with Mrs Retallick.'

'I don't want them there. I'll go and fetch them back.' There was the sound of a chair moving across a stone floor.

'I think you'd better leave them there for tonight and speak to Mrs Retallick about it in the morning. She'll be coming to Ruddlemoor to see you. In any case, Mrs Bolitho isn't fit enough to travel tonight. I doubt if she'll be able to make up her mind about what she wants to do for a few days yet.'

'What do mean . . . what she wants to do? She'll come home here, where she belongs. They both will.'

'That's up to them, but if I were you I'd listen to what Mrs Retallick has to say before making any demands. After seeing what you'd done to your wife, she wanted to dismiss you from Ruddlemoor. If Tessa hadn't pleaded with her, you'd not have had a job to go to tomorrow.'

'Tessa pleaded with Mrs Retallick for me? After what had happened?'

'That's right.'

There was a long silence in the darkness of the kitchen before Captain Bolitho spoke again. 'Tell her I'm sorry for everything.'

Incredibly, Darley thought the other man sounded almost humble. He would never have believed it possible.

'Tell her. Tell her . . . if she and her mother come back, I promise it won't ever happen again.'

'I'll tell her, Cap'n Bolitho, but your wife won't even be fit enough to walk for a few days. I doubt if Tessa will come back before then.'

Chapter 19

Arriving at the Retallick house, Darley found Jo and Jim Bray there. They had been out when the violence erupted in the Bolitho house next-door, but other neighbours had told them what had happened. Jo made an inspired guess about where they might find Tessa and her mother. From the Shovell home they had gone on to the Gover Valley.

Seated around the kitchen table with Tessa, Miriam and the Brays, Darley and Lily gave an account of their visit to Abel Bolitho at Stenalees.

Doris was upstairs in bed. A doctor had been called to the house earlier to examine her. He had diagnosed a broken nose and expressed the opinion that two of her ribs were cracked.

When Darley ended his account, Lily added, 'I think Captain Bolitho's sorry for what he did to Tessa's ma. He said he is.'

'He always does,' declared Tessa, bitterly. 'But it never stops him doing it again when he's had a few drinks and something's happened to upset him. Mind you, Ma and I have never left home when he's hit us before. It might just bring him to his senses.'

'We'll give him ample time to think about it,' declared Miriam, firmly. 'You and your mother can stay here until everything has been sorted out and you both decide you want to return.'

To Darley, she said, 'It seems to me you said everything that needed saying, young Darley. You take after your pa, you know. He's never been frightened to go anywhere, or talk to anyone – however fearsome their reputation. Keep it up and one day you'll probably find yourself managing the two works for Josh and me.'

Darley was still glowing from Miriam's compliment when he and Lily left the house to return home in the pony trap she had arranged for them.

Jo came outside with them while her father was still talking to Miriam in the hallway. As she walked beside Darley in the darkness, she unexpectedly found and held his hand. 'I'm proud of you for doing all you have for Tessa and her mother today, Darley. They've put up with a lot from Captain Bolitho. They should have left him years ago. Everyone says so.'

Tongue-tied as a result of the unexpected pleasure of holding hands

81

with Jo, he said, 'It . . . it was Miriam who did everything. I just went and spoke to Cap'n Bolitho.'

'No, Darley, you did far more than that. Tessa told me that after the fight, when her mother was hurt and her father was lying unconscious, she didn't know what to do. Then, when the preacher came along and asked where he could take them, she thought of you. Somehow she knew that if she came to your house and you were there, things would be sorted out. They have been. At least, for the time being. I know just how she feels, Darley. You give people confidence.'

They had reached the pony and trap now and Jo shivered. Although Darley was glowing from the warmth of Jo's praise, it was a cold night. He realised that she had left the house without her coat.

'You'd better go in and get your coat, before you catch a cold.'

'Yes.'

Jo suddenly moved close to Darley and kissed him quickly. 'Good night, Darley. Thank you again. For everything. For just being you.'

He climbed into the trap and Lily clambered in after him.

They set off along the road to St Austell and it soon became evident that their driver was not a talkative man. Peering into the darkness, he concentrated his attention upon keeping the pony on the road.

After some minutes, Lily said quietly, 'You like Jo lots, don't you?'

There was a long pause before Darley said seriously, 'Yes, Lily, I do.'

'She likes you lots too. I can tell.'

'Do you really think so? Perhaps it's just because we've been able to help her friend.'

'You don't believe that any more than I do. Besides, I saw her kiss you.'

Darley's fingers went to his mouth. 'She's the only girl who's ever kissed me, Lily – except for you, of course.'

'Are you going to marry her?'

'You've asked me that before and the answer's the same. It's a foolish thought, Lily.' There was bitterness in the tone of his voice but Lily persisted.

'Why is it silly if you and Jo like each other so much?'

'I can't marry *anyone*. Not the way I am.'

'You've been a lot better lately, Darley. You haven't had a bad attack for weeks. Ma was saying only the other day that you've been a different person since you started working at Ruddlemoor.'

When the words failed to draw any response from her brother, Lily said unhappily, 'People who have lung disease can get better. Pa said so only the other day.'

Darley realised he had made Lily unhappy. Putting an arm about her, he teased, 'You just want to see me married off, so you can move in to my bedroom.'

Darley had a good-sized bedroom, while the room where Lily slept was little more than a large cupboard.

It was a lighthearted remark, but she took it seriously. 'I don't want you to leave home, Darley. Not ever, if you don't want to. But if you ever *did* get married, I'd like it to be to Jo.'

Darley squeezed his young sister to him as they approached the street lights of St Austell. 'That's about the way I feel, Lily. If ever I could marry, I'd want it to be to Jo.'

Tessa and her mother remained at the Retallick house for a full week. By the end of this time Doris Bolitho was up and about, worrying because she was not in her own home, attending to the things that would need doing.

Jo was a constant visitor. She said she came to see Tessa, but Miriam thought otherwise.

For Tessa, the week spent at the Retallick house was a time when she enjoyed more freedom than she had ever known before. At home, in Stenalees, it felt as though her every moment was monitored and controlled by her father. Here, she was able to make her own decisions. She was also able to leave the house for hours at a time without having to face angry questioning about her movements.

Darley came to the Retallick house most nights, ostensibly to keep Miriam up-to-date on the progress in the new workings. He would discuss with her the fittings and equipment they were likely to need in the new buildings being erected there.

However, when his business with Miriam was over he spent even longer telling Tessa and Jo about the plans he had for the new office. He spoke in glowing terms of how things were beginning to move ahead in the whole works, despite the absence of Josh.

The office work was increasing in proportion to all that was happening at Ruddlemoor. In particular, the proportion of the cost to be borne by each of the companies sharing the railway link was already causing a considerable number of problems.

The Varcoe solicitor was of the opinion that when the new pit was fully operational, the Ruddlemoor workings would be despatching more clay to Fowey than the Varcoe works. They should therefore bear a greater percentage of the cost.

It had taken Darley a couple of days to persuade the solicitor that half the cost was a fair share. Had the Ruddlemoor and Retallick works not decided to be linked to the line, the Varcoe works would have needed to find the *whole* amount.

He declared that Josh Retallick would contribute half – but no more than half – to the cost of maintaining the line and the rolling stock. Eventually, the Varcoe solicitor grudgingly accepted the arrangement.

It was a very busy time and Darley was relieved that Abel Bolitho had not made life difficult for him while Tessa and her mother were still at the Retallick house.

In fact, he hardly saw the works captain. When Darley was in the office for a few hours Abel was usually in the pit, where a large area of pit-face had collapsed due to a period of heavy rain.

The fall had carried away the tramway carrying clay waste to the spoil-heap, burying a large number of skips. Continuous heavy rain was hampering all efforts to put things to rights.

However, when Friday arrived, Darley returned from yet another visit to the Varcoe works and found Abel Bolitho waiting for him at the new office.

Darley was immediately apprehensive. Captain Bray was away at Charlestown harbour. He was negotiating the fees to be charged for the clay taken there from the new Daniel workings. Darley and Abel were alone in the office.

Much to Darley's relief, Captain Bolitho spoke to him more civilly than at any time since their first meeting.

'I want to speak to you, Shovell. Have you seen Tessa and Mrs Bolitho since last weekend?'

'I saw them both last night, at Mrs Retallick's house.' Darley did not add he had also seen them every other night of the week too.

'How are they?'

'Tessa seems well enough and Mrs Bolitho is making progress. She's out of bed now and says her ribs aren't hurting her too much. Mind you, she has two of the most colourful black eyes I've ever seen.'

A pained expression crossed Abel's face as he said, 'I'm glad she's getting about again. Did she say anything about coming home?'

'Not to me. I don't know whether she's discussed it with Mrs Retallick.'

'Will you be seeing Mrs Retallick tonight?'

'I could if you wanted me too.' Darley thought it inadvisable to tell the works captain that he fully intended visiting Miriam's house again because Jo would be there.

'Will you ask Mrs Retallick if it's all right for me to come calling on Mrs Bolitho and Tessa on Sunday? Tell them too that I want to talk to them.'

'I'll tell them, certainly – but I can tell you right away what Miriam Retallick's reply will be.'

'Oh, and what's that?'

'She'll say that you're welcome to come calling – provided you're sober when you arrive there.'

Abel glared at Darley for some moments and the younger man tensed. He thought he might have overstepped the mark with the volatile works captain. Much to his surprise, Captain Bolitho nodded his head.

'If that's what she says you can tell her she has my word – I won't touch a drop before I pay my call.'

For a few moments more, Abel seemed to be struggling to find words for what he wanted to say. Then he said in a gruff, strained voice, 'You can tell Tessa and her mother I'm wanting them home again.'

With this, Captain Abel Bolitho turned away abruptly and walked back towards the Ruddlemoor pit. Behind him, Darley realised he had just witnessed a proud and lonely man being as humble as he knew how.

Chapter 20

It was an unfamiliar Abel Bolitho who called at the Retallick home the following Sunday. Dressed in a navy blue serge suit that was reserved for special occasions, he stood waiting for the door to be opened to him. In his hands he nervously held a black bowler hat. Bluster and aggression were totally absent from his manner.

The door was opened by Lily. Today she was not with Darley. He had thought it neither desirable nor advisable to be at the house when Abel arrived.

This decision had been made after he and Miriam had spoken at some length the previous day. They had discussed the works captain's visit. Darley believed Abel Bolitho was genuinely sorry for what he had done, but whether his contrition would last was another matter.

'Come in, Captain Bolitho. Great-aunt Miriam's waiting in the lounge for you.'

The works captain entered the house in the uncertain manner of a nervous schoolboy. After diligently scuffing the soles of his boots on the wool-bordered Vandyke mat inside the hallway door, he followed Lily to the lounge.

Although Abel had worked for the Rosevear family for all his working life, this was the first time he had been farther than the back door of their former home.

The house was much grander than he had imagined it would be. The furniture was tasteful – and expensive. There were imported carpets on the floor such as he had never seen before. Nothing here was calculated to make the captain feel less ill-at-ease.

Miriam was seated in the large lounge with Tessa and Doris Bolitho. Jo was in the kitchen, out of sight.

Whether by accident or design, the women were seated in armchairs on different sides of the room. Abel was waved to a seat against the fourth wall and Lily was sent from the room.

Abel could not look at more than one of the women at a time, and this served to increase his discomfiture.

For two or three minutes after he had seated himself, the occupants of the room sat in an increasingly unnerving silence. Abel had actually begun to squirm before Miriam spoke.

'Have you come here because you have something to say, Captain

Bolitho?' Nodding to where Doris Bolitho sat with gaudily discoloured eyes, she added, 'Or are you here to admire your handiwork?'

The question brought a sudden flush of anger to the Ruddlemoor captain's cheeks. He was not used to being spoken to in such a manner. Especially by a woman.

'I came here to speak to my wife and daughter. I want them to come home.'

'Really, Captain Bolitho? Well, at least the reason for your visit is clear to us now. We certainly won't labour under a mistaken belief that you might have come to say you are sorry for the injuries you've caused.'

Abel struggled to remain calm in the face of Miriam Retallick's provocative sarcasm. 'I'm sorry for hitting Doris, of course I am. That's why I'm here. She knows that.'

'I'm pleased to hear you say it, Captain Bolitho. You'll pardon me if I think it more likely that you're here because you have had enough of trying to wash, cook and clean for yourself. But that's between you, and your wife and daughter. Now I've satisfied myself there's not likely to be any immediate violence, I'll leave you to talk things over with them.'

Miriam rose from her seat. Turning her back on her works captain, she said to Doris, 'I'll be in the kitchen if you want me. I have no wish to come between a woman and her husband, but you're welcome to remain in this house for as long as you wish. It's a large house and I don't enjoy being here on my own.'

'I'll come to the kitchen with you,' said Tessa, unexpectedly.

Both Abel and Doris protested immediately, but Tessa said firmly, 'This is a matter you need to sort out between the two of you, without my opinions. I won't always be living at home. One day it'll be just the two of you, once more. If you can't live together without Mother being constantly in fear of her life, it's best if she decides to leave now, before she's hurt even more seriously.'

Tessa's statement was brutally truthful and she hoped it might have an effect on her father. That had been her intention, but when the woman reached the kitchen, Miriam said, 'I hope your words bring your father to his senses, Tessa, but he's never impressed me as a man who can be easily persuaded – especially if the suggestion comes from a woman.'

'That's true,' she agreed. 'But it's given him something to think about. While they're talking I think I'll go for a walk. I feel I have need of some air.'

When Tessa had left the kitchen, Miriam stirred up the kitchen fire with a long, twisted iron poker. When she had settled a heavy, smoke-blackened kettle more firmly into the glowing coals, she said to Jo, 'I don't know where that young lady goes for her evening "walks", nor is it any of my business – but it's not for the good of her health, I'm quite certain of that.'

Taking down a teapot from a shelf over the fire, Miriam said, 'Tessa was speaking of leaving home just before we left Abel Bolitho and Doris alone in the other room. How do you see your future, Jo? Does our Darley figure in it in any way?'

Miriam's forthrightness brought colour to Jo's cheeks. 'I like him. I like him very much,' she admitted. 'I think – I believe, he feels the same about me, but he's never said anything to make me hope it will ever go any farther than that.'

'I doubt if Darley will ever say anything more, especially if he's really fond of you – and I happen to know he *is*. Darley has always believed his illness sets him apart from others. Makes him something less than a man.'

'He's more of a man than most of those I know,' said Jo immediately. 'He's proved it, too. He saved my uncle and the others at the Notter mine. Then he fought off those men who tried to steal the Ruddlemoor wages . . .'

Miriam smiled at her spirited defence of Darley. 'You don't have to convince me, Jo. Or anyone else who knows him, come to that. The only person you've got to convince is Darley himself!'

Jo believed she had allowed her feelings for Darley to show a little too much. In a bid to change the subject, she said, 'I've seldom seen Captain Bolitho as subdued as he is today.'

'It will be good for him. Mind you, it's wonderful what a week without a woman in the house can do for a man.'

The kettle on the fire had begun to steam, the lid dancing noisily. Shifting it to the hob, Miriam said, 'Have you ever thought of leaving home and going your own way?'

'Often, even though I'm very happy at home. We only have a small house and it seems crowded sometimes, even with just the three of us there. I sometimes think I'd miss my mother and father, but they get along very well. They'd hardly notice if I wasn't there.'

'Then I've an idea that I've been thinking about since you started visiting here. If it appeals to you, I'll put it to your father.'

By the time Miriam and Jo carried tea and biscuits to the lounge, Doris and Abel Bolitho had reached agreement on their immediate future. Doris had agreed to return to their Stenalees home, in return for a promise from Abel that he would forego his Sunday lunch-time drinking.

Doris was well aware it was a promise he would probably not keep for very long, but it was a beginning. It was certainly more than he had ever conceded before.

'When do you plan to leave?' Miriam asked Doris as she passed her a cup.

88

'If Doris and Tessa can be ready, they'll return home with me now,' said Abel. He would not breathe freely until he escaped from this house. He felt overawed both by his surroundings and by Miriam.

'Doris isn't fit enough to walk all the way to Stenalees, if that's what you have in mind. I'd send her off in the pony and trap, but my driver has Sunday off. It will be far more convenient for her to return home in the morning. As for Tessa, no doubt she'll want to be with her mother.'

Doris Bolitho's face showed her uncertainty. 'I think I can manage now, Mrs Retallick. I *will* manage with Tessa's help.'

'Of course you'll manage. You're almost well again now, Doris. But if it will make you feel better, I'll call and see how you're getting on in a couple of days time.'

The thought of having Miriam Retallick calling at his house did not suit Abel Bolitho. He resented having this woman dictate to him the running of his family life, but he said nothing. Mrs Retallick was his employer and she did not look favourably on him at the moment. Besides, he desperately wanted Doris and Tessa to return home.

'I'll be happy to have you call on Doris, Mrs Retallick. I'm grateful to you for taking care of her. I want to have her and Tessa home again and you have my word that nothing like this will ever happen again.'

'I sincerely hope not, Captain Bolitho. If it does, I believe you'll lose your family for good. You'll certainly lose your post as captain of Ruddlemoor.'

Chapter 21

Jo walked back to St Austell with Lily that evening, an hour after Abel had left the Retallick house.

It was a pleasant night for a walk. Crisp and fresh, a half moon hung like a lop-sided lantern in a sky liberally sprinkled with stars and small, high clouds.

Jo found Lily bright and amusing, and her devotion to Darley was apparent whenever his name came up in conversation. Lily told Jo a story of the time when she had broken a leg, a couple of years before, and Darley had carried her everywhere on his shoulders.

'You love Darley very much, don't you, Lily?' Jo laid an arm across her slight shoulders in a spontaneous gesture of affection.

Suddenly serious, Lily replied, 'Yes . . . do you?'

The unexpectedly forthright reply caught Jo off balance. She was silent for so long that Lily thought she had offended her. When she made an effort to apologise, Jo silenced her. 'It's all right, Lily. It's a question I've been asking myself for a long time. I don't have to any more. Yes, I think I do love Darley. Does that make you unhappy?'

'No, I'm glad. He loves you too, you know.'

When Jo had recovered her composure for a second time, she asked, 'How do you know that, Lily?'

'Because I know him. Anyway, he told me so.'

'He told *you*? Why hasn't he told me?'

'Because of his illness. He'll never say it – unless you tell him first. Then he might.'

Jo thought about the younger girl's revelation for the remainder of the walk to the Shovell house. She only half listened to Lily's happy chatter. Fortunately, Lily neither demanded nor expected constant replies. An occasional grunt was perfectly acceptable.

Jo had a great deal to think about this evening. Uppermost in her mind was Lily's disclosure about Darley's feelings for her. There was also the offer Miriam Retallick had made to her and to which she had yet to give a definite answer.

Because she felt she needed some thinking time, Jo resisted Lily's plea that she should go into the house with her. Jo left Lily at her doorstep and set off for home.

It was almost four miles to Stenalees, for the most part along a dark and lonely lane. However, it was a walk Jo had made many times before and it had no fears for her.

She had just cleared the lights of St Austell when she heard the sound of running footsteps behind her. Suddenly nervous, Jo drew back into the shadow of a giant granite arch, part of the railway viaduct which bridged the valley at this spot.

The footsteps almost reached the place where she stood – then they slowed to a walk. There was the sound of laboured breathing before a voice said, 'Is that you, Jo?'

She found she had been holding her breath and released it now in a great sigh of relief. 'Darley! You frightened me for a moment. What do you think you're doing, running like that?'

'Sorry. I didn't mean to scare you. I thought you shouldn't walk all the way to Stenalees alone in the dark. Especially through the Menacuddle Woods. The Ruddlemoor men cleared everyone out after they tried to steal the wages, but the vagrants are drifting back. There are gipsies there too, at the moment.'

'I'm not frightened of the gipsies, they don't bother women, but some of the others I've seen around give me the creeps.' Jo took hold of Darley's arm. 'It's kind of you to come after me like this, Darley.'

'I must admit I felt a bit hurt that you didn't come in and at least say hello before going on home.'

'I should have done, I know, but there are a few things I need to think about. I thought I could do it on the way home.'

'What sort of things?'

'Well, for a start, Mrs Retallick would like me to go and work at her house as a companion, until Mr Retallick comes home. I'd work and stay there all week and go home from Saturday night to Monday morning.'

The news took Darley as much by surprise as it had Jo.

'But . . . that means you wouldn't be coming to work in the office, at Ruddlemoor.'

'That's right. Not for a while, anyway. When Mr Retallick comes home from Africa I can either stay on at the house, come to work at the office – or do anything else I feel I want to do. Mrs Retallick says she'll help me, whatever I decide to do.'

'I was looking forward to us working together.' Darley sounded deeply disappointed.

'So was I, but then I started thinking about it. Really thinking. Working together at the office is fine. We're together – but there's always someone else there. If it isn't Tessa, it's my pa, or Captain Bolitho, or someone else coming in for something. If I worked for Mrs Retallick we could meet each other in the evening as we have while Tessa and her ma have been staying at the house. Summer isn't very far away. We'd be able to go for walks in the evening, or sit in the garden and talk, depending on what you wanted. In fact, we'd be able to see far more of each other than we do now, and without having other people around us all the time.'

There was just enough light beneath the trees for Darley to see that her face was turned towards him. 'Of course, it depends very much on what it is you want. You might be happier if we only met at work.'

'That isn't so, Jo, as well you know. You surely don't think I've been coming to Great-aunt Miriam's house every night this past week just to see how Tessa and her mother were?'

'Isn't that what you want me to think, Darley? I've been going to the Gover Valley every night too. You and I have walked and talked together so much I feel I know you better than I've ever known anyone else in my life. Yet I still don't think you've moved any closer to me, Darley. Not *really* close. Why? Is it because you don't want to? Perhaps you find me a nuisance?'

Jo closed her eyes and hoped that the all-seeing being to whom she prayed every Sunday was looking down on her at this moment. She was taking the greatest gamble of her life. The outcome mattered more than anything she had ever done before.

'*No*!' The word was torn from him.

In a more normal voice, he said, 'I'd happily exchange a year of my life for every hour spent with you, Jo – but I don't think I have that many years to give away. Not enough to ask anyone to gamble their own life on them.'

'If you're not prepared to share your life with me, then don't try to tell me what I should do with my life, Darley Shovell. You have no right. No right at all.'

'It isn't that, Jo. I'm a sick man – oh, I know you'll say I've been much better lately. Everybody says so, and they're right – but only partly right. I'm the only one who really knows how I am. I wouldn't ask anyone to take me on. Especially not you.'

Jo unlooped her arm from his. 'Then there's no more to be said, is there?' She stopped and turned to face him. 'You needn't come any farther with me, Darley.'

When he began to protest, she cut him short. 'No, I don't want you to. I said I needed to think, but I don't any more. You've answered all the questions I would have asked myself. I won't be taking up Mrs Retallick's offer. I'll carry on working at the office – unless I decide to leave Ruddlemoor altogether. Goodnight, Darley.'

Jo turned and began walking away from him. She hoped she was going in the right direction. At that moment she was so blinded by tears that she could have walked off the roadway.

'Jo?'

Either she had not walked as far as she thought, or Darley had been following her.

She did not reply and a moment later he spoke again. This time she knew he *was* following her.

'Jo . . . I love you.'

Now she was forced to stop. She could not see a thing. Then it was too late. He had caught up with her and was turning her to him.

'Jo, I don't want to rob you of your future. But if it's what you really want, I'll give you mine – and willingly. I've never wanted anything the way I want you, and I never will. If you marry me I can't promise you a lifetime of happiness, but I promise that for however many years we have together I'll never do anything to make you unhappy. Will you settle for that, Jo?'

'Yes, Darley.' Jo's arms held him close. 'If you really love me I'll settle for whatever comes – just as long as we're together.'

Chapter 22

'Thank you for walking Jo home last night, Darley. There'll be no need of such a walk once she becomes a companion to Mrs Retallick.'

It was Monday morning. Darley and Jim Bray were on their way to the Varcoe works from the new office. It was hoped they would be able to finalise the last few details of the rail link shared by the two companies.

'You've decided to let her take the post then?'

'Her mother and I could hardly refuse. It's an opportunity for her to see a little more of the grand side of life than we can offer her at Stenalees.'

It would also enable her to save more money for married life. Jo and Darley had discussed it during the walk to her home. Darley was disturbed that Jim Bray had said nothing about that. He wondered whether Jo had decided not to say anything about it to her parents just yet.

It was too important a matter to leave unanswered.

'Did Jo say anything else about . . . about things she and I talked about last night?'

'She said the two of you'd discussed marriage.'

When Jim Bray looked at Darley there was an enigmatic expression on his face. 'I thought that was a matter for you to bring up, not me.'

'Of course.' Darley cleared his throat, nervously. 'I want to marry Jo more than I've ever wanted anything in my life.'

Darley gave Jim Bray a sideways glance, but the works captain was looking straight ahead. It was impossible to judge what he was thinking.

'I . . . I don't expect you to be overjoyed about the idea, Cap'n Bray. I wouldn't be if I was Jo's father.'

'Oh? I may be wrong, but shouldn't you be trying to persuade me what a fine husband and son you'll make?'

'That wouldn't be any use with you, would it? You know better.'

Jim Bray made no reply and they walked on in silence for a full minute before Darley blurted out, 'I *do* love Jo. If you'll let her marry me, I'll do my very best to make her happy.'

Still Jim Bray said nothing and Darley felt a tight knot of unhappiness growing inside him.

'I can understand your not wanting her to marry me. Ever since last

94

night I find it difficult to believe that *she* really wants to marry me, but she does. I'd never have dared say anything to her about it if she hadn't made it clear it's what she wants too.'

Jim Bray suddenly halted and turned to face Darley. 'The way Jo feels about you may have come as a surprise to you – her mother and I have known for a long time. Longer than Jo herself, I suspect. Because we've seen this coming we've discussed it at some length. We both wish your health was more certain, if only for your sake, but there's very little that's guaranteed in this life. As Jo's mother said, if you were a miner, or a fisherman, you'd face the risk of death every day of your life. To my knowledge it's never stood in the way of any girl who wanted to marry a miner or a fisherman. It certainly wouldn't stop a girl like our Jo!'

Jim Bray smiled at Darley's expression of delight. 'Besides, we've all noticed the improvement in you since you've been at the works. We all hope you continue to improve. In the meantime, you and Jo have our blessing. We hope you'll enjoy a long and happy married life.'

The works captain held out his hand and Darley took it eagerly, feeling far too emotional to say more than, 'Thank you, Cap'n Bray. Thank you very much!'

As they fell into step again, Jo's father said, 'Having Jo working and staying at Mrs Retallick's house will help her mother and me get used to not having her around. I've no doubt you will want to marry soon after Mr Retallick returns.'

Darley's plans had not advanced as far as the actual marriage, but thinking about it now gave him a warm glow that left him impervious to the cold wind.

When Darley returned to the works office after a successful meeting with the Varcoe owner he was greeted by Tessa who gave him a hug and a kiss that raised the eyebrows of old Winnie Gilbert. The elderly bal maiden had come to the office to request a small advance on her wages with which to buy a present for her niece who had just given birth to a son.

'You're a dark horse, Darley Shovell. There's us working in this office together and you've never breathed a word about it. As for Jo! I knew she was taken with you, but I didn't know things had gone this far.'

'If Jo sees you kissing her husband-to-be that way, they're not likely to go any farther,' declared Winnie, disapprovingly.

Releasing Darley with a deliberately exaggerated reluctance, Tessa said provocatively, 'What the eye don't see, the heart won't grieve over, Winnie. So unless you say anything she's not likely to be the least bit upset, is she?'

Moving away from Darley, she added maliciously, 'Anyway, I'm always happy when I hear of someone getting married. It's the natural thing to do when two people love each other, isn't it? They want to be together, set up home and have babies. I mean, it's what we're put on this earth for.'

'That's as may be, but there's some who don't get things in the right order. When that happens they're likely to find a lot more trouble for themselves than they've bargained on.'

'What do you mean by that?' Tessa rounded on the old bal maiden so ferociously that Darley thought for a moment she was about to attack the older woman.

Winnie Gilbert was not in the least perturbed by Tessa's question. 'I mean exactly what I've said, girl. No more, and no less. But I'll tell you for nothing that I don't lose any sleep because *I'm* not wed.'

To Darley, Winnie Gilbert said, 'I'll come back for that money later, Mr Shovell. When I can collect it without a lot of backchat from them as'll one day wish they'd lived life the way I have.'

As Winnie Gilbert left the office cackling quietly to herself, Darley said to Tessa, 'What was that all about?'

'Who knows?' Tessa lied. 'Winnie's like one of they old prunes. All dried up and wrinkled, with no juice left in her. Live life like her, indeed! But let's forget about her and talk about you and Jo. When did you decide you'd be married? When will the wedding be? Do you think Jo will let me be a bridesmaid?'

Chapter 23

The next few weeks were very happy ones for Darley and Jo. Most evenings he would visit her at Miriam's house, where she was now working. If the weather was wet, he would remain in the house talking to Jo and Miriam.

On these occasions Miriam would always find something to do for an hour elsewhere in the house, leaving them alone in the kitchen.

On fine evenings, they would go for a walk in the countryside around the Gover Valley, sometimes climbing above the valley to look out at the sea, no more than a couple of miles away where there were always ships to be seen. Tall sailing ships leaning gracefully before the wind; rusty old coasters belching black smoke and wallowing their slow way along the English Channel; menacing warships, en route to and from the Royal Naval dockyard at Devonport; great majestic liners, sailing to and from the great ports of the world.

To the north and west the skyline was becoming increasingly dominated by the waste-heaps from the numerous clay workings. By this industry, man was changing the landscape as nothing else had done since the great Ice Age.

Despite this, it was a very pleasant place to be. Especially when they were able to enjoy the pleasure of sharing the things they saw and did.

There was an increasing awareness by both of them of the depth of their feelings for each other. More recently they had begun to make tentative plans for a late-summer wedding, the actual date dependent upon Josh's return from Africa.

Miriam had received a number of letters from Josh after his safe arrival at Insimo. They gave details of the tragic deaths of Daniel and Wyatt, and informed her of the situation there now.

It seemed Elvira had no intention of returning to England with her surviving three sons, even though unrest persisted in that troubled land. Josh would be remaining with them for a few months more, planning to return to Cornwall before the end of the summer.

The only thing that cast a shadow, albeit a small one, on Darley's present happiness, concerned Tessa. She was showing far more affection towards him than was good for his peace of mind.

On one particular occasion, she had been absent from the office for

97

almost an hour when a messenger was sent from the Ruddlemoor works to say her father wanted to speak to her. Darley had been obliged to go in search of her.

He eventually saw her coming from the boiler room at the far end of the new Daniel 'dry'. She appeared flustered and dishevelled. She tried to excuse her appearance by saying that she had muddied the hem of her dress, had washed it out, and dried it by the furnace fire.

On the way back to the office they met up with Captain Bolitho who had come to find Tessa for himself.

The Ruddlemoor works captain had viewed them both suspiciously and demanded to know where they had been. Darley said Tessa had been sent by him on an errand and he had gone to find her when he learned her father wished to speak with her.

It was evident that the works captain had believed Darley no more than *he* believed Tessa's story. However, although sceptical, Captain Bolitho had not pursued his doubts.

Later, when Tessa returned from her father's office, her gratitude to Darley had been so over-effusive, it embarrassed him.

Partly because of this, and also to keep a check on her during his own enforced absences from the office, Darley took on an elderly ex-teller from a St Austell bank. Unfortunately, the retired bank clerk was not in the best of health and was frequently absent himself.

On one of their walks together, Darley decided to tell Jo of his concern about Tessa and her over-friendly manner towards him.

Much to Darley's surprise, Jo treated the whole matter as a huge joke. She told him it was no more than a ruse to deflect attention from the affair she was having with Tom Sparrow.

'You're not the only one she's using in this way,' Jo told Darley. 'I believe she's making visiting me an excuse to get out of the house and see Tom. She's telling her mother she's coming to see me at Miriam's house a couple of evenings a week. It came out when we were all at church last Sunday. Her mother said how nice it was that we hadn't lost touch and that she was pleased Tessa was coming here to see me. She even suggested I should send her home earlier so she wouldn't have to walk home in the dark and arrive home so late! In fact, Tessa's only been to see me once – and that was weeks ago!'

Jo's disclosure took Darley by surprise. He was aware that Tessa's morals were not high, but was unaware she had been carrying on an affair.

'Isn't Tom Sparrow one of the wagoners we employ to carry clay to Charlestown?'

The railway link with the Varcoe works took the bulk of the China clay to Fowey, but low-grade clay was still taken by wagon to Charlestown harbour. About twenty self-employed wagoners performed this work.

'That's right. The wagon and horse were a gift from the family of Tom's wife when they married. They're gipsies. I believe Tom is part gipsy himself. It worries me sometimes to know that Tessa has got herself mixed up with him. If his wife's family ever find out about them there'll be all hell let loose. They look upon such things as an affront to the whole family. I've told her she ought to end the affair before it's too late.'

'I hope it's not too late already. Twice in the last few days we've found gipsies wandering around the works. When they've been challenged they've refused to say why they were there and have been ordered off. I saw one of them myself. He seemed to be looking for something. I thought he was looking around to see what he could steal. After what you've just said, it seems he might have been looking for *someone*. Perhaps either Tom or Tessa.'

'He probably came from the gipsy camp I saw when Miriam and I were on our way to Ruddlemoor yesterday. They're in the woods at Menacuddle. About eight or nine caravans.'

Jo used her employer's first name now, instead of the more formal 'Mrs Retallick'. Miriam had said that as Jo was likely to be family before very long, she might as well get used to what she would call her then.

That night, as Darley walked home, he thought of what Jo had told him about Tessa and her liaison with Tom Sparrow. He had no doubt at all that the visit of the two gipsies to the works were connected with the affair. He felt he should warn Tessa, but it would not be easy.

Tessa Bolitho was every bit as stubborn and unwilling to listen to reason as her father.

Chapter 24

Two days after he and Jo had discussed Tessa, Darley was in the office with the Ruddlemoor captain's daughter when Jim Bray came to the office.

'Is young Tom Sparrow due to pick up another load for us today?'

It was late afternoon and Darley shook his head, 'He's already taken two. He might have managed another, but there's been a bit of a hold-up at Charlestown. They're taking an hour or two longer than usual.'

Tessa sat at a desk behind Darley. Aware of her interest, he added, 'Why do you ask?'

'One of the men has just come in with Sparrow's horse and wagon tied behind his own. He found it making its own way along the road from town with no sign of a driver.'

'I expect he stopped off at the General Wolfe and spent longer there than expected.'

It was by no means uncommon for wagoners to stop off for a drink, leaving their horse to make its own way back towards the pit. Usually, the wagoner would catch up with his horse and wagon before they reached the clay works, sometimes by taking a short cut.

This theory was unexpectedly ruled out by Tessa. 'Tom doesn't drink. Anyway, he's got a new horse that doesn't know the road as the last one did. He wouldn't have left it to make its own way back here.'

'You seem to know a great deal about Tom Sparrow, young lady,' Jim Bray said pointedly to Tessa. He had heard rumours about her and the wagoner. Her words served to confirm them.

Darley saw that Tessa was really anxious, her eyes dark and fearful in her suddenly pale face. 'If he's not in the General Wolfe, do you have any idea where he might have gone?'

'No. Unless . . . He might have stopped off to speak to the gipsies camping in the Menacuddle Woods. He's not on the best of terms with them, but I believe they're related to his wife.'

'I'll speak to some of the wagoners when they come to the office. They might know where he is,' said Darley.

'When you find him, tell him I want to speak to him. If any man's going to do work for us he needs to be responsible. I'll not have a man who allows a horse and wagon to wander the countryside unattended unless he has a very good excuse.'

When Captain Bray had left the office, Tessa turned to Darley. 'Will you go and ask after Tom now . . . please?'

Darley hesitated. 'He's not officially employed by the company, Tessa, he can please himself what he does. He's certainly not the first wagoner to allow his horse to stray.'

'Not Tom. *Please*, Darley. I'm afraid he might have met with an accident, or . . . something.'

'What's the "or something"? Why are you so worried about him?'

'It's just a bad feeling I have. Please, Darley, ask among the wagoners if anyone's seen him.'

Few of the wagoners to whom Darley spoke showed any interest in the whereabouts of Tom Sparrow. Independent men, they minded their own business, and expected others to do the same.

Not until Darley had despaired of learning what had happened to the wagoner did he find someone who had seen him leave St Austell.

'He was close behind me when we came under the viaduct, but I didn't see him after that. Come to think of it, I don't think I even looked back. He might have been behind me for most of the way, or could have stopped soon after I saw him. I just don't know.'

'Were there many people on the road? Anyone I could ask about him?'

The wagoner shrugged. 'I wouldn't say it was crowded, not as many wagons as this morning, but there were one or two. There were also a few of they gipsies hanging around the track down to the Menacuddle well. Why don't you ask them about him. They probably know him better than any of us do.'

'I might do that. Thanks.'

Darley repeated his intentions to Tessa, adding, 'I'll look in on them on my way home. I doubt if they'll so much as pass the time of day with me, but I'll try.'

'Are you going to see Jo tonight?'

'I might, why?'

'I'll come over there to see her. Then you can tell me if you've learned anything.'

Darley was not at all certain he wanted to have Tessa's company when he visited Jo, but there was nothing he could do about it. He realised she really was anxious about Tom Sparrow. In passing, he wondered whether Sparrow's wife would be equally as concerned? Perhaps the missing wagoner had felt ill and gone straight home?

He decided not to pursue this line of thought. He had no intention of wasting half his evening by tramping to Stenalees to find out. Enough of his evening would be disrupted as it was.

On the road to St Austell, Darley fell in with Jeremiah Rowe, the

101

Varcoe works captain, who was on his way to St Austell too. They walked together along the road, discussing the satisfactory state of the neighbouring works.

When they entered the Menacuddle Woods, Darley mentioned his intention to speak to the gipsies about the missing wagoner.

'I'll come with you to their camp,' said Jeremiah Rowe, unexpectedly. 'I occasionally employ gipsies on a casual basis. If some of them are in the camp they're more likely to speak to me than to you. They're a close-mouthed lot, especially with strangers.'

The two men left the road and took the steep track which led from the road to an old well, beside which the gipsies were in the habit of camping.

To Darley's surprise, there was no one here. No caravans, no horses – and no gipsies. Looking around him at the rubbish strewn about the clearing, and the blackened mounds which were all that remained of camp fires, hot until a few hours before, Darley expressed puzzlement.

'I can't understand it. They usually stay much longer than they have this time and one of the wagoners saw their men lounging around up at the road, only hours ago.'

'It's no good trying to understand the gipsy mind, Darley. Their ways are not ours. Whatever the reason, they've certainly gone now.'

Taking a last look around, he shrugged, 'Oh, well, I tried. I couldn't do any more.'

As the two men walked away from the clearing, Darley headed back the way they had come, but Jeremiah Rowe said, 'There's a quicker way back to the road. The river's fairly shallow a little way along and strewn with enough large stones to make stepping across on them easy. At least, it's easy if you take it slowly. We used to have races across the river when I was a boy. Many's the ducking I've had here, I can tell you.'

Jeremiah Rowe was still reminiscing about the past when he ducked beneath a low hanging tree. 'Through here. Ah, yes, I remember it well.' Pointing to a tall beech, he said, 'If you were to climb to the top of that you'd probably still see my initials carved there. I used to doubt whether anyone had ever climbed so high before. It doesn't look so big now, somehow. But here we are, these are the stepping-stones.'

Following the Varcoe mine captain, Darley was halfway across the river, balancing carefully on a rounded boulder, when his companion stopped abruptly, just as Darley was about to move to the stone on which he stood.

'What is it?' Something in Jeremiah Rowe's frozen pose caused him to ask the question urgently.

'Over there . . . in the water by the far bank. See? Wedged between the stones . . .'

Jeremiah Rowe shifted one foot to another stone and his change of

102

balance enabled Darley to see past him. In the water, half-submerged, was the body of a man, lying face downwards.

The mine captain leaped from stone to stone to the far bank and Darley followed him as quickly as he could.

The stones against which the body of the man was wedged were too far from the bank to be used to stand on and Jeremiah waded thigh-deep into the fast-flowing stream. After only a moment's hesitation, Darley followed him.

Jeremiah had difficulty dislodging the body, but with Darley's help he was able to drag it to the bank. Once here, their combined efforts succeeded in dragging it from the river and they laid it gently down among the decaying leaves of the wood.

The Varcoe mine captain turned the body over, but Darley knew who it was, even before he saw the sightless eyes staring up from the bloodless face.

They had found Tom Sparrow. He would never again cheat on his gipsy wife.

Chapter 25

Darley and Jeremiah Rowe hurried to the St Austell police station to report what they had found. Constables were immediately despatched to locate the body of Tom Sparrow and arrange to have it conveyed to the mortuary.

A cursory examination by the police sergeant revealed no marks of violence on the body. He ignored a tentative suggestion by Darley that the disappearance of the gipsies from the Menacuddle Woods might be connected with the death of the wagoner.

The sergeant expressed the opinion that Tom had somehow slipped from the road when he was walking beside the horse and wagon. Knocking himself out when he fell into the river, he had subsequently drowned before regaining consciousness.

Both Jeremiah and Darley were required to give lengthy statements about their reason for being at the spot where they found the body. While they were engaged in this activity, a constable was sent on horseback to find Tom's wife. She would need to come to St Austell and make a positive identification of her late husband.

They were still at the police station when the constable returned to say there was no one in the house. Neighbours were unable to say where she was, or when she was likely to return. They had, however, been able to provide the constable with the address of the deceased man's mother. She lived at a village some four miles away. The sergeant arranged to send another man to bring her to the police station.

'Do you think it was an accident?' Darley asked Jeremiah, as they left the police station.

'No. I'm inclined to think you're right, that the gipsies had something to do with Sparrow's death,' said the Varcoe works captain. 'But you and I are clay workers, Darley, not policemen. This is one for them – and for the coroner. No doubt we'll both be required to attend the coroner's court to give evidence of finding him. Until we hear what is said there, we'd be wise to keep out theories to ourselves. You cross just one gipsy and you'll never be short of enemies for the remainder of your life.'

It was ten o'clock that night when Darley reached the Retallick house in the Gover Valley. It had been his intention to break the news of Tom

Sparrow's death to Miriam, have a few words with Jo, then return home. His hopes plummeted when Jo opened the door to him and he saw Tessa standing in the doorway behind her.

'Have you found him?' Tessa put the question to him even before Jo had time to greet him.

'Yes, Tessa, I'm afraid I have. But let me come in – and fetch Miriam too. It's not a story I want to tell more than once.'

Darley told his story to Tessa, Jo and Miriam when all four were seated in the lounge of the Retallick house. Darley was relieved he had decided not to tell his story when at the front door with the two girls. When he spoke of finding Tom Sparrow's body lying in the river at Menacuddle, Tessa gave a low moan of despair and slid in a faint from her chair to the floor.

'Quick, Jo. Fetch the smelling salts. You'll find them on the dressing-table in my bedroom.'

As Jo hurried from the room, Miriam said, 'Darley, help me lift her to the settee. You take her shoulders, I'll take her legs . . . mind her head!'

She called out the warning as Darley began to lift Tessa's limp form and her head dropped back, narrowly missing the wooden arm of a chair.

It took only a few moments to lift Tessa and lay her on the settee. As Miriam fumbled with the buttons at the neck of Tessa's dress, she asked, 'Tell me what this is all about, Darley? Why should the accident to Tom Sparrow cause Tessa to faint? Wasn't he a married man?'

'Yes. He was married to a gipsy girl.'

'Then why is Tessa so affected by news of his death? She doesn't strike me as being the sort of girl who would faint at news of the death of someone she hardly knows.'

When Darley made no reply, Miriam said, tight-lipped, 'Your silence is answer enough, young man. What a foolish girl she is! I realised when she was staying here with her mother that she must be carrying on with some man. She might have thought she was sneaking out of the house every opportunity she got without being noticed, but she wasn't. It was nothing to do with me, so I said nothing. But to get mixed up with a married man! Heaven help her if her father ever finds out.'

Miriam looked down at the girl lying on the settee and added enigmatically, 'And I very much suspect he will find out . . . and soon.'

At that moment, much to Darley's relief, Jo returned to the room carrying a small crystal bottle which she handed to Miriam.

A few minutes later Tessa came out of her faint, making choking sounds and attempting to brush away the bottle being wafted beneath her nose.

When she tried to sit up, Miriam said, 'Come on, my girl, upstairs with you.'

'No. I must get home or I'll be in trouble with my father.' Tessa began looking about her, showing signs of panic and Darley thought she might make a break for the door at any moment.

'You can go home soon enough. I'll have you taken in the pony and trap, but you'll rest here for a while first. If you won't go upstairs and lie down, you can stay here. Darley, you know where Dick Lowe lives. Go and tell him to get the pony and trap ready. He can take Tessa home.'

Dick Lowe was the elderly handyman who had worked for the Rosevears and now took care of things about the Retallick house and garden.

'Jo, go to the kitchen and make us all a cup of tea. I'll stay here with Tessa.'

It was close to midnight when Tessa arrived home. As she had feared, her father was waiting up for her. He heard the pony come to a halt outside the house and was halfway down the path to meet her by the time she opened the garden gate.

'Where have you been? I hope you've got a very good explanation for arriving home this late? If you haven't you'll feel my belt, young lady, I promise you that . . .'

'I went to visit Jo Bray and stayed much later than I'd intended – talking to Miriam Retallick.'

Tessa hoped desperately she had been able to eliminate all evidence of the tears she had shed for Tom Sparrow in the trap on the way home.

'It was so late that Miriam Retallick sent for one of her staff to bring me home in the pony and trap.'

'Mrs Retallick should know better than to keep a young girl out to this hour of the night.'

Abel Bolitho was still grumbling at her as they entered the house, but her explanation had taken the fire out of his anger. He could hardly complain too much if she was kept out late by his employer, and Mrs Retallick had behaved responsibly by having her sent home by pony and trap.

Neither could there be any doubts about Tessa's story. The pony and trap now turning around in the road outside the house bore testimony to that.

Nevertheless, Abel Bolitho still expressed his displeasure at having his daughter return home at such a late hour.

In the passageway, he said, 'You go straight up to bed now and I'll tell your mother you've returned home at last. She's been worried sick about you . . .'

As Tessa thankfully climbed the stairs, her legs feeling as though

106

they were weighted with lead, her father called up after her, 'It's all right for Mrs High-and-Mighty Retallick. She doesn't have to get up for work in the morning. She should have some thought for those of us who do.'

Chapter 26

Tessa found sleep an elusive ally during a long, long night. Lying in the darkness she shed many tears while she tried to find a single glimmer of hope in the bleak future she foresaw.

It was a relief when the light grey of morning showed through her curtains and familiar objects in her room became discernible.

The relief did not last long. When she rose from her bed to prepare herself for work, a wave of uncontrollable nausea swept over her. It was not a new experience. She had suffered morning sickness for the past two weeks, but this morning she faced it with increased dread.

Always before she had been able to keep going with the thought that at some time during the day she would have a secret liaison with Tom. They had talked about what was happening to her and he had been able to calm her fears. He was even able to persuade her it was a wonderful thing to happen and not the disaster she believed it to be.

Tom had told her it was all the incentive he needed to leave his wife and go away with her. They would take the horse with them, perhaps the wagon too. They would go far away, to some place where they were unknown and he would take work as a wagoner. They would have a good life. He, Tessa . . . and the baby.

But that had been yesterday. Today, Tom was dead. Tessa had to face the future on her own – and with a dead man's baby in her belly.

She was sicker than usual this morning. She was glad the small, wooden privy was at the bottom of the garden, well away from the house. Her retching and gasping for breath would have left no one in any doubt about what was wrong with her.

Eventually, feeling exhausted, ill and close to despair, Tessa rose from her knees, squared her shoulders, and pulled back the bolt on the inside of the privy door.

Stepping outside the small building, she came face to face with her father. One look at his face told her all the subterfuge was over.

'Come into the house, you *slut*!'

'No!' Terrified by the expression on his face, Tessa looked around her for a means of escape. There was none.

Before she could even move from the spot, he reached out and grabbed her long, uncombed hair. Twisting his grip painfully, he forced her in front of him along the path and into the house through the kitchen door.

Doris Bolitho was in the kitchen preparing breakfast. One look at Tessa being propelled through the door by her husband caused the two eggs she was holding to drop to the kitchen floor.

All the fears which had been allayed in recent months rushed back, 'What's the matter? What's happening . . . Abel?'

'Shut up and mind your own business. When this little *slut* has told me what I want to know, then I'll deal with you. I can't believe you didn't know.'

'Know *what*?'

Doris's stomach contracted in fear at his words. She did not know what he was talking about, but he was in one of his violent moods and that terrified her.

She received no reply from her husband. He had gone through the kitchen into the passageway outside, driving Tessa before him, her head twisted painfully as a result of the grip he still maintained on her hair.

Too frightened to follow after them, Doris started as she heard a frightening thud. Abel had hurled Tessa from him, throwing her against the wall at the foot of the stairs.

'Go on upstairs.'

'No.'

There was another heavy thud, and once again Tessa cried out, 'No!' But this time there was pain in her voice.

'Very well, we'll sort it out down here. First of all, how long have you been pregnant?'

Doris drew in her breath in dismay. Tessa pregnant? It could not be true. And yet . . .

'Don't lie to me, you dirty little slattern. I heard you out there being as sick as a dog – or should I say the bitch that you are? How long?'

There was the sound of another heavy thud, and then again, as though Abel had struck his daughter with his fist.

'I don't know. I tell you, I don't know!' This time Tessa screamed out the words, her pain evident.

Overcoming her fear of her husband, Doris went from the kitchen to the passageway. 'Abel, leave the girl alone. Please. Let's talk this over.'

'Talk! The time for talking is past. If all she'd done was "talk" she wouldn't be in the trouble she is now – and we wouldn't have shame brought into this house.'

'All the same . . .'

'Shut up and get back in that kitchen, or I'll deal with you in the same way. I'm probably the last person in the house to know about this.'

Doris backed away. Behind her, in the passageway, Abel resumed the violent 'questioning' of his daughter and Doris waited to hear no more. Rushing from the kitchen she went in search of her nearest neighbour: Jim Bray.

Tessa knelt on the floor in the passageway, clutching her stomach and rocking in pain. Abel stood over her, his whole being trembling in anger.

'Answer me, girl. Who's the father of the bastard you're carrying?'

When she continued her rocking without answering, Abel reached down and seized her hair once more, twisting her head so she was forced to look up at him.

'You heard me. Who's the father of this baby?'

When she still made no reply, he hit her on the side of her face with his fist. Her head snapped back against the wall and he was left holding a handful of hair.

'Tell me . . .' A sudden thought came to him and he seemed to swell with renewed anger. 'I know who it is. It's that Shovell boy, isn't it? I knew there'd be trouble with the two of you working in the office. It's him, isn't it?'

'No!' It came out as a wail of despair.

'Don't lie to me!' This time the words were accompanied by a kick that caused her to scream in pain.

'No . . . it isn't his.'

'I said, don't lie to me.'

Another kick, and then another, this one fairly and squarely in her stomach as she lay on the floor.

'It's Shovell, isn't it? Tell me. Tell me the truth. Tell me the father is Darley Shovell.'

The kicks were coming more frequently now and Tessa lay on the passageway floor in a haze of pain, barely hanging on to her senses. She knew that nothing other than the reply he wanted would stop him from continuing to kick her. If he would kill her and be done with it, she would willingly have died, like Tom. But the pain was unbearable . . .

'Yes . . . Yes, Darley's the father.'

One more kick left her moaning in agony and then she realised there were others in the passageway with them. Raised voices. An argument. A scuffle: But the kicking had stopped – and Abel Bolitho had left the house.

A few moments later, her mother was kneeling beside her. 'Tessa. Tessa. Can you hear me?'

'We'd better get her upstairs to her bed.'

'NO!' The word came out through thick and cut lips. 'No, I'm not stopping in this house. Not now. I never want to see *him* again.'

'All right, but for now . . .'

'No, Jim, she's right.' Dabbing blood from around Tessa's mouth,

110

Doris looked up at her neighbour. 'We've both taken more than enough from Abel. I'm going too.'

'Where? Tessa can't travel far in her state.'

'Yes, I can . . . and I will.'

Tessa struggled to a sitting position on the passageway floor. 'I don't care where we go. But I'm going as far from Stenalees as I can.'

'Can you arrange a carriage to take us to St Austell station, Jim? In the meantime, I'll gather together a few things.'

'Where will you go? What will you do?'

'Anywhere and anything. It doesn't matter. I've got a few pounds put by – so has Tessa. Abel has money saved too, quite a lot. We'll take that as well. He owes us more than money can ever repay. I can work, and so can Tessa when she's well again.'

'If you're quite certain.' Jim Bray looked down at them pityingly. 'I can't say I blame either of you. I'm surprised you've stayed with him for so long. I don't know many women who would. I'll send someone across to help you and then arrange a carriage.'

'Cap'n Bray!'

Tessa's call came as Jim Bray was letting himself out of the front door. When he turned, Tessa pushed her mother's hand away so she could speak clearly.

'You must find Darley. Catch him before he leaves home. Tell him he's not to go to work today. If he does, my father will kill him.'

'Why?'

'Because Father will be looking for him.' Memories of the fate of Tom Sparrow flooded back to her and her face screwed up in anguish, although her mother and Jim Bray thought it was pain.

'I . . . I'm having a baby. Father thinks Darley is the father.'

Jim Bray looked at her in total astonishment. 'A baby?' When the news had sunk in, he asked, '*Is* Darley the father?'

'No.'

Seeing the reply was insufficient, she added, 'It was Tom Sparrow, but Father wouldn't have believed that. He *wanted* to believe it was Darley.'

Chapter 27

Darley left his St Austell home and set off for work accompanied by Lily. She was enjoying a few additional days away from school because her teacher was ill once more.

Darley was of the opinion Tessa would probably not be at work for a day or two. Lily was coming with him to Ruddlemoor to 'help' in the office. She would be able to do some simple filing and a number of the less important tasks, but Darley did not expect too much of her.

Lily was happy to have the opportunity to spend a whole day with Darley. She would not mind what he gave her to do. Skipping along beside him, she asked, for the fourth time that morning, 'Do you think Tessa *will* be at work today?'

'No.'

'What exactly *is* wrong with her?' Lily was bursting with curiosity. Everyone was being very secretive about the nature of Tessa's illness.

'She went to visit Jo at Great-aunt Miriam's house last night and was sent home in the pony and trap because she didn't feel well, that's all.'

'What if she never comes back? Could I take her place in the office? I'd learn everything very quickly.'

Darley smiled at her eagerness. 'Once you start work you'll wish you'd been able to put it off for a few more years. But you'll need to stay at school for a while longer yet. Learn all you can and I don't doubt we'll find a place for you in the works office.'

'I'd like that,' said Lily seriously. 'I expect you'll be married to Jo and will have left home by then. Unless I'm working with you I'll hardly ever see you at all.'

Finding a new home was something Darley had not yet put his mind to. He had hardly come to terms with the idea of getting married to Jo.

It set him off on a happy train of thought that stayed with him through Lily's chatter all the way to Ruddlemoor.

Once in the office, he was still showing Lily what to do when the door was flung open and Captain Bolitho entered the office.

The works captain was momentarily taken aback at seeing Lily. Jabbing a finger in her direction, he demanded, 'What's she doing here?'

'She has a day off from school so I told her she could come and help

112

in the office. We can always do with extra help. Especially if it involves no extra cost.'

Darley carefully refrained from asking about Tessa. It might prompt some awkward questions from the Ruddlemoor captain.

'Then she can take care of things in the office until you get back. My daughter's not feeling too good. She won't be coming to work today.'

'Until I get back from where?' Darley had not made any plans to go anywhere.

'From the old workings at the far end of the Ruddlemoor pit. There's a lot of useable equipment there and someone's coming to make an offer for it later this morning. I want to make a list of exactly what they'll be buying.'

Darley wished the Ruddlemoor captain had not left it until the last minute before making such a list, but it would have to be done.

'I could go,' said Lily, brightly.

'You'd take too long,' growled Abel Bolitho. To Darley, he said, 'Well, are you coming, or shall we still be making a list when the buyer arrives?'

'I'm coming.' Darley picked up a number of sheets of paper and a board on which to rest them when he was writing. To Lily, he said, 'If anyone comes to the office with a query you can't answer, tell them I'll be back in about an hour. Until then you can tidy up – and put the kettle on. We'll have a cup of tea when I return.'

Outside the office, Abel Bolitho made no attempt at conversation. Striding out towards the Ruddlemoor pits, he left Darley hurrying along in his wake.

He kept up the same pace through the two pits that were operational and on to the smallest of the Ruddlemoor pits. It had ceased working only a few months before and rails, broken tramway wagons and disused pipes were strewn about the edge of a deep water-filled pit. It had rained during the early hours of the morning and the water in the pit was the colour and consistency of creamy milk.

'Up the other end,' said Abel Bolitho, tersely.

Darley followed the other man until they were out of sight of the other two pits, the sound of working greatly muffled. At the edge of the man-made lake, the older man halted.

Taking out a pencil and straightening out the paper on the piece of board, Darley said, 'Where do we begin?'

'*I* begin with you!' Abel Bolitho spoke with such venom in his voice that Darley looked up, startled.

The Ruddlemoor captain was standing hands on hips. The expression of malice on his face struck immediate fear in Darley.

'What are you talking about?' Darley tried to behave naturally. It was not easy. 'There doesn't appear to be as much machinery here as

113

you thought. Listing this will only take ten or twelve minutes. Fifteen at the most.'

'I haven't brought you here to list machinery, Shovell. I wanted you out of the sight and hearing of everyone so I could talk to you about Tessa – and the baby. You'll know about the baby, of course?'

After a moment's surprised hesitation, Darley said, 'Yes, I know.' He was genuinely puzzled by Abel Bolitho's manner. Why should he go to all this trouble to talk to *him* about the baby Tessa was expecting.

'I thought you would. I knew something like this would happen if I allowed Tessa to work in that office, with you.'

'It's got nothing to do with the office . . .'

'No? It might not have happened there, but I'd say the office has *everything* to do with it. Well, Shovell, isn't there something you'd like to say to me? "Sorry", perhaps, or something equally meaningless?'

'Why should I be sorry? I'vc got nothing to be sorry about. The baby is nothing to do with me . . .'

'So *that's* the way you intend playing the game, is it? Denying all responsibility? I should have expected it. Like father, like son. He's always denied all responsibility for the death of my father. Well, I know better. Tessa has already admitted to me that you're the father of the bastard she's carrying. But the Shovell family isn't going to get off scot free this time. My only regret is that no one will ever know how the settling up was done.'

'I . . . I don't know what you're talking about. Why should Tessa lie about me?'

Darley felt the hairs on the back of his neck rising. He was beginning to believe the Ruddlemoor captain was actually insane.

'You disappoint me, Shovell. I thought you were going to plead with me that you wanted to marry Tessa. Then I'd have been able to tell you that I wouldn't let her marry you. No, not if you were the richest man in Cornwall.'

'Why would I want to marry Tessa? I'm going to marry Jo Bray.'

As he was speaking, Darley became aware that Abel Bolitho had laid his plans carefully. At Darley's back was the lake of milky-white clay water. The edges were wet and slippery . . . The Ruddlemoor captain stood between him and escape and there was no one to see or hear what happened here.

'Is it supposed to make it better that you make one girl pregnant and plan to marry another?'

'I've told you, I have nothing to do with Tessa being pregnant. She'd tell you that if she was here. Let's go back to your house and ask her.'

'I've already asked her – and you're not going anywhere, Shovell. Your last glimpse of this earth will be of a disused clay pit. I hope, for your sake, you can't swim. That would only prolong the agony for you.'

Darley found he was having difficulty in breathing. He knew it was

114

caused by fear and not by his lung sickness, 'Look . . . You've got this all wrong. I'm nothing to do with the baby Tessa's carrying.'

'That's better! I hoped to see you grovel before you died.'

As the Ruddlemoor captain was talking, Darley tried to move to one side, hoping to make a desperate dash past him, but Abel anticipated him and moved to block his escape.

'I know the name of the child's father. So do others. They'll tell you . . .'

'That's it. Keep it up, Shovell. Aren't you going to go down on your knees and plead with me? It wouldn't make any difference either, but I'd enjoy it.'

Darley realised that whatever he said, or did, would make no difference. It was the Ruddlemoor captain's intention to throw him in the waters of the disused pit. Whether or not he was the father of the baby Tessa was bearing made no difference. It was what Abel wanted to believe.

Suddenly, and quite unexpectedly, there was a shout from the other end of the quarry. Abel Bolitho spun around. Seizing the unexpected opportunity to escape, Darley sprinted past him, avoiding the hand that reached out too late to prevent his escape.

Coming towards them from the working part of the Ruddlemoor works were Jim Bray, Lily – and Darley's father.

Jim Bray had called at the Shovell house hoping to prevent Darley from going to work. When he told Jethro of what had happened at Stenalees, Darley's father put on his coat and both men hurried to the Ruddlemoor works.

Behind the two men were a number of the Ruddlemoor pit workers, following out of sheer curiosity, wondering what was going on.

Darley met them halfway across the floor of the pit.

'What's been going on?' Jethro put the question to his son.

'Cap'n Bolitho's gone mad! He accused me of being the father of the baby Tessa's expecting. He was going to drown me in the pit. He'd have done it too, if you hadn't come along.'

Suddenly aware of how close he had come to death, Darley found he was shaking.

'Would he? We'll see about that . . .'

Jethro began to walk towards the Ruddlemoor captain, but Jim Bray took his arm. 'Don't do anything foolish, Jethro. Darley's right, Abel Bolitho isn't wholly sane.'

'Don't stop him, Cap'n Bray. One Shovell has got away from me for the time being, but the other one will not. My father will rest more easily in his grave if I do to Jethro Shovell what was done to him.'

'What is it you think was done to your father, Bolitho? After all these years, let's exorcise the cancer that's been eating at your heart for all this time.'

'You know very well what happened. Your Union men attacked him because he wouldn't join the strike that *you* called . . .'

'You've believed that for too many years, Abel Bolitho. It's coloured your attitude towards the Shovell family and to the Trades Unions. I think perhaps it's time you learned the truth. I couldn't have called a strike, even had I wanted to. I'm an Association man, not a Unionist. Besides, your father was not beaten by Union men but by the clay men who were his workmates. It had no more to do with a Union than had his reason for not joining the strike. He daren't join for fear he'd be dismissed from the works. If that had happened it would have been discovered how he'd robbed everyone – both the men and his employers – during all the years he was in charge of the works store. Selling the men who worked there goods at high prices. Not only that, but charging them an outrageous interest on top of the normal price. When the men found out, they used the strike as an opportunity to pay him back for all the years he'd robbed them.'

'That's a lie, Shovell! An evil, warped lie against a man who's no longer here to defend himself. A man who was respected by everyone who knew him. I'll have you for this.'

'Save your breath, Abel Bolitho. I can find you a dozen men who knew what happened, and why. Everyone kept quiet in the early days out of respect for your mother – and for you, his young son. But your mother's no longer with us and a man needs to earn the respect he's given.'

The men from the Ruddlemoor pit who had followed Jim Bray and Jethro to the disused pit, had heard all that had been said. They drew closer as Jethro continued, 'We might as well clear up another matter while we're at it. Your Tessa may or may not be pregnant. Either way, Darley has nothing to do with it.'

'You're lying again, Shovell. She told me herself it was him.'

'She *told* you? Or did you *force* her to say it was him, because that's what you wanted to believe? Having seen some of your handiwork on your own wife, I've no doubt she would have said it was the Duke of Cornwall if it would have stopped you beating her.'

'It *is* his child. I warned of this when she went to work in the office with him . . .'

'I suspect she was expecting the baby when she began work there – and there's not a man in Ruddlemoor who couldn't name the father. Jim?'

'He's right, Abel. Tessa was carrying on with young Tom Sparrow for many months. You're probably the only one on the works who didn't know.'

'I don't believe it . . . You're both in this together!' Despite his assertion, Abel had seen the nods of agreement that came from the works men standing behind Jim Bray when he named the wagoner.

116

'Bring him here and let's see what he has to say about it.'

'He'll never be able to say, one way or the other, Abel. Tom Sparrow was found dead last night. He was lying in the river, close by the gipsy camp in Menacuddle Woods. The camp occupied by the family of Sparrow's wife.'

'That's right,' Jethro spoke again. 'When Tessa heard the news at Miriam Retallick's house, she fainted and had to be sent home by pony and trap.'

'It's not true. I won't believe it until I hear it from Tessa's own lips.'

'You're going to have to believe us, Abel,' said Jim Bray. 'Half an hour after you left the house, Doris and Tessa left too. They've left you for good this time. Left Cornwall too – and I can't say I blame either of them. The best thing you can do is follow their example, Abel. When Mrs Retallick hears of this, you'll be finished here.'

'It isn't true. None of this is true.'

Abel Bolitho stood facing them, but looking at none of them. Shaking his head in a refusal to accept all he had just learned, he seemed thoroughly bewildered. A man caught up in a bad dream.

'Let's leave him to sort it all out in his own mind,' said Jim Bray. 'No one else can help him.'

Jethro nodded. 'I feel ashamed of myself for telling him about his father, but there was no other way. It should have been done many years ago.'

'All right, you men,' Jim Bray called to the Ruddlemoor workers. 'Back to work now, all of you.'

The men did as they were told, speaking excitedly among themselves as they went.

One of the younger men in the group looked around when they were almost out of the disused pit and his expression underwent a dramatic change. For many moments he seemed to be trying to say something and then he screamed one word.

The word was: 'NO!'

As his companions turned to him, he pointed back the way they had come.

Darley and the others turned around. Behind them there was no one. Captain Abel Bolitho had disappeared. All that was to be seen was a circle of ripples slowly spreading out across the surface of the milky water of the flooded clay pit.

Both groups of men ran back to the water's edge. By the time they reached the pool even the concentric circle of ripples had disappeared.

'What happened? Did you see?' Jim Bray put the question to the worker who had shouted.

The man nodded, trying hard to gather his wits together. 'He . . . picked up one of the trolley wheels . . .'

117

A number of rusting iron wheels lay about on the pit floor and the workman pointed to them.

'He . . . he stuffed it inside his jacket and . . . just jumped in. He didn't make a sound!'

The silence that greeted his words lasted a full two minutes. Then Jim Bray said, 'We'll need to borrow a rowing boat. I'll have men go out with grappling hooks. We'll find him.'

Addressing Darley, he said, 'Borrow a horse from the stables. Get down to the station and see if you can catch Doris and Tessa before they leave. They ought to know what's happened.'

Darley hurried away. Just before he left the pit he looked back. His father, Jim Bray, Lily and the workmen still stood at the edge of the deep pool which held the body of Abel Bolitho in its depths. But for their timely arrival it would have been *his* body that lay somewhere in the milky depths of the old Ruddlemoor clay pit.

Chapter 28

Darley was not an experienced rider, but that did not matter today. The horse given to him from the works stable was advanced in years. Although occasionally saddled, the animal was more used to pulling skips along the works tramway than carrying a rider on an urgent mission.

The horse adamantly refused to rouse itself to anything more energetic than an uncertain trot all the way to St Austell. Nevertheless, Darley reached St Austell more quickly than had he travelled on foot.

Upon reaching the railway station he tied the Ruddlemoor horse to the railings and entered the station. Walking through the entrance hall he passed a small, arched window behind which sat a ticket clerk.

The station had two platforms, linked by a bridge painted cream and brown. Behind the second platform was a siding where a number of wagons were unloading bagged clay into a railway truck.

The platforms were deserted except for a uniformed porter wielding a wide, soft-haired broom in an unenthusiastic manner.

'Has a train left the station in the last hour so?' Darley put his question to the porter.

'Going where?'

'Anywhere.'

The porter gave him a quizzical look. 'Most folks who ask about trains like to know where they're going. Still, that's your business, I suppose. There's been four trains this morning. Two to Penzance, two going t'other way. The last two were the eight-forty to Penzance, and the nine-twenty to London. Was you hoping to catch either of them?'

'No. When is the next train?' Darley hoped that if Doris and Tessa had missed either of the earlier trains, they might have decided to wait where they would be less conspicuous to catch the next one.

The porter had resumed his sweeping. Now he ceased once more and with a sigh leaned heavily on the broom before speaking again. 'There's the eleven-thirty-five to Plymouth, change for London, and the twelve-thirty to Penzance. Will either of those suit you?'

'I don't know.' Darley was uncertain what he should do next. 'I was hoping to catch up with two travellers, but I suspect I've missed them already.'

'What were the travellers? Men? Women? A married couple?'

119

'Two women. A mother and daughter. They probably had a lot of luggage with them.'

'Thin-faced woman, scared of her own shadow? Travelling with a girl of about sixteen who looked as though she'd taken a good beating.'

'That's them! You've seen them. Which train did they catch?'

'They arrived to catch the nine-twenty.'

'Then I *have* missed them.' Darley made a gesture of frustration.

'They didn't catch it. The young girl collapsed on this platform, not a foot from where you're standing now. Blood everywhere there was. I should know, I had to clear it up. Someone said she'd had a miscarriage, but she hardly seemed old enough to be carrying. Anyway, they took her off to the hospital and her mother went with her. We've got all their luggage in the baggage office. You a relative of theirs?'

'A friend. Thank you very much. I'll go to the hospital and find them.'

'When you see them, remind 'em as there's a daily charge for baggage . . .'

Darley retrieved the horse which appeared to be asleep on its feet. It was a reluctant starter. Fortunately the hospital was only on the other side of the small town.

When he reached the hospital, Darley was asked to wait in a corridor. It seemed a doctor was examining Tessa and Doris was with them.

'What's going to happen to the girl . . . to Tessa?'

'That depends upon the doctor, but she'll be here for a day or two. If you'd care to go away and come back later . . .'

Darley received the information with a deal of relief. He had not been looking forward to breaking the news of the death of Abel Bolitho to his wife and daughter.

He believed he knew someone who could do it far more successfully. Gover Valley was not far away. He would go there and tell Miriam all that had been happening at the works.

Jo let him into the house but her pleasure at seeing him changed when she saw his expression. 'What is it, Darley? Why are you here? Has something happened at Ruddlemoor?'

'You'd better come in and listen while I tell Great-aunt Miriam.'

She was in the lounge, a letter on the small table beside her. Had Darley not been so full of the information he had to give her, he would have been aware that Miriam was looking pale and drawn.

She listened in silence while Darley told the story of Tessa's beating and the events that had led to the suicide of the Ruddlemoor works captain. He then gave her the present whereabouts of Tessa and Doris Bolitho.

Both women listened to the story in shocked disbelief. Jo made

120

occasional sounds of distress, especially when Darley told how close he had come to losing his life at the hands of Abel Bolitho.

When the tale came to an end, Miriam said, 'You did the right thing coming to tell me all that has happened, Darley. I'll go to the hospital and break the news to Doris. We'll make some arrangements for them to be looked after for a while until Doris feels able to cope by herself. Do you know whether their house at Stenalees belongs to us?'

'Yes, it does,' said Jo. 'Ours does too.'

'That will make things easier. Darley, when you return to Ruddlemoor, tell Captain Bray to take over the running of the whole of the works. I envisage it as a permanent arrangement, if it's acceptable to him. Tell him I'll be along to see him just as soon as it's possible. In the meantime, tell Dick Lowe to have the pony and trap ready – and, Darley!'

'Yes, Aunt Miriam.'

'Don't stay here talking to Jo for too long. Too many things are happening around us. We've got to try to stay on top of it all.'

'I won't stay for many minutes. This isn't the right time to be discussing wedding plans – but I do want to make some plans with Jo soon.'

'Make your plans by all means, but don't get fixing a firm date. I had a letter from Josh this morning.'

'Did he say when he's coming back?' asked Darley, eagerly.

'He couldn't. He's been thrown into gaol in South Africa.'

BOOK TWO

1894

Chapter 1

The train on which Josh had travelled from Cape Town for three days and nights, steamed laboriously into the recently completed station at Johannesburg. This was the northernmost point of the South African railway system. Only the needs of the goldminers had brought it this far, against the inclinations of 'Oom' Paul Kruger, President of the South African Republic.

Slowly, with seeming reluctance, the train came to a juddering halt. Leaking steam, it added its accompaniment to the myriad sounds of Africa's busiest rail terminal.

Uniformed staff moved along the platform crying out the name of the station lest any passenger be in any doubt.

On the platform, African porters jostled each other as they vied for business. Excited men, women and children sought friends and relatives they had not seen for months, or years. Shouts went back and forth from open window and platform when recognition came.

Quickly spilling from the train, the new arrivals added to the cosmopolitan confusion of the scene. Here were returning businessmen, hopeful would-be miners, wives and families joining miner husbands, and girls arriving to marry miners. Other women had come here to sell their charms to the lonely men who frequented Johannesburg's many bars and brothels.

'Johannesburg is quite a town.'

The man who spoke the words to Josh was standing at an open window beside him. He had boarded the train only at Kimberley. Before this moment he and Josh had nodded a greeting to each other, no more.

'It certainly looks pretty lively,' agreed Josh as a brass band began playing at the far end of the platform. In the midst of the band a banner was unfurled. It declared, 'Welcome to Annie Carne. Arriving to marry Sam Whittle'.

'It's a *wicked* place. Africa's Sodom and Gomorrah. Spawned in the greed for gold and breeding the evils of lust and blasphemy.'

The impassioned words spoken in Afrikaans were uttered angrily by a young man dressed in the manner of a 'predikant', a preacher in the Dutch Reformed Church.

'Perhaps you might suggest to President Kruger that he stop taking a very hefty slice of the profits from such an evil undertaking?' said the

125

man who had boarded the train at Kimberley.

'On the contrary, President Kruger should tax Johannesburg out of existence,' declared the angry predikant. 'One day he might.'

Johannesburg was in Transvaal. Unlike the Cape Colony, it was not ruled by the British, but by Boers. Part of the South African Republic, it was occupied by burghers whose ancestors had trekked to the interior many years before to escape British rule.

It was twelve years since these men had fought and won a war against the British, in defence of their independence. Most bitterly resented the presence of so many non-Afrikanders – 'Uitlanders' – in their land, digging out the gold they had found in Johannesburg. The influx of these foreigners, the arrogant Britons in particular, filled them with a smouldering resentment.

President Kruger had been pressured by the Church to which he belonged to throw them out. On a personal level he would have been happy to oblige, but his country desperately needed the money they were pouring into the Transvaal coffers. All he could do was make things as difficult as possible for them. He levied taxes when and where he could and refused to allow the vast majority of them to have any say in the country's affairs.

'The Dutch Reformed Church might stick its head in the sand and pretend there isn't a world beyond the Transvaal borders, but that doesn't mean it's going to go away. Johannesburg will expand. No doubt Transvaal will grow rich too, as a result.'

'Never! God will prove he is with *us* and against those who scorn his laws.' The predikant stepped from the train and pushed his way through the noisy crowds. His disapproval was evident in the stiffness of his body as he disappeared from sight.

It had been very many years since Josh had lived in Africa and learned the language of the Afrikander. There had been an opportunity to recall some of it whilst on the boat from England and during his brief stay in Cape Town. He knew enough to have followed the conversation between the two men.

'I gather that not all Afrikanders are enamoured of Johannesburg and its gold mines?' he said to his companion.

The other man shrugged. 'How would you feel if such a place as this sprang up in England? Populated by foreigners who made little attempt to learn your language and didn't bother to hide their contempt for you? Oh, no need to answer. Would you like some help with your luggage?'

'I have only this one small trunk.' Josh lifted the object in question in his arms and stepped from the train behind his companion.

'Where are you staying?'

'I don't know Johannesburg,' he replied. 'Can you recommend anywhere?'

'Your accent is that of a Cornishman. You'll feel at home in the Petroc Hotel.'

Josh's fellow traveller beckoned to an African porter and spoke to him in a native language.

The porter picked up Josh's bag and the other man said, 'I've told him to take the bag to the hotel. They'll tip him there and charge it to your account. Don't worry, your bag will be there when you arrive, however long it is. You have my word. But you're travelling light. Are you here as a miner or an engineer? Johannesburg has plenty of the one, and not enough of the other.'

'Neither. I don't intend being here any longer than is necessary. I'm on my way to Matabeleland.'

They were pushing their way through the noisy crowd but at Josh's words the other man turned to look more closely at him.

'Matabeleland? Why . . .?'

He got no further with his question. From somewhere close at hand there came a massive explosion that seared Josh's ear-drums. At the same time it created a vacuum that squeezed his lungs painfully. A moment later there was a rush of hot, dust-laden air that threatened to choke him.

From somewhere beyond the end of the platform, a huge pall of smoke rose high in the air, swirling and billowing upwards until it blotted out the sun.

As the roar of the great explosion died away, it was replaced by the sounds of screaming and confused shouting. As the noises swelled, Josh, his companion and a number of other men began running towards the source of the calamity.

Beyond the station they could see twisted rails scattered about a huge hole in the ground where the railway track had been minutes before. All around for a frightening distance were the ruins of buildings, many of them now no more than a heap of rubble.

A wagon loaded with dynamite for the miners had been left in the fierce heat of the sun for too long and exploded.

A man ran to one pile of rubble and began digging with his bare hands, shouting that there were women beneath the shattered building. Josh and his companion from the train began digging beside him. Soon they were joined by many others.

Suddenly, one of the men shouted. He was immediately surrounded by a gang of frenziedly digging men. Minutes later the body of a girl wearing a gaudy red dress was passed over the heads of the men and laid in what had been the road. Another rescue worker murmured to Josh that this particular heap of rubble had once been a bar, much favoured by the younger, single miners.

Suddenly, the angry predikant from the train put in an appearance. Standing on a faintly smoking heap of rubble, he held up both arms in a gesture that embraced the whole of the town and cried, 'You have just witnessed the wrath of the Lord, sent down from Heaven to punish the evil that is Johannesburg.'

The oaths that were hurled at the predikant should have brought another bolt from heaven had he truly been 'the Lord's messenger'.

Two men carrying a ladder which was needed to climb down inside a hole uncovered beneath a nearby shattered building pushed the predikant to one side. One of them said roughly, 'If you're not going to help, Predikant, get out of the bloody way of those who are!'

The Afrikander preacher relinquished his vantage point only long enough for the two men to pass by. Then, ascending his smouldering pulpit once more, he cried, 'Take this as a warning from the Almighty. Continue in your wicked ways and next time there might be no survivors. None at all.'

There was an angry murmuring from the men who had pulled the body of the saloon girl from the wreckage of the bar – suddenly a number of them rushed at the predikant. They grasped him beneath the armpits and lifted him from the ground.

Ignoring his protests, the men ran with him to a waste pit which was at the rear of the demolished bar. The hole was half-filled with rubbish and water. For a moment it seemed all the men would end in the mud and filth of the pit.

Not until they reached the very edge of the pit did the men carrying the struggling victim come to a halt. Not so the predikant. Still shouting defiance, his arms flailing, he landed in the middle of the pit and disappeared from view.

For a few moments Josh thought he had disappeared for ever. Then, minus his wide-brimmed hat and unrecognisable as a man of the cloth, his head rose above the filthy water. To the accompanying jeers of the watching men, he fought his way to the edge of the waste pit and dragged himself out.

The predikant and the wrath of the Almighty were soon forgotten as yet another young body in a gaudy dress was exhumed from the ruins of the shattered saloon.

In the next few hours a hundred more would join the bar-girl, laid out with respect, but little dignity, in the dusty streets of Johannesburg.

Whether it was the wrath of the Almighty, as the predikant had claimed, or appalling human error, it was a tragedy that none who witnessed it would ever forget.

Chapter 2

It was not until the early hours of the next morning that Josh and his recent travelling companion left the now-dwindling army of men who still searched the rubble of demolished buildings for survivors of the explosion. Nobody, alive or dead, had been found for three hours.

'Will the Petroc Hotel have escaped the blast?' Josh put the question as the two weary men reached an area where at least some buildings had escaped the full force of the gigantic blast.

'Almost certainly. It's a little way from the railway line.'

They were in a prosperous area now, with bright lights shining from windows and doors. Suddenly, Josh's companion said, 'Let's have a drink before we go to your hotel.'

It was his intention to refuse. He wanted some sleep before making an early start that morning. He needed to make arrangements for the remainder of his journey to Matabeleland and was determined to reach his destination as quickly as possible.

However, before Josh could express his thoughts, his companion was halfway up a small flight of wide steps that led to a substantial building. Josh decided that one drink would do no harm.

He followed the other man into a foyer that was out of keeping with anything he had yet seen in Johannesburg – or anywhere else, for that matter. Dark wood panelling covered the walls from floor to a very high ceiling where a chandelier, six feet in diameter, dispensed sparkling light to every corner.

Josh became suddenly aware of his appearance. His hands, and no doubt his face too, were filthy as a result of the recent rescue work. His clothing was covered in dust.

'I'm not dressed for such a place,' he protested. 'I'll probably be thrown out.'

'The man who tries will be out through the door before you. Many others will have been doing the same as us tonight. Anyway, most of the men you'll meet here were probably scrabbling in the dirt at the bottom of a gold claim only a year or so ago.'

At that moment a very smart man wearing evening dress hurried towards them, his appearance serving only to emphasise their dishevelled state.

'It's nice to see you again, Mr Selous . . . Sir.' A nod of his head in

129

Josh's direction acknowledged his presence before attention was returned to his companion. 'Would you care to take advantage of a bathroom? While you're bathing I'll have someone brush and freshen up your clothes. When you come out you'll find a bottle of your favourite Champagne waiting for you, Mr Selous. It's on the house tonight for all those who've been involved in rescue work.'

The opulence of their surroundings and the attitude of the man who had greeted them was totally unexpected. Yet it surprised Josh far less than learning the identity of the man in whose company he had been for so many hours.

As the immaculately dressed manager called on employees to take Josh and Selous to the bathrooms, Josh said to his companion, 'You're Frederick Selous, the famous hunter? The man who guided Rhodes's pioneer column to Mashonaland?'

Selous smiled. 'I can claim some experience in hunting and, yes, I guided the column to Mashonaland. I never realised news of my exploits had reached Cornwall.'

There was a hint of humour in Selous's remark, as Josh realised. Until comparatively recently, Cornwall's geographical situation and the independence of its inhabitants had made it the most remote area of England.

Selous was speaking again. 'You have the advantage of me. We've worked together all day and for half the night without exchanging names!'

'I'm sorry. With all the drama and tragedy I never thought . . . I'm Josh Retallick and, as you guessed, I'm from Cornwall.'

It was immediately apparent that the name meant something to Selous.

'Retallick? And travelling to Matabeleland? Then you must be related to Dan Retallick. He and his fine young family live in the beautiful valley of Insimo.'

Josh felt the pain of Selous's words, and it showed in his expression. 'Daniel was my son. My *only* son. He and my eldest grandson were killed in the recent Matabele uprising.'

'Daniel and Wyatt dead!' Selous was genuinely distressed. 'I'm sorry, Josh. Deeply sorry. Please accept my sympathy. I've stayed with the family on more than one occasion and have grown very fond of them all.'

When Josh had murmured his thanks, Selous said, 'What will his widow – what will Elvira do now? Will she and the children leave Insimo and return to England with you?'

'I doubt it very much, but I won't know until I reach Insimo and am able to discuss the future with her and the boys.'

At that moment two servants came to take Josh and Selous to the bathrooms.

130

As he and Josh parted company, Selous said, 'I've just realised I'm ravenous. You must be too. We'll eat afterwards and talk more about your journey.'

As he stepped through the door to his own bathroom, Selous spoke to one of the servants. 'Give Mr Retallick a glass of Champagne to drink while he's having his bath. He's earned it today.'

Not until he stepped into the hot water did Josh realise how much the muscles of his body ached. It had been a long time since he had performed such hard physical work.

It had been a day of tragedy for a great many of the residents of Johannesburg. He hoped there might never be another such day for them.

As he soaked away the aches from his body, Josh thought of the many and varied tragedies he had encountered during his lifetime.

As a young man he had been wrongfully convicted of sedition against the British government. Sentenced to transportation, he had been shipwrecked here in Africa, on the notorious Skeleton Coast, whilst on his way to servitude in Australia.

During the years he spent in this vast continent he had become embroiled in tribal warfare, seen friends die, and witnessed heartbreak and many other sufferings.

Both here and in Cornwall he had been present at too many mine disasters where men died and women were widowed.

Now he was back in Africa because Daniel and Wyatt had been killed and he had become embroiled in yet another tragedy, one on a frightening scale.

As he soaked away his physical aches and pains, he wondered what else his African visit held in store for him.

Chapter 3

'What route are you taking to Insimo, Josh?' Selous asked the question as the two men ate.

It was almost three o'clock in the morning, but most of the tables in the club's restaurant were occupied by men consuming meals more suitable for late-evening. The explosion on the railway had disrupted any routine the easy-going town might have had and few men would see their beds tonight.

Swallowing the piece of rather tough steak he had been chewing, Josh replied, 'I believe the route to Matabeleland is through Bechuanaland. The only reason I came to Johannesburg is because it's as far north as the railway could carry me. I'll buy a couple of horses, head for Bechuanaland and find the road there.'

'It's the route most men take to Matabeleland,' agreed Selous, pouring more Champagne for Josh as he spoke. 'It's the best route if you're taking wagons, but it means you'll be travelling three sides of a square, instead of just one. If you're travelling light and are in a hurry there's a more direct route to Insimo. In fact, it's almost a straight line from here. You could be there in about two weeks.'

Josh was startled. He had estimated it would take him at least twice that time – even longer unless he had help along the way.

'You'll be talking of a cross-country route. If I were to try it I'd get hopelessly lost. Besides, what of the Tsetse fly? It's always been particularly bad along the border between Matabeleland and the Transvaal.'

Tsetse fly was the scourge of the area along both banks of the Limpopo river, boundary between Transvaal and Matabeleland. It transmitted a disease that was usually fatal to both horses and cattle. Many travellers straying from the established routes between southern and central Africa had lost all their animals to the depredations of the Tsetse.

Stranded on foot in a relentless land, many men and their families had died too.

'Tsetse *is* bad – in places. I've found many areas that are clear. I've never worked out why the fly should infest some places and not others, but I've taken horses across the river on a number of occasions, and will again.'

132

'I wouldn't dream of arguing with someone who knows the country as well as you, but how can *I* find safe crossing places?'

Selous grinned. 'That's easy. I'll take you.'

Raising his glass to Josh, he said, 'Here's to a speedy and safe journey.'

Only thirty-six hours after Selous's offer to guide Josh to Insimo, the two men set out from Johannesburg. They were riding horses chosen by Selous and each man led two more. Although Selous did not expect to encounter the deadly Tsetse fly, four of the six horses were 'salted'. This meant they had been infected by Tsetse, but were among the very few to have survived. As a result, they were considered to be immune from any further sickness.

It was rare to find salted horses this far south of the Matabeleland border. They had been expensive to buy but, as Selous pointed out, it would give them additional insurance should something unforeseen drive them from his proposed route.

The road to the north passed through Pretoria, the capital of the Transvaal, but Selous left the road and skirted the town.

He did this for the same reason he insisted that Josh practise speaking the Afrikaans language with him. It was many years since Josh had used the almost-forgotten language, but he found it returned remarkably quickly.

Selous declared that while they were in the Transvaal it would be advisable to avoid using English whenever others were around to hear them.

'The English are unpopular here and are looked upon with suspicion,' he explained.

'Is there any justification for the Boers' suspicion?'

Josh was aware that his companion knew Rhodes and every other man of note in Southern Africa. If there was any conspiracy against the Boers, Selous would know about it. Whether or not he would tell Josh was another matter. It would depend on how far Selous felt he could trust him.

'Yes, there is,' said Selous, with only a momentary hesitation. 'The Transvaal stands between Rhodes and his ambitions of expansion to the north. Rhodes is not a man who will be thwarted, whether it's by one man or a whole nation. Another reason is the town we've just left behind – Johannesburg. There's enough gold still in the ground to finance whole countries for many years to come. President Kruger is playing into Rhodes's hands by imposing petty restrictions on the British miners and the men who are paying them. One day he'll go just a little too far and Rhodes will be justified in calling on British troops to come to their aid. Most Boers, outside of government, are aware this might happen and they're becoming increasingly jittery.'

A slow moving ox-cart was on the road ahead of them and they were forced to pass in single file. Waiting until they were riding side by side once more, Selous said, 'We'll avoid the Boers as much as is possible. If we're forced into their company, leave me to do the talking.'

Josh was perfectly happy to agree to the arrangement. All he knew of the situation in this part of Africa was that it was volatile, to say the very least.

Pretoria was by-passed successfully, and the country to the north rapidly became more sparsely populated. There were farms here, but the Boer character worked in favour of the two travellers.

The trekkers who had made their way here fifty or more years before had come seeking a place where they could live their lives in the manner they chose. They resented interference from anyone. In order to achieve this they built their farmhouses out of sight of both their nearest neighbours and the road that ran through the various settlements.

Consequently, it was possible for Josh and Selous to make their way through the settled lands without challenge and virtually unnoticed.

Two days beyond Pretoria the more populous farming areas had been left behind. There *were* still Boer farms to be found here, but when smoke was sighted it was more likely to be rising from the cooking fires of a native kraal.

Selous was more relaxed now and they spent the next night sleeping in a native hut, sharing with their hosts a kudu shot by Selous. Listening to the natives, Josh became aware of the great respect in which they held his travelling companion.

Late one afternoon Selous said they were within twenty-four hours of the Limpopo river. This constituted the border between Transvaal and Matabeleland. At the time they were in a wide valley, heading towards a water-hole. As they drew closer they saw a large party approaching from the opposite direction.

The other party comprised eight horsemen and a wagon, together with more than thirty native men and women who were accompanied by a couple of children.

Selous swore beneath his breath. He would have avoided the others had it been possible, but these were not 'town Boers', they were men brought up on the veldt. As wise in bush-craft as Selous himself, they were heading for the same water-hole.

The Boers had seen Josh and Selous at the same time as they were themselves spotted. Two of the riders immediately detached themselves from their own party and rode towards them.

As they neared, Selous said, 'I've met one of these men before. Say as little as possible to them and remain on your guard.'

Apprehensively, Josh asked, 'Who are they?'

'Slavers. They capture natives in Northern Transvaal and sell them to slave dealers in Portuguese East Africa.'

Josh looked at Selous, unwilling to believe he was serious. The expression he saw on the other man's face confirmed that Selous was deadly serious.

'I thought slaving had been stamped out years ago?'

'It has in all civilised countries, but not in Portugal's African territories – or places like this. There's no one would dare come here and try to enforce any kind of law.'

The two heavily bearded Boers were close enough now for Josh to see the bandoliers of rifle bullets they wore over one shoulder and long-barrelled rifles held across the pommel of each man's saddle.

As they drew nearer one rider spoke to the other and both appeared to relax. When they were a few horse lengths away, one man produced a smile and extended a hand.

'Selous, man! I haven't seen you for years. You're famous now, eh?' He spoke in Afrikaans, with the accent of a man who had spent many years away from the main centres of his own language.

'Paul Jacobs!' Selous shook the Boer's hand warmly enough. 'I heard you'd been killed by an elephant in South West Africa a couple of years ago.'

'It takes more than an elephant to kill a Voortrekker, but he trampled me a little. I still look good on a horse, but on the ground I walk like a chameleon.'

Indicating his companion, who had said nothing so far, Jacobs said, 'This is Pik Erasmus. He doesn't say much because he's too deaf to hear a reply, but he's as fine a shot as you'll find anywhere.'

Selous nodded to the silent Boer horseman and then pointed to Josh. 'This is Josh. His son and grandson have been killed by the Matabele, up north. We're on our way to find out what's happened to the rest of the family.'

Jacobs nodded his sympathy to Josh, but addressed his next words to Selous. 'You English have been too soft with the Matabele, that's why you're having trouble. You should have led Rhodes's column straight through the middle of Matabeleland. Showed Lobengula right at the beginning who was boss. That's what these people need.'

Selous produced a smile. 'Lobengula had forty thousand warriors waiting for us to do just that. We had three hundred men. I didn't like the odds.'

The main body of Paul Jacobs's party was approaching now. Josh could see that the adult natives with them were linked together by a chain.

Nodding his head in their direction, Selous said, 'Aren't they Bechuanas? They're a long way from home.'

'We found them in a place where they shouldn't have been,' lied Jacobs. 'We're moving them on. To somewhere where they'll be more

135

appreciated. But come and meet the others. We're just about ready to outspan. We'll camp together.'

Josh waited for Selous to refuse, but his companion knew that the place where the Boers had already stopped their wagon had the only water within many miles.

At the Boer camp the two men were introduced to Paul Jacobs's companions. Josh thought he would need to go a long way to find a more villainous band of men. He felt uneasy at being camped so close to them.

He also found the condition of the natives upsetting. Chained together, they looked as though they had been kept this way for many days. A number had sores where the iron bands around neck and wrist had chafed. One man also bore weals across his back, indicative of a severe beating.

As he and Selous spread their blankets a short distance from the wagon of the Boers, Josh voiced his misgivings to Selous.

'I feel the same as you,' said the hunter. 'But keep your thoughts to yourself and try not to take too much notice of the slaves.'

'That's not easy,' said Josh as a Boer cuffed one of the children who had strayed too close to their cooking-fire.

'*Make* it easy if you want to help them.' Something in Selous's voice made Josh look at him sharply, but the other man was saying nothing more.

Chapter 4

It was a night Josh would remember for the remainder of his life. It began sociably enough. He and Selous were invited to the Boer camp fire to share a klipspringer that had ventured too close to the crowded water-hole. The animal was killed by an incredibly long shot from the rifle of one of the Transvaalers. The feat earned genuine applause from Selous.

'It was a good shot,' admitted the Boer marksman, displaying no false modesty. 'But you're the famous hunter. Do you think you could do better?'

'I doubt it. I don't think I've ever seen a better shot.'

'Let's have a shooting match,' said Paul Jacobs. 'We'll all join in. You too, Englishman. Let's see what you can do with that pretty little English gun you have in your saddle holster.'

Josh was not aware the Boers had even noticed the gun he carried in a saddle holster. It was a Holland and Holland double-barrelled rifle. Josh had bought it from the London gunsmith only hours before boarding the ship from England.

'It's a long time since I did any serious shooting,' he admitted. 'But I don't mind trying my hand.'

Selous agreed reluctantly, but it was he who proved to be the finest shot of them all. It was decided in a shoot out with the Boer who had killed the klipspringer. Josh did not disgrace himself, ending the match ahead of two of the Boers.

The Boer who had lost to Selous was an ungracious loser, but Paul Jacobs was jubilant. It seemed he had laid bets with his countrymen after declaring that Selous was: 'The finest hunter in the whole of Africa.'

'Now we've seen Selous shoot we have something to celebrate. Pik, bring the brandy from the wagon.'

To Selous and Josh, he said, 'It's not every day a man meets up with an old friend. It calls for a celebration.'

'Sorry, Paul, but you can count me out. The only thing I ever drink is Champagne, and that only in moderation – as you know. Besides, Josh and I want to be on the move before dawn tomorrow. We're likely to run across Matabele before the day's out. I'll need a clear head to deal with them.'

'Agh, man, you English are too serious. You should learn to relax a little.'

'Call on me when we're both in Johannesburg, Paul. I'll relax with you there. Not out here.'

Paul Jacobs shrugged. 'Well, how about one of the kaffir women? It'll have to be one of the ugly ones, the others are already booked, but it'll be better than nothing.'

'Again the answer's no, Paul – and for the same reasons. An early start and a clear head.'

'Then it's a good job you've laid your blankets a fair way from the wagon. *We're* in the mood for a party tonight.'

It was no idle boast. The noise from the Boer camp increased with the passing of the brandy jar and the night hours. At the height of the party the cries of one of the native women were added to the sounds emanating from the group around the camp fire.

Eventually, Josh sat up. 'Listen to that! What are they doing?'

'They're having *fun*, Josh. At least, that's what they'd tell you, if you were to ask them.'

'And the woman?'

'No one's asked her opinion. She's a kaffir woman.'

'You know very well what I mean. She's human, the same as you and I. How can you just lie there and listen to it without doing something about it?'

As he spoke the woman screamed again. It was the sound of pain, rather than fear.

When Selous made no reply, Josh asked, 'Did you see the slaves while we were eating? Each of them was chained by one wrist and linked to another chain padlocked about a tree. Their eyes never left us but no one thought of taking food to them.'

'They'll be fed. The Boers want to sell them in Portuguese East Africa. They won't fetch a worthwhile price unless they're in a reasonable condition.'

'Is that your only thought on the matter?'

'No, but I've been hunting in Africa for twenty-two years now. I've learned that there's a time for action, and a time for doing nothing. If I were to go to the Boer camp right now and remonstrate with them, I would be a dead man within minutes – and so would you.'

Selous lay down and pulled a blanket over himself. 'Had we not met up with Paul Jacobs and his friends this would have been happening anyway and we'd have been none the wiser. All you have to remember is that we want to be on our way before dawn in the morning. Pull the blanket up around your ears and pretend you can hear nothing.'

It was an unsatisfactory reply and Josh lay beneath his blanket quietly fuming. Yet he knew Selous was right. Any attempt to interfere would lead to both their deaths. All the same, he found their impotence humiliating.

* * *

Josh was woken by Selous shaking him. He sat up, startled. It was still dark, although there was a faint grey light in the sky to the east.

'Wh-what?' For a moment he had forgotten their promised early start.

'Shh! Be as quiet as you can. We don't want to wake our friends over by the wagon.

Suddenly, memories of the previous evening came flooding back to Josh. He rose stiffly to his feet and cast a glance in the direction of the Boers' camp. The fire had burned low and there was nothing to be seen except the outline of the covered wagon against the pre-dawn sky.

'I've saddled and loaded up the horses. All you need do is pack your own blanket.'

Ten minutes later, they were on their way, riding through the thick scrub, leaving the Boers and their evil trade behind them.

They had been riding for about two hours when Selous reined in. 'There's someone over there, hiding behind that small baobab tree.'

He drew his rifle from the saddle holster. Josh did the same, but Selous said, 'You wait here and cover me while I go and see who it is.'

He was halfway to the tree when a man stepped from behind it and took a pace towards him. An African, he was followed by a woman. They looked familiar.

Selous slipped his rifle back in his saddle holster. Dismounting, he signalled for Josh to join him. Then he disappeared from view behind the tree with the other two.

Josh kneed his horse forward, still holding his gun. As he approached the woman stepped into view and now he recognised her. When he had last seen her she had been chained to a tree beside the Boer camp he and Selous had just left!

'What medical kit are you carrying in your bags, Josh?' Selous stepped into view.

'A few bandages. Lint. Iodine . . .'

'Iodine is just the thing. Find it for me, will you? And some lint too.'

Puzzled, Josh did as he was told. He pulled the pack containing the medicine kit from a saddle-bag, extracted the iodine and walked around the tree to find Selous.

The hunter was bending over a young woman who sat on the ground behind the tree, bending forward.

At sight of her back, Josh sucked in his breath in horror. It was criss-crossed with weals, apparently inflicted by a cruelly wielded whip. The skin on many of the weals had broken open and Selous was finding difficulty in keeping the flies at bay.

A glance from him spoke more than words as he took the iodine. Josh protested, 'You can't put that on such wounds. The pain will be excruciating.'

'Putting nothing on and leaving it open for the flies will be worse.'

139

Pouring iodine on the lint, Selous applied it to the woman's back. Just the thought of it was enough to cause Josh to wince. As Selous worked on her wounds, the woman kept her head down, looking into her lap. Not a whimper passed her lips.

After a few minutes, Josh went to where the horses stood. He returned with a soft white shirt. The crude medical treatment had just been completed and he thrust the shirt at the woman, saying to Selous, 'Tell her to wear this. It will cover her back and keep the flies away until the wounds are a little better, at least.'

When Selous spoke to the woman she glanced up at Josh for the first time. The look in her soft, brown eyes reminded him of a wounded doe he had once found.

'Can she keep the iodine?' asked the hunter.

'Of course.'

Selous spoke to the woman who gave Josh another glance. Then he had a lengthy conversation with the man in a native language Josh did not understand, punctuated with much gesticulating. It appeared that Selous was directing the small party to head north, and then west.

After a while the injured woman climbed painfully to her feet. Selous went to his own saddlebags and came back with a quantity of biltong, strips of dried meat carried by most travellers in this part of Africa. Handing it to the other woman, he turned and Josh followed him to the horses.

As they rode away, Josh said, 'How did they escape from the Boers? And what about the others?'

'The Boers probably got drunk and careless during the night,' said Selous, non-committally. 'They kept the key ring on a hook on the back of the wagon. All their slaves escaped during the night.'

Josh looked back and saw the three figures, one wearing a white shirt, trekking across the veldt.

'But the Boers will come after them – and they can't fail to see the woman in a white shirt.'

'They will have other things to think of today,' declared Selous. 'All their horses were run off at the same time as the escape was taking place. By the time they retrieve even one of them the Africans will be halfway back to Bechuanaland.'

Josh thought the wily hunter's story was too pat. Besides, the escape was too well planned to be entirely the work of the freed slaves. He believed that Selous had played a major part in the happenings of the night that had just ended. Yet he knew better than to ask any questions.

Frederick Courtenay Selous was a man who preferred to keep some things to himself.

Chapter 5

Josh and Selous were involved in one further incident before reaching the Insimo Valley. It occurred as they crossed a wide but shallow expanse of the Limpopo.

Leading two horses, Josh was following the hunter when there was a sudden commotion behind him. A great threshing of water was accompanied by the whinny of terror-stricken horses. As his own mount tried to leap forward, Josh was almost pulled from the saddle by the lead rope.

Selous turned in the saddle, at the same time dragging his rifle from the holster close to his leg. Josh was still having great difficulty controlling his own horse and the report from Selous's large-bore rifle did nothing to calm the animal.

The last horse in Josh's string of three had gone down in the water and now the cause of the commotion came into view.

Struck in the brain by the bullet from Selous's gun, a huge crocodile reared from the water, contorting its body like a snake, the scaly tail beating the water to foam as it writhed in its death throes.

The horse too had been mortally wounded, the powerful jaws of the crocodile snapping one of its rear legs. Once dragged to shallow water, Selous fired again to end the animal's agony and Josh transferred its load to the other unsaddled horse while Selous kept guard lest the crocodile have a companion.

'Damn! I should have been watching out for crocodiles,' said Josh despondently, as he secured his pack on the still frightened horse. 'That was a good animal. I'm afraid I've been out of Africa for too long.'

'Don't blame yourself,' said Selous, philosophically. 'I *was* keeping a look-out, but I missed seeing it. The croc must have come from behind us. With the state of this water you couldn't see anything until it leaped out at you.'

The water in the sluggish river was as muddy brown as the banks on either side. 'We must be thankful it was a horse and not one of us.'

The two hundred miles to the upland valley of Insimo took them a full week, but they were involved in no further incidents to mar the journey.

Along the way they passed close to a number of Matabele villages. Here, outside the beehive huts, women crouched close to the ground,

141

preparing meals for their families. Children, shielding their eyes against the sun, gazed at the two men as they rode by. Others, less overawed at the sight of two armed white men, ran after them hurling insults.

Ominously, they saw no warriors in any of the villages. It was possible they had gone off on a great hunt to bring meat and skins back to the villages. Selous tended to believe they were off planning less acceptable activities.

'I've heard Rhodes's men boasting that the Matabele are a defeated nation. They even advocate cutting the numbers of the Company's police because they're no longer needed. For the most part the advisers are men who have never come face to face with a Matabele warrior. They judge him by other Africans they've had dealings with. They'll have a rude awakening!'

'You think there'll be more fighting to put those in the Insimo Valley at risk?'

'I didn't say that. Folk at Insimo do understand the tribes. No one will touch them there. Daniel and Wyatt would have been safe had they remained in the valley, but I suppose it might have been difficult for your son to allay his conscience by staying put when others were at risk.'

When the two men came within sight of the wide valley of Insimo, they were presented with a scene of well-ordered prosperity. Herds of cattle grazed the sides of the hills, watched over by herd-boys, proud of their responsibility.

There were crops here too, well fenced against domestic stock and the plundering of wild animals. At the far end of the valley were the neat, stout houses built by Daniel Retallick for his family and the friends who had joined them over the years.

There was also a small, fenced graveyard on the side of the hill beyond the Retallick house. It gave Josh a moment's pain when he noticed the sunlight glinting on two newly worked gravestones.

The riders had been observed the moment they entered the valley and a chain of Matabele workers passed word along the valley to the main house.

When Josh and Selous were still a few hundred yards from the small group of houses, a man came out to meet them, flanked by three boys, the youngest not much older than Lily Shovell. All carried rifles.

Beyond the three, and situated only a short distance from the houses, was a stout, squat tower. It had a thick, ironbound door and no windows. In their place were narrow slits situated some twenty feet from the ground. It seemed the residents of Insimo were prepared should they be caught up in another Matabele insurrection.

As the two parties drew nearer to each other, the oldest boy said something to the man. A moment later the middle of the three boys

142

called 'Grandpa!' and ran towards Josh. Behind him the other two boys grinned, but did not follow their brother. Nathan, the oldest surviving brother, was almost fourteen and too old to show such emotion. Benjamin was ten and too shy. Only eleven-year-old Adam was not afraid to show his delight.

Josh swung from his horse and hugged Adam. Then he did the same to Benjamin, overcoming the boy's shyness. He gravely shook hands with Nathan as the others addressed Selous by name, and with obvious respect.

The man who had come from the house with the boys was not much younger than Josh. His beard was as grey as the hair that showed beneath his floppy-brimmed hat. Holding his hand out to Josh, he introduced himself. 'I'm Jaconus Van Eyck.'

'I'm very pleased to meet you at last.' Josh shook the other man's hand warmly. 'You've taken good care of all the family for very many years. It's been a comfort to me and Daniel's mother to know you were with them.'

'I'm only sorry it took a tragedy to bring you here,' said Jaconus. 'I was with Daniel and Wyatt when they died. They were both as brave as any men I've ever known. But if I hadn't been there to prevent young Nathan from going to their aid, you'd have lost another grandson that day. They're fine boys. You can be proud of every one of them.'

Suddenly embarrassed by handing out such fulsome praise, Jaconus Van Eyck released Josh's hand and nodded in the direction of Selous. 'I see you travel in good company.'

'We met in Johannesburg. Selous showed me a quick route to Matabeleland.'

'I'm sure he did. There's no one I'd rather ride with myself. But we'd better make for the house. Elvira ran off to preen herself a bit when we heard riders were on their way. When she knows who's come visiting she'll play hell with me for keeping you out here for one moment longer than is necessary.'

As they walked towards the house Benjamin ran ahead to tell his mother who it was who had come to Insimo. He had been in the house for less than a minute when the door was flung open and Elvira came running to meet her father-in-law.

'Papa Josh! Papa Josh!' She flung herself at him and, as he held her, she burst into tears. 'You have come all this way because . . . because . . . It is so good of you. So good!'

It was many minutes before she regained control of herself. Those about her waited with averted eyes, their pity tinged with the embarrassment of witnessing such raw grief.

Suddenly, Elvira pushed herself away from Josh and smiled up at him apologetically. 'So many tears! Not since Daniel and Wyatt were killed . . .'

Taking his arm, she said, 'But come inside. You must be exhausted after such a journey.'

As they went up the path to the house she turned to Selous. 'It is so good to see you too, Frederick. We do not see enough of you these days.'

He murmured words of condolence, but Elvira had full control of herself now and cut him short. 'We will talk about it later. For now, you must be hungry. Tell me, how did you two meet each other . . .'

Chapter 6

Josh soon realised that many things had changed in Africa since he was last here, thirty years before. One of the greatest advances was in the field of communications. He was able to send a telegram from Fort Victoria, some fifty miles distant, informing Miriam of his safe arrival. The message would be with her before he had returned to Insimo.

Josh rode to Fort Victoria accompanied by his two youngest grandchildren, Jaconus Van Eyck, and Selous. Nathan had remained behind in the valley because of the uncertainty of the times.

Selous would not be returning to Insimo with Josh and the others. He was riding north, to Mashonaland to meet the administrator, Starr Jameson. It seemed there was a great move afoot to have the whole country between the great Rivers Limpopo and Zambezi named after Cecil Rhodes. It was to be called Rhodesia – Southern Rhodesia. This was because Rhodes already had plans to expand northwards, across the Zambezi. The land there would be Northern Rhodesia.

As Josh rode back beside Van Eyck, he said, 'Rhodes is building his own private empire here. I'm surprised he hasn't tried to get hold of Insimo.'

'I believe he once had thoughts about it. However, Daniel met him and they made a deal. Not that Rhodes could be trusted to keep his word, he's far too ambitious. But Daniel tied the ownership of the valley up so tightly it should be secure for all time. The valley belongs to the Retallicks and it always will.'

The Afrikander hunter's words went a long way towards answering one of the main questions Josh had come to Africa to clarify: whether or not Elvira was likely to return with him to England with the boys.

He doubted he would be able to persuade her to leave. There was far too much for the family here. Daniel had carved out an empire in Matabeleland. Elvira was unlikely to throw up everything he had worked for and move to a country that was virtually unknown to any of them.

A couple of evenings later, Josh's conclusions were confirmed when the whole family discussed the matter around the table during the evening meal. With them were Jaconus Van Eyck and Victoria, daughter of a man who had been Josh's friend during his own years in Africa. She had a house nearby in the valley.

'Insimo is our home, Papa Josh,' said Elvira. 'The boys have never known anywhere else. They will never find anywhere better for them.'

'Even with the ever-present danger of another Matabele uprising?'

'They won't attack us here,' declared Jaconus, confidently. 'Their grievances are with Rhodes, and the settlers he brought in. Not with us. Besides, they no longer have a king to rally them and command their support. Any trouble will come from local groups – and we are capable of dealing with them.'

'Well, if you ever change your mind about coming to England, remember there's a place for you in Cornwall. I have enough business interests there to ensure you'll be comfortably off. Besides, I'm no longer a young man and all I have will come to the boys one day. As it is, I don't doubt that Miriam is going to be very disappointed that I won't be bringing all of the family with me when I return.'

'I don't know about the boys,' said Jaconus. 'But I could never live in England. There are too many people there for my liking.'

Josh looked at him in surprise for a moment, then he said, 'I keep forgetting you took a Matabele delegation to England a few years ago on behalf of Lobengula. You're so much a part of all that is Africa that it's difficult to imagine you anywhere else.'

'I'll never be happy anywhere else for very long, but I take great pride in the fact that I once met and spoke to Queen Victoria.' Jaconus shrugged. 'Not that it did Lobengula any good. Rhodes took over the country and Lobengula is dead as a result. All the trip did was convince me that I'd rather live at Insimo than anywhere else. Mind you, young Benjamin might come to England one day. He's the one who's always asking me question about life there.'

'He's been asking me questions too.' Josh smiled at his youngest grandson. 'Perhaps he'll be the one who'll take over the Ruddlemoor China clay works for me.'

'I'd like that!' said Benjamin, eagerly. Then, looking at the family and friends sitting at the table about him, he added, 'But not just yet.'

When the laughter had died down, Josh said, 'I don't think I am going to be able to change anyone's mind, so there's really no excuse for me to remain at Insimo. I will merely be indulging myself by staying on.'

There was a chorus of protest and Elvira said, 'You've come thousands of miles to be here and show your support for us. To let us know there is someone who cares. That we have family beyond Insimo. It is very important to all of us. The least you can do is remain here for a little while, at least. Let us show you Insimo and all get to know each other a little better.'

Josh remained at Insimo for almost three months. During this time he came to know his son's family well and his love for them grew – as it did for the beautiful Insimo Valley.

Of the boys, Nathan was the strong, practical one. He would run the valley enterprises well and they would prosper under his management.

Adam had a wilder streak in his make-up. He was eleven now, but already he would go off on his own, hunting – and he never returned empty-handed. He was the member of her family about whom Elvira was most concerned.

Benjamin, the youngest of the brothers, was ten years old and by far the quietest of the three boys. He was also, according to Elvira, the child most deeply affected by the death of his father and brother at the hands of the Matabele. He, of them all, was least inclined to trust the tribesmen now.

Benjamin attached himself to Josh wherever he went and asked him numerous questions about England.

One day, about a month before the date Josh had set for his return to England, Benjamin was with his grandfather walking back from the small gold mine they had on the property. They had gone to gather enough gold for Josh to take back to England to make a ring for Miriam. It would be a very special present for her.

They were almost at the house when Benjamin turned to Josh with sudden tears in his eyes and said, 'I miss my pa.'

Putting an arm about his shoulders in an affectionate gesture, Josh said, 'Of course you do. You always will. Your grandma and I have missed him since the day we both said goodbye to him, and that was many years ago. It will be far worse for you, but you'll always have your brothers to turn to.'

'I wish you'd stay here with us for ever.'

'Seeing all you have here, I must admit I sometimes feel the same way. But soon England won't seem so far away for you. When I was in Cape Colony I was told they would soon be extending the railway here. You'll be able to catch a train to Cape Town, take a ship from there and be in England within a few weeks. When you do that, I promise that your grandma and I will be there to meet you.'

'When can I come?'

'As soon as you like – or you can leave it for as long as you like. Whenever you decide to come, you can be absolutely certain that we'll both be delighted to have you there with us. You just remember that. Always. You hear me?'

Benjamin nodded. They had grown very close during the couple of months Josh had been at Insimo. It would be a wrench for both of them when the time came to part.

Chapter 7

Josh's last view of the family was of them all standing in the doorway of their Insimo house, waving to him as he rode away in the company of Jaconus Van Eyck.

Jaconus was riding with him as far as the Bechuanaland border. Josh intended travelling by the more usual route back to the railhead at Johannesburg.

There were two reasons for this. The first was that he was not as confident alone on the open veldt as was Selous. The second was that he did not want to risk meeting up with the Boer slavers on his route south. He was convinced Selous had been far more involved with the release of the slaves than he had admitted.

At the Border, Jaconus Van Eyck introduced Josh to the inspector in charge of the border post. The policeman was a man Van Eyck had once hunted with. As a result, Josh rode down the Hunter's road heading south in company with two members of the border police.

It was an interesting ride. On the nights when they were forced to camp in the open there was no shortage of game to shoot and they ate well. On other occasions they stopped at various kraals where they were welcomed as guests by chieftains and headmen.

There were also a couple of hostelries along this well-travelled route. They had been opened in anticipation of a railway being built to link the Cape Colony with the new lands to the north. It was one of Rhodes's stated ambitions to build a railway that would link the Cape with Cairo – and those around him were used to the great man succeeding in his aims.

There was a strong British presence in Bechuanaland too and Josh found it comforting to meet so many Britons along the road.

After six days of travel they met up with a small party of Afrikanders who had just crossed the Kalahari desert from German West Africa. They were heading for Pretoria and Josh decided to ride with them. Pretoria was only a few miles from Johannesburg and the Afrikanders would provide company and protection along the road.

They reached Pretoria early in the afternoon, after another four days on the road. Leaving the others to go their own way, Josh found a small but clean hostelry and booked a room for the night. He would leave early in the morning and arrive in Johannesburg in time to find somewhere to stay while he checked on the times of trains to Cape Town.

Once on the train he would really feel he was on his way home. Riding across the vast tracts of Southern Africa, Cornwall seemed worlds away – and he was missing Miriam very much now. Before this occasion they had not been parted for more than a few days during the whole of their married life and he felt he had been away from her for long enough.

After putting up his horses and settling his possessions in his room, Josh thought he would take a walk and see something of the Transvaal capital.

It was a very pleasant city, quiet and well laid out. Everything, in fact, that Johannesburg was not. There were also a great many places of worship belonging to the Dutch Reformed Church in the town. As Josh walked past one, situated on a wide, tree-lined road, two predikants, dressed in sober black and wearing wide-brimmed hats, walked from the building.

Glancing at them, Josh was surprised to recognise the smaller of the two. When Josh had last seen him he was crawling from a Johannesburg rubbish pit, on the evening the dynamite train had exploded.

The memory brought mixed feelings in its wake. Amusement at the thought of the Afrikander preacher's deserved fate. Sadness when Josh remembered the many residents of Johannesburg killed and injured in the mighty explosion.

Predikant Pieter Vanderbyl recognised Josh too. Had he turned around as he walked along the street, Josh would have seen the Boer preacher pointing in his direction, talking excitedly to his companion.

Josh had walked the length of the tree-lined street and was turning the far corner into a shopping area when he heard a shout behind him. Looking back, he saw the two predikants hurrying after him. With them was a man wearing the uniform of a Transvaal policeman.

He shouted once more when he saw he had Josh's attention and waved his hand, calling for Josh to come to him.

Josh had a sudden sense of foreboding and his immediate instinct was to turn and run.

He dismissed the thought immediately. He did not know Pretoria and the constable and the two predikants were younger men. He could not outrun them. He also believed he had no need to run. He had done nothing wrong. Yet he had an uneasy feeling that all was not well.

As the three men reached him, with the policeman in the lead, Josh said, 'You want to speak to me?'

He spoke in English and it brought a strange expression to the face of Predikant Vanderbyl. 'There! I told you he was English,' he said to the policeman, triumphantly.

'You understand Afrikaans, *Uitlander*?' The policeman spoke in his own tongue to Josh, calling him by the somewhat contemptuous name which the Transvaal Boers gave to those who did not belong in the Transvaal. To those who were 'foreigners'.

'I understand it well enough,' he replied. 'Is there something I can do for you?'

'Yes, you can come with me to police headquarters.'

'Why? I'm only passing through Pretoria. I'll be leaving for Johannesburg in the morning.'

'Not *tomorrow* morning you won't. Predikant Vanderbyl has made a complaint to me that you assaulted him in Johannesburg, about three months ago . . .'

'That's *absurd*!' Josh replied angrily. 'I did no such thing.'

'It's no good you telling *me*,' said the policeman, nonchalantly. 'The predikant has made a complaint. My duty is to take you to police headquarters. The *landrost* will decide whether or not you've done anything wrong. Come along with me, please.'

'But . . . this is quite ridiculous. I have just booked a room at a hotel. My belongings and horses are there. I'm travelling on in the morning. Returning home – to England.'

'You can tell all that to the *landrost*, when you see him. As far as I'm concerned you could have been on your way to the moon. For now you're coming with me.'

Chapter 8

The police headquarters cells turned out to be a series of iron-barred 'cages' set around the walls of a very large room. Only two were occupied, yet instead of being put in a cell on his own, Josh was thrust in a cage that already contained three other men.

Two of them were evidently drunkards. Breathing out stale alcohol, they lay on wooden cots, sleeping off the after-effects of the excesses which had landed them in a police cell.

The other occupant was a morose Boer who chose to sit on the floor, staring out through the bars with hardly any movement.

'If you know what's good for you, you'll leave him well alone,' advised the policeman, turning the heavy key in the cage lock. 'He's due to appear before the *landrost* charged with murder. That's his sister in the cage over there. I believe she's the reason he committed the crime, so if I were you I shouldn't try to strike up a conversation with her. He's a jealous type.'

Josh soon learned that 'striking up a conversation' with the Boer murderer's sister was well-nigh impossible. She berated her brother in a loud, shrill voice that went on and on, once the policeman had left.

It was evident that she, and probably her brother too, were both mentally retarded. However, it did enable Josh to learn something of the crime for which they had been arrested. It seemed the girl and her brother shared a house because both parents had died – fortunately, as the girl told her brother in every other shouted sentence. Had they not already been dead, they should surely have died of shame.

The girl had become involved with a man of whom her brother had not approved. It led to many arguments between them, culminating in the shooting to death of the man when he visited the house one day.

The police, unable immediately to ascertain the true facts of the case from the hysterical sister and silent brother, had arrested them both.

Sitting on the edge of a cot, the Boer woman's tirade assailing his ears, Josh thought it could have been worse. He might have been sharing a cell with thieves – and he had been allowed to keep a great deal of his money. The remainder was lodged in the police headquarters' safe.

He was wondering what course his own arrest would take, when he heard the second women in the other prison cage speak for the first time. Evidently exasperated by her companion's ceaseless tirade against her brother, the woman pleaded with her to keep quiet, if only for a few minutes.

It was not the woman's words that caused Josh to take immediate notice, or the fact that she had spoken in English. It was her accent.

The girl was Cornish.

Rising to his feet and crossing to the bars nearest the other 'cage', Josh called above the sound of the woman's voice, 'You there! The woman in the other cell. Are you from Cornwall?'

'That's right. Oh, shut up a moment, will you, you silly cow?' The last words were directed once more at her cell-mate. 'So are you by the sound of it. Where are you from?'

'St Austell now. Before that I spent my life on Bodmin Moor.'

'I had a brother on Bodmin Moor. He worked in one of the Caradon mines. I'm from a small village, just outside Camborne . . .'

For a few minutes their surroundings and the incessant haranguing of her brother by the Boer woman were forgotten. The minds of Josh and the girl – her name was Martha Doney – were back home in Cornwall.

Suddenly the Boer woman dropped to her knees and began crying – and Josh and Martha were back in a police cell in Pretoria.

'What are you doing here, in a cell?' Josh put the question to the girl.

Martha jerked her head in the direction of the weeping woman who clung to the bars beside her. 'Same reason as her, I reckon. Because of a man. Me and Danny Spargo was going to be married back in Cornwall, before he lost his job in the mines. There was no work to be had around Camborne way. Then someone came around offering work for miners in Johannesburg. Made it sound as though there was a fortune just waiting to be picked up. Danny spoke to me about it. Said if he came here he'd work all hours of the day and night to send my fare home so as I could join him.'

The Boer woman had begun screaming at her brother once more and Martha had to raise her voice.

'I should have known better than to let him out of my sight. I never heard a word from him for more than six months. Then an old aunt of mine died. Left me a little money. It weren't much, but it was enough to pay my fare to Johannesburg, so I came looking for Danny.'

Martha shrugged, 'Of course, I couldn't find him, could I? My money ran out and I had to find work. If you've been to Johannesburg you'll know there's only one place where a girl with no money ends up. I found work in one of the bars. Called the Duchy Arms, it is. It's used by a lot of the Cornish miners and I hoped I'd get word of Danny there . . . Oh, shut up, for Christ's sake, or I'll give you one!'

After rounding on her noisy cell-mate once more, she resumed her story. 'Well, I did get word of him. Someone told me he'd come here, to Pretoria. Had opened a shop.'

Martha gave a short, humourless laugh. 'It was something we'd often talked about when we were both back home in Cornwall. Making enough money to marry and open a small shop somewhere. It was a dream we'd always shared. I thought he'd gone halfway towards making the dream come true. Like a fool, I believed that perhaps he'd waited until he'd bought it and then wrote to me to come out here. Probably the letter had been on its way to Cornwall while I was on a ship bound for South Africa. So I came to Pretoria.'

Martha fell silent then. She said nothing for so long that Josh prompted her, 'So you came to Pretoria. Did you find him?'

'Oh, yes, I found him all right,' she said bitterly. 'What the man in the Johannesburg bar *hadn't* told me was that Danny is now married to an Afrikander girl. The money for the shop hadn't come from his hard work in the mines, it had come from the girl's parents. It wasn't our dream that had come true – but *his*. Him and his cross-eyed wife. He'd married her for her money, nothing else. I could see that as soon as I saw her. That only made it all worse somehow. If she'd been attractive, someone he'd fallen for despite himself, I might have understood.'

'So what did you do? How did you end up in here?'

'I started wrecking their shop. Threw things everywhere. Most of it I threw at him. When he was hiding out of the way beneath the counter, I broke everything I could lay my hands on. *That's* why I'm in here.'

'How long have you been in these cells now?' Josh wanted some idea of how swiftly justice was administered in Pretoria.

'Two weeks,' came the startling reply. 'But that's nothing, really. The day I came in two men were going up for trial. They'd been waiting for six weeks. Mind you, I could get out of here today if only I had money to pay for the things I broke. Danny's wife has said she won't press charges if the damage is made good.'

Dismayed at the prospect of having to spend anything up to six weeks locked in a police cell, it was some moments before Josh asked, 'Would you go back to Cornwall if you had the chance?'

'Like a shot!' the answer came back immediately. 'But it seems likely I'll have to spend the next few years here, paying for the damage I caused.'

In a brief lull between the rantings of her cell-mate, Martha Doney mused, 'I wish I'd never left Cornwall. It's summer there now. Summer makes me think of those Sundays when I'd go to chapel and in the afternoon take a walk around the countryside. Sometimes, when there was no work to be had, we'd walk to the beach over by Portreath. Once we helped the fishermen to haul in a seine net to the beach and came home with a basket of fish.'

Josh could see tears in her eyes now. He thought these were genuine

153

tears of nostalgia, unlike the Afrikander woman who seemed to be able to turn her emotions on and off at will.

Suddenly a new sound was added to the din of the police cells. One of the men who had been arrested for drunkenness awoke. Still affected by the alcohol he had consumed, he began calling for the gaoler to take him to the toilet.

A constable came and led the drunken man away. After a few minutes they returned and Josh took the opportunity to speak to the policeman. He asked if he might be moved to a cell away from the noise, adding, 'I've been trying to talk sensibly to that young woman over there.'

Josh pointed to where Martha was peering at them, between the bars of her cell. 'I can hardly hear myself think, far less hold a conversation.'

The constable's expression indicated disapproval. 'You haven't been brought here so you can chat with young girls.'

'I've just learned we both come from the same place in England. She's in trouble and I might be able to help her.'

'The only way you could help is to pay for the damage she caused at the grocery store.' The constable grinned, evidently conversant with her story. 'Mind you, I can sympathise with her. She was let down badly.'

'I sympathise too and would like to help – not only to get her out of here, but back to England. I want to discuss it with her, but we can't hear ourselves speak. Is it possible to move to empty cells farther away from this?'

The Afrikander woman had begun shouting at her brother once more and further explanation was unnecessary.

The constable shrugged. 'The trouble is that whenever a cell is occupied it has to be cleaned afterwards – and the African cleaner needs to be paid.'

Josh reached inside his pocket and extracted two notes. 'Would this cover it?'

The constable took the money and pocketed it quickly. 'I'll see what I can do.'

Half-an-hour later Josh was still in the same cell. He thought he had probably parted with his money for nothing. Then yet another constable arrived with a number of keys jangling on a large iron ring. Martha was moved to a cell on her own and, minutes later, Josh was transferred to a cell alongside her.

Martha had seen him pass money to the constable and was aware of what he had done. When she thanked him, Josh replied, 'I needed to talk more privately. I hope I might be able to help you.'

Now he was closer to her, Josh realised she was even younger than he had at first thought. She was probably no older than seventeen or eighteen years of age.

'How can you help me – and why?' She was looking at him uncertainly.

'How much damage did you cause to the shop owned by your ex-sweetheart?'

'Thirty-three pounds worth, so they said.'

Josh looked at her with a grudging respect. 'You certainly expressed your feelings to the full!'

The girl smiled somewhat sheepishly. 'I *was* very angry.'

'All right, I'll pay for the damage – and give you a little money to live on until I get out of here. Then we'll talk about paying for your passage back to England. To Cornwall.'

A variety of expressions chased each other across Martha Doney's face – and Josh recognised the last as suspicion.

'You mean – you want me to travel back to England with you? To share your cabin?'

'No, that's *not* what I mean. I'll pay for you to return to Cornwall. There are no strings attached to my offer.'

Still suspicious, she asked, 'Why? Why should you spend so much money on someone you hardly know?'

'There are a number of reasons, Martha. We're both from Cornwall, and I've just lost a son and a grandchild. Wyatt, my grandson, was almost your own age. I'd like to think that if I had a grand-daughter who was in the trouble you're in, someone might come along and help if they were able to.'

Martha was still uncertain and he added, 'Besides, I'd like you to help me too. I want someone to contact the British diplomatic agent in Pretoria and telegraph a Mr Selous at the Rand Club in Johannesburg. I should also like to send a telegram to my wife in Cornwall. To tell her I'm likely to be delayed coming home.'

Chapter 9

The British diplomatic agent in Pretoria was an apologetic, ineffectual man who looked as though he was in need of exercise to tighten up the flabby muscles that put a severe strain on the waist buttons of his trousers.

'I received your message from the young lady who was in here,' he said when he arrived at the police headquarters to visit Josh, the day after Martha's release. 'I'm afraid there's very little I can do except ensure you are treated correctly. We British are held in considerable contempt in this part of the Transvaal. It's all due to the poor showing we made in our little misunderstanding with the Boers back in '81. Because they beat us then they're convinced they can do it again whenever they wish. It makes life very difficult for a diplomatic agent, I can assure you.'

The agent's fatalism did not reassure Josh in the least, but the man was speaking once more. 'I must say, the young lady you sent with your message seemed extremely grateful to you for arranging her release.'

'Where is she now? Staying at the hostelry where I left my horses?'

'I must confess I don't know. I never thought to enquire.'

'I would have thought that as the British diplomatic agent you would have felt it your duty to enquire. The girl can be no more than eighteen and is probably younger.'

'Quite possibly, but from what I understood of the matter for which she was arrested, the girl is not without considerable experience of . . . for the sake of delicacy, shall I say, "life"?'

'You can be as delicate or indelicate as you like. A young girl like that needs protection. I've promised to pay her fare back to England when I'm released. I'd be obliged if you'd offer her some protection until then.'

'I have my own business to attend to, Mr Retallick. Should she need my assistance I will, of course, do my best. However, I can't chase around Pretoria in the hope of finding her and offering help she would probably not appreciate.'

Josh knew he would not change this man's mind. He was not the type to put himself out for someone unless he was forced to.

'Have you heard anything of the ridiculous charges that have been laid against me? When am I likely to appear in court?'

'I haven't been told anything, but if you can get a message to me when the time comes, I will do my best to be present in court.'

Josh tried to persuade the diplomatic agent to find out more for him, but the consul would not be pushed. A few minutes later he excused himself, promising to call again in a week's time if Josh's case had not come to court by then.

Josh was left fuming at the agent's unhelpful attitude and wondering whether Martha had sent the telegraph messages to Selous and to Miriam. He was disappointed that she had not paid him a visit since being released from custody. However, he realised she might be reluctant to return to police headquarters.

The British diplomatic agent returned to visit Josh much sooner than either he or Josh had anticipated. He had hurried all the way from his home and was hot and out of breath.

'Mr Retallick, I have just received a telegram from Cape Town.'

Josh was puzzled. 'Cape Town? You're sure it's not from Johannesburg? From Frederick Selous?'

'No, it's from Cape Town. From Mr Rhodes, the Cape Prime Minister – but he mentions Mr Selous. It seems a message from you to Mr Selous was passed to the Cape. Mr Selous was about to take passage to England but passed details of your predicament to Mr Rhodes. He has sent me a telegram telling me to help you and asking if he can be of assistance.'

The diplomatic agent paused to mop his brow. 'Of course, had I known you were a friend of Mr Selous's and were acquainted with Mr Rhodes . . .'

The handkerchief circled the inside of the British agent's collar. 'I have already lodged a complaint with the *landrost*. I have told him your arrest must be a dreadful mistake and requested that he have it rectified immediately.'

Josh felt it unnecessary to tell the consul that he had never met Cecil Rhodes. Silently, he gave thanks to Frederick Selous for once more proving himself a good friend.

'Thank you. When can I expect to be out of here?'

'I don't know, dear boy. The *landrost* will hesitate to offend the Prime Minister of the Cape, but this will put him in a quandary. On the one side he has you and your very influential connections. On the other side is the Church. I think he will need to put the matter before President Kruger himself.'

Josh groaned. If there were unnecessary complications he could be held in the police cell for weeks!

'Can't you at least see if I might be released into your custody until a date is set for me to appear in court?'

'Of course, dear boy. I hadn't thought of that. I'll go and see about it right away.'

As the diplomatic agent turned away, Josh said, 'By the way, have you seen anything of Martha Doney since she delivered my message to you? I'd like to thank her. She sent off the telegram to Selous for me.'

'Ah! Well...' The consul turned back to Josh, seemingly embarrassed. 'Well now, I think it might be as well if you did not talk about your acquaintanceship with that particular young lady. Let everyone remember only that you are a friend of Cecil Rhodes and Frederick Selous. We must hope they forget you helped Martha Doney to gain her release from custody.'

'Why, what has she done? Where is she now, by the way? Did you try to find her after your last visit here?'

'No, I did not, I am very pleased to say. As for her present whereabouts . . . I think the Pretoria police would very much like to have an answer to that question!'

Josh waited impatiently while the British diplomatic agent gave him a smug 'I told you so' look.

Finally, Josh said, 'Well, are you going to tell me about her, or go away and leave me guessing?'

'Well, of course, nothing has yet been proven, but there was a fire that almost completely burned out one of the premises in the heart of Pretoria. It is strongly believed that your Miss Doney was responsible.'

'She's not *my* Miss Doney – and why should it be thought she is responsible?'

'Because the premises that burned down happened to be the shop where she caused the damage that resulted in her arrest in the first place! As I said, nothing has yet been proven, but a girl answering her description was seen in the area and Miss Doney is nowhere to be found. If she has any sense she will be well on the road to the Cape Colony by now and planning to catch the first boat to England.'

The British diplomatic agent smiled through the bars at Josh. 'I repeat, Mr Retallick, I think it might be wise if you were to forget you were ever acquainted with Miss Martha Doney.'

Chapter 10

James Deakin, the British diplomatic agent, visited Josh daily for the remainder of his stay in the police cells. The agent offered platitudes and made optimistic comments, but was unable to give Josh a hearing date for his appearance before the *landrost*. Neither was he able to offer any hope of bail.

There was no news of Martha Doney. Every time a new prisoner was brought to the cells, Josh thought it might be the Cornish girl. However, she seemed to have made good her escape from Pretoria.

Although Josh was not released by the Transvaal authorities, he had been allowed several small privileges since special interest had been taken in him by the British diplomatic agent. He remained in a cell on his own, was brought reasonable food from a nearby eating-house and taken from the cell for exercise in the prison yard both morning and evening.

Josh had been imprisoned for ten days when a constable came to the cell at the usual time for his morning exercise and opened the door. However, instead of taking him out to the yard, today the constable led him through the main building to a small, side door.

'Where are we going?' Josh asked his escort.

'You're appearing before the *landrost* this morning,' was the unexpected reply.

Josh was thrown into some confusion. He had been given no warning to pay special attention to his appearance, or steel himself to face the charges made against him. Nevertheless, it was a great relief to know that the end of his ordeal might be in sight.

The court was a high-ceilinged, austere room with no members of the public present and only a handful of officials. The *landrost* sat behind a large, polished table at one end of the room. Josh stood beside a chair facing him, some distance from the table.

Looking up from a document he was studying, the *landrost* stared at Josh for a few moments before asking, 'You are Joshua Retallick?'

To Josh's surprise, he spoke in English.

'That's right.'

'And your address?'

'The Gover Valley, St Austell, Cornwall. That's in England.'

'I'm not interested in that. What is your address in this country?'

'I have no address in Transvaal, or anywhere else in South Africa. I am passing through after a visit to my daughter-in-law and her family in Matabeleland.'

The *landrost* wrote something on the document in front of him before saying, 'Joshua Retallick, a complaint has been made against you that on a day in January, 1894, in Johannesburg, you, with others, assaulted Predikant Pieter Vanderbyl. How plead you?'

'Most definitely "Not Guilty",' declared Josh, emphatically. 'The accusation is an out-and-out lie.'

'You'll have time to give your story later, Mr Retallick. For now "Not Guilty" will be sufficient. You may be seated.'

As Josh seated himself, the *landrost* said in a loud voice, 'Call the first witness, please.'

A constable at the back of the room opened a door and called a name. In response the officer who had arrested Josh entered the court. He told of receiving the predikant's complaint and of arresting Josh. He spoke in Afrikaans and when he ceased talking, the landrost asked Josh, 'Do you understand what has been said?'

He nodded. 'I do.'

'Are there any questions you wish to ask this witness?'

'None. It happened as he said.'

The constable was dismissed and Predikant Vanderbyl was called to the courtroom.

Taking the stand, the preacher swore the oath, avoiding looking at Josh. When asked to give his evidence he said, 'I was in Johannesburg – an *evil* place – preaching the word of Our Lord to the *uitlander* miners there. Including this man . . .'

The predikant pointed to Josh but before he could continue his story, the *landrost* interrupted him. 'Just a minute, Predikant. You said a group of miners. The prisoner is not a miner, but a visitor to this country.'

'Most of the Johannesburg miners are visitors to our country. *Uitlanders* who have brought their evil ways with them.'

'We will keep the record straight, Predikant Vanderbyl. The prisoner is not a miner.'

'Nevertheless, he was with miners. Men who were jeering at my preaching. When I persisted, he and the others took hold of me and threw me into a pit containing all manner of filth.'

'That's a downright lie!' Josh started to his feet to challenge the preacher's statement.

'Silence, Mr Retallick! You will have an opportunity to state your case in a few minutes.' The *landrost* glared at Josh and, reluctantly, he sat down, still fuming at the lies told by the Boer preacher.

Receiving a nod from the *landrost*, Predikant Vanderbyl continued, 'I was left to climb unaided from the filthy pit and went in search of a

Transvaal policeman. There was none to be found. Even policemen keep away from such a place. Had I not seen this *uitlander* here, in Pretoria, every one of them would have escaped justice. I told the previous witness what had happened and this man was arrested.'

'Were there any witnesses to this assault, Predikant?'

'Many, but they were all *uitlander* miners.'

'Thank you. Mr Retallick, do have any questions you wish to put to Predikant Vanderbyl?'

'A great many, sir.'

Rising to his feet, Josh spoke to the Afrikander preacher. 'You say I was with miners, yet only a few minutes before we had both arrived on the same train from Cape Colony.'

'So? It does not mean you are not a miner.'

Frowning, the *landrost* asked Josh, 'Were you with miners in Johannesburg, Mr Retallick?'

'I was with Mr Frederick Courtenay Selous, sir. We had been travelling together. As for being with miners, there were a great many men searching the rubble for survivors after the explosion. No doubt many of them were miners. I don't know.'

'Explosion!' The *landrost* appeared startled. 'Are you talking of the disaster involving the dynamite wagon?'

'That's right. Indeed, the predikant chose a pile of rubble for his pulpit when he decided to warn all and sundry of the dangers of Sodom and Gomarrah. Every other man in the vicinity was trying to save lives. I believe that is why he was thrown into the rubbish pit, because he was hindering the rescue work.'

The *landrost* looked thoughtful. 'So you are not denying that you were present when this incident occurred? Did you make any effort to prevent it?'

'At the time in question, I and Mr Selous were pulling a young woman from the rubble, not knowing whether she was alive or dead.' Josh paused. 'As it happens, she was dead.'

'This Mr Selous of whom you speak . . . is he the hunter? The man who led the pioneer column to Mashonaland?'

'Yes. He guided me from Johannesburg to Matabeleland.'

'And he witnessed this incident too?'

'Yes. He would no doubt have been here today had my telegram reached him, but he is on his way to England.'

'You have told me you are resident in England, Mr Retallick, yet you speak our language surprisingly well. Will you explain this to me?'

'I lived in Africa for eighteen years, but that was a long time ago. I left my son in Matabeleland. He later married the daughter of a Portuguese official who became Governor of Portuguese East Africa. Unfortunately, my son and grandson were killed in the Matabele rising last year. As soon as I received the news, I came from England to visit the family. I was on my way home from Matabeleland when I was arrested.'

The *landrost* nodded in apparent sympathy, but his thoughts were racing. Unknown to Josh, the mention of Elvira's father had made more of an impression upon the *landrost* than anything else that had been said in court that morning.

The Transvaal government was desperate to obtain an outlet to the sea. Surrounded as they were by British territory and protectorates on almost every side, their only hope lay in persuading the Portuguese government to allow them access via a railway line through Portuguese East Africa.

The *landrost* was a politically ambitious man. He hoped to gain a senior post in government before very long. Such hopes would be dashed if he were responsible for antagonising the Portuguese authorities by convicting the father-in-law of an ex-governor's daughter. On the other hand, if he informed President Kruger that he had freed Retallick and done his best to soothe his feelings . . .

'Are there any more witnesses to be called?'

There was much shaking of heads among the few officials and constables present.

Sitting back in his chair, the *landrost* frowned at the man who had caused Josh to be arrested. 'Predikant Vanderbyl, you have failed to prove your case against Mr Retallick. Indeed, it is my opinion that he has been the victim of a grave miscarriage of justice as a result of your accusation.'

Predikant Vanderbyl jumped to his feet, his face flushed with anger. 'You are doubting my word? The word of a minister of the Church?'

'I am saying that you have allowed yourself to believe that because Mr Retallick was present when this assault was carried out, he was involved. My finding is that he was *not*. You are free to go, Mr Retallick. I regret that you were ever arrested in the first place and I can only offer my apologies on behalf of the Transvaal government.'

Josh left the court with the angry protests of Predikant Vanderbyl sounding in his ears. He was so happy that even the chatter of James Deakin failed to annoy him. The British diplomatic agent had entered the courtroom halfway through the hearing. Now he was suggesting that his hard work 'behind the scenes' had played a large part in Josh's acquittal.

It did not matter to Josh now. Nothing mattered except that he was going to collect his belongings from the police clerk. Once free, he would send a telegram to Miriam – and then he would be going home. To Cornwall.

Chapter 11

Josh arrived in Johannesburg to find he had twenty-four hours to wait before he could catch a train to Cape Town. Taking a room at the hotel where he had stayed three months before, he was able to sell his two horses at a reasonable price to the stable from where they had been purchased.

He had sent a telegram from Pretoria to tell Miriam he was on his way home once more and now found himself with time on his hands.

He decided he would have a walk around the bustling and fast-growing town of Johannesburg. His first visit was to the gold-mining district. The sheer scale and variety of the mining operations there amazed him.

Lone miners and groups of two or three, with tiny claims, toiled in the shadow of huge machines owned by vast and powerful syndicates. Such machinery would soon take over from the independent operator as more and more claims were bought up. The amount of money being made and spent was such as Josh had never experienced in the tin and copper mines of Cornwall.

It was evening before he left the diggings. He was filled with wonderment as he made his way back through a part of town where the miners would come after dark to spend their money on drink and 'entertainment'.

Walking along a dusty and particularly noisy thoroughfare, he glanced up to the sign above an open door. In bold, gold letters on a black background, it read: The Duchy Arms.

Josh came to a sudden halt. This was the saloon where Martha Doney had said she once worked. He had thought about the young girl once or twice on his ride from Pretoria. Perhaps someone here might know her whereabouts?

The saloon was quite busy even though it was still early evening. There were a number of tables and chairs dotted about the room, with men and gaudily clothed girls sitting about them. The dominant feature of the saloon was a long, wooden bar counter which ran the full width of a wall at the rear of the saloon.

Behind the bar five men were busy serving drinks. Josh chose to order his from a short stocky bartender with a full dark beard. To Josh, it seemed that the man might have come straight from a Cornish mine, and his accent appeared to corroborate such an assumption.

'What can I get for you, me handsome?' asked the man.

'I'll have a beer,' said Josh.

As the bartender pulled the drink from one of the many pumps behind the bar counter, Josh said, 'I'm looking for someone. A girl named Martha Doney.'

'Are you now?' said the man, without taking his eye from the glass he was holding. 'And who might you be, may I ask?'

'The name's Retallick. Josh Retallick.'

The bartender looked up at him quickly. 'That's as good a Cornish name as any I know. But if I might say so without causing offence, you're a bit old for Martha. If it's a woman you're looking for, I'm sure Dolly would be happy to oblige you. I've never heard anyone complain about her yet . . .'

'I'm sure she's as good as any of the other women in here,' said Josh amiably. It sounded hopeful that Martha might be found here. 'But that isn't why I want Martha. She said I might find her here. I'm returning to Cornwall tomorrow. I said I'd take a message home for her.'

'I wish I was returning to Cornwall tomorrow,' said the bartender, fervently. 'But it'll take a year or two living here before I can earn enough to pay off the debts I owe back home. As for Martha . . . Well, she's a bit busy right now, if you understand me?'

The bartender gave Josh a wink and inclined his head in the direction of the stairs that led up from a corner of the saloon. 'I'd say you've got time for another drink or two before she comes down.'

'Fine. I'll wait.'

Josh carried the drink to a table from where he had a clear view of the stairs.

The Duchy Arms was a busy establishment. As darkness fell it became even busier. Josh waited perhaps half-an-hour during which time many men and women came downstairs. Most of the women returned up the stairs with different men before many minutes went by.

Then Josh saw Martha. She came down the stairs with a young and self-conscious young man. At the bottom of the stairs she gave him a brief kiss then walked towards the bar, looking about her as she went. Josh thought she was probably searching for potential customers.

When she was no more than a few paces from him, he stood up. Martha's glance passed over him – and then returned sharply.

Her astonishment was tinged with fear. For a moment, Josh thought she might run. Then she hurried towards him.

Clutching his arm with both her hands, she exclaimed, 'Josh, you're free! What happened? Did they decide not to put you on trial?'

Her voice was loud and excited. At nearby tables, heads were turned towards them.

164

'I appeared before the *landrost* and was found not guilty. But I want to know what happened to you?'

Their conversation was being listened to with great interest by all those close enough to hear. Josh said, 'Is there anywhere we can go to talk?'

Martha shook her head. 'Not unless you want to come upstairs with me? If you do, I'm afraid you'll have to pay for the privilege.'

She inclined her head towards the bar where the bearded Cornish barmaid was frowning in their direction. 'Jannie owns this place. Every girl here works for him. He doesn't miss a thing. He knows exactly how many times each girl goes upstairs. At the end of the night we have to hand the money we've made over to him and he gives us a small percentage as our "wages".'

Josh said quietly, 'Why do it, Martha? I've offered to pay your fare back to Cornwall. That offer still stands.'

'What would I do when I got back there, Josh? Everyone at home knows I came here to marry Danny Spargo. Would I tell them that he'd married someone else? That while I was trying to find him I worked in a saloon-cum-brothel, taking men upstairs to bed at three pounds a time? Oh, yes, and I spent a couple of weeks in a prison cell because I'd smashed up the shop run by Danny and his wife. How do you think they'd take that in Cornwall, Josh?'

While they were talking, the bearded barman had come from behind the bar and now he stood at the table. Addressing Josh, he said, 'Can I get you another drink, me handsome?' To Martha, he said, 'Shouldn't you be working, Martha? We're getting busy now . . .'

Josh took a five-pound note from his pocket. Handing it to the barman, he said, 'Here, that's to pay for Martha's time for the next half-hour. You can use the change to pay for a couple of drinks.'

Waving the man away, he said to Martha, 'I heard that the shop owned by your ex-fiancé and his wife was burned down soon after you were freed. The police and the British Agent in Pretoria seemed to think you had something to do with it. Did you?'

Another of the bar-girls had joined the men at the nearby table and persuaded them to buy a couple of bottles of Champagne. Their attention diverted, they were no longer listening to the conversation between Josh and Martha.

'It's a pity Danny wasn't inside when it went up!' she said fiercely.

'So you *did* set fire to the shop?'

Instead of answering the question direct, Martha said, 'Do you know what Danny did? After I'd paid his wife the money you gave me, Danny found out where I was staying. He came there to see me. Said he'd made a mistake by marrying a Transvaal girl. He said he couldn't very well leave her after such a short time, but he would eventually. He swore on it. Then he wanted me to go to bed with him, there in the hotel! I got

165

angry with him and he tried to quieten me, saying I'd bring some of the staff running to find out what was wrong. I began to scream then, hoping they *would* come, but he ran off. I was still angry that night when I went out for a walk. Somehow – and I swear it wasn't deliberate – I found myself walking past his shop.'

Martha shrugged. 'Acting on impulse, I broke a glass pane in the door, got inside, and set fire to the place. Then I collected my things and walked back here, to Johannesburg.'

'Well, I'm not denying you had provocation,' said Josh. 'But what are we going to do about you now, Martha? If the Pretoria police catch up with you, you'll go to prison for a very long time.'

'They won't catch up with me,' she declared, confidently. 'The police don't come here. If they did come looking, someone would tell me and I'd be out of here like a shot, I tell you.'

One of the barmen brought drinks to the table, sent by the manager. When he had gone, Josh said, 'This is no life for you, Martha. Where can you go from here? The only way is down. Surely you can see that for yourself?'

'That isn't so.' Her chin jutted defiantly. 'Three of the Duchy Arms girls have been married while I've been here. One of them to a partner in a gold syndicate. None of 'em was as good-looking as me. I'll do all right, don't you worry.'

'I will worry, Martha, and my offer remains open until the train leaves for the Cape tomorrow. I'll be on it – and you'll be with me if you have any sense. Don't worry about what might happen when we reach Cornwall. I'll find work for you in China clay country.'

Martha smiled sadly. 'Working as what, Josh? A bal maiden? Can you imagine me slaving all day, my hands cut and sore, for a few shillings a week? If I please a miner here he might give me five pounds on top of what I have to pay to Jannie. Money flows freely in Johannesburg. No, Josh, it's a very kind offer but it's not for me. I'll stay here and take my chances. You go home to your wife and everything else you've got there. I'll be all right.'

He stood up. 'As I said, the offer is open until the moment the train leaves. Think about it.'

'I will . . . but the answer's going to be the same tomorrow as it is today. All the same, thank you, Josh. Thank you for your help when we were in Pretoria – and thank you for caring, even if it's just a tiny bit.'

She stood up too and gave him a warm kiss that brought a chorus of cat-calls from the nearby tables. Then, as Josh walked out of the saloon, Martha ran upstairs alone, ignoring the calls of Jannie the bar-owner.

The Johannesburg railway station was crowded when Josh boarded the Cape Town train the next day. Many of the men who were travelling in this direction had made money in the gold mines and were returning to their home countries to put it to some good use.

A few, travelling at the rear of the train in carriages little more comfortable than stock cars, were those who had failed to achieve the dream which had brought them to Johannesburg. They would hang around the docks in Cape Town, hoping to sign on as a crew member in order to work a passage back to their home country. They travelled in the certain knowledge they would fare no better when they reached England.

From his compartment, Josh spent much of the time looking out of the open window of the carriage. He still nursed a hope that Martha might change her mind. That in the cold light of day she might reassess the doubtful opportunities offered to her by the life she led in Johannesburg and return to the land of her birth.

It was a hope he nurtured until the moment a whistle blew on the platform and the train jerked into motion, accompanied by the cheers of the passengers.

Not until the sprawling gold town had been left behind and open veldt unfolded to view did he put Martha from his mind. He accepted that she was now as much a part of the past as was Insimo, Matabeleland and his adventures in Pretoria. He would never see any of them again.

He was returning home. To Miriam. To Cornwall. The Gover Valley – and to Ruddlemoor.

167

BOOK THREE

1902

Chapter 1

'Josh . . . Miriam . . . it's over! The war's over. The Boers have surrendered!' Lily ran to the room where Josh and Miriam were eating breakfast. In her hand she held a newspaper, delivered by a boy from the St Austell newsagent.

Miriam took the newspaper from her. The headlines announcing the end of the war in South Africa were a quarter of a page high. Glancing quickly through the first page she passed the newspaper to Josh.

'Thank God! It's a war that should never have begun. Now it's over perhaps some sanity will return to that part of the world.'

Glancing up from the newspaper, Josh said, 'It's reported here that it might take a while for news of the surrender to reach all the Boer commandos. It seems most have been operating entirely independently of their governments. Adam might be unaware the war is over.'

Adam, their grandson, had been fighting on the side of the Boers in one of their far-ranging and hard-hitting commando units. Nathan, his brother, had also been involved in the fighting. Drawn into the war against his own inclinations, he had acted as a scout for the British Army.

'It must have been heartbreaking for Elvira to have two of her sons serving in the war on opposite sides,' said Lily. 'Fighting against each other . . .'

'Many families in Southern Africa had to face a similar problem,' replied Josh. 'But it proved a blessing for Nathan on one occasion. Adam was able to save his life.'

'At least *Ben* wasn't caught up in the fighting,' said Lily. 'He stayed at home taking care of Insimo.'

'It's a good job somebody in the family showed some sense,' said Miriam. 'I'll write to Elvira right away and find out what's happening.'

'In the meantime I'll send her a telegram,' said Josh. 'I'll tell her how happy we are that the war's over and ask for news of the boys. I'll go and do it right away.'

'Aren't you going to Ruddlemoor today?' called Miriam as he walked from the breakfast room.

'Jim Bray manages very well without me,' he replied over his shoulder. 'In fact, I think he gets things done more easily if I'm not around.'

171

'I suppose that means you'll spend most of the day poking about the house, making a nuisance of yourself and finding things for other people to do?' complained Miriam, but her expression belied the words.

'Most men have retired by the time they reach his age,' she said as she and Lily heard the door close behind Josh. 'But not my husband. He'll carry on until the day he's too ill to walk to Ruddlemoor. Talking of which, how's that brother of yours? Any better?'

Lily shook her head as she straightened the chairs about the breakfast table and began gathering up the dirty crockery. She had been employed taking care of Miriam and Josh in their Gover Valley house for more than a year now.

'He hasn't left his bed for three weeks. Poor Jo is more worried about him than I've ever known her. I am too. For a few years after Darley and Jo were married, I thought a miracle had happened. That he was going to be all right. It didn't last. He's worse now than ever before.'

'It's *so* sad,' said Miriam. 'The only small consolation is that he's enjoyed some very happy years being married to Jo.'

'That's true,' agreed Lily. 'But she will be inconsolable if anything happens to him. We all will be.'

'Well, don't let's talk of Darley as though all hope has gone,' said Miriam, firmly. 'That young man has a habit of confounding those about him.'

She had seen the tears well up in Lily's eyes as they discussed Darley. Lily had always been fond of her older brother, but it was time she found a young man to take her mind off Darley's problems. She was now an attractive girl of eighteen and popular with the young men of the district.

'Have you heard anything of that young man of yours recently? The one you've been writing to? No doubt he'll soon be home now the war in South Africa is over.'

'Eddie Long is not my young man,' retorted Lily.

'Oh! Then perhaps the letters that have been coming here from South Africa were for someone else, even though they had your name on them?'

'I've been writing to him because his mother asked me to. She said that with him being so far from home, it might be nice for him to have letters from someone who went to school with him.'

'Does Eddie Long know that's all there is to it?'

Lily shrugged. 'If he doesn't know it now, he will when he gets home and I tell him.'

Miriam's bid to change the subject from Darley's illness had succeeded better than she realised. Lily had become concerned recently about the increasing warmth and seriousness of Eddie Long's letters. What she had told Miriam was the truth. She had begun writing to him only at the request of his mother, but he seemed to have assumed a

172

relationship that was never intended. She consoled herself with the thought that she would be able to explain the situation to him when he returned to Cornwall.

She tried to push to the back of her mind the memory of Eddie Long as he had been when she knew him at school. A couple of years older than her, he had possessed a temper that had more than once brought him into conflict with authority. When he joined the Imperial Yeomanry and sailed for South Africa there were many who expressed an opinion that it was the only thing that saved him from becoming involved in more serious trouble.

However, his family were near-neighbours of the Shovells and they had always been on good terms. Lily would discuss the matter with Eddie's mother before his return. It would prevent any unpleasantness if his mother explained to her son that Lily's letters to him had been at her request.

Neither his father nor mother could write. Lily's letters were intended only to keep him in touch with news of home. Any romance with Lily did not exist outside the mind of Eddie Long.

Besides, there was someone else: Simon Kendall. Quiet and serious-minded, Simon had come from London to set up an office that would represent the Trades Union movement in Cornwall among the clay workers. It was perhaps natural that he should turn to Jethro Shovell for advice and, through him, get to know Jethro's daughter.

Simon Kendall cared for his fellow men and intended devoting his life to helping them. He was all that Eddie Long was not.

Chapter 2

The war in Southern Africa came to an end on 31 May 1902. Ten weeks later the first soldiers returned to Cornwall from the battlefields. Eddie Long was not one of their number.

Three days before their leaders agreed the terms of surrender, a Boer commando derailed a train travelling southwards towards Cape Town from Mafeking. On board were soldiers of the Imperial Yeomanry, Eddie Long among them.

Eddie was trapped in the wreckage of a carriage for more than three hours. When he was finally released, army medical staff discovered that his right leg was shattered.

The injured Cornish soldier was transported to the hospital ship *Maine*, berthed at the Royal Navy's Cape base of Simonstown. Surgeons operated on the leg but were unable to make good the damage that had been sustained in the derailment. They were forced to amputate below the knee.

Eddie returned to Cornwall a bitter man late in October of that year.

The Long family had been notified that their son had been wounded, but the extent of his injury came as a great shock to them. Lily had written to express their sympathy, but the letter failed to reach him.

Eddie had not written at all. At first, his physical condition had prevented him from writing a coherent letter. Then, as he improved, he had felt unable to put into words his feelings about losing a limb.

Lily went home late one Saturday evening in October to spend the remainder of the weekend with her parents, and was told that Eddie Long had returned home that day.

The news of his war wound upset her, but only as much as it might have done had anyone else she knew suffered the same loss.

On Sunday she was on her way to chapel with her mother when she found Eddie waiting for her at the gate. Standing with a crutch tucked beneath each armpit, he said accusingly, 'I waited up until late last night. I thought you'd come to the house to see me.'

'Why?'

'Well, you must have known I was home. My ma came over to tell your mum and dad.'

174

'They told me you were home, yes. I intended coming to see you today. I didn't know until last night just how badly you'd been wounded. I'm very sorry about your leg, Eddie.'

'Yes. It makes all the difference, doesn't it?'

'Difference to what?' Lily was not quite clear what he was talking about.

'To you and me. You won't want to tie yourself to a man with only one leg.'

'As far as I'm aware there was never any suggestion that I should tie myself to you when you had two legs, so it makes no difference to *me* at all.'

'That isn't the way you came across to me in your letters, Lily.'

'I certainly never said anything to make you think any differently, Eddie Long.'

'Then why did you write to me all the time I was in South Africa, if you didn't have some feelings for me? Why write to me in the first place? There must have been something. And don't tell me you weren't aware of the way I felt?'

'I wrote to you because your ma asked me to. Because neither she nor your pa can write. She wanted me to keep you up to date with everything that was going on here.'

'I don't believe you, Lily Shovell.' He looked at her accusingly. 'Why did you suddenly stop writing when I was wounded? Because you were afraid I'd come back from the war less than a man? Because you thought I might come back like this?'

'I wrote to you as soon as we heard you'd been wounded. You should have received the letter. As for your leg . . . Whether you came back from the war with one, two, or even *three* legs would have made no difference to me. You're a neighbour and I've known you since I was at school. You're someone I wrote to because you were away at war and probably feeling lonely. You've never meant anything more to me, and you never will.'

With this final statement, Lily hurried off to catch up with her mother. She was glad she had been able to straighten things out with Eddie Long, although she felt somewhat guilty because she might have spoiled the homecoming of a wounded soldier.

Lily also had a nasty feeling that Eddie would have already told others there was far more to their friendship than was the truth. Unless the war had changed him a great deal, he would no doubt explain away his lack of progress with her by the fact he had returned with a permanent disability.

It was unlikely to do her own reputation much good.

Lily forgot about Eddie Long when she arrived at the chapel. Simon Kendall was here. He smiled at Lily and her mother when they entered and they sat beside him, Lottie separating her daughter from the young Trade Unionist.

Simon was not a Methodist, but he sometimes came to chapel to hear Jethro Shovell preaching. Lottie thought it was probably politically expedient on the part of the young Londoner. Jethro Shovell headed a very influential Benevolent Association movement in Cornwall. Whatever the reason, Lottie knew his presence always brought pleasure to Lily, although she had yet to make up her mind whether or not she fully approved of him.

During the service, Lily tried to analyse what it was she enjoyed about Simon Kendall's company. He was a good-looking young man, but she did not find him attractive in a physical sense. She decided it was because he had seen the world that was beyond Cornwall's borders and had a lot more to talk about than most of the men she knew.

Even while she was reaching this conclusion Lily realised that Eddie Long had *also* seen the world beyond Cornwall, yet she was not anxious to know more of him.

Simon was returning to the Shovell house for lunch. As he and the three members of the family walked together, Simon said, 'You preach a powerful sermon, Mr Shovell. I'm beginning to understand why you're so persuasive when you talk about your Association business.'

'He's never been any different since he was Lily's age,' said Lottie. 'Religion and politics have always been the two most important things in life. Making money for his family has never come very high on his list of priorities.'

The smile Lottie gave Jethro took all the sting out of her words, and she added, 'Mind you, we've never gone without any more than most folks in these parts.'

'Working people shouldn't have to go without *any* of the necessities of life,' said Simon, somewhat pompously. 'That's what Trades Unionism is all about. When . . .'

Before he could amplify on his theme, Lottie interrupted him, 'Young man, I've sat in chapel and listened to one sermon this morning. That's as much as I can take in for one day. If you want to practise your sermonising then you and Lily can walk on ahead while her father and I call in and see how Mrs Carne is today. She was ninety-six last Tuesday. Apart from a touch of arthritis she looks good for another ninety-six, but I like to keep an eye on her.'

As Simon and Lily walked off together, Lottie said, 'That young man reminds me a lot of you when you were that age, Jethro. Out to change the world and convinced that unless everything's white then it must be black.'

'Don't get any romantic notions about Simon Kendall, Lottie. Especially where our Lily is concerned. There's a very big difference between that young man and the way I was. You and I both knew what it was to live in a poor community. I set out to change things that I could see were wrong. I could see them because I'd experienced them for myself. I'd felt them – and still do. Young Simon comes from a very different background. There's no religion in his family and very little hardship as far as I can make out.'

They had reached the home of Mrs Carne now and Jethro held the garden gate open for Lottie to pass inside. He resumed talking as they walked up the path together to the house.

'Simon looks upon the Trades Union movement as an up-and-coming arm of politics. He's chosen it as a *career*, not because he regards it as a personal crusade. When he comes to choose a wife it will be his head and not his heart that will make the decision. That wasn't the way I chose you, Lottie – and it isn't what I want for Lily.'

Chapter 3

'What have you and Pa been doing this week?' asked Lily conversationally as she and Simon Kendall walked homewards through the streets of St Austell from chapel.

'He's helped me to organise a couple of Union meetings in the evenings. But in the main we've spent our time waiting outside one or other of the clay works, trying to persuade the men coming off shift to join either the Union or his Association, if they weren't already members. We haven't had a great deal of success this week. It seems the China clay business is a bit slow at the moment. Besides, a lot of men are returning from South Africa and looking for work. The clay men are nervous about doing anything that might put their jobs in jeopardy.'

'It's nice to know Pa has someone going around with him who thinks as he does. For as long as I can remember he's fought a lone battle on behalf of the men – and they haven't always appreciated it.'

'Things are changing now, Lily. The Unions are taking over Associations like those founded by your father. They're becoming a force to be reckoned with. One day employers – and the government itself – will have to take their views into account before making decisions that are going to affect the lives of everyone in this country of ours. In my father's time it would have been unthinkable for a man to consider taking up a career in a Trades Union, but not now.'

'What sort of a family do you come from, Simon?'

'Oh, a pretty ordinary one. My father is a teacher – quite a good one, actually. He has his own small school in Essex. He taught me, and then I managed to get a place at Cambridge University. It was there I became interested in Trades Unionism. When I left university I started work in the movement, and here I am.'

Lily looked at Simon with the respect of someone with a little learning for a man who had been educated at a university.

'My brother Darley is interested in the Trades Union movement, but he's never really had the strength to get too involved with it.'

'So your father has told me. With the views that the two of them hold, I'm surprised that Darley and you are so close to the Retallick family. Oh, I know Josh Retallick is your great-uncle, but he's still an employer.'

'He's a *good* employer,' said Lily, defensively. 'And so is Aunt

178

Miriam. They have been since the days when they lived on the moor and owned a mine. They care about people.'

'Well, that's nice to know,' said Simon, adding wryly, 'mind you, if everyone were like them there wouldn't be any work for men like me or your father.'

They were approaching the Shovell house now and Lily saw Eddie Long slouched over his crutches, close to the garden gate.

He was not someone she wished to meet while she was with Simon. She would have ignored him, but as Simon opened the gate for her, Eddie called, 'So this is the new man in your life, is it, Lily? He's the one you'd throw over a wounded soldier for.'

'I can't throw over something I've never had, and certainly never wanted,' retorted Lily as she walked up the path to the front door.

'You can't deny you wrote to me all the time I was in South Africa, Lily. I've kept all your letters. Every one. They're upstairs. I keep them in the ammunition pack I wore as a soldier of the Queen.'

'Then I suggest you read through them all again. There's nothing in any of them that I would mind the whole world knowing about. They are letters written to a soldier who was far from home – and written at the request of your mother!'

Lily could see even while she was talking that her words were having no effect upon the wounded ex-soldier. He had been drinking – and drinking heavily, judging by his manner.

'What sort of a homecoming is this for a man who almost died fighting for his country? I've lost a leg, I've lost my girl too, and I doubt if I'll ever be given a chance to work again. I fought for nothing.'

'Come on, Simon. Let's go indoors.' Lily took his arm to lead him away from Eddie who had lurched awkwardly in their direction.

As they turned to walk away there was a sudden clatter. Looking back, Lily saw he had dropped one of his crutches.

It would have been difficult for him to pick it up at the best of times. In his present condition it would have proved impossible.

Simon walked a few paces to the gate. Bending down, he picked up the crutch and handed it to Eddie who promptly tucked it beneath his arm without a word of thanks.

Simon would have returned to Lily, but at that moment Eddie reached out quickly and gripped the sleeve of the other man's coat, high up on his arm.

'What sort of a man are you, who'd steal a wounded soldier's girl, eh? Tell me, what sort of man would do a thing like that?'

Simon was not physically a large man, but he showed no fear of Eddie. 'I've stolen no one's girl. Lily and I are just friendly because I work with her father.'

'Just friendly!' mimicked Eddie, and Simon smelled ale on his breath. 'Have you ever been a soldier? No, of course you haven't.

You're not even a Cornishman. What are you doing here?'

'I don't think I need to explain that to *you*. If you really want to know what I'm doing in Cornwall then come and speak to me tomorrow – when you're sober. I'll tell you all about the Trades Unions. You might even find we can help you to find work. That's if you really *want* work.'

'I'm a better man than you, mister. Even if I've only one leg and have been drinking more than I should.'

'I don't doubt it,' said Simon, amiably. 'All the same, if there's something you have to say then I suggest you leave it until tomorrow.'

At that moment Jethro and Lottie appeared. Lottie appeared to have noticed nothing untoward. She nodded a greeting to Eddie before saying to Lily, 'Old Mrs Carne had a niece there. She's such a cantankerous woman you'd think she was the one who is old and not her aunt. But what are we doing out here? Let's go inside and have a cup of tea before I get us something to eat. How about you, Eddie? Do you feel like a cup of tea?'

Jethro was more observant than his wife. When he and Lottie were approaching the house he had seen Eddie's hand drop from Simon's arm.

'I expect young Eddie wants to be getting on home for his dinner. It's nice to have you back home, boy. I'm sorry about your leg, of course, but I was at a meeting yesterday. We were making out a list of names to be included on a memorial tablet in Truro Cathedral. It's in memory of those who'll never return to Cornwall from South Africa. It was tragically long. Enough to make a man think very deeply about the folly of war. It couldn't have been easy for you out there, boy.'

'It's not very much easier now I'm home,' complained Eddie bitterly. 'Who'll want to employ a one-legged man? What could I do anyway?'

Jethro had detected the slurring of Eddie's voice and he said, 'Folk in Cornwall are more patriotic than you realise. But we won't talk about it now. Come and see me tomorrow. If you really want work, I might be able to help you.'

When they were inside the house, Lily said to her father, 'Simon said the same as you to Eddie, but he doesn't want work. He's trouble, the same as he's always been. Nothing has changed.'

'Perhaps not, but he's earned himself a chance. I might be able to get it for him.'

'From Josh Retallick?' The question came from Simon.

'That's right.'

Simon hesitated before saying, 'I know he's a relative, but in view of all that's being planned for the Trades Unions in this area, do you think it's wise to be beholden to an employer? Any employer?'

Jethro gave the younger man a direct look. 'I know you've come from London and are probably more in touch with Trades Union affairs than I, but don't get to thinking you can't learn from the experience of others. One of the lessons I've needed to learn the hard way is that more can be achieved by talking to employers – Cornish employers in particular – than in setting out to fight them. Besides, no man has ever had to fight Josh Retallick in order to get fair working conditions. I might also remind you that fifty years ago, long before the Trades Unions got themselves properly organised, Josh Retallick was transported for his views. He was one of the first Trades Union martyrs, although he'll never be recognised as such.'

Chapter 4

Josh looked up from the sheet of handwritten paper he held in his hand and nodded at Eddie Long. 'This looks all right to me. What do you think, Cap'n Bray?'

Jim Bray removed the pipe from between his teeth to say, 'I agree with you. If Eddie can count too then I'm happy to give him a trial in the office.'

'I can count as well as anyone else who's attended school,' said Eddie, ungraciously.

'Then it's settled.' Josh chose to ignore Eddie Long's abrasive manner. 'You're now employed in the Ruddlemoor works office, Eddie.'

The three men were in the office where Eddie had just been interviewed for employment. Also in the room were Jo Shovell and Tessa Bolitho.

'Jo and Tessa will be pleased.' Josh smiled at the two women in question. Jo was working at a nearby desk, Tessa filing some papers in a cabinet. 'They've been hard pushed to keep up with the work since Darley went off sick. How is he today, Jo?'

'Not very good. He had a restless night and didn't want any breakfast.'

Turning back to Eddie, Josh said, 'You can start tomorrow morning at eight o'clock. Can you make it to the office by then?'

'I'll be here.'

'Fine. I hope you'll enjoy working at Ruddlemoor. You'll soon settle in to the routine and Jo and Tessa will tell you anything you want to know.'

'Who's in charge of the office?' Eddie asked.

Josh frowned. 'If Darley comes back then he's the office manager. In the meantime nobody else will take his place. Jo and Tessa know everything you need to know. They'll tell you what to do. If you have any problems they can't solve, then Captain Bray is your man.'

When Eddie Long had gone, Josh followed his works captain out of the office and voiced his thoughts to Jim Bray. 'I hope I haven't made a mistake taking on that lad? Young Lily thinks I might regret it.'

Jim Bray shrugged. 'You're giving him a chance he's not likely to get anywhere else. What he does with it is up to him. If he's got any sense he'll buckle down and be thankful he's got work. If he doesn't then he'll go. It's as simple as that.'

'I agree, Jim – and I'll leave that entirely in your hands.'

'I don't know what my pa was thinking about, allowing Eddie Long to come to work at Ruddlemoor. He's been nothing but trouble all his life. Losing a leg won't have changed his ways. In fact, from what Lily was telling me last night, it's made him worse than ever. He's convinced the world owes him something.'

'Well, he fought for his country and was wounded. Shouldn't he expect something in return?'

Jo looked suspiciously at Tessa across the office. 'It's unlike you to take the part of someone you hardly know. Unless . . . You're not setting your bonnet at Eddie Long, surely! Why, you're almost old enough to be his mother.'

Tessa had gone through her life bouncing from one affair to another since her involvement with Tom Sparrow had ended so tragically.

The latest man in her life had been the village blacksmith in her home village of Stenalees. It was brought to a halt when the blacksmith's wife confronted her husband in the village public house.

Almost as powerfully built as he, the woman wielded a pair of giant-sized blacksmiths' pincers. Using descriptive language seldom heard from a woman, she loudly proclaimed her intentions. If her husband did not end his affair with Tessa Bolitho, she would use the pincers to castrate him when he returned to the matrimonial bed.

She left the public house with the uproarious approval of the customers ringing in her ears, and Tessa's latest romance was at an end.

'What do you mean, I'm old enough to be his mother? I'm barely six years older than he is. That's hardly any difference at all.'

Tessa's indignation was not feigned. Even so, she was fully aware that most women of her age were married and had a home and children of their own. It was a fact of which her mother was constantly reminding her.

'That's as may be. But he's a baby compared to you.'

'How do you know? He's been off to war in the army, hasn't he? He couldn't have spent every minute of the day and night fighting. I've heard all about what soldiers get up to when they're away from home.'

'All the same, you'll be a fool to get involved with a man who's working in the same office as you.'

'Not unless someone goes blabbing to your father about it – and if they do, we'll all know who it must be, won't we?'

Jo shrugged. If Tessa had made up her mind to have Eddie Long then nothing she said would make any difference. It was none of her business, anyway, but it *would* make working in the office extremely difficult.

* * *

183

It became evident from the moment Eddie Long began work in the Ruddlemoor works office that he was a grumbler. The lay-out of the office was not right; the desk allocated to him was not as good as those used by Jo and Tessa. Most of all, it was evident that he resented working with two women, both of whom were senior to him in years and office experience.

Eddie Long would plough on with a task blindly, even if he knew nothing at all of what he was supposed to be doing. The result was that instead of there being less work to do, there was more. Most of the work he undertook had to be done again, usually by Jo.

Tessa's plan to ensnare him with her charms proved equally ineffectual, at least at first. When it was apparent that he was struggling to learn the office routine, Tessa offered to remain behind in the office in the evening to help him.

Eddie's reaction was typical. 'I'm paid to work here from eight in the morning until six at night. No longer. When six o'clock comes I have my own life to lead. I forget about Ruddlemoor.'

'I'm sure I could make it interesting for you,' Tessa persisted. 'Why don't you give it a try? Tonight, perhaps?'

'You'll never be able to make it interesting, no matter what you did,' declared Eddie, adamantly. 'It's woman's work and nothing you say can change that.'

'It's work that's bringing you in a weekly wage,' said Jo, angrily. 'It's high time you stopped feeling sorry for yourself and faced up to the facts. You're not the only wounded man to return from the war. There are a lot of men far worse off than you who would like to be *able* to work. My Darley for one.'

'He's welcome to have it whenever he likes,' retorted Eddie. 'He's never been able to do anything more than office work. I have.'

Jo would have said a lot more had her father not entered the office at that moment. With him he had the monthly attendance record for all the Ruddlemoor employees and he stayed in the office for the remainder of the day.

That night Lily came from the Gover Valley to visit her brother and Jo told her of the frustrations of working with Eddie Long.

'Great-uncle Josh should never have taken him on,' agreed Lily. 'But he feels very strongly that Eddie should be given one chance, at least. Anyway, you're not likely to get any sense out of him now – or from Miriam either.'

'Oh, and why is that?' asked Jo as she prepared a meal for Darley, in the kitchen.

'They've had a letter from Africa from one of their grandsons. From Benjamin. It seems that when Josh went there he told him that if he ever decided to come to England he could take over Ruddlemoor. After all these years it seems Benjamin has decided to take up the offer. There was a letter from him today. He'll be setting off from Insimo in the New Year. It's not only the Ruddlemoor office that's likely to be different in the future. It could be that *everything* will change – for all of us.'

Chapter 5

Young Ben Retallick stood at the rail of the *S.S. Dungannon Castle*, well wrapped up against the cold as the great liner edged slowly sideways towards the jetty, bullied by two diminutive tugs.

Another liner belonging to the same shipping company passed by, outward bound, four funnels billowing smoke. A long streamer of steam escaped from the whistle as the captain saluted his colleague on the incoming ship.

Around the quays of the busy port were wagons and carriages of all descriptions. Passengers and goods bound to and from all the continents of the world intermingled. At the dockside station, trains pulled by mighty locomotives were dwarfed by the great ocean liners.

Beyond this network of activity were the roofs of houses, shops, churches and warehouses, varnished red and grey by recent rain. The buildings extended in uneven uniformity as far as could be seen in every direction.

This was Southampton, England's premier port for the ocean-going liners of the world.

'Are you returning home from a holiday, young man?'

The question was put to Ben by an elderly woman who had come to stand beside him at the crowded rail. He had nodded a greeting to her on the occasions when they had met in the corridors of the *Dungannon Castle*. She always seemed to be accompanied by a girl of about his own age. He had never heard the girl speak and she seldom raised her gaze from the deck at her feet.

Sure enough, when he looked past the woman he saw the girl standing in her shadow now.

'No, I came here on a visit once, but I was too small then to remember anything.'

'Really!' It seemed to Ben the woman was suddenly less interested. 'So you're here on a visit?'

'Not exactly. My grandfather wants me to take over his business interests. I'm here to give it a go and see if it's what I want.'

'Oh!' The interest suddenly returned. 'Where are these business interests?'

'In Cornwall. He owns some clay workings. I believe he still has an interest in mining too.'

186

'Well, fancy that! Do you hear, Deirdre? This young man is also going to Cornwall. What a pity we never struck up a conversation earlier on the voyage. We could have told you much about Cornwall, couldn't we, dear?'

The question was directed at the young woman, but without waiting for a reply, the woman continued speaking. 'It would also have been company for Deirdre. I think she has found the voyage somewhat boring with only her grandmother for company. What's your name, young man?'

'Ben Retallick, ma'am. I was named for my great-grandfather.'

'Well, it's certainly a Cornish name. I am Lady Tresillian, and this is my granddaughter, Deirdre Tresillian.'

The young girl in question raised her head momentarily and Ben glimpsed a pair of striking blue eyes in a look that was not at all demure before she returned her glance to the deck once more.

'How are you travelling to Cornwall? Will there be someone to meet you here?'

'There will be nobody to meet me, Lady Tresillian. I'm not even certain my letter telling them I'm on my way will have arrived yet. As for travel . . . I'll make some enquiries when I go ashore.'

'There is no need for that, dear boy. I have a carriage arranged to take us to the Royal Hotel in Salisbury, where we will stay the night. Come there with us. Tomorrow we will take a train to Cornwall. We will guide you on your way and it will be a great relief to have a young man escorting us.'

Ben found Lady Tresillian somewhat overbearing, but it would have been churlish to refuse her offer. Besides, although he would have felt perfectly happy travelling through unknown veldt in Africa, he was nervous about finding his way around England.

At the hotel that evening, Lady Tresillian questioned Ben closely about his life in Africa. She seemed impressed that his mother was the daughter of a Governor of Portuguese East Africa, but looked sceptical when he told her of the vast land-holding held by the Retallick family in the Insimo Valley.

In a bid to change the subject and bring the reticent Deirdre into the conversation, Ben asked, 'Have you both been on holiday to Southern Africa?'

Glancing quickly at her granddaughter, Lady Tresillian replied, 'Not so much a holiday as a pilgrimage. My husband was killed in the war against the Zulus in 1877. He is buried in Natal. Deirdre's father, my oldest son, died at Paardeberg during the late war. We visited their graves and made arrangements for them to be cared for as we would wish.'

Ben murmured his sympathy to both women, but Lady Tresillian was not a woman to wallow in misery. 'They both died as they would have wished – in the service of their country. You've told us of your mother, is your own father still alive?'

'No, he and my eldest brother were killed by the Matabele in the uprising of '93.'

For the second time that day Ben was the recipient of a glance from Deirdre and there was sympathy in the look.

'You weren't involved in the recent war, of course?' said the older woman.

'We were raided once by a Boer Commando, but beat them off – and both my brothers fought in the war. Nat was a scout for the British, Adam fought for the Boers.'

Deirdre was staring at Ben quite openly now but it took more than his revelation to put Lady Tresillian out of countenance. 'It must have been very difficult for your mother, having two sons fighting against each other.'

'It was difficult for all of us, but it all worked out. As it happened, Adam was able to save Nat's life on one occasion.'

'Where are your brothers now?'

'They both found wives during the war. Adam is living on a farm in the Transvaal, Nat has returned home with his new wife to run things at Insimo.'

'And you're heading for Cornwall to take over a clay works from your grandfather?'

'That's the idea, but I have a lot to learn. I know absolutely nothing about the China clay business.'

'You'll learn, young man – and you'll learn fast. Besides, you will no doubt have a good Cornish captain to run the works for you. Then you can find time to enjoy the Cornish social life, I have no doubt.'

Pushing back her chair noisily on the polished stone floor of the dining-room, Lady Tresillian said, 'We have an early start in the morning, so I'll be off to bed now. You can stay, Deirdre – for twenty minutes, but not a minute more. Good night, young man – no, don't stand up. Finish your meal and escort Deirdre to our room when you're ready.'

For a few minutes after the older woman had gone, Ben and Deirdre sat in an uncomfortable silence before Ben said, 'Did you enjoy your visit to South Africa?'

Deirdre shook her head. For a few moments, Ben thought she was going to maintain her silence. Then she said softly, 'Not very much.' They were the first words he had heard her say.

'No, of course not. It was unthinking of me. I couldn't have been a happy journey for you.'

'It wasn't that.' Deirdre looked up at him and once more he was aware of the startling blue of her eyes. 'I never really knew my father.

He was first and foremost a soldier and chose to spend most of the time fighting someone, somewhere in the world. Actually, it could have turned out to be a very pleasant journey. I loved the country – and the sunshine.' Deirdre smiled but Ben thought it only served to accentuate a deep unhappiness within her.

Dropping her gaze again, but this time only momentarily, she added, 'But it wasn't much fun travelling with my grandmother. She was convinced that if she left me alone with anyone my own age for even a few minutes I'd rush off and disgrace the family, or something equally dreadful. This is the first time she's let me out of her sight – and for a whole twenty minutes! You're honoured, Benjamin.'

He smiled. 'It's because she cares about you, I've no doubt. But as we have a whole twenty minutes, would you like to take a walk outside? It's quite a cold evening but it would probably be a very pleasant walk alongside the river.'

She seemed uncertain at first, but Ben said quickly, 'Please! I've seen absolutely nothing of England yet. It's my first opportunity to walk about an English town – and I'd enjoy it more if you were with me.'

Deirdre hesitated no longer. 'All right, but we mustn't go far, just in case my grandmother comes looking for me.'

The River Avon flowed close to the hotel and on its bank they paused to watch some young children feeding a number of swans and ducks.

'I presume there are no crocodiles here?' queried Ben.

His question brought a laugh from Deirdre. It was the first time he had seen her looking happy and it was a pleasant sound.

'No, you'll find no crocodiles here.' Looking up at him and still smiling, she said, 'You *do* have a lot to learn about this country.'

At that moment one of the small girls offered Deirdre a piece of bread to feed to the ducks.

Kneeling on the river bank, she coaxed one of the ducks to come close and feed from her hand.

'I like ducks,' said Deirdre suddenly. 'They are gentle creatures, yet the drakes are very brave. We had one in Cornwall that tried to protect our ducks from a dog. He had nothing with which to ward off a dog, but he saved the ducks, even though it cost him his own life.'

'There are many creatures like that,' agreed Ben. 'I've watched them in Africa.'

Throwing the last small portion of bread into the water, Deirdre stood up and brushed the crumbs from her hand. 'You're going to find things very different in this country, you know.'

'Yes – especially the weather. But it's a challenge and I'm looking forward to it. If things don't work out I can always go back to Insimo.'

'You're very lucky. For some of us there's no going back. No alternative to the life we are expected to lead.'

189

Ben waited for her to continue. When she made no attempt to amplify her brief statement, he said gently, 'It sounds as though you've had a very unhappy life?'

'Not unhappy exactly, but it's always been lonely. Grandma has never understood that.'

They were walking along the river bank now and Ben said, 'Talking of Lady Tresillian, we had better return to the inn now.'

'Yes.'

They walked in silence for a brief while before Deirdre suddenly blurted out, 'It wasn't the whole truth you know. The reason Grandma gave you for why we went to South Africa. We *did* go to see the graves of my father and grandfather, but that wasn't the main reason. I was taken there "for my own good". I think that's how they put it. It was felt I had become too fond of someone. A *married* someone at that.'

She looked at Ben to judge his reaction. Perhaps expecting him to be shocked. His expression showed nothing.

'I had a tutor, a woman who lived in Truro – that's our nearest town. Her husband has travelled the world and he knows something of just about any subject you can think of. He's a poet too. He was very kind to me and I began to tell him my troubles. He would always listen – and that is something no one has *ever* done. Just sit and listen to me. Sometimes, when I was particularly unhappy, he would hug me too. That is something else no one has ever done. Then, one day, one of Grandma's friends was passing by the house and saw him give me a hug in the garden of my tutor's house. She didn't notice, or didn't *want* to notice, that my tutor was at a window speaking to us at the time. Not that it would have mattered to anyone, I suppose. I had allowed him to behave with "undue familiarity".

'Half an hour later a servant came to the house to take me home. By the time I arrived there I found that everything had been blown up to such proportions it verged on a scandal. No one would listen to *my* version of the story. Before I knew it I was on a boat to South Africa and my tutor and her husband were told to leave Cornwall by the time we returned.'

With fierce bitterness, Deirdre added, 'Their only offence was to show me some affection. I believe the very word strikes horror in the hearts of my grandmother and her friends.'

Ben thought it was a very sad observation for such a young girl to make, especially if she believed it to be true.

'Why have you told this to me?' he asked her.

Deirdre lifted her eyes to his face. 'Because . . . because I *need* to tell someone. I *have* to tell someone. I need a friend, Benjamin. I know my grandmother is going to invite you to visit us when we reach Cornwall. Please accept. *Please*!'

190

Ben thought it was a tragedy that this young girl should need to make such an appeal to him.

'Of course I will. I'll visit you as often as I can.'

Chapter 6

Thanks to the recent installation of a telephone in the Gover Valley house, Ben was able to ring ahead and let Josh and Miriam know he was on his way. As a result, they were waiting excitedly for him when the train steamed in to the platform at St Austell railway station. Lily was with them.

Miriam greeted him with affection, but also a certain amount of awe. 'Look at you!' she said, standing back after giving him a hug. 'There's me remembering you as you were when you visited us as a tiny baby all those years ago, and here you are a good six feet tall!' She hugged him again. 'All the same, I think I would have recognised you. You have your mother's skin and hair, but you have the features of your father.'

Ben shook hands warmly with Josh, then more formally with Lily. Meanwhile, his luggage was being unloaded by a porter. No sooner was this operation completed than a whistle blew farther along the platform. With a rush of escaping steam, and a preliminary skidding of iron wheels on iron track, the engine began slowly drawing the train out of the station on its journey towards Truro.

Ben had to run alongside the train in order to call a farewell to Deirdre and Lady Tresillian. Deirdre was hanging precariously from the carriage window and still waving when the train passed from view, and Miriam said: 'Well, it didn't take *you* very long to make friends here. Who was that?'

'Lady Tresillian and her granddaughter. We travelled from South Africa in the same ship, yet didn't talk to each other until we were docking at Southampton. Since then Lady Tresillian has rather taken me under her wing. She made certain I reached St Austell safely.'

'Hmm!' It was an expressive sound. Miriam was determined not to appear impressed that Ben had travelled to St Austell in the company of a titled lady. 'But it wasn't Lady Tresillian who was almost falling from the train in her determination to wave to you until the very last moment!'

Ben grinned at his grandmother, making no attempt to reply to her observation.

It was a very happy party who rode in the carriage to the Gover Valley. Lily was relieved. She had nursed a great many misgivings about having someone new living in the same house. However, she discovered that Ben was a very easy-going young man.

He was attractive too, but she tried not to think of this. Josh had told her of the vast landholdings Ben's family had in Matabeleland – now part of Rhodesia, the country named after the man who had engineered its acquisition on behalf of Great Britain. He had arrived travelling in the company of a titled woman and her daughter. Lily reminded herself that Ben would regard her only as a distant relative. A *poor* distant relative. One who worked in the house of his grandparents.

The lights burned late that night in the Retallick household. The talk was of family, of the past, and of Ben's future role in the Ruddlemoor China clay works.

Josh's proposals were generously simple. He had, he said, accumulated sufficient wealth to enable Miriam and himself to live in considerable comfort for the years remaining to them.

His will had been made and there were generous legacies for all members of the family. If Ben found he enjoyed being involved in the production of China clay, Ruddlemoor would become his.

Josh added he was confident Ruddlemoor possessed considerable scope for expansion. A shrewd and determined businessman could not only expand the existing workings, he might merge with others in what had become a very lucrative market.

Josh enthused about the prospects for Ben as owner of Ruddlemoor for so long that eventually Miriam said firmly, 'You men can save the rest of your business talk for tomorrow. It's way past my bedtime – yours too, Josh, although I doubt if any of us are going to sleep. It's so exciting having a grandson in the house.'

'Miriam's right, Ben,' agreed Josh, rising stiffly to his feet and helping Miriam from her chair. 'You know where your room is. You've had a long day, so there's no need to be in a hurry to get up in the morning. It doesn't matter what time we get to Ruddlemoor.'

When Josh and Miriam had made their way upstairs, Lily busied herself straightening cushions and rearranging the chairs in the room.

Ben was not quite at ease with Lily yet. He felt there was a certain coolness in her attitude towards him. He had not been in the house for long enough to know whether it was her normal manner. He thought she might resent his presence here.

He told himself it would be quite understandable if she would have preferred him to remain in Africa. Quite apart from the extra work his presence made for her, he would also be taking a large share of the inheritance she could, with some justification, have expected to come her way.

'I think I'll have a drink of water, then I'll go to bed too,' he said to her.

'I'll get it for you,' said Lily, unexpectedly.

When Ben protested that it was not necessary for her to wait upon him, she said, 'It'll be easier if I get it. You don't know where the cups or anything are kept.'

Ben followed her uncertainly to the kitchen and she drew a glass of water for him from the tap. As she handed it to him, she said, 'That wasn't entirely true what your grandfather was saying just now.'

'What wasn't?' Ben could not think to which part of Josh's conversation she was referring.

'That bit about it not mattering what time you got to Ruddlemoor. He'll be down here first thing in the morning, pacing around and getting under everyone's feet. He's told anyone who'd stand still long enough to listen that you were coming to England from Africa. He can't wait to take you to Ruddlemoor and show you off.'

'I'm glad. Pa would have been delighted to know I was in Cornwall and planning on staying. Although if he and Wyatt were still alive, I doubt if I'd be here now. Everything would have been very different.'

'Your pa's death hit both Josh and Miriam very hard,' said Lily. 'You won't find Miriam saying too much about it now, but she's as happy as your grandad that you've come here to live.'

Ben downed the water from the glass Lily had given to him before saying, 'How do *you* feel about me being here, Lily?'

She looked startled. 'Why should it make any difference to me? It's a little extra to do around the house, that's all. I'm not exactly overworked. It might even make it easier for me, especially now my brother Darley is so poorly. I'll be able to leave the house knowing there's someone to keep an eye on Josh and Miriam. That's until *your* social life picks up, of course. I don't suppose that will be far off, having travelled to Cornwall in the company you were keeping on the train.'

'That side of English life is something that I'm going to find difficult to get used to,' admitted Ben. 'Back home my socialising never got far beyond attending a wedding in the African compound.'

He hesitated before saying, 'How about you? Do you get out and about very much?'

'Certainly not with the likes of Lady Tresillian and her granddaughter,' replied Lily. 'I might go to fairs and feast days and the like, but I don't see much outside of this house and my home in St Austell.'

'How about men friends? Is there anyone in particular?'

To Ben's consternation Lily rounded on him immediately. 'What business is that of yours, Ben Retallick? As a matter of fact, there *might* just be, but that's between me and him. If you take a tip from me, you'll save your questions for asking about the China clay workings. You've got enough to learn there, so keep your mind on things that

194

concern you. I'm going to bed now. You can put the lights out before you go upstairs.'

Lily swept from the room leaving Ben open-mouthed, wondering what he had said to upset her so much.

When she reached her room, Lily sat down on her bed and she too wondered why Ben's question about 'men friends' had triggered off such an explosive reaction. It was still bothering her when she fell asleep.

Chapter 7

Ben rose early the next morning and was downstairs only minutes after Josh. Miriam would follow in a few minutes. In the meantime, the two men sat down to a breakfast cooked by Lily.

'I'm glad you're up and about early,' said Josh, having apparently forgotten all he had said the previous evening about there being no hurry to get to the clay works. 'We can get to Ruddlemoor in time to catch Jim Bray before he begins his morning inspection. He can take you with him. You'll get an idea then of the extent of the workings.'

'Don't try to push too much down the boy's throat in one day,' said Miriam, entering the breakfast room and hearing her husband's plans for Ben. 'Give it to him all at once and you'll find he'll be off to catch the next boat back to Africa.'

Lily was going back and forth to the kitchen while this conversation was taking place and Ben wondered what her thoughts were on the matter. After their brief and rather acrimonious exchange shortly before bedtime the previous evening, he thought she might be happier were he to return to Africa. However, she said nothing and bade him a polite farewell when he and Josh left the house.

They travelled to Ruddlemoor by what Josh called a pony and shay, a small light carriage. Along the way, he said, 'Remind me to get a horse for you sometime this week. I might send one of the men to the market on Tuesday.'

'If you don't mind, I'd rather choose my own animal. We had some wonderful horses at Insimo and I'm afraid I'm a bit particular about them.'

'Of course, of course!' said Josh. 'You'll be far more of an expert than me. I'll give you the money . . .'

'You don't need to do that, Grandpa. The Retallicks of Insimo are a wealthy family too, you know. Pa planned everything very carefully before he died. I probably wouldn't ever need to work, if that's the way I wanted things – but I don't. I've come here because you want me to take over Ruddlemoor and because I think it's what I want, too, but I have no intention of living off you.'

Ben's independent attitude pleased Josh and he said, 'That's fine. I understand the way you feel, but the horse will be a welcoming present from your grandma and me. So let's have no more arguments about it.'

196

Ben's arrival at the Ruddlemoor China clay works caused a great deal of interest among the workers. The head of every man and woman in sight turned towards Ben and Josh as they drove towards the office.

There had long been some concern among the men because of Josh's advancing years. They knew the time was fast approaching when Ruddlemoor would pass into new hands. This would inevitably bring changes – and changes of ownership rarely brought benefits to employees.

Jim Bray saw their approach and was waiting outside the works office to greet them. His open, welcoming smile brought an immediate response from Ben. Josh was watching both men closely and felt a great sense of relief. He had always hoped and believed Ben and the works captain would get along well together. Now he was certain of it. He felt the future of Ruddlemoor would remain in good hands.

Inside the office, Tessa, Jo and Eddie were introduced to Ben. He nodded acknowledgement to Eddie and Tessa. To Jo, he said, 'I've been talking to Lily about you and Darley. I hope he isn't feeling too bad at the moment? I believe we're paying you a visit tomorrow evening. I look forward to meeting Darley, I've heard a great deal about him over the years.'

After a brief familiarisation with the office and what went on here, the three men left. Josh was returning to the Gover Valley, while Captain Bray took Ben on a tour of the workings.

Behind them, Tessa made an exaggerated show of collapsing limply in her chair, saying, 'What a wonderful piece of young manhood that is! He's made me go all weak at the knees.'

'You'd go weak at the knees if he was ninety years old and as weedy as a violet,' retorted Jo. 'He's a man, and that's always been enough for you.'

'Oh, he's a man all right,' agreed Tessa, totally unabashed. 'But *what* a man! Do you think you might need some help entertaining him tomorrow night, Jo? I'll be happy to come around to your place and help you out . . .'

'Did you hear that *accent*?' Something in Eddie's voice brought the light-hearted banter between the two women to an immediate halt. When they looked at him they could see he could hardly contain his fury.

'What's wrong with it?' demanded Tessa. 'I think it adds something a little *romantic* to him. It sort of makes him foreign, although not foreign, if you know what I mean?'

'It makes him a *Boer*! A bloody South African. One of the men I was fighting for almost three years. It was men like him who killed dozens of my mates and caused me to lose my leg.'

'You'd better watch your language if you intend to stay working in this office, Eddie Long – and for your information, Ben Retallick comes from Rhodesia, not from South Africa.'

Despite the years he had spent in South Africa – in fact, it was a year and a half and not the three years he had stated earlier – Eddie's knowledge of Southern Africa geography was decidedly sketchy.

'What's the difference? He's a Boer. I should know, I heard enough of them talking when we took them prisoner. What's he doing here?'

'He's Josh Retallick's grandson,' said Jo. 'And if you want to continue working at Ruddlemoor, I suggest you keep your thoughts to yourself. Ben Retallick will probably take over one day.'

'That will be the day I leave,' declared Eddie. 'I've not been out in Africa fighting a war just to come home and find I'm working for one of the men we spent three years defeating!'

Jo gave a sigh of exasperation, and said to Tessa, 'It's simply no good talking to him, is it? He's got it into his thick head that Ben Retallick is a Boer and no amount of proof is going to change that. You're heading for trouble, Eddie Long. When it comes I'll be the first to say it serves you right.'

'I for one would be glad if Ben Retallick brought trouble my way,' said Tessa. 'Boil up the kettle in case he comes back to the office, Jo. We might be able to persuade him to stop for a cup of tea with us . . .'

Ben's tour of the Ruddlemoor China clay works took the whole of that day. By the end of that time his mind was in a complete whirl. He had not realised there was so much involved in quarrying, recovering and refining clay. It would take him weeks to learn the many processes through which the raw mineral would pass before it became marketable.

Yet he found it exciting too. From the top of the great pit from which the China clay was dug, he looked around and as far as the eye could see there were similar works being operated. No doubt each one was striving to achieve greater efficiency in a bid to produce more clay than the others.

There was a challenge about the whole business that Ben found strangely stimulating. Back in Africa, in the Insimo Valley, it had been possible to stand and look about him with the knowledge that everything within sight belonged to the Retallicks. Within that area the family ruled with absolute power. No man, white or black, had been able to wrest the land from them and Ben could not foresee that they ever would.

Here, in the St Austell area, every clay producer was competing against his neighbour. Some would succeed, others would fail. A shrewd, efficient and determined businessman might one day control most of the workings hereabouts. All of them, perhaps.

That man would be the virtual ruler of an area that almost matched the Insimo Valley for sheer size. He would be the acknowledged, if uncrowned, 'king' of clay country. It was a thought that appealed to Ben Retallick. It gave him the incentive to learn everything there was to know about the business in which he was going to stake his future.

Chapter 8

The next evening Ben walked with Lily to the St Austell home of Darley and Jo Shovell. It was a fine, crisp evening and, although Lily did not go out of her way to make conversation, she was not unpleasant. Ben found he was enjoying her company more and more with each passing day.

As they walked he asked polite questions about her family and life in St Austell. She filled in the details of much that he already knew about her and declared that she particularly enjoyed working for Josh and Miriam.

When the talk turned to Ruddlemoor, it was Ben who suddenly waxed enthusiastic. He told her of the clay processing and the work involved as though it must all be as new to her as it was to him.

After listening to him at some length, Lily said, 'I'm impressed. I thought life here in Cornwall would prove very boring after the life you've led in Rhodesia.'

'Far from it. I find everything here *very* exciting. Not only that, I believe there's tremendous potential for modernisation and expansion. I want to look into that.'

'You must mention it to Darley if he's well enough to speak at any length. He always believed Great-uncle Josh could have made a lot more money had he been a little more adventurous.'

'What a pity he's so ill. He sounds just the sort of man I'd like to have working at Ruddlemoor . . .' Observing the sudden brief raising of Lily's eyebrows, he added hastily, 'That's if I do ever take over Ruddlemoor.'

'Oh, I don't think there's any doubt about that,' she said. 'It's what Josh and Miriam want – and after listening to you, it's quite obviously what you want too.'

'Yes, it is,' agreed Ben, in a sudden moment of complete honesty. 'I loved Insimo – I still do – but I always knew it would never be *mine*. There were three brothers ahead of me. When Wyatt was killed it still left Nat and Adam. I was always aware that Nat would one day take over. Adam knew it too, that's why when he married he stayed on his wife's farm in the Transvaal. The menfolk in her family were all killed during the war. The farm is his to run as he sees fit now. If I take over Ruddlemoor it means that I too will have something of my own.

Something that, I hope, will be *my* success story.'

Lily said nothing, but she realised in that moment that although Ben Retallick was not much older than herself, he possessed a fully matured ambition. Ruddlemoor would probably prosper under his ownership, but she doubted whether those who needed to do his bidding would find him a comfortable young man for whom to work.

Darley had insisted that he leave his bed and dress himself to welcome Ben to the house. He was seated in an armchair in the lounge, beside a crackling fire with a rug about his knees. He looked even more frail because he was dressed in clothes that had fitted him when he was a more active man and many pounds heavier than now.

Darley had other visitors too. Jethro and Lottie were also paying a call on their son. With them they had brought Simon Kendall.

Darley was surprised at the familiar manner with which Simon greeted Lily. She too was startled by his unusually effusive greeting, but tried not to allow it to show.

By contrast, Simon's handshake with Ben was formal to the point of coolness. In view of the way he had greeted Lily, Ben thought it must be because he had accompanied her to the house. He was unaware that Jethro had told Simon of Ben's future role at Ruddlemoor. Even had he known, Ben had yet to learn of the attitude of Trades Union officials towards employers. There had been no Trades Union at Insimo.

After about half-an-hour, when conversation about the various members of the Retallick family was flagging, Ben managed to broach the subject of Ruddlemoor with Darley.

He found him as enthusiastic about the future of the clay works as Lily had suggested he would be. Soon the two were deep in conversation about Ruddlemoor and the clay area. Jethro and Simon were drawn into the discussion when they began making suggestions about various innovations to improve the lot of the clay worker.

In the kitchen, Jo and Lottie questioned Lily about Ben.

'He's all right,' she replied, in answer to a question from Jo. 'But he's very ambitious, I can tell you that! He's already thinking about taking over the whole of the clay country when Ruddlemoor is his. Mind you, it wouldn't surprise me if one day he *did*. There's a whole lot more to Ben Retallick than meets the eye.'

'Then set out to catch him now, our Lily,' said Jo, jokingly. 'He'll be a very rich man one day and there's no one who stands a better chance. You're both living under the same roof!'

'He's a rich man *now* from all I understand,' replied Lily. 'The trouble is, I don't think I *want* to catch him.'

'Well, that's one less for Tessa Bolitho to worry about then. She's ready to throw herself at him whenever he looks in her direction.'

'She'd throw herself at *any* man,' said Lottie. 'Whether he looks at her or not.'

'That's what I said,' agreed Jo as she cut bread to make sandwiches. 'But it won't stop her.'

'Tessa's a whole lot older than Ben,' said Lily. 'He'll not look at her.'

'Don't you be too sure,' said Lottie. 'Tessa's not *that* much older. Besides, she's an attractive young woman and certainly knows how to turn a man's head.'

'Anyway, it won't concern Lily,' said Jo. 'She's got Simon Kendall to think about.'

'What's that supposed to mean?' asked Lily, heatedly.

'The way he greeted you when you came in, I thought there must be something going on that no one had bothered to tell me about,' commented her mother.

'I thought the same,' agreed Jo. 'He never greets me like that.'

Lottie and Jo were still teasing Lily about Simon when Ben put his head around the door of the kitchen.

'I thought I'd leave now,' he said. 'I think all my talk of Ruddlemoor has tired Darley a bit more than is good for him.'

'But I'm just making sandwiches.' Jo pointed to the heaped plates on the kitchen table. 'You'll at least stay for something to eat?'

'I think it's probably best if I don't. Darley really is tired. If I stay he'll want to talk some more about Ruddlemoor. It's my fault really, and I'm sorry, but he does know a lot about the works and I enjoyed talking with him. I'd like to come again soon, if you don't mind. Next time I'll try not to talk with him for so long.'

'He loves talking about the clay works – any clay works,' said Jo. 'Call on us any time you like. There's no need to let us know in advance. Just drop in whenever you feel like it. It's nice for Darley to have someone to talk to.'

When Ben left the house dusk was beginning to fall. Lily, Jo and Lottie had taken the sandwiches to the lounge at the front of the house – the house's 'front room', kept exclusively for visitors.

Through the window the women watched Ben walking away and Lottie said, 'He's a handsome young man. Reminds me somewhat of his great-grandfather. He was Ben too and I believe he set many a heart fluttering in his time.'

'Well, Ben Retallick doesn't make my heart flutter,' said Lily.

'I'm pleased to hear that,' said Simon Kendall, who was standing just behind her.

Lily had turned to speak to him when Jo said suddenly, 'Who's that talking to Ben on the corner?'

Something in her voice caused Lily to return her attention to the street outside and brought Jethro to the window.

Two men on the corner had moved so that Ben would be forced to step from the pavement to pass them by.

'I don't know their names,' said Lottie. 'But I've seen them before. They were both soldiers who fought in the South African war. I saw them earlier today. They were talking to Eddie Long.'

'Then Ben's in trouble,' said Jo, sharply. 'Eddie's convinced he's a Boer. He's going to need help.'

Without waiting to see if anyone was following her, Lily ran from the room and out of the front door.

Recovering from his initial surprise, Jethro ran from the house after his daughter. Simon Kendall was a somewhat tardier third.

Ben had enjoyed talking to Darley. He possessed a lively mind and was as enthusiastic about the China clay industry as was Ben himself. However, their talk had visibly tired the invalid and Ben suspected the sick man had a limited reserve of strength on which to call.

Ben also suspected, rightly, that Darley would not admit his physical weakness in front of him. As long as he remained in the house, Darley would not retire to bed, where he so obviously belonged.

Besides, Ben did not feel entirely at ease with the others in the house. It was nothing he could define, but he believed it might have something to do with Simon Kendall. He felt the man resented him.

Walking away from the house, Ben thought it would be quite pleasant to walk back to the Gover Valley on his own. It would give him time to gather his thoughts together.

Since arriving in Cornwall he had seen much that was new to him. Ruddlemoor posed a big challenge to the way of life he had known until now – albeit a welcome challenge.

As he approached the corner of the street, he noticed two men standing together. He took little notice until, as he drew near, both moved so he would need to step off the pavement in order to pass them.

It made little difference to him, so he stepped from the pavement to the road.

The two men also stepped on to the road, blocking his path once more.

They were barely an arm's length from him now and Ben stopped and looked at them. For a moment he thought they intended to try to rob him, but dismissed the thought immediately. They had obviously been standing here waiting for him to leave the Shovells' house.

He said nothing, waiting for them to speak. After glancing at each other, the older of the two men said, 'We want to talk to you.'

'I doubt if there's anything to talk about that couldn't be said at the Ruddlemoor works office. Come and see me there tomorrow.'

The man who had spoken looked at his companion, triumphantly. 'You hear that, Harry? You hear that accent? It's him, all right.'

Returning his attention to Ben, he said aggressively, 'We were fighting in the war in South Africa against men like you. A lot of our friends were killed or maimed.'

'I feel sorry for them. A lot of Rhodesians fought in South Africa. Many of them were killed or wounded too.'

'I never met any Rhodesians there. The only men we met who spoke like you were Boers – and we don't like Boers. In fact, we *hate* Boers.'

Ben breathed in the beer fumes as the man thrust his face towards him as he spoke. He realised that nothing he said would make any difference. These men had been waiting for him and were determined to make trouble.

He decided he would meet it head on. 'I don't suppose the Boers liked you either. So what? The war's over now.'

'Not for us, it's not. We're not going to have any Boers coming here and trying to lord it over us Cornishmen.'

Now Ben knew for certain this was no chance encounter. This meeting had been planned with the connivance of someone from Ruddlemoor – and he believed he knew who that someone was. 'I can see it's no use trying to talk to you. If you intend making trouble you'd better start now because I'm going past you.'

As Ben finished talking, he took a step forward. One of the men put out a hand to stop him.

Without further ado, Ben swung a punch that landed on the other man's nose and sent him staggering backwards.

He turned to face the other man and they collided. Too close to throw punches, Ben wrestled the man to the ground.

As they struggled, the first man returned and aimed a kick that landed on Ben's thigh. It was sufficiently painful to distract him and allow the man he was holding to wriggle free.

Help arrived in the form of a very angry Lily. Arms flailing and shrieking her wrath, she fell upon the man who was about to kick Ben for a second time. He retreated, holding his hands up to his face in a bid to protect himself from her clawing nails.

Jethro arrived upon the scene at that moment. Suddenly the odds were too great for the two young veterans of the South African war. They both fled as Ben climbed to his feet and dusted himself down.

'Are you all right?' The question came from Lily.

'I'm fine.' He grinned at her. 'Thanks to *you*. You were magnificent, Lily.'

'She was that,' agreed Jethro. 'But she has had practice. She and Darley once saved the Ruddlemoor wages from a whole gang of would-be robbers – but what was this all about?'

'They thought I was a South African and wanted to declare war all over again.'

'I know where they will have got *that* idea from,' declared Lily. 'I'll have something to say to him when I see him . . .'

'I think I know, too,' said Ben. 'And I'd rather you left it to me to deal with. But I'm grateful for your help. As a boy I learned how to fight with the Matabeles and I think I could have handled those two, but you saved me from taking a bit more punishment than I would have enjoyed.'

'Won't you come back to the house, clean up and settle your nerves before you return to Josh and Miriam's?' asked Jethro.

'No, I'd like to be back there before dark.'

'I'll come with you,' said Lily, unexpectedly. 'Just wait here for me while I return and say goodbye to Darley and Ma. I won't be a few minutes.'

As Lily returned to the house, Simon Kendall hurried after her. When he caught up with her, he said, 'You don't need to go back to the Retallicks' house just yet, Lily. I was hoping to walk back with you and have a talk about things . . . about us.'

It was what Lily had wanted for some time. To have Simon say something to her about the future. Now he had actually broached the subject, it no longer seemed quite so important.

Cuttingly, she said, 'I doubt if you'd be able to walk that distance, Simon. It took you so long coming from the house to the fight there's obviously something wrong with your legs.'

'So that's it! You've fallen for Ben Retallick.'

As they reached the door of Jo and Darley's house, Simon Kendall said, 'Don't get any high-and-mighty ideas about him, Lily. He's an ambitious man. You and he are worlds apart.'

'I'll work out my own ideas, thank you, Simon, and I don't think I need share them with you.'

'Please yourself, Lily, but remember what I've said. I may not be a fighting man, but I'm a patient one. I'll still be around when you've become disillusioned with Ben Retallick.'

Chapter 9

When Eddie Long lowered himself gingerly from the clay wagon which had given him a ride to work, he found Ben waiting for him. With the single crutch, which was all he now used, tucked firmly in his armpit, Eddie would have passed by the prospective owner of Ruddlemoor without acknowledging his presence.

Ben had other ideas. He came alongside Eddie, who immediately quickened his pace.

'You can go as fast as you like,' said Ben, sounding surprisingly amiable. 'If I haven't finished what I have to say to you by the time we reach the office, it can be said there, in front of others.'

Eddie knew Captain Bray was always in the office early. Reluctantly, he slowed.

'I met two of your friends last evening, Eddie. Like you, they seem to have a grudge against anyone they believe to be a South African. Again, like you, they are under the mistaken impression that I'm one.'

Eddie had not spoken a word since Ben caught up with him and he remained silent now.

'Your friends also believed they were going to give me a thrashing. Perhaps they thought they might persuade me to go back to Africa. They were wrong on both counts. I learned all about fighting among young Matabele men and boys. Zulus, Eddie. They learn to fight – really fight – so that one day they'll be warriors like their fathers. Part of the finest fighting force in the whole of Africa. I learned well from them, Eddie. Because of what I learned I've tracked Boer commandos and fought them when they raided our farm. Fought them face to face, not at a distance. How many men did *you* kill face to face, Eddie?'

When he still remained silent, Ben said, 'I'm not telling you this because I want to brag or to make an impression upon you. I'm not even trying to prove I'm as patriotic as you think *you* are. I really don't give a damn what *you* think. I'm telling you this to show you I don't scare easily – and I don't play at fighting. You can tell your friends I've come here to take over Ruddlemoor. I'm making Cornwall my home and I'm here to stay. The stupidity of you and your friends won't make me change my mind, Eddie. All that will happen is that you'll lose your job and your friends will end up hurt and with the prospect of long prison sentences ahead of them.'

They had reached the works office now and at the door Ben stopped. 'That's all I've got to say to you. Remember it. I certainly shall.'

Inside the office Captain Bray had been watching through the window and seen Ben and Eddie approach. He was aware that Ben was doing all the talking and could guess what it was about.

When Eddie came inside and went to his desk, the works captain said, 'I've heard what happened last night. I had intended giving you a very strong warning, Eddie. I might even have dismissed you. I believe you deserve it. However, it seems young Ben Retallick has probably said all that's necessary – for now. Whatever he said to you, I suggest you take it to heart. If you don't, you'll have me to answer to.'

It was a very subdued young man who sat at his desk to commence the day's work, but his discomfiture was not yet at an end.

Jo was the last to arrive and her greeting was, 'I want words with you, Eddie Long – and you're not going to like what I have to say . . .'

In a sudden outburst of anger, he said, 'If it's about what happened to Ben Retallick last night, I don't want to hear it.'

'I'm sure you don't – but you're going to. If ever there was a cowardly, unwarranted attack, that was it.'

'Look!' said Eddie, angrily. 'I can do without you raking over it again. I've had Ben Retallick and Cap'n Bray on my back already. I don't know anything about the attack. I wasn't even there.'

'You wouldn't have the guts to take him on even if you had both legs. You got others to do your dirty work for you. No, don't try to deny it. You knew he'd be at my house last night and my ma saw you talking to your two mates earlier in the day.'

Unable to contain her curiosity any longer, Tessa said, 'Will someone tell me what all this is about? What have I missed? Did something happen last night? I told you I should have come to your house, Jo . . .'

'Ask our war hero, here. He can tell you all about it while I go to collect the attendance figures from the "dry". They've forgotten to bring them to the office.'

When Ben arrived home from Ruddlemoor that evening, Lily greeted him with the words, 'There's a letter arrived for you.'

'That's good! Is it from Rhodesia?'

'No, from Tresillian. Isn't that where your travelling companions came from?'

Ben was startled. 'Her name was Lady Tresillian, so I suppose it probably is. Where's the letter now?'

'I put it on the table in the dining-room. I'll go and get it for you. I thought we'd be eating right away, but Josh and Miriam aren't home yet.'

'Where are they?'

'They've gone into St Austell to see Darley. I told them I didn't think he was too well last night.'

Lily left the room and returned with the letter. Handing it to him, she asked, 'Have you spoken to Eddie today?'

'I have.' As he spoke, Ben was opening the envelope she had handed to him.

'Well? What happened?'

'Pardon?' Ben had been reading from a gilt-edged card that had been contained in the envelope. Looking up suddenly, he said, 'Sorry . . . Nothing happened. I just put him right about a few things, that's all . . . Good Lord!' He appeared startled. 'Lady Tresillian has invited me to attend a welcome home ball at her home.'

'Well! Aren't we moving in exalted circles now? You've only been in Cornwall a few days and are already being invited to the homes of titled ladies! You'll be charging us to speak to you before long.'

Ben seemed not to hear her, but he was looking at her speculatively. Suddenly, he said, 'Will you come with me, Lily?'

'Me? Come to a society dinner with you? Why would you want *me* to go with you?'

'Because I can't think of anyone I'd rather have with me on such an evening.'

'You're just saying that to stop me teasing you, Ben Retallick. All right, I won't tease any more, if that will make you happy.'

'The thing that would make me happy would be for you to come with me.'

'You're definitely accepting then?'

'Yes. Will you come?'

Lily looked at him searchingly for a few moments. Then she said, 'I think you really mean it.'

'I do.'

'Thank you for that, Ben. I'm honoured. Very honoured indeed that you'd really take me to a ball with your titled friends, but the answer is no. I wouldn't be at home among such people. I wouldn't know what to wear, or what to say and do. I'd be unhappy and I'd only embarrass you.'

'You wouldn't. I'd . . .'

'No, Ben. Nothing you say would make me go there with you, but I really am flattered that you've even considered it. Now, sit down and I'll get your meal – if it isn't cooked to a cinder by now. Then you can tell me everything that went on between you and Eddie Long. I doubt if I'll get the true version from anyone else.'

Chapter 10

Ben's entry to the upper echelon of Cornwall society had a dramatic beginning.

The lodge to Lady Tresillian's estate stood beside the river which bore the family name. A tidal water, it curved its way between wide mud flats to join the Rivers Fal and Truro on their way to the superb anchorage that stretched inland from Falmouth.

Today there was an exceptionally high spring tide. It had turned in the last hour, but still lapped at meadow and woodland on either bank.

A number of village children and others from the house had gathered to watch the arrival of well-dressed gentlemen and bejewelled, immaculately attired women. Most guests were arriving in coaches and carriages of various sizes. Only a very few single men rode horses.

The horses and carriages had been arriving for half-an-hour, by which time some of the younger children had become rather bored with the proceedings.

As each coach arrived and slowed almost to a halt to enter beneath the arched gateway, the children would rush to catch a glimpse of the occupants. The moment this was achieved they would run back to the river bank and throw sticks and twigs into the dirty brown water, watching them swirl downstream with the outgoing tide.

A light carriage was ahead of Ben when he turned off the road and the children were already running back to the river bank as he reached the gate. Suddenly there was a shriek of alarm and a number of the children began screaming.

Turning in his saddle, Ben was in time to see the head of a frantically struggling little girl disappear beneath the surface of the water.

Reining in his horse, Ben pointed it towards the river bank, heading for a spot downstream from where he had last seen the girl. He was fortunate to see her arm appear briefly above the water, some distance from where she had gone under. It gave him an idea of the speed of the current.

Leaping from his horse, he flung off his jacket, kicked off his shoes and dived in the water.

It was colder than he had imagined, and the current was stronger, but luck was with him. As he came to the surface, so too did the child – and she was only just beyond his reach.

She went under again almost immediately, but when Ben reached the spot and dived beneath the surface his outstretched hand caught in her long hair.

She was still struggling, but her efforts were weak and spasmodic now. Dragging her to the surface, he struck out for the bank.

A number of men and women had joined the children on the bank, among them a couple of men who were obviously dressed for Lady Tresillian's grand ball.

When he reached the bank, Ben pushed the now limp girl towards the onlookers and she was taken from him and pulled ashore.

Moments later he too was hauled to dry land where he was thumped on the back by a number of appreciative onlookers. As he sat down to regain his breath, he heard the young girl he had rescued coughing and retching. Then she began to cry in a jerky, painful way and Ben sighed with relief. His rescue had not been in vain. She was going to be all right.

As he sat, head back, trying to recover his breath, a voice said, 'That was quick thinking, young man, and splendidly executed. The child owes her life to you.'

Ben looked up to see a tall, elderly man looking down at him. Dressed, as Ben had been, for Lady Tresillian's ball, the man looked extremely distinguished.

'You were on your way to Lady Tresillian's house, I presume?'

Ben nodded. He would not try to speak just yet.

'I'll take you to the house in my carriage. We'll bring your coat and shoes too. The gateman can bring your horse along later.'

'It would . . . be better . . . if I walked.' Ben's breath was returning now. 'Get the inside of the coach . . . all wet.'

The man smiled. 'That's all right. My wife and I can occupy one seat while you take the other. We'll get you to the house and see about finding something dry for you to wear. At least your jacket and footwear are dry.'

As he rose to his feet, Ben looked down at his trousers and shirt. Both were muddy and wet. It was not an auspicious social debut.

When they reached the very large house of Lady Tresillian, Ben was hustled in through a side door and taken upstairs to a guest bedroom. After a hastily prepared bath he emerged to find a selection of shirts and trousers laid out on a bed for him to try.

He found a suitable shirt and a pair of trousers that *almost* fitted. The addition of a bow tie, his own jacket and shoes meant that he was now ready to join his hostess and the other guests downstairs. The maid who conducted him from the room assured him that his own clothes would be washed and ironed by the time he was ready to go home.

The maid added, 'They're all waiting for you in the ballroom, Mr Retallick.'

Ben did not take any particular notice of her words, but they were brought home to him when he entered the high-ceilinged ballroom that was almost large enough to have housed a small African village.

As he entered the room, the orchestra subsided unevenly into silence. A liveried footman took the place of the maid and indicated that Lady Tresillian was at the far end of the ballroom.

As Ben followed the footman across the dance floor, the guests began to applaud. Ben thought it in appreciation of the orchestra. Not until they had formed two deep ranks on either side did he realise they were clapping *him*.

By the time he reached Lady Tresillian and her granddaughter, Ben's cheeks were a fiery red. His pleasurable embarrassment was not helped when his hostess greeted him with a hug and a kiss instead of the customary handshake.

'Well done, indeed, Benjamin,' she beamed. 'We've all been hearing how you dived in the river and saved a young girl. We're all extremely proud of you. You're quite the young hero.'

'Thank you, Lady Tresillian – but Deirdre must take some credit for it too, you know.'

She looked startled and Lady Tresillian said, 'Deirdre? But she was here at the time. How . . .?'

'When we were staying at Salisbury she assured me there were no crocodiles in English rivers. Had she not done so I might have thought twice before diving in today!'

Lady Tresillian still looked puzzled, but Deirdre was delighted that Ben had remembered their brief time together at Salisbury.

'Oh, well, it was a splendid thing to do,' said Lady Tresillian. 'We are all proud of you. Now, I'm sure you wish to meet some of our younger guests. Deirdre will remember their names far more readily than I. Off you go and have an enjoyable time. You have thoroughly earned it.'

The orchestra had begun to play once more. As couples took to the floor, Deirdre said, 'It was very brave of you, Benjamin. General Grove told us all about it.'

'General Grove?'

'General Sir Robert Grove. The man who brought you to the house in his carriage. I thought you must know him? He lives somewhere near you. He also owns some clay works.'

Ben expressed immediate interest in the man who had brought him to the house, and when he looked about the room for him he saw the general standing with a group of friends on the far side of the ballroom.

Ben remained with Deirdre for the next fifteen minutes. However, as people came up to congratulate him on his successful rescue, she became once more the girl he remembered on board the *S.S. Dungannon Castle*. Seemingly stricken dumb with shyness by the numbers of people about her, she made no attempt to introduce him to any of those who came up to speak.

Only when Ben spoke to her did she raise her glance from the floor and look up at him, her eyes as lively as they had been during their sojourn at Salisbury.

After a particularly attractive, albeit effusive, young lady had spoken to him, Ben reminded Deirdre that her grandmother had said she would introduce him to the young men and women in the room.

Suddenly distressed, Deirdre said, 'I *can't*, Benjamin. I hardly *know* anyone myself. Grandmother thinks that because she knows so many people in the county, and they all know her, that it is the same for me. It isn't. Grandmother has kept me away from people. Tonight is probably the first occasion most of them have met me.'

Deirdre seemed so distressed Ben thought she was about to burst into tears at any moment. 'I . . . I'm sorry, Benjamin. I'm the last person you should be saddled with on your first social occasion in Cornwall.'

'Nonsense,' he said, cheerfully. 'To be perfectly honest with you, I'm extremely flattered that Lady Tresillian should consider me as a suitable companion for her granddaughter – but I have a confession to make to you.'

Deirdre looked up at him with an apprehensive expression, and Ben said hastily, 'I can't dance. I just don't understand the first thing about it.'

Relief flooded Deirdre's face and on the spur of the moment, she asked, 'Would you like me to teach you the basic steps?'

'I would be very grateful to you if you could.'

The floor was extremely crowded, despite the great size of the room, but the guests made room for them when they made their way to the floor.

Deirdre felt very light and fragile as he held her in his arms, but he soon discovered that dancing did not come naturally to him.

After apologising on three occasions for treading on her feet, he felt relief when the dance came to an end. The sight of Deirdre dancing gave one of the young men in the room courage to ask her to dance with him and he claimed her as they left the floor.

Somewhat at a loss as to what he should do next, Ben found he was standing close to General Grove and his friends. At that moment the general saw him and beckoned to him.

As Ben approached the party, the general smiled and said, 'I'm pleased to see they were able to fit you up with a pair of trousers, young man. You look a damn sight more presentable than when you crawled out of the river. All the same, you did well. Damned well.'

His sentiments were echoed by the other men in the group.

212

Embarrassed, Ben said, 'With all that was going on, I feel I didn't thank you as I should. It was very kind of you to bring me to the house in your carriage. I couldn't have been the most acceptable of passengers.'

'Nonsense, my boy. We were delighted to be able to help.'

After a brief silence, the general asked, 'Are you by any chance related to Joshua Retallick, owner of the Ruddlemoor China clay works?'

'I'm his grandson.'

'Ah! I thought you might be. I'd heard he was bringing a young grandson from Africa to take over Ruddlemoor. So that's you, eh?'

'That's the idea, but I have a lot to learn first. Grandfather won't hand Ruddlemoor over until he's satisfied I know what I'm doing.'

'That shouldn't take you too long, my boy. You have a good mentor in Captain Bray. I've tried to get him to come to work for me on more than one occasion, but he's too damned loyal. However, where are my manners? Allow me to introduce you to my friends. Most of our little group here are involved in the China clay business. Some, like your grandfather, came to it through mining. It's a more stable business, certainly.'

'I've already formed the opinion that it might be even more stable if each clay company worked with the others instead of against them,' said Ben boldly, deliberately seeking a reaction.

Some of the men exchanged glances with each other, but no one made any comment while introductions were being made all round.

While this was going on the music stopped once again. Ben never even noticed, he was too busy trying to memorise the names of the men in General Grove's circle. All were men he would one day be dealing with as friends – or rivals.

He was not aware of Deirdre leaving the dance floor. She walked towards him before she noticed he was engaged in conversation. After hesitating for a moment, she turned away.

Ben would have liked to stay longer with General Grove and his friends, but the impression grew that he had interrupted a business discussion between the men.

Ben was interested in what was being discussed, but General Grove said, 'We mustn't monopolise you, young man. If you don't hurry you'll be pipped at the post for the company of that very attractive young lady you're with. Come and pay a visit to my works sometime. If I'm not there then give me a call at home. Damned useful gadgets, these telephones. I wish we'd had them when I first joined the army. They would have changed the course of many a battle, I can assure you.'

Chapter 11

When Ben reluctantly left General Grove and the other clay works owners, he went in search of Deirdre. She was not where he expected her to be, although he could see the young man with whom she had been dancing, and her grandmother. She was with neither of them.

After a while, he found himself by the table where they were serving drinks and snacks. As he accepted a drink, one of Lady Tresillian's senior footmen who was standing beside the table, said quietly, 'Are you looking for Miss Deirdre, sir?'

'Yes. Do you know where she is?'

'I saw her leave the ballroom through one of the French windows on the far side of the room, sir.'

'Was she alone?'

'Oh, yes, sir. Miss Deirdre's not a great one for company, even on such a splendid occasion as this. That's why it was such a pleasure for us all to see her enjoying your company so much, sir. I'm quite sure Lady Tresillian will be delighted if you were to find her and bring her back here.'

The footman could hardly have been more charming, yet Ben realised there was a hidden criticism of Deirdre in his words. She was, after all, joint hostess of the ball with her grandmother. She should not have left the house and her guests.

Outside the French windows was a long terrace, extending for almost the whole length of the rear of the house. The terrace was surrounded by a stone balustrade. Beyond this was a sharp drop to an extensive lawn that extended well beyond the area illuminated by lights from the great house.

There were a number of seats and tables here, many of them occupied by young men and women undeterred by a cool breeze blowing in from the south-west.

It was not very well lit, but there was sufficient light to see – and to be seen by. One of half-a-dozen young girls sitting at one of the nearby tables called to him, 'Are you looking for somewhere to sit? We have room for you here.' She indicated a vacant chair beside her.

The girl's forwardness had been fuelled by the amount of drink she had consumed. The expressions on the faces of a couple of her companions showed amused disapproval.

Ben grinned, 'Keep the place for me in case I come back.'

As he walked away he heard the giggles of her more inhibited friends, but there was still no sign of Deirdre.

After searching for a while longer, he decided she must have returned to the house. He was actually on his way back to the ballroom when he glimpsed a light-coloured dress in a corner of the terrace where the lights did not quite reach.

He turned to look and here, almost hidden by luxuriant shrubbery, he found her. Part of the balustrade had broken away and she was seated on the stonework with her legs dangling over the side.

Ben had the quiet tread of a man who had spent a great deal of his time tracking game in Africa and dropped to a seat beside her before she knew he was there.

'Surely you can't have had enough of the ball after only two dances? Mind you, my efforts were enough to put a girl off dancing for a lifetime, I'll give you that.'

His sudden arrival startled her and she exclaimed, 'I didn't expect anyone would find me here.'

'Don't you want to be found? I would have thought this to be a special occasion for you. Your very own ball.'

'Not really, it was Grandmother's idea.'

'All the same, you can't just wander off as though there was no one else around.'

'I came looking for you but you were busy talking to General Grove and the other men.'

'Yes, I'm sorry about that, but I discovered we all share a common interest in China clay. It's the first opportunity I've had to meet and speak to other owners.'

'You'd better go back and talk to them, then. I am quite all right out here.'

'I can't do that, Deirdre. They know I came looking for you. If I go back alone they'll think we've had a quarrel – and that would set them gossiping. I suppose I'll just have to remain out here with you. Mind you, all your guests will probably imagine far worse things if we both disappear for too long.'

'I've already told you to return to the house, if you want to.'

'So you have.'

Ben made no move to leave. Instead, he said, 'It's an unfair world really, isn't it?'

'Why?' Her face turned towards him and he could just make out the puzzlement on her face.

'Well, we'll sit out here for a while, talking in all innocence of nothing in particular. After a while we'll go back inside. If we've been missed then your reputation will be in tatters, while mine will receive a considerable boost – at least, it will among all the young men in there.'

Deirdre was quiet for a while and then she said, 'Did my grandmother send you to find me? Are you taking her side against me?'

'No to both counts. I'm on *your* side, Deirdre.'

'Do you mean that, Benjamin?'

'I certainly do.'

'All right, let's go inside again, but I honestly don't enjoy occasions like this, do you?'

Helping Deirdre to her feet, Ben replied, 'I can't really answer that. This is the first ball I've ever attended.'

'Honestly?!' There was astonishment in Deirdre's voice.

'Honestly. The closest I've ever come to an occasion like this was when I was invited to a coming-of-age ceremony for some of the Matabele girls in our compound, in the Insimo Valley. There was a lot of dancing there, but the music was a little wilder and the girls certainly weren't as well dressed as you and your friends . . .'

Lady Tresillian was a wily and very observant old woman. She had seen Deirdre leave the house and correctly guessed the reason why.

She had also observed Ben leaving and knew exactly how long he had been outside. It was not long enough to cause a scandal, or indicate irresponsibility on his part. It had been just long enough to confirm to the shrewd old hostess that Ben had the ability to influence her granddaughter as no one else could.

She was pleased too to see that Deirdre was laughing happily as she came through the door with the young man. Her granddaughter had laughed all too infrequently in recent years. Ben Retallick was good for the girl. He might not be a member of one of the more established Cornish families, but the fact that he was a 'colonial' could be used to excuse this failing. Besides, there was aristocratic blood on his mother's side of his family, albeit *foreign* aristocracy.

He was also a very wealthy young man. That would compensate for any shortcomings in his blood line – and Deirdre *was* a very difficult young girl.

All in all, Lady Tresillian decided that Benjamin Retallick might prove to be quite acceptable as a husband for her granddaughter.

Chapter 12

'What time did you get back from your party last night – or should I say this morning?'

'I don't know. Somewhere around two o'clock, I think.'

This was a deliberate lie. It had been after four o'clock before Ben returned from Tresillian.

Lily sniffed her disapproval. 'You're going to feel like death warmed up all today. I hope it was worthwhile?'

'It was. I met a number of the clay works owners there.'

'So? You could have met them by just riding to their works. You didn't need to stay up all night just for that.'

'It wouldn't be the same. Meeting them somewhere like Lady Tresillian's house puts everything on a different footing, somehow. Makes it all more friendly.'

'If you believe that then Ruddlemoor will soon be in trouble. There are a lot of clay workings around St Austell. Competition between them is fiercer than you'd find in a wagonload of fighting cocks. I've no doubt they're friendly enough when you meet them at some society ball. Most would be so delighted to be invited they'd be on their best behaviour. But when it comes to business you'll find it a different story. They'll cut your throat as soon as look at you. You ask Great-uncle Josh. He's managed very well for all these years without getting too friendly with any of the other owners.'

'I know he has, Lily. In his time he's put new ideas into practice before many works owners had even heard of them, but he's probably the oldest owner in the business now and methods are changing quicker than ever before. If we're not careful, we'll be left behind.'

'My, we are ambitious, aren't we? And all this before we've been in the business long enough to tell the difference between a barrow-load of clay and a heap of spoil! But you're the clever one, I'm only the cook.'

Lily had intercepted Ben coming downstairs and now she asked him, 'How many eggs do you want with your breakfast?'

'None, thanks. I'll just have toast and a cup of tea.'

Josh entered the room in time to hear Ben's breakfast order and he grinned. 'It must have been quite a ball if you can't face bacon and eggs this morning. Mind you, when you're beaten home by the sun it's difficult to work up an appetite much before midday. I heard you come in.'

'It seems the sun must have come up early this morning,' said Lily, stiffly. Giving Ben a frosty look, she stalked from the breakfast room, heading for the kitchen.

'Have I said something wrong?' asked Josh as his stiff-backed niece passed from view.

'No.' Ben looked sheepish. 'It was me. I told Lily I thought I must have arrived home at about two o'clock.'

Josh looked at him thoughtfully as he sat down at the table. He was not particularly concerned about the small lie Ben had told to Lily. He was more interested in the reason *why* he had lied to her. It was a matter he would discuss with Miriam when they had a quiet moment together.

'General Grove and several other clay works owners were at Lady Tresillian's ball. The general suggested I should call on him at his works some time. Have you ever been there?'

'I've never felt a need to go there,' replied Josh. 'It's known to be one of the more efficient workings, but it has a bad labour record. It's said the general insists things are run along military lines. Either the men do exactly as they're told, or they're out. I've heard them grumbling that he'd introduce flogging if he had his way.'

'Is that so? Nevertheless, I think I'll pay a visit there sometime.'

Aware of Josh's disapproval, he added, 'I'd like to see as many works as possible. The more I know about the China clay business, the better I'll be able to understand its problems.'

'True,' agreed Josh. 'But have a word with Jethro before you go. The general won't have Union labour at the Grove works, but so many complaints have been made about it that Jethro probably knows as much about the works as the men employed there.'

A couple of days later Ben was at Ruddlemoor when Josh's odd-job man rode from the Gover Valley to say visitors were at the house to see Ben.

Sitting in the office, Ben was puzzled. 'To see *me*? Who are they?'

The odd-job man shrugged. 'They didn't come and make themselves known to me. I'm just the one Mrs Retallick sent to come and fetch you. All I can tell you is that it's a well-dressed young woman, another not a lot older, and a young child. They all arrived in a carriage, the likes of which we don't often see around this way.'

When Ben had gone from the office, Tessa said mischievously, 'Two young women and a child, eh? Could this be some of young Master Ben's past catching up with him, d'you think?'

'He's not old enough to have *that* sort of a past,' retorted Jo. 'They are probably friends he made on the way to England.'

'Tomorrow's past is today's fun,' declared Tessa. 'And I'd be more than happy to provide *that* for our young master-to-be.'

'You're showing all the symptoms of a frustrated woman,' said Jo, scornfully. 'The best thing you can do is find yourself a man.' Looking pointedly at Eddie, who had remained silent, she added, 'I suggest you find him well away from Ruddlemoor.'

'A fat chance I've got of that,' said Tessa, bitterly. 'I'm here for most of my working hours, and so tired when I get home I'm not fit for anything.'

Suddenly more cheerful, she said, 'Mind you, there was a very attractive young man from the Varcoe workings came here to deliver a letter yesterday. I've never seen him before. I'll have to make some enquiries and see if any of the men know anything about him . . .'

Chapter 13

When Ben reached the Retallick home in the Gover Valley he realised immediately that the carriage standing outside the house belonged to Lady Tresillian. The coat-of-arms on the door was a duplicate of the one above the fireplace in the entrance hall at Tresillian House. But who could the passengers be? Two young women and a child . . .?

Part of the mystery was solved when he entered the lounge and saw Deirdre seated there. Josh, Miriam and Lily were also in the room, but he failed to recognise the other two, neither of whom was dressed as expensively as Lady Tresillian's granddaughter.

Deirdre greeted him with a warm smile that was not lost on either Miriam, or Lily, but it was Josh who spoke.

'Here's the hero himself! Why didn't you tell us of the adventure you had when you went off gallivanting the other evening?'

Ben had a glimmer of understanding. Although he did not immediately recognise the small girl with Deirdre and the other woman, there was something familiar about her. But this was a clean little girl, wearing her best dress. He believed that the last time he had seen her she was bedraggled and half drowned, weeping on the bank of the Tresillian river.

'I forgot.' His reply brought a chorus of disbelief.

'I'm glad to see you looking fit and well,' he said to the child who clung shyly to the other young woman.

Crouching down before her, he said, 'I don't even know your name, do I?'

'It's Sapphi — that's short for Sapphire, sir,' said the woman. 'Sapphi Smith. I'm Ann Smith, her mother. My husband is a gardener at Tresillian House. Lady Tresillian very kindly let Miss Deirdre bring me here to say "thank you" for saving Sapphi from the river. I do thank you, sir, from the very bottom of my heart. If you hadn't dived in the river to rescue her, I don't dare think of what would have happened.'

Tears welled up in her eyes as she said, 'We'd have lost her, sir. For sure we would.'

Highly embarrassed, Ben said, 'Well, it's all ended happily, I'm pleased to say. Sapphi looks well enough now, even though she's too shy to speak to me.'

'Me and my Tom, that's Sapphi's father, would like you to take this, sir. As a keepsake to remind you of how brave you were. It's a very small token of our gratitude.'

It sounded like a speech that had been well rehearsed and she handed Ben an unwrapped tan pigskin wallet.

He was about to protest that he could not possibly accept such a present from the woman. It was a very fine wallet and must have cost her and her husband far more than they could afford. Then he saw the expression on her face and realised this was a very important moment in her life.

'You shouldn't have done this, you know,' he said. 'But it's a truly magnificent wallet. I shall treasure it and think of Sapphi every time I use it. Thank you.'

Beaming with pleasure, Ann Smith said, 'Miss Deirdre helped me to choose it for you, sir. You'll find a threepenny piece inside because Tom says it's unlucky to give anyone a wallet without money inside.'

'Then please give my thanks to Tom too.'

The presentation over, there was a short and slightly awkward silence before Deirdre spoke for the first time since Ben had entered the house. 'Now Ann has expressed her gratitude and delivered her gift, I suppose we should be returning to Tresillian.'

'You can't come all this way just to say "Hello", "Here you are", and "Goodbye"' declared Josh. 'Besides, you're the first friend Ben has made since coming from Rhodesia. Have you ever been to China clay country before, Miss Tresillian?'

Deirdre shook her head. 'No.'

'Then you must let Ben show you around Ruddlemoor. I'll have Dick Lowe get the pony and shay ready. He'll take you there.'

'Ann and Sapphi can stay with us until you come back,' said Miriam. 'It's a delight to have a young child in the house. I've always felt it's something this house needs. I doubt if there's been a child in the place for more than fifty years.'

'If Miss Tresillian is going to Ruddlemoor she'll need something different to wear. She'd better come upstairs and borrow something of mine.'

Lily's offer surprised even herself. In truth, she felt jealous of this well-dressed, well-bred and rich young woman. Jealousy was not a familiar emotion for Lily, but Deirdre Tresillian had so many material advantages. Enough, certainly, to turn the head of a young man like Ben.

It was with a sense of shock that Lily realised that *he* was at the root of her jealousy. She had fallen for Ben Retallick!

In her bedroom, Lily found a dress, cloak, and a pair of rather well-worn boots to fit Deirdre. 'It's not exactly what you're used to,' said Lily. 'But you'll find them practical when you're tramping through mud and wet China clay.'

221

'What fun!' exclaimed Deirdre. 'And what a charming room you have.'

Lily looked at the other girl quickly, but there was no hint of derision in Deirdre's expression.

'Are you a member of the Retallick family?' asked Deirdre, a little too casually. She remembered that Lily had been at St Austell station with the others on the day of Ben's arrival. It was apparent to her that although Lily did much of the fetching and carrying in the household, she was not a servant.

Lily realised the other girl was trying to establish her position in the household and it amused her.

'I'm a distant cousin of Ben's,' she said, non-committally.

'Do you live here with Mr and Mrs Retallick?'

'I've been running the house for them for the last couple of years. I enjoy it.'

'It must be wonderful to have the freedom to decide for yourself what you're going to do with your life.'

Deirdre spoke wistfully, but Lily found it difficult to pity her.

'I need to work. I'm fortunate to have found something I enjoy doing, with people like Miriam and Josh. Most other people need to do whatever work is available.'

Deirdre thoroughly enjoyed her visit to Ruddlemoor. She found pleasure in the mud and dirt and noise and bustle of the works. It was all the more pleasurable because she had never before been allowed to do anything like this.

As they walked back towards the office from the quarry, Deirdre said, 'This has been a wonderful day, Ben. I've enjoyed having you show me around Ruddlemoor, and also meeting your grandmother and grandfather too. They are lovely people.'

'Yes, I think so.'

'I like Lily too. She's very kind.'

It was a hesitant attempt to learn Ben's feelings for the girl who had loaned her the clothes she was wearing.

'Don't you think she's nice?'

'Yes, but she can be quite fierce too. She came to my aid when I was being attacked by two men. I'd only been here a couple of days.' Ben told Deirdre of the attack on him by the two ex-soldiers.

She was appalled. 'That is quite dreadful, Benjamin. The men should have been arrested and thrown in prison.'

She glanced sideways at him as they walked. 'Things *do* seem to happen to you. Hardly anything ever occurs in my life.'

'There are some things I'd rather not have happen to me.' He met her glance. 'What about the couple you were telling me about? The tutor and her husband?'

Deirdre looked away. 'They've left Cornwall.' After a moment's hesitation, she added, 'Grandmother was right, you know. I was so unhappy. So lonely . . . he could easily have taken advantage of me. I realise that now.'

'Your grandmother is a very astute woman.'

'I'm glad you think so. She is extremely impressed by you. She's suggested you might like to accompany us to the Duchy ball being held in Truro in a few weeks time. She's invited you to stay at Tresillian afterwards.'

'That's very kind of her. Would you like that too?'

'I'd like it very much,' she replied without looking at him.

'Then I'm happy to accept.'

She gave him one of her rare, happy smiles. 'Of course, I hope we'll see you again before then.'

They walked on in silence for a few more minutes before Deirdre said, hesitantly, 'I enjoy being with you, Benjamin. I can talk to you. Tell you things. How I'm feeling . . .'

'I like being with you too, Deirdre.' As they spoke they passed through a narrow gap between small railway wagons, turned on their side for repair. As they moved closer together their hands touched and her fingers gripped his hand momentarily.

It was a small gesture of affection on her part, but when she released her grip she would not look at him.

Ben realised she was probably growing fond of him. He had told her he *liked* her and this was perfectly true. However, he was not yet certain whether he wanted things between them to go beyond that stage.

Chapter 14

Over the next few weeks it became increasingly obvious to Jo that Eddie and Tessa had become lovers. It was none of her business, but she was concerned. For Tessa it was merely one more in a long string of liaisons. It meant nothing more to her than the thrill of the moment. But Jo realised it was more than this for Eddie. For all his expressed worldliness and having fought in a war, he was inexperienced with women – especially those like Tessa. He was taking the affair far more seriously.

Jo said nothing until one lunchtime, after the affair had been carried on for some time. She had left Ruddlemoor to call in on the wife of one of the workers who lived in a cottage close to the works. The woman was expecting a baby any day.

However, when Jo arrived at the house she found the woman's mother and other members of the family with her. Jo returned to Ruddlemoor, arriving much earlier than expected.

There was a frantic scramble as she opened the door. Inside the office Tessa was straightening her skirt, while Eddie balanced precariously against the desk, facing away from the door, fumbling with his trousers. Jo felt it was time she issued a warning to the amorous couple.

'Look, I don't care what you two get up to when you're away from Ruddlemoor, but I have no intention of making a noise or knocking at the door before I enter this office – and I don't like feeling embarrassed because I know I'm disturbing something. Do you understand?'

Reaching out for the crutch which leaned against a wall, Eddie growled, 'You're just bitter and jealous because you're getting nothing. It's high time you remembered what a man – a real man – was like.'

Jo rounded on him and for a moment it seemed she might strike him. Indeed, she stood before him, her nostrils flaring angrily. 'If you dare say anything like that again, Eddie Long, I'll cripple your other leg. Ill as he is now, Darley is more of a man than you ever were when you had two legs. Just because you've been wounded in a war doesn't make you a hero in my eyes. It could just as easily have happened in an accident in this country. I don't believe you've ever fired a shot in anger. If you did, it was no doubt while you were running away. Simply putting on a uniform wouldn't have changed you from the man and boy you used to be. You were despicable then and you haven't changed a bit.'

Turning her back on him, Jo said to Tessa, 'I'm going to check the loading figures. If you've any sense you'll find something to do outside the office too. You can do better than Eddie Long, Tessa.'

When Jo had left the office, an unrepentant Eddie said, 'I seem to have annoyed her.'

'You've annoyed me too, Eddie. Darley's a good man and Jo's been a friend for many years. If you're going to go around saying things about either of them then I don't want any more to do with you either.'

'I was only joking with Jo. She took it the wrong way, that's all.'

'Then you can say sorry to her when she comes back to the office.'

Eddie pulled a face. 'I might . . . if I thought she'd accept it, but she won't.'

'You'll say it all the same, unless you want me to go off you as well.'

Eddie shrugged. 'All right, if it's going to keep you happy. Not that you'd give *me* up, Tessa Bolitho. I've got too much of what you need.'

'Don't you be so sure of yourself. There are plenty of men in the world willing to run after me – and they can run a sight faster than *you*!'

When Ben had been in Cornwall for some months, Josh called a meeting of the workers at Ruddlemoor. The clay works had expanded over the years. Now, with three pits working, it employed three hundred men and women.

They gathered outside the office. Speaking from the top of the office steps, Josh made his announcement: when Ben reached the age of twenty-one, Ruddlemoor would become his.

Until then, Ben would assume full responsibility for the day-to-day running of the works. Josh would not leave the scene entirely; at least, not immediately. He would remain in the background, acting as an advisor – but only until Ben came of age.

Every one of the Ruddlemoor workers had been aware since his arrival that Ben would one day be the works owner. Nevertheless, the news was given a mixed reception. One of the reasons was that Eddie Long's constant and bitter resentment of Ben was beginning to take effect.

Few of the men and women who worked at Ruddlemoor had travelled any farther than a few miles from their homes. The geography of their own county was a mystery to them. African geography was as mysterious as that of a star in the Milky Way.

Eddie Long was one of their own. If he said Ben Retallick was a Boer, they were prepared to accept it.

Ben knew there was some resentment against him in the works and, when Josh had made his statement, took his place at the top of the steps and gave the Ruddlemoor men a brief address.

'I'm very grateful to my grandfather for allowing me to take over

225

Ruddlemoor. I've spent some months now learning what goes on. I know it's going to take me a lot longer than that. During my time here I've managed to speak to most of you and I believe Ruddlemoor has a happy and efficient workforce. In fact, I'd say Ruddlemoor is better than any works in the whole area.'

The declaration brought a few cheers at least. Encouraged by this, he said, 'It's my hope that we'll continue to expand, as we have during my grandfather's ownership. We *must* expand if we're to remain at the top. We must also embrace change, because we're living in exciting times and many of the changes will make life easier for all of us. The one thing I do want to assure you of is that every one of you here is as important to me as you always have been to my grandfather. Without you, Ruddlemoor wouldn't be the great clay works it is today. I want you to always remember that. I certainly shall.'

Beside Ben, Josh said something and Ben leaned towards him to catch his words. Straightening up once more, he said, 'My grandfather has asked me to say something else to you. To celebrate my taking over Ruddlemoor, and as Summercourt Fair opened yesterday, tomorrow will be a holiday for everyone. Wagons will be leaving for the fair at eight o'clock in the morning, returning at eight tomorrow night.'

Ben's earlier words had received a mixed reception, but news of the day off and transport to Summercourt Fair brought forth a great roar of approval.

Retreating to the office, Josh said, 'That was a good speech, Ben. It should have reassured them at any rate.'

He shook his head. 'They cheered at the news that they were getting a day off to go to Summercourt Fair. I don't think they're too keen on the idea of my taking over as owner.'

'They are suspicious of change, Ben. That's all it is. Once you take over, you'll be all right. Give them a couple of years and they'll have forgotten they once worked for *me*.'

'I hope you're right. Now I've committed myself, I'm determined to keep Ruddlemoor in profit. It's a good works. I intend that it will be an example to every clay works in the district.'

'I don't doubt it will be, Ben, but bide your time. Don't rush into anything, and when you tackle something new take the men along with you. When you get down to it it's *them* who will make or break Ruddlemoor – and they'll make or break you too.'

Chapter 15

'So you're running Ruddlemoor now? Does that make you happy?'

Lily asked Ben the question that evening as she busied herself in the kitchen of the Retallicks' Gover Valley house. Ben sat at the table, drinking a cup of tea.

'It's why I came to England in the first place. And, yes, it does make me happy. Ruddlemoor is a fine clay works. All the same, I want to increase its profits. From all I've heard we're doing better than most but one bad year will cancel out all the profits of the last three. Two bad years and half the works in the district will be forced to close down. What it needs is for all the clay owners to get together and not try to undercut each other. That way spells ruination for all of us.'

'I'll take your word for everything you say. All I know is that Ruddlemoor has always been a good works. A happy place – at least, since Jim Bray has been captain.'

'I hope it's going to stay that way, but sometimes I get the feeling the men and women working there resent me. It's probably because I've come here from Africa with little knowledge of Cornwall – and suddenly I've got the power to control a large part of their lives.'

'You're too sensitive, Ben. They haven't fully accepted you yet, that's all. It would be the same whoever took over Ruddlemoor – and somebody would have had to do it very soon. Josh couldn't have held on for very much longer. Besides, people always resent someone who has more than they have. I don't suppose you learned very much about that when you were living at Insimo?'

'There are so many things I didn't learn. About Cornwall especially. For instance, what goes on at a fair?'

'You're asking about Summercourt Fair? Well, that's something special. It's held once a year and people come there from miles around. There'll be all sorts of amusements and entertainments; things for sale; food of every sort. It's great fun! Miriam's given me the day off so I can go.'

'Can we go together?' Ben asked, eagerly.

Some of Lily's enthusiasm faded. 'I'd like to say yes, Ben, but I've already promised Simon I'll go to the fair with him. Besides, we'll be travelling in one of the Ruddlemoor wagons. It might not be such a good idea for you to be on the wagon with us, especially on the way back.

227

Most of the young men will have had too much to drink and if there is any resentment among them, they might make things unpleasant for you.'

'Yes. You're quite right.' Ben was deeply disappointed, and it showed.

'Perhaps we could meet up at the fair and you could come around with Simon and me?'

'I don't think that would meet with Simon's approval, somehow. No, it's all right, Lily. I probably won't go.'

Josh decided that Ben *would* attend Summercourt Fair. He travelled there in the Retallick shay, in company with Jim Bray, the Ruddlemoor captain, driven by the Retallicks' handyman.

Jim Bray would not normally have attended the fair, but Jo was going. Lottie and Jethro thought it was time she took at least a brief break from taking care of Darley. They would spend the day and evening with their son. Jo would travel to Summercourt on the wagons with Tessa and the bal maidens, and would meet up with her father at the fair.

Ben and the works captain found Jo waiting impatiently for them when they finally reached the fair. The pony and shay had been held up on the road by the sheer volume of traffic. The Summercourt Fair was one of the highlights of the Cornish calendar and it seemed to Ben that most of the county's inhabitants were attending.

Jo had not known that Ben would be accompanying her father and greeted him somewhat uncertainly. She was even more disconcerted when, no more than ten minutes after their arrival, her father saw one of his fellow clay works captains and left her with Ben.

'You don't mind, do you?' he said to Ben. 'I haven't seen Charlie Grigg for a year or two and I'd like to learn what his company is up to.'

Jim Bray did not wait for a reply and a moment later Ben said apologetically to Jo, 'You don't have to stay with me. If you'd prefer to be with Tessa . . .' He had seen Tessa and some of the younger bal maidens in the company of Eddie Long and a group of young men.

'Tessa's the *last* one I want to be seen with! My reputation *would* be in tatters if I were seen without Darley, and in her company!'

'But it's all right to be seen with me?'

The question seemed to take Jo by surprise. 'I don't see why not. After all, we are related, in a distant way. Besides, I'm a lot older than you.'

There was possibly six or seven years' difference between them, but Ben decided not to make an issue of it. Instead he said, 'Well, I hope you're not too old to go on one of those roundabouts? I've never even seen one before. They look like fun. Come on, we'll just make it before it starts up again, if you're quick.'

Once again Jo tried to plead her age, but Ben would not listen. Grabbing her hand, he forced her to run with him to the roundabout. They clambered aboard just as the owner was warning the other riders to hold tight in preparation for the beginning of the ride.

The ride was much faster than Ben had expected it to be. It seemed it was also too fast for Jo. She screamed as loudly as any of the other girls on the roundabout.

Too busy trying to keep her dress down and her hair in some sort of order, Jo did not see Lily staring up at her from the crowd gathered about the roundabout. It was a look tinged with envy. Lily too had wanted to ride on the roundabout, but Simon Kendall would not take her. He felt it would be undignified for him to be seen on a roundabout . . .

Ben helped Jo down from the wooden dragon on which she had been riding and she clung to him for a few moments, giddy from the experience of whirling around and around in tight circles.

'That was fun!' exclaimed Ben, happily. 'Would you like to go on again?'

'Never!' declared Jo, vehemently.

'Then we'll go and enjoy a good haunting instead,' he declared, and promptly led her by the elbow to a marquee. Daubed with lurid posters, it invited all those with sufficient courage to enter the tent and sample the thrills of a haunted house.

Once again, Jo was hustled inside despite her protests. It was another deliciously frightening experience for her and she came out chattering as excitely as any young girl.

There were many other fairground entertainments to be enjoyed and Ben was determined to miss none of them. The 'human skeleton'; a bearded lady; two-headed calf; fire-eaters; jugglers; knife-throwers. The fair was filled with new experiences for Ben. He seemed intent upon sampling them all – and sharing them with Jo.

When they met up with Lily and Simon, Jo was red-faced and breathless after just sharing a boat-swing with Ben. 'I swear he was trying to make the thing turn a complete circle,' she said breathlessly. 'Are you having a good time, Lily?'

'It's all right. I suppose one fair's the same as another, really.' Her reply was far from enthusiastic.

'Oh, no. I think this is one of the best fairs I've been too. They seem to be better than when I last went.'

Suddenly, Jo's face contorted as she fought with an unhappy thought. 'The last time I went to a fair was with Darley. I wish he'd been well enough to come to this one. He'd have loved every minute of it.'

'Perhaps he'll be well enough to bring you next year?' said Ben, in an attempt to cheer her. 'If he is, you'll enjoy that even more. Now . . . I want to visit the boxing booth. Shall we all go?'

'I have no intention of paying to watch two men beat the living daylights out of each other,' declared Simon, immediately. 'I never used to enjoy it when it was provided free outside the London public houses, when I first joined the Trades Union movement.'

'I'm going to give it a miss too, Ben,' said Jo. 'But you go. I'll stay with Lily and Simon for a while, until I meet up with Pa again.'

Ben looked from Jo to the boxing booth. He felt he would be deserting her. She was enjoying the fair and he doubted whether Simon was capable of making her forget for a brief while the sadness that lay in store for her with Darley.

'I didn't know you were interested in boxing,' said Lily.

'I've been enthusiastic about it since I was a small boy. I was taught to box by Selous, the hunter – the man who accompanied Grandad Retallick to Rhodesia on his last visit. Selous learned at school, I believe. Then an ex-prizefighter stayed with us at Insimo for a while. He taught me and some of the Matabele to fight and I used to spar with them quite often. More recently, I sparred with a South African on the boat. He was coming to England for a world championship fight. I enjoy boxing very much. Will you come in with me?'

For a moment, Lily was tempted. She had never seen a boxing match. But then she saw the expression of disapproval on Simon's face.

'No, I don't think I will.'

'You go on your own, Ben. I'll meet up with you somewhere around the fair afterwards.'

'All right. I'll catch up with you later.' Ben had seen the look Simon had flashed at Lily. He had believed Lily to have cooled towards the Trades Union man recently. He was not to know she was fulfilling a long-standing promise. He wondered how serious their relationship was. He hoped it was no more than a passing romance. Lily deserved far better than the sober-sided Trades Union official.

Chapter 16

A showman stood on a platform outside the huge canvas boxing booth. In a voice coarsened by years of shouting and seasoned with an excess of gin, he tried to coax the crowds to come inside. Here, he promised, they would witness the fighting prowess of 'some of the finest fighters in the land – no, in the *world*'.

Ben paid a shilling, the canvas flap doorway was held to one side, and he entered the noisy, smoke-filled interior.

Spectators surrounded a ring set up on a platform in the centre of the great tent. A fight was in progress between a squat, powerfully built, balding man and a slow, cumbersome giant.

The smaller of the two men was a fairground fighter, the other a fancied local man. It was a one-sided contest. The big man had strength and courage, but he was no match for the vastly more experienced professional.

The Cornishman plodded doggedly after his opponent, being stopped every couple of paces by the taunting, accurate jabs of the other man. The blood from his nose mingled with that from a cut lip, but the shouts of his friends – and everyone in the booth seemed to be his friend – kept him on his feet.

Suddenly, at a signal from his corner, the fairground pugilist ceased retreating. Taking the Cornishman by surprise, he moved forward and lashed out with a barrage of well-aimed, skilful blows.

The Cornishman rocked back on his feet and in a few more seconds the bout was brought to a close. A left-handed blow to the stomach from the fairground fighter folded the bigger man over. A vicious uppercut almost straightened him up again, then his legs buckled and he crashed to the ground.

The fight was over and a groan arose from the spectators.

As friends of the defeated man lifted him from the ring, another fairground boxer climbed into the ring. Lighter and smaller than the previous fighter, he looked to be extremely fit.

A bowler-hatted man now took the centre of the ring and lifted two hands, calling for silence. When he had the attention of the spectators, he called, 'I think you will agree, that was a splendid fight. A gallant challenger, and a worthy champion.'

There was sporadic applause from the watchers, but the fairground boxing promoter was already issuing a fresh challenge. Pointing to the boxer who had just entered the ring, he shouted, 'You see before you one of the newest of my boxers. Bombardier Wright, fresh from the British Army. How good he is . . . I don't even know.'

Ignoring the jeers of his audience, the promoter continued: 'He might be a great find for me . . . he might cost me a fortune. I'm willing to take a chance on him. How about you?'

There was little reaction from the crowd, none of the men meeting the promoter's glance as it swept about the tent.

'Come along now. There must be someone in the crowd willing to take his chances with this inexperienced young fighter. It's a chance to go home with a pocketful of money. *Five* pounds to the man who can last three rounds with Wright. *Fifteen* to anyone who can beat him. Knock him out for the count of ten and you'll go away with *twenty* pounds. More than most men earn in three months. Come along now, who's willing to test his skill against my boy?'

Bombardier Wright danced about the ring, shadow boxing, but still there were no takers.

'Come along, you have my guarantee you won't be hurt . . .'

This remark was greeted with derision by the crowd. The big Cornishman had been the fourth to be carried from the ring that evening.

'All right! All right! I tell you what I'll do. I'll raise the prize money. *Twenty* pounds to anyone who can beat him. *Twenty-five* for a knock-out. Not only that, if a man lasts for three rounds and knocks Bombardier Wright to the canvas just once, I'll double his prize money to ten pounds. Now, is that generous or isn't it? Come along, young gents. Who'll take my man on for a prize that's better than you'll find in any other boxing booth in the land?'

'I will.'

Ben took up the challenge, without knowing quite why he was doing it. Bravado, perhaps. A need to prove himself in front of a Cornish crowd . . . especially those Ruddlemoor men who were here. He was not even certain himself. But as he pushed his way through the crowd hands reached out to pat him on the back.

'Good lad!' said the promoter. 'You look a likely contender.' Behind him Bombardier Wright paused in his prancing and eyed Ben as he climbed to the ring.

'Who are you, son? What's your name?'

'Ben Retallick.'

From somewhere in the crowd there was a sudden buzz of excitement and he heard his name repeated.

'That's a good Cornish name, if ever I heard one. Where are you from?'

Insimo would have meant nothing to anyone here. Rhodesia would have been equally obscure and he would not use the address of Josh and Miriam.

'Ruddlemoor. I'm from Ruddlemoor.'

There were many clay men among the spectators and the name brought a cheer.

'Well, you've got some friends here to cheer you on, son. Now. Listen carefully while I tell you the rules of the fight. Then you can strip to the waist, put on a pair of gloves, and the fight will begin . . .'

Outside the boxing booth, news of the impending bout between Bombardier Wright and the new owner of Ruddlemoor was spreading with astonishing speed.

Jo, Lily and Simon were walking slowly together when they saw Tessa, Eddie and a number of Ruddlemoor workers hurrying towards them.

Tessa paused to say, 'I thought you'd be in the boxing booth with everyone else from Ruddlemoor.'

Lily looked puzzled. 'Why?'

'Don't you know? Ben Retallick's going in the ring with one of the fairground boxers.'

Jo and Lily looked at each other in disbelief.

'Come on, Tessa,' said Eddie, irritably. 'This is one fight I don't want to miss. It's high time Mr Retallick got his come-uppance.'

Leaning heavily on his single crutch, Eddie swung away, pushing his way through the crowd.

'What on earth does Ben think he's doing?' asked Jo, in alarm.

'I don't know, but I'm not staying here while someone tries to knock his head off. Come on, Jo.'

Lily and Jo hurried away without asking Simon whether or not he was coming with them. Reluctantly, almost sulkily, he brought up the rear.

The man taking the money at the boxing booth did not know what had caused the sudden influx into his tent, but he made no complaint. The boxing booth had been doing reasonable business at the fair so far, but the present interest was totally unexpected. There were a number of women among the customers too and this was also unusual.

Almost every one of those eager to pay their money and enter the tent was a Ruddlemoor employee, but the boxing booth proprietor could not know this.

By the time Lily and Jo passed into the tent the first round had begun. The fairground fighter came out of his corner with a rush, hoping to catch his opponent off guard.

Ben side-stepped him easily and slipping past his guard got home a couple of crisp punches, but they were not very heavy blows.

After another minute it was evident to Lily that the spectators were almost equally divided in their support for the two fighters. Those who were not Ruddlemoor men were for Ben. Those who were, seemed to be against him.

Ben seemed to be holding his own in this first round until he misjudged his timing and a heavy blow caught him on the side of the face and staggered him.

There was a roar from the spectators as Wright moved in after him. Ben slipped inside the other man's blows and clung to him. By the time Wright extricated himself Ben had recovered sufficiently to defend himself until the bell sounded for the end of the first round.

There was an immediate roar from the spectators. This was the first fight of the day which had gone beyond the first round. It was also the most exciting.

Suddenly, Jim Bray put in an appearance beside Lily and Jo. 'What's going on? I've just been told that young Ben Retallick is in the ring with the fairground boxer. I thought he was looking after you, Jo?'

'I didn't want to come in here. He did, so he left me with Lily and Simon and came in here on his own. Mind you, he didn't say anything about wanting to *fight*. If he had I'd have tried to stop him.'

'I don't think Ben would take any notice of you, or anyone else, if he really wanted to do something,' said Lily. 'Besides, I think there's more in this than wanting to fight. I think it's his way of getting the Ruddlemoor men to look up to him.'

The others looked at Lily quizzically and she felt obliged to explain, 'It's been difficult for him, coming in to the business from outside Cornwall. He's very young and he's not one of them. I think he wants to prove something to them.'

'If that's what it's about then he's failed miserably,' said Simon, spitefully. 'The Ruddlemoor men are cheering the other man.'

'Then we'll need to do something to bring them over to his side,' said Jim Bray. As the bell rang for the commencement of the second round, he cupped his hands to his mouth and shouted, 'Come on, Ben Retallick. Remember you're fighting for Ruddlemoor.'

Many faces in the crowd turned towards the works captain for a moment, but then the fight began once more.

During the interval the fairground boxer had been ordered to go out and finish Ben in this round. He came out of his corner determined to carry out his instructions. Instead, he walked into a barrage of punches. Ben too was determined to bring the fight to a close – but in favour of himself.

For at least a minute the two boxers stood toe-to-toe in the centre of the ring, swapping punch for punch, and the spectators were roaring their approval. Both men carried a hefty punch and for the second minute they were somewhat more circumspect. Then the fairground boxer swung a blow that landed decidedly low.

With a grimace of pain, Ben dropped to one knee. The other fighter should have stood back until he recovered his feet. Instead, he struck two more blows, knocking Ben to the canvas.

The howl of protest from the spectators could be heard all over the fairground – and it came from the Ruddlemoor men now, as well as the others.

The sound was heard in every corner of the fairground, rising above the music of the roundabout and the shouts of the barkers. It drowned the rapid count of the referee too. Despite this, Ben rose to his feet before ten fingers were held in front of his face and he spent the remainder of the round evading the onslaught of his eager opponent.

During the brief interval before the third and last round, Ben did his best to gather his senses and recover his wind.

Bombardier Wright was desperate to finish the fight now and in the third and last round he tried every trick, fair and foul, that he had learned during a hard apprenticeship as a fairground pugilist.

For half the round Ben ducked and weaved, retreating before the other man's attack. Then, without warning, he stopped. Standing his ground, he launched his own attack on the other man. He put every ounce of power and all the skill he had learned in Africa into the punches he threw.

One of them landed flush on the chin of the bombardier and he sagged at the knees. Another punch to the side of the jaw knocked him down.

The spectators in the boxing booth went wild with delight and Lily's shrill, excited voice could be heard above their jubilation.

The shouting did not die down until it became apparent to everyone that the referee was giving the fairground fighter a count that would give him at least thirty seconds to recover and rise from the canvas.

The cheers changed to howls which increased when Bombardier Wright staggered to his feet only to have the clamour of the bell bring the contest to a close at least twenty-five seconds before it should have been ended.

However, their anger turned to cheers when the proprietor of the boxing booth made a great show of congratulating Ben and handing over ten pounds. He was greatly relieved that he was not parting with twenty-five.

Ben was aware that the proprietor was offering him a place in his entourage, but now he had made his point, he was eager to leave the ring.

Ducking between the ropes, he dropped to the floor and made his way towards the entrance. On the way he had to run a gauntlet of spectators, many of them Ruddlemoor men.

'You were robbed, Mr Retallick.'

'You should have won.'

'He ought to have been counted out when you had him down.'

The comments of the men were accompanied by a pummelling of his back that dealt him almost as many blows as had Bombardier Wright.

Before he reached the canvas-flap door, he was confronted by Jo and Lily, with Captain Jim Bray standing behind them.

Ben was surprised to see them here, in the boxing booth, but was riding high on the knowledge that he had acquitted himself well in the ring. He grinned at them. 'If I'd known *you* were here watching me, I'd have fought harder and made certain of him when I put him down.'

Lily suddenly gave vent to her feelings. 'From what I saw earlier you're lucky it wasn't *you* being carried from the ring. What on earth got into you?'

In truth, she had been scared for him until the final minutes of the last round. Then she had screeched encouragement more loudly than anyone else.

'I knew what I was doing,' Ben lied. 'I realised I had the beating of him after the first minute.'

Before Lily could say any more, Jo said, 'You weren't only fighting Bombardier Wright. The referee and timekeeper were on his side too. But we'd better find some water and a cloth. If I don't clean up that face for you, you'll have a hard time convincing Josh and Miriam that you *won* a fight.'

Chapter 17

Behind one of the many fairground beer-tents, Jo dipped Ben's own handkerchief in a bowl of water, squeezed out the excess water and began cleaning his bruised and grazed face.

'I've done this before. When Darley first came to work at Ruddlemoor. He'd gone to St Austell to collect the men's wages, taking Lily with him. On the way back with the money they were set upon by a gang of would-be robbers. He and Lily saw them off, but his face was worse than yours.'

'I didn't know Lily went in for such violence,' said Ben, squinting at the girl in question, hoping he was not going to develop a black eye.

'The difference with me and Darley was that we were doing it for Ruddlemoor,' retorted Lily.

'Oh, and what was different today? Unless I'm mistaken Ben went into that ring for the same reason,' said Jo.

'How do you make that out?' retorted Lily.

'Well, it's been clear just lately that he wasn't getting the respect he deserved from the men at Ruddlemoor – due largely to having Eddie Long poison their minds against him. Today Ben became one of them – and every man and woman who works there will be proud to tell others they work for Ben Retallick of Ruddlemoor. It was a clever move, Ben – but a risky one. Had you lost it would have been a different story.'

'But I didn't lose – and I came close to winning.'

He took the handkerchief from Jo as she began drying his face. 'Thanks. That feels much better. Am I too much of a sight?'

'No, you'll do.' She smiled at him. 'I'll tell you something, though. You can thank Eddie Long for rescuing you from Tessa. She got herself all excited seeing you fighting. Had he not been there she'd have latched on to you for sure and there would have been no escape. The scandal would have undone all you've achieved today.'

Lily made a disparaging noise. 'I'm glad things have worked out so well for *you*. I doubt if Simon will ever speak to *me* again. He says I made a spectacle of myself by shouting so loudly in the boxing booth.'

She had spoken without thinking. Now realisation of what she had said brought the blood to her cheeks.

'In that case, I'd say Ben deserves to make it up to you,' said Jo. 'There's my pa coming now. I'll go off with him. It's a long time since he and I spent a few hours together. It'll be a treat for both of us. Ben's a glutton for fairground punishment. He can take you on all the rides he made me go on – and all the others I refused. You've got far more energy than me.'

Lily protested, albeit not too vehemently, but Ben said, 'That sounds like a very good idea. There's no reason why your day should be entirely spoiled because you supported me. Come on, Lily. Let's start with the shooting gallery. I'll win one of those dolls for you . . .'

Because of Lily's over-enthusiastic support of Ben in the boxing ring, Simon Kendall had determined to leave her to her own resources for a while in order to demonstrate his displeasure.

He fully expected her to come and find him and apologise for her behaviour. He would forgive her, of course, but not until he had pointed out that a man in his position needed to maintain a dignified demeanour at all times.

The Trades Unions were working hard to consolidate the gains for which they had fought and suffered during the nineteenth century. At the next General Election they hoped to be represented in Parliament by a strong Labour Party. One day they would come to power in a bloodless revolution destined to change the shape of British politics for ever.

Simon Kendall intended to play an important part in that future. He would not allow accusations of frivolity to be levelled against him and spoil his chances.

He continued to believe Lily would come to her senses – until the moment he saw her accompanying Ben on the roundabout. Head thrown back, she was laughing uninhibitedly. Thoroughly enjoying the childish ride. At that moment he realised he had lost her for good this time. Suddenly the fair lost all its appeal for him. He left the ground and set off on the long walk back to St Austell.

Along the way he thought of what had happened and became consumed by an increasingly bitter hatred. It was aimed not at Lily, but at Ben Retallick. The young man to whom life had given everything without demanding anything in return.

He epitomised all that Simon Kendall most hated. Men who by an accident of birth were more privileged than himself. Simon enjoyed opposing such men whenever and wherever he encountered them. It was the reason he found it so easy to throw himself wholeheartedly into the Trades Union cause and convince fellow members of his dedication to their movement.

Ben took Lily on the roundabout and gave her the ride she had wanted so much earlier in the day. She also sampled many of the other fairground pleasures denied by her more staid escort.

Once or twice she felt a twinge of conscience about Simon, but

238

refused to allow it to spoil the day. He had chosen to go his own way. She had not walked off and left him on his own.

It was late evening before Ben decided he would call it a day and return home.

'I'll go and find Jo,' he said to Lily. 'I expect she'll be wanting to leave by now and get back to Darley. But there's no need for you to go until you're ready. You can return on a wagon with the others.'

'No, I've had enough,' said Lily. 'It's been a wonderful day, Ben. The best fair day ever – thanks to you.'

'I've enjoyed it too. It's been a day to remember – but here's Jo now.'

She was ready to go home, so too was Jim Bray. They agreed with Lily and Ben that it had been a marvellous fair day.

'Everyone from Ruddlemoor says the same,' added the works captain. 'Mind you, that fight of yours had a lot to do with it for them, Ben. Ruddlemoor men are walking tall as a result.'

'I doubt if Josh and Miriam will be as pleased,' commented Jo, touching a graze high on Ben's cheekbone. 'Still, I've seen worse. There's just enough there to remind folk at Ruddlemoor of Summercourt Fair for a few days, at least.'

The pony and shay took Jo home to St Austell first of all. Before leaving she gave Ben a quick kiss on the cheek, thanking him for giving her such a fun-filled day.

'Give my regards to Darley,' said Ben. 'Tell him that next year we'll all go to Summercourt Fair together.'

'If I thought that was a possibility I'd be the happiest woman in the world, Ben,' said Jo as she went in through the garden gate of the house she shared with her sick husband.

Jim Bray was also being returned home in the shay. Ben and Lily dropped off close to the entrance to the Gover Valley and walked along together in the darkness.

'I'm glad Jo had such a happy day,' said Lily. 'She doesn't have much in life to cheer her these days.'

'I'm pleased too. She's a very nice person. Caring for Darley day after day must place a dreadful strain on her. Can nothing be done for him? I'd be very happy to help if it was felt there was someone who could offer him any chance of a cure.'

'That's a very kind offer, Ben, but he's been seen by all the doctors who claim to be experts on lung sickness. There was a Swiss doctor somewhere up on the Mendip Hills in Somerset who offered a faint hope that he might do something. The trouble was he wanted Darley to stay there for about a year. It was Darley himself who refused the offer. He's no fool, Ben. He knows he's living on borrowed time now.'

'I'm sorry for Darley, for Jo – and for you too. I know how close

239

you've always been. Josh has mentioned it many times.'

They walked in silence for a while before Lily said, 'Don't let's think about unhappy things tonight, Ben. It's been a wonderful day, although you're going to feel your bruises tomorrow. You were absolutely mad to go into the ring in that boxing booth. Mind you, it certainly brought everyone at Ruddlemoor on to your side – with the possible exception of Eddie Long, of course. But even he will need to hold his tongue for a while.'

Ben grinned in the darkness. 'It's the best day I've had since coming to England, thanks to you and Jo.'

'Better than the ball you went to at Tresillian?'

Lily did not bring Deirdre's name into the conversation, but the aristocratic young girl was in her thoughts as she asked the question.

'Lady Tresillian's ball and Summercourt Fair can't be compared, Lily. Today I could be myself and think of nothing but enjoying the day. At Lady Tresillian's house I needed to be on my best behaviour, aware that people were watching me, summing me up. Perhaps it was the same today, really, but I could still relax and enjoy myself. All the same, when I was at Tresillian I met some people who will be important to Ruddlemoor in the future.'

Breaking off the conversation for a few moments, he resumed it by saying, 'That reminds me, I must follow up the invitation from General Grove. It might prove to be important to the future of the China clay industry as a whole.'

'Oh, Ben! You're *impossible*.' Suddenly and unexpectedly, Lily linked her arm with his. 'Forget Ruddlemoor. Forget China clay. It's a moonlit night and you've just enjoyed a lovely day at Summercourt Fair.'

'Yes, and now I'm walking home in the moonlight with the most attractive girl I've ever met. You're right, Lily. There's a time and a place for everything. Just at this very moment I think it's the time and place for this.'

Bringing Lily to a halt, he turned her to face him and then he kissed her.

Lily tried to convince herself that he had taken her by surprise, but she knew it was not so. She had been half expecting – half *hoping* – this was what he would do.

She could have stopped him *before* he kissed her. Instead, she allowed it to happen and it was some moments before she broke away.

'No, Ben. We mustn't.'

'Why not, Lily?'

'You must *know* why not. We're both living under the same roof, at Josh and Miriam's house. If there was anything going on between us it would cause a scandal that would do nobody any good. Besides, it could only cause a lot of unhappiness for both of us if we were to grow fond of each other.'

'You're too late, Lily. I'm already fond of you.'

'Don't fool yourself as well as me, Ben. It's moonlight, you've had a happy day – and I'm *here*. By the time morning comes you'll have recovered your senses and I don't want you to have anything to regret.'

'I still don't see . . .'

'Yes you do. You're the new owner of Ruddlemoor and one day you're going to be a force to be reckoned with in the China clay industry. In Cornwall too, I've no doubt.'

'So? You're a relative . . .'

'A *poor* relative. I'm employed in Josh and Miriam's household. A servant.'

When Ben began to protest, Lily cut him short. 'I don't want to argue with you, Ben. Shall we talk of something else and go on as we were before, or walk home separately, in silence?'

Ben's grin was visible in the moonlight. 'That would probably make me feel at home. In Africa you'll see the women walking behind their men, but they're usually balancing something on their head too. All right, you can take my arm again and I'll try not to get any more romantic notions – for tonight, at any rate. But this isn't the end of it, Lily Shovell. I promise you that.'

Chapter 18

Darley Shovell died the day before Ben was due to attend the Duchy ball in Truro with Deirdre Tresillian.

The news was brought to the Retallick house at breakfast-time by Jethro and broken to Lily with the Retallicks and Ben present.

'Last night he told Jo he'd had a very happy day and was feeling better than he had for many weeks. This morning she went to his room and he'd gone. Died in his sleep as peacefully as could be wished. Your mother's at the house now, Lily. I thought you'd like to go there too.'

'I'll fetch a coat . . .' Ashen-faced, Lily fled from the room.

Ben met her coming down the stairs as he went up to his room. The tears had not yet begun, but her distress was clear to see.

'I'm very, very sorry, Lily. Please give my sympathy to Jo and your mother too. I'll call at the house when I feel I won't be getting in the way. In the meantime, if there's anything I might do . . .'

Lily swallowed hard and nodded, before hurrying past him to the hall where her father waited for her. When they had left the house together, Miriam said, 'We'll give the family an hour or two together before we call on Jo.'

Josh nodded. He had known Darley as well as any man. Had given the sick young man work when he would not have found it elsewhere.

'I'll go to Ruddlemoor and break the news to Jim Bray,' said Ben. 'He'll want to be with Jo. I'll call in at the house about midday. I'd only be in the way of family if I called any earlier.'

Despite her faults, Tessa Bolitho was a warm-hearted girl and she shed genuine tears for Darley after Jim Bray left the office.

'Poor Jo,' she said, accepting the handkerchief proferred by Ben. Dabbing at her eyes, she said, 'She'll be inconsolable. She fell for Darley the first time she ever saw him and there was never anyone else for her.'

'She'll find life a lot easier once she's got used to not having him,' said Eddie Long, unfeelingly. 'She might realise what she's been missing all these years by having an invalid husband.'

'It's people like you who are missing out on life,' said Tessa, rounding on Eddie. 'Because you're incapable of loving anyone as much as Jo and Darley did. They found more happiness together than you ever will, Eddie Long.'

'I shall be going to see Jo at midday,' said Ben to Tessa. 'I'll take you along if you'd like to come.'

'Thank you.' She handed back the damp handkerchief. 'I'm glad someone around here has feelings.'

By the time Ben and Tessa arrived at Jo's house, Miriam and Josh had both left. Jo was doing her best to hide her grief and Ben's heart went out to her. He gave her a warm hug that would have raised eyebrows on any other occasion.

It was in sharp contrast to the cold formality shown by Simon Kendall when he came to the house. He offered only stilted condolences to the whole of the Shovell family.

Ben had thought the young Trades Union official would take the opportunity to make up his quarrel with Lily. Instead, Simon was even cooler towards her than he was with any of the others.

It seemed that others had noticed it too. Simon did not remain at the house for every long. As he left, Tessa said softly to Ben, 'I'm not sorry to see the back of *him*. I've seen more emotion on the face of a pilchard down on Mevagissey quay! I don't know what Lily sees in him.'

'Not a lot at the moment,' said Ben. 'I don't think she's forgiven him for his behaviour at Summercourt Fair.'

'If *you've* got any sense you'll step in before they make it up, or before someone else steps in to snap up young Lily,' said Tessa in a moment of rare generosity and selflessness. 'She's got more about her than any other young girl you're likely to meet up with in Cornwall — and that includes all the fine ladies you've met at places like Tresillian House.'

Shortly afterwards, the subject of their conversation came and spoke to Ben.

'Let me know when you're leaving to come home. I'll come with you.'

'I thought you'd be staying with Jo. She'll need someone here with her tonight.'

'I think Ma's going to stay with her. Besides, Miriam and Josh need someone too.'

'You needn't worry about them. They've got the granddaughter of their handyman coming for today and tomorrow.'

'I don't think that's such a good idea. She's done some work at the house before and proved to be a disaster.'

'Yes, Miriam did say something of the sort, but she'll be all right for this one night. You stay here, Lily, and try to persuade your ma to go home. I think you'll be able to provide the sort of comfort Jo needs tonight.'

When Lily had left them to go and speak to her mother, Tessa said, 'You're very fond of Jo, aren't you?'

Aware that Tessa was an incorrigible gossip, Ben said, 'Yes, I am. Had I been lucky enough to have a sister, especially an older sister, I'd have liked her to be just like Jo.'

When Lily returned to the Gover Valley the following evening she was as surprised to see Ben as he was to see her.

'What are you doing here? I thought the grand Duchy ball was on in Truro tonight?'

'I couldn't go, not with all that's happened, and with the funeral tomorrow.'

'Everyone would have understood. You said yourself how important it was to you, and to Ruddlemoor.'

'I'm sure it would have been, but I can see the other clay owners some other time. But why have you come home? I thought you would stay with Jo until after the funeral.'

'She wanted to be on her own tonight.'

'I think I can understand her feelings,' said Ben, sympathetically. 'I remember very clearly when they brought the bodies of my pa and Wyatt home. My brothers and I went to bed eventually, but Ma stayed up all night. She spent the whole time praying in front of the little altar she had in her room.'

'That must have been a dreadful time, Ben. I remember how upset Miriam and Josh were when the news reached us here. I was a very young girl then and never did really understand what had happened, but I can remember their grief.'

'It was one of those tragedies that should never have happened. People in that part of Africa are still arguing about who was to blame. Pa had been friends with the Matabele king and his people for very many years. In fact, it was the king who gave Insimo to us. But there had been a lot of dishonesty and misunderstanding between the Matabele and Rhodes. Eventually, the Matabele rose in rebellion. One of the sons of the king was jealous of the influence Pa had with him and the uprising gave him the opportunity to kill Pa. Wyatt died trying to help him.'

Lily shuddered. 'At least poor Darley died peacefully. Rhodesia sounds a horrible place.'

'No, Lily. It's an absolutely beautiful country. I'd very much like you to see it one day.'

He paused, his thoughts very many miles away from the Gover Valley. 'Africa is so vast and so different to anything you've ever known that it's difficult even to attempt to describe it to you.'

He looked at Lily once more. 'But Africa isn't like England. It doesn't always give a person a second chance.'

244

Chapter 19

The weather on the day of Darley Shovell's funeral was as sombre as the occasion with the sun well hidden behind low, grey cloud. It was a 'walking' funeral, the cortège setting out from the house on foot behind the coffin. This was borne by four of the men Darley had once saved from the Notter mine and two men from Ruddlemoor. The workers of Ruddlemoor had been given the day off as a mark of respect for Darley and many of them followed family and friends in procession.

It was the first such event witnessed by Ben. He was very impressed by the homage paid by mourners and those who stood along the route. The Shovell family were highly respected in the small market town and residents came out of their houses to line the pavements. Behind them, shops were closed for the passing of the procession and every house had its curtains drawn.

Many years before, the teachings of Wesley had greatly influenced the residents of the town and the impressive Methodist church to which the coffin was taken reflected the grip the young religion had once held.

The church was filled to capacity for the simple but moving funeral ceremony. After sending Darley's soul winging heavenward to enjoy eternal life, his coffin was lowered to the darkness of the damp and cold earth while those who had known and loved him shed their tears.

Miriam complained that the graveside ceremony had thoroughly chilled her even though the weather was quite mild. After only a half-hour at the Shovell house after the funeral, she asked Ben to take her home. Josh and Lily would follow later.

Wrapping a blanket about her knees in the open shay, Ben flicked the reins and the pony set off at a gentle trot.

'That's better,' said Miriam as they drove from the street where the Shovell house was situated. 'I can't stand funerals. Never could. I prefer beginnings to endings. A wedding, no matter how simple, pleases me far more than the most elaborate funeral. Talking of which, I'd like to see young Lily settled down before it's my turn to go.'

'You'll outlive us all, Grandma,' replied Ben, hoping to by-pass the dangers inherent in this particular conversation. 'I've heard people say you're virtually indestructible.'

Ben had a very easy relationship with Miriam. He could chide her in a manner which no one else would dare to contemplate.

'No one's indestructible,' she retorted. 'That's why we all need to get on with enjoying life – and the best way to do that is to find someone you want to share it with.'

'I'll remember that, Grandma.'

'I'd be happier if you acted on it instead of committing it to memory. Memories are for when you reach my age. Young Lily's going to be a good catch for some young man, Ben. Far better than all the hoity-toity friends you've made since coming to Cornwall, I can assure you.'

'I wouldn't argue with that. I happen to think Lily's a very special girl too.'

While this discussion was taking place they had turned in to the Gover Valley. The pony knew it had only a short way to go before it was unharnessed and turned out in a field so speeded up its gait. By the time Ben had managed to slow the animal, the Retallick house was in sight. Outside stood a carriage and pair.

'Talking of hoity-toity friends, haven't I seen that carriage somewhere before?'

'It looks as though it's the one belonging to Lady Tresillian.'

'What's she doing in St Austell today of all days?'

As Ben brought the pony and shay to a halt, the Tresillian coachman walked back from the house, where he had been knocking futilely at the door.

The occupant of the carriage heard the pony and shay come to a halt and a head appeared from the open window. It was Deirdre.

'What are you doing here?' asked Ben, somewhat ungraciously.

Opening the carriage door and stepping to the ground, she said, 'I was so upset that you didn't come to the ball that I just had to come here and find out what was wrong.'

'Didn't you get my message? I telephoned and spoke to Lady Tresillian . . .'

'Grandmother said you couldn't come . . . for family reasons. That was all.'

For the first time Deirdre seemed to notice that both Ben and Miriam wore mourning clothes. 'I'm terribly sorry, Benjamin. Has there been a bereavement?'

'Yes. We've just come from the funeral of Lily's brother.'

'I'm sorry, Benjamin. I really am. I shouldn't have come here.'

'Well, you're here now,' said Miriam. 'You'd better come inside. I'm ready for a cup of tea. I don't doubt you could do with one as well.'

'I won't stop. Please accept my apologies for intruding on such a sad occasion.'

'If you want to use formal words then write them on a postcard and send them to Ben. I've had enough of people being all stiff and starchy today. Poor Darley was never one to stand on ceremony. He was a warm and caring young man. He'd have been as impatient with all this

246

pomp and ceremony as I am. There's a lot to commend the Methodist Church, but when it comes to funerals they're as long-winded as the Church of England. Let Ben help you out of that carriage and come inside. I'll go ahead and put the kettle on.'

Miriam hurried up the path to the house and as Deirdre was handed out of the carriage by Ben, she said, 'Your grandmother has very strong views about life, doesn't she? In her own way she's quite as positive as my grandmother.'

'She's never been one to mince words,' he agreed. 'But she's a wonderful woman. One day I'll tell you the story of her life. It will make your hair stand on end.'

'I'd love to hear it,' said Deirdre. 'But before we go inside, can I ask you to accept an invitation to join a shooting party and stay at Tresillian next weekend? Please say yes. Grandmother found someone to partner me to the Duchy ball when we learned you couldn't come. If you don't come to Tresillian for the weekend she'll ask him instead. Please come.'

'I'm not quite sure what's happening,' said Ben. 'I will if I can . . .'

'General Grove is going to be there. So too are a number of his friends from this area. You'd find it very useful, I am quite certain.'

Ben thought quickly. It could be just the opportunity he had been seeking. A chance to talk to the other clay owners in relaxed surroundings.

'All right, I'll be there.'

'Oh, Benjamin, that's wonderful! It makes me so happy.'

In the house, Deirdre behaved with all the correctness that had been instilled in her by her tutors and by Lady Tresillian herself.

When it was time for her to leave, she apologised once more for arriving uninvited on a day when the family were in mourning.

Ben escorted her outside to her waiting carriage. Here she reminded him once more about the weekend shoot at Tresillian and he reiterated his intention of being there as a guest.

Once in the carriage, Deirdre waved from the open window until the vehicle disappeared from sight around a bend in the Gover Valley road.

Back inside the house, Miriam moved away from the window and was seated in her favourite chair by the time Ben came in.

'She's a very pleasant young woman, Ben, for all she's county aristocracy.'

'Yes, she is quite nice.'

'Is that all you have to say about her? How serious are you about that young lady, Ben?'

'Not very serious at all, really. I like her, but I wouldn't rate my feelings as being any more serious than that.'

'Then be careful, Ben. Very careful – for her sake, if not for your own. Unless I'm very wrong, that young lady is seriously smitten with you.'

Chapter 20

When Ben arrived at Tresillian House for the weekend shooting party he carried a new shotgun, purchased only the day before.

He was met by a servant who took gun and saddlebags, promising that his clothes would be ironed before being placed in his room.

No sooner had the luggage and horse been taken than Deirdre came bounding down the steps to meet him with an enthusiasm that brought frowns of disapproval from two women alighting from a nearby carriage.

'I'm *so* pleased to see you, Benjamin. I was afraid you might not come today.'

'I said I would.'

'I know, but I had chosen the time of my visit to you so badly I thought you might decide to change your mind.'

Seemingly aware for the first time of the two women who had disembarked from the carriage and were now standing with their husbands, Deirdre said, 'I must go and meet some of the other guests, Benjamin. I doubt if I'll see much of you for the next hour or so, but I'll be with the other women bringing food out to you on the shoot.'

An hour and a half later, Ben was standing at the edge of a wood, nursing his new shotgun in the crook of his arm. Beside him was General Sir Robert Grove.

'Have you done much shooting, young Retallick?' The general's voice carried to each of the armed men who stood in a long line at the edge of the wood.

'Not this sort of shooting.'

'Never mind, you'll soon catch on and you're in good company. Don't shoot at the bird when it's too close to the ground and be careful not to shoot one of the beaters.'

Calling to someone farther along the line, the general's voice boomed out, 'Remember that "colonial" we had with us a few years back, Charles? Came from Trinidad or some such place. Went back to the house bragging that he'd enjoyed the finest day's shooting he'd ever known. Damned chap shot a peacock, a beater's dog, and peppered a gamekeeper's backside!'

When the general's chortling subsided, Ben said seriously, 'I'll try not to do the same, sir.'

As they were speaking, the first bird came whirring noisily from between the trees.

The general called, 'He's mine . . .' but before he raised the shotgun to his shoulder, Ben had fired. As the sound of the shot echoed through the wood the bird's wings stopped beating and it plummeted to the ground.

General Grove was somewhat peeved, but farther along the line a couple of men called out, 'Good shot!' and Ben acknowledged their praise with a cheerful grin.

A few minutes later everyone in the shooting party was blasting away at pheasants as the birds fled the cover of the wood in ones, twos and small coveys.

Behind the birds, beaters and gamekeepers created a continuous cacophony of sound. Shouts, bugles, whistles and barking dogs drove the birds before them to almost certain death. The din continued until the first of the beaters emerged from the trees, when all firing ceased.

A number of dogs had been busily retrieving downed birds and now they were assisted by beaters and gamekeepers.

When the pheasants were heaped up behind the shooters, men came around and began filling small sacks with the empty cartridge cases which were scattered in profusion around each of the shooting men.

This was the moment when Deirdre and a number of the wives arrived in a light carriage, bringing baskets containing food and drink. The contents were swiftly transferred to small tables previously set up by servants from the house.

Deirdre was as busy as any other woman helping with the picnic meal, but she was never far from where Ben stood. When he was alone for a few minutes she hurried to him with a plate of food.

He already had some and would have refused, but she exchanged the full plate she was carrying for the half-empty one he held and said quietly, so her voice carried no further than Ben, 'Be careful what you say to General Grove and his wife.'

Startled, Ben asked, 'Why?'

'My grandmother has asked their opinion of you. Lady Grove is notoriously insensitive. She'll ask the sort of questions that no one else would dare put to you, and they might offend you.'

'Why should your grandmother go to such trouble to learn about me?'

Deirdre looked suddenly coy. 'She wants to be absolutely certain you're a suitable . . . companion for me.'

'Why doesn't she ask *me* about the things she wants to know? Anyway, I would have thought you quite capable of choosing your own friends.'

Deirdre wondered whether Ben really did not know why Lady Tresillian was taking such an interest in him. She decided he did not.

'I have already told you the reason I was taken on the cruise to South Africa. I am afraid it will be a very long time before I am trusted to use my own discretion about anything . . . but here comes General Grove. We must talk more later. Are you quite certain you won't have another drink, Benjamin? How about you, General?'

'What?'

The general was rather hard of hearing and Deirdre repeated her question.

'No, thank you, my dear. Need a clear eye and a steady hand for the shooting this afternoon. Has this young man told you what a fine shot he is? No? Well I'm sure he will later. I'm going to take him away from you for now. Want him to meet some of the men who share our interest in the clay business.'

'Of course, General. Shall I take your plate, Benjamin?'

Stepping close to him, she said quietly as he handed back the plate she had only just given to him, 'Try to find time to speak to me before we return to the house, Benjamin. There's not a woman here less than three times my age. I shall be bored to tears if I have no one else to talk to for the remainder of the day.'

In spite of Deirdre's request, Ben was not able to speak to her again before the afternoon shoot commenced. His fellow guests were the men who owned the major clay works in the St Austell district. They were the backbone of the industry.

There was a great deal of discussion about the various clay workings and Ben tried to remember as much as possible of what was being said, without saying too much himself. He had been warned by Josh before leaving the Gover Valley not to say too much about what was going on at Ruddlemoor.

'Remember,' Josh had said, immediately before Ben set off, 'clay works owners are in the habit of playing their cards close to their chests. We're all in competition with each other. I've had Ruddlemoor for ten years but they've never invited me to one of their meetings. That could be because of my background, but it's suited my way of working. They'll probably treat you differently. You've started off on the right foot by making the right connections on your way to Cornwall. All the same, listen to all that's being said, but tell them nothing of your plans for the future. This is a cut-throat business, Ben, and the market for clay isn't expanding as fast as clay production right now. Some owners are likely to go under – although they'll use every means at their disposal to remain afloat.'

It was apparent from the way many of the owners were speaking that Josh's grasp of the current situation was a sound one.

It was equally obvious that many of the owners had more than a passing interest in the affairs of Ruddlemoor. Fortunately, Ben's excuse that he had not been in command of Ruddlemoor long enough to have a full grasp of the situation there was accepted.

The men talked for so long that he was not able to return to the tables to speak with Deirdre again.

Eventually, General Grove pulled out a watch from his pocket and announced to his companions that it was time they moved on to the new shooting stand.

'This time you can take your place in the line at the far end from me,' the general said to Ben. 'I noticed a few pheasants getting past the guns up there. You'll steady them up a bit, I daresay. We'll talk more business tonight after dinner, my boy. Some of us have a few ideas we'd like to discuss with you.'

Ben turned to give Deirdre a wave before he and his fellow shooters passed out of sight of the women. Even at this distance he could make out her disappointed expression and remembered what Miriam had said to him on the day of Darley's funeral, when Deirdre had come to the Gover Valley house.

'That girl is smitten with you . . .'

Chapter 21

At dinner that evening, Ben was seated between Deirdre and Lady Philomena Grove. It proved to be not the most relaxed of meals.

Deirdre had warned Ben of Lady Grove's insensitive way of questioning and she had not exaggerated. It took the form of a blunt interrogation that bordered on rudeness.

The general's wife questioned him closely about his mother, father, brothers and grandparents, their present whereabouts and activities, or wanted details of the manner of their passing. She was also curious to know everything about Insimo and how it came into the hands of the Rhodesian Retallicks.

Ben was reluctant to boast about the vast landholding that was Insimo and said no more than was necessary. Consequently, he sensed that she believed him to be lying. But by this time he did not care.

Even the frequent pressure of Deirdre's leg against his own when Lady Grove asked a particularly impertinent question was insufficient to prevent him becoming extremely irritated with her.

When Lady Grove supposed he had never experienced shooting parties of the nature they were enjoying today, he thought of the dead pheasants piled in heaps behind the shooters and agreed with her.

'In Africa I've hunted elephant, buffalo and all types of game. Mainly it was with the Matabele who went out armed only with spears, risking their lives in order to provide meat for their families. I've also shot crocodiles when they've proved particularly troublesome and I've stalked rhino with Selous. But, no, I've never before taken part in a shoot like the one we had here today.'

Much of the table had become quiet while Ben talked and his words travelled farther than he had intended.

A few places along the table, General Grove heard only part of Ben's statement and misinterpreted his words.

'We enjoy many days like this during the winter months, dear boy, and have a wonderful time. It's exhilarating to spend a day out in the healthy air – and in such good company too. Sport such as that you've enjoyed today has made a marksman of every Englishman worth his salt. That's the reason we win wars and have acquired the greatest empire the world's ever known.'

'Oh! I didn't know Cecil Rhodes was a marksman. My father knew

252

him and told many stories about him, but I never heard him mention Rhodes's hunting prowess.'

General Grove never entertained the slightest suspicion that there might be a hint of sarcasm in Ben's reply, but it seemed he did not hold the empire builder in high regard. 'I'm talking of *gentlemen*, young Retallick. Rhodes was an administrator. As administrators go, he was quite a good one, despite one or two errors of judgement. There's a need for such men once the army's done its work, but it's the gun that's the conqueror, not the pen. I remember having a similar discussion with General Gordon before he set off for Khartoum. "Charles," I said . . .' It was a story that most of those at the table had heard before and conversation resumed, making it unnecessary for Ben to hear it through to the end.

Dinner at Tresillian House seemed to have gone on for an exceptionally long time before the butler entered the room to announce that coffee was awaiting the ladies in the drawing-room. The gentlemen would be served at the dining table.

As the men stood up and the ladies made their exit, Deirdre said softly to Ben, 'Be on your guard. I will try to speak to you later.'

When the women had gone, General Grove suggested the men should move to one end of the table where they could converse with greater ease.

It was not until some time later, when brandy, port and coffee was circulating freely, that they began discussing business. At first it was no more than a general conversation regarding the state of the China clay industry, but eventually it turned to measures that might be taken to improve matters.

Ben was by far the youngest clay works owner in the room. This, coupled with the advice given to him by Josh, meant he deemed it wise to remain silent whilst the discussion was taking place. Not until one of the men asked his opinion on a particular point did he make an observation.

'From what I've seen so far of the China clay business it seems to me that every works is going its own way, regardless of what's best for the industry as a whole. This means that for much of the time each company is competing against the others. Surely this doesn't make a great deal of sense? In these difficult times – and you all seem to be in agreement that things are indeed hard for the industry – we ought to form some sort of an Association. If we agreed on a common policy and no one owner tried to undercut the price of another, we could force up the price. This would ease the pressure on those works that are struggling at present.'

'That's what I've been advocating for years,' said Augustine Steen. The oldest man present, he owned one of the larger workings and had been the first to bring in a rail link. 'It's the commonsense thing to do.

253

Benjamin Retallick is new to the clay business and can perhaps see things more clearly than those of us who are bound by the way we've always done things in the past. I endorse his suggestion wholeheartedly.'

'I don't hold with Associations,' declared General Grove. 'Form an Association and you'll have every two-man working in the district clamouring to join. Before you know it *they'll* be running things and we'll need to get permission from them before we can do a damned thing.'

It was evident from the number of nodding heads at the table that General Grove had the backing of the majority of clay works owners.

Satisfied he had their approval, the general continued, 'No, gentlemen. While I agree with much of what Augustine and our young friend have suggested, I will not be drawn into any form of Association. I believe the interests of every one of us here are best served by the discussions we have on occasions such as this. Now, shall we debate the proposal that we agree on a common price for our clay?'

'But if we don't consult the smaller workings on a mutual price, they will sell at less than us and the buyers will take from them instead of us.' The protest came from Ben.

'That is not so. The smaller companies can produce neither the quantity nor the quality that the large buyers require. Besides, we are powerful enough to order the smaller companies to raise their prices to our own level, if need be. If they refuse we will merely need to drop prices for long enough to put them out of business. Then we can raise them once more. They are well aware of this, I can assure you.'

General Grove sounded both smug and confident. As the discussion continued, Ben decided he liked him even less than before.

The talk between the clay works owners continued until very late in the evening, but it ended in agreement between them. The price of China clay would be raised by each of them on the first of the following month. The price set would be that achieved earlier in the year.

The men were congratulating each other on a highly successful meeting when suddenly the door of the dining-room was flung open.

Lady Tresillian's butler, looking uncharacteristically flustered and unkempt, burst in upon the assembled guests, 'Gentlemen, I beg your assistance. We have a serious fire in the kitchen. Unless something is done very quickly, I fear it will spread and destroy the whole house . . .'

Chapter 22

As the men hurried from the dining-room and along the corridor to the kitchen, led by the Tresillian butler, smoke was very much in evidence. It rolled past them like a moorland mist, catching at throats and irritating eyes.

'Where's the nearest tap?' Ben snapped the question at the butler who had stopped short of the kitchen. The smoke seemed to have induced a state of shock in him.

'In the kitchen.'

'*Another* tap. We can't get in the kitchen.'

'Outside. By the kitchen door.'

They were close to the kitchen now and orange flames could be seen through the smoke. There was a window nearby and Ben said to the butler, 'Go out through there. Get buckets, bowls, anything that will hold water and have them passed in through the window to us. We'll form a chain and see if we can put the fire out from in here.'

The first bucket of water had come through the window when Ben heard screaming. Moments later a young assistant cook staggered from the kitchen. Her dress was on fire and she was close to hysteria.

Throwing the water from the bucket over the girl's blazing dress, Ben grabbed her before she could flee past him. He beat at the remaining flames with his bare hands before one of the clay works owners took off his coat, wrapping it around the girl's legs where it effectively stifled the last of the flames.

'How long had you been in the kitchen?' Ben questioned the girl who was sobbing uncontrollably. '*Answer me, girl!* Is anyone else in there?'

'I came in through the other door . . . I could smell smoke. Everything was alight.'

'So you don't think anyone else is still in there?'

'I . . . I don't know.'

As the girl spoke, the owner of the coat removed it from about her legs. He looked up at Ben and grimaced. She was very badly burned.

'Did you close the other door?' He spoke to her more gently now.

'I don't know . . . No, I didn't. All the smoke poured everywhere. I didn't know where I was . . .'

The girl began crying once more and he said, 'Get her back to the women. She'll need a doctor, but we must get to that other door and

255

close it or it will fan the flames and spread them to other rooms.'

'I'll go.' One of the servants who had come along the corridor behind the guests turned and hurried back the way they had come.

At that moment another bucket of water was passed through the window. Ben took it and advanced to the kitchen doorway. He threw it into the room, aiming at the spot where he could see flames rising through the smoke.

Another bucket followed, but they seemed to make little difference to the conflagration. Suddenly, someone came through the smoke from behind Ben. In his hand was a hosepipe, already spraying water from a brass nozzle.

The hose was handed to Ben and he advanced into the blazing kitchen, directing the water ahead of him to wherever he could see flames.

His efforts had some effect and he persisted in his fire-fighting until choking throat and streaming eyes drove him back to the corridor. Here a young servant took the hose from him and continued the dangerous task.

Some minutes later, there was the sound of hooves clattering on the cobbled courtyard beyond the window and helmeted men seemed to be everywhere. The Truro fire brigade had arrived, answering an earlier telephone summons from a quick-thinking servant.

Coughing and spluttering, his eyes smarting so much he could not see clearly, Ben was led away along the corridor by one of the servants.

Somewhere along the way, Ben was met by General Grove and some of the others.

'Bring him in here,' said the general. Although Ben would have preferred to have been taken to his room, he was led into the drawing-room. The women seated in here gasped at his appearance as he was seated in a comfortable armchair.

'Get the lad something to drink,' said the general. 'Champagne's best to clear smoke from the throat. Quickly, someone, before he chokes.'

In no time at all, it seemed to Ben, he was being helped by Deirdre to raise a glass of Champagne to his lips.

It went down well, despite some initial choking. A second glass swiftly followed while Deirdre dabbed intermittently at his heavily watering eyes with a dainty lace handkerchief.

When he could see once more he saw that almost everyone invited to the shooting party was here, even though smoke seemed to have seeped into this room too. Not until he had gathered more of his senses did he realise that much of the smell of smoke was coming from his own clothing.

'Are you all right, Benjamin?' On her knees before him, Deirdre asked the question anxiously.

'Yes.'

His voice sounded rough and strange. Not certain he could be understood, he nodded his head.

'I'm so relieved. I feared you'd swallowed so much smoke you would choke!'

Embarrassed by the hero-worship he could see in her expression, Ben croaked, 'How's the girl? The servant who went into the kitchen during the fire?'

'A doctor's on his way to her now. Her legs are burned, but I don't think it's as bad as it might have been had her clothes not been extinguished in time.'

There seemed to be servants and guests hurrying in all directions, when suddenly a distressed maid came to where Deirdre still kneeled in front of Ben.

'Miss Deirdre . . . I think you had better come quickly. It's Lady Tresillian. All the excitement's proved too much for her. We think she's had a heart attack.'

The remainder of the evening at Tresillian House was thoroughly chaotic. Lady Tresillian had been taken to her room, accompanied by the doctor who had already been in the house, treating the assistant cook. Deirdre had deserted her guests to be with her grandmother.

Meanwhile the Truro fire brigade was doing its best to ensure there was no danger of the fire re-igniting in the kitchen.

Towards the end of the evening the efforts of the fire brigade were hampered by an army of servants, determined to clear up the kitchen area and make it functional as quickly as possible.

Meanwhile, in the drawing-room, General Grove was regaling his fellow guests with a long story of a fire that had occurred in the British residence of an obscure Indian state where he had been a member of the garrison. It seemed the general, then a very junior officer, had shown such conspicuous bravery that he had earned for himself immediate promotion and a handsome reward from the local rajah.

When this story led to another, telling of the general's exploits during the attempts to relieve Khartoum and the ill-fated General Gordon, Ben decided he had listened to enough reminiscences. The drink and the fire had taken its toll on him. He wanted nothing more than to go to bed.

Slipping quietly from the drawing-room, he made his way upstairs to his room. He felt it might have been more helpful had he and the other guests returned home and allowed the servants at Tresillian to bring some order back to the great house.

He had tentatively suggested as much to another of the guests, only to be told it would be impractical. Such a change of plans would seriously disrupt the households of many of the guests. They would

257

remain at Tresillian for the night and reassess the situation in the morning.

In his room, Ben stripped off his clothes which still reeked of smoke and had a good wash, using cold water from the large jug on the washstand.

When he had washed and dried himself, Ben blew out the lamp on the nearby table. Climbing into bed he contemplated all that had happened during that eventful day and evening.

He wondered how Deirdre was coping with the attack suffered by her grandmother. He was not at all certain she was a girl used to facing up to such emergencies.

He was concerned too about the seriousness of the heart attack. None of the guests had been told and the doctor had still been with the elderly lady when Ben came to bed.

It had been a most unexpected outcome of the fire. Lady Tresillian had always given the impression that she was virtually indestructible. He wondered what would happen to Deirdre if her grandmother were to die.

Chapter 23

Still thinking about the possible repercussions that the death of Lady Tresillian would have on her granddaughter and the household in general, Ben had almost dropped off to sleep when he thought he heard a sound. It sounded like a soft tapping on the door.

He listened and heard the sound repeated. This time there could be no doubt. Someone was knocking very quietly on the door of his room.

He sat up. 'Who is it?'

Instead of a reply, the tap was repeated, but it was more urgent this time.

Puzzled, he threw back the bedclothes and put his feet to the floor. What would a servant want with him at this time of the night? Unless something had happened to Lady Tresillian and the guests were being gathered for the news to be broken to them . . .

'Just a minute. I'm coming.'

He should have lit the lamp, but it would take time because he could not remember seeing any matches on the table nearby.

At the door he turned the key and opened it. To his astonishment he saw Deirdre standing there. Before he could recover from his surprise she had slipped past him into the room.

'Close the door quickly, Benjamin. I thought I heard someone on the stairs. If any of Grandmother's friends knew I had come to your room there would be the most awful scandal.'

He did as he was told before saying, 'Just a minute, I'll see if I can find some matches and light the lamp.'

'No! I'm in my night things. I was going to bed but suddenly I felt that I didn't want to be there on my own. One of the servants had told me earlier that you'd come to bed and I came straight here.'

Almost fearing to ask the question, Ben said hesitantly, 'How is she . . . your grandmother? Is she going to be all right?'

'I don't know.' Deirdre sounded distraught. 'The doctor hasn't long gone. He's given her something and she's sleeping soundly. He says he'll be back again in the morning . . .'

Suddenly, her voice broke. 'Oh, Benjamin! What am I going to do if anything happens to her? How will I cope? I have no one . . .'

She began to cry. At a loss as to what he should do, Ben reached out to her. A moment later she was in his arms and crying against him.

When the racking sobs stopped Ben said consolingly, 'I'm sure things will be all right, Deirdre. I've heard of people who have lived for many years after having a heart attack. Do you have any relatives who can be contacted to come and stay at Tresillian for a while? Until your grandmother is back on her feet, at least?'

Deirdre shook her head, rubbing her face against his pyjama top.

'There's no one except a brother of Grandmother's who lives in India somewhere. I know he's still alive, but he married an Indian wife and no one has mentioned him for years.'

'Well, I'll always do anything I can to help, I hope you know that. But Lady Tresillian has very many friends, there will always be someone to turn to.'

'I can't speak to them, Benjamin. They're all so old and set in their way of doing things. I know Grandmother is the same, but I'm used to her.'

'Well, try not to think the worst. You said yourself that your grandmother was sleeping soundly when you left her. She might be feeling a whole lot better in the morning. Things will seem so much better then.'

As he held her, Ben was disturbingly aware that she was wearing only the flimsiest of nightwear. He really should not be holding her quite so close, but releasing her was not going to be easy until she made a move – and this she seemed very reluctant to do.

'I don't know what I – what *we* would have done without you tonight, Benjamin. First the fire, and then Grandmother's heart attack. Everything's been racing around in my brain since it all happened. I feel I would have become demented had I not come along to see you.'

She began to cry once more and he said, 'Try not to cry, *please*! The fire might have been a lot worse, and your grandmother is still with us.'

Deirdre's crying gradually subsided and then she spoke again. This time her voice was so quiet, Ben had to put his head down in order to hear her.

'Benjamin, can I stay here, with you, tonight?'

'What do you mean . . . neither of us go to bed?' It was a foolish question, but he could not believe she meant that they should sleep together.

'No. I want to lie with you . . . and feel safe. I don't want to be on my own. Not tonight.'

'I . . . you . . . What would Lady Tresillian say if she ever found out? Besides, there are the guests and the servants. They might come looking for you, for something or another.'

'Most of the guests have gone to bed and they won't be up until late in the morning. As for the servants, they wouldn't dare say anything, even if they found out. But they won't. I locked the door of my room

260

when I came out. They'll think I'm in there asleep. I'll return to my room in the morning and no one will be any the wiser.'

Ben had the uncomfortable feeling that Deirdre's presence in his room was no spur of the moment whim.

'We can't.'

'*Please*, Benjamin. Don't make me beg you to let me stay here.' Deirdre began crying once more. 'If I go back to my room I'll lie awake all night, my mind filled with horrible and frightening thoughts. I need someone to cuddle me, Benjamin, and I feel safe when you're holding me. Please let me stay here with you.'

Ben should have known better than to give in to her. But she was a lonely and frightened young woman and he sensed her desperation was not entirely simulated. Besides, he had drunk rather more Champagne than he was used to.

'All right, but . . .'

He was able to say no more. Deirdre gave him a hug that took his breath away. Then she said, 'Let's lie down, Benjamin. With you holding me, neither of us saying anything.'

They lay down together and as he held her, Deirdre turned towards him. Now he was as aware of his own body as he was of hers – and so was she.

They had not been lying there very long when she put a hand to his face and whispered, 'I *am* glad we met, Benjamin. I like you very, very much.'

He tried to move his body away from her slightly as she hugged him, believing she would find it embarrassing, but her arm went about him and stopped him from moving away.

'You do like me too, don't you, Benjamin? Yes, I can feel you do . . .'

The next moment they were kissing. He was uncertain whether it was on his initiative or hers. Suddenly he was holding back from her no longer and as his hands explored her body she did nothing to stop him. Indeed, she moved to make it easier for him.

Then Ben forgot all his misgivings and they were making love. He had made love to a couple of Matabele girls from the compound in the Insimo Valley, but those had been stolen moments in the long grass. It had never been like this.

When Ben could love her no more and lay gasping, her body still trapped beneath him, Deirdre begged him not to stop. He made love to her again as soon as he was able and then, totally exhausted, fell asleep beside her, holding her in his arms.

When he woke in the morning, she had gone. For a moment, Ben wondered if it had all been some incredible, unbelievable dream.

Lying back on his pillow he knew it had been real enough. Not only that, he was fairly certain that Deirdre was not the innocent young woman she would have him – and everyone else – believe.

He lay there for a long time, wondering where they would go from here.

Chapter 24

By the time Ben had washed and dressed, he was feeling increasingly apprehensive about going to breakfast. He eventually gathered the courage to leave his room and go downstairs. Somewhat to his surprise he discovered that most of the guests were already in the breakfast room. He had expected them to be late rising in view of the previous evening's excitement.

It seemed they had reached a joint decision late the night before. They would return early to their own homes in order that the Tresillian household might return to some semblance of normality.

The talk at the breakfast table was of Lady Tresillian. Wakening early after her induced sleep, she had declared she felt hungry and demanded something to eat. Once this need had been satisfied she had to be dissuaded from leaving her bed and joining her guests downstairs.

Although it was still early, the doctor had already been to the house and examined his titled patient. He had expressed amazement at her remarkable recovery. Nevertheless, he stressed that she had suffered a serious heart attack and suggested she should regard it as a warning. In future she must take life at a more leisurely pace and pass much of the responsibility for running the great house to others.

To her granddaughter, for instance.

Deirdre was much in evidence at the breakfast table and seemed already to have taken the doctor's advice to heart. She divided her time between the breakfast room and the greatly reduced facilities of the fire-damaged kitchen.

Ben had been apprehensive at the thought of facing her this morning. He was quite convinced their manner towards each other would arouse the suspicions of the other guests – in particular the inquisitive wife of General Sir Robert Grove.

His concern proved unnecessary. Deirdre greeted him with a warm but correct friendliness. Not even Lady Grove could have read anything more in her greeting, or her reply to Ben's question about Lady Tresillian's condition.

When he took his place at the breakfast table, the woman seated next to him commented, 'Isn't it wonderful to see how happy Deirdre is to have been given such good news about Lady Tresillian?'

Still feeling embarrassed, Ben agreed that it was indeed.

'Yes, indeed. Last night I looked at poor Deirdre and thought the poor girl was heading for a breakdown. Yet this morning she is all that one would expect of a young woman of such breeding. I really must remember to mention it to Lady Tresillian when I next speak with her. She will be very proud of her granddaughter.'

This seemed to be the consensus of opinion of most of those breakfasting at Tresillian House. Only Lady Grove seemed to find the world less than perfect. Ben decided this was probably the fault of General Grove. He had clearly drunk far more than was good for him the previous night and was nursing a severe headache this morning. It was due, he insisted, to the excitement of the previous day.

Ben was very glad he was not seated close to either Lady or General Grove. He did not feel capable of coping with either of them this morning.

Back in his room, he dawdled over the task of placing his things in the saddlebags. He thought Deirdre was probably awaiting an opportunity to visit him.

Ben believed they needed to talk about all that had happened between them the previous night. He felt guilty. Facing up to everything in the cold light of day he believed he had taken advantage of her at a time when she was particularly vulnerable.

When she did not put in an appearance he reluctantly handed the saddlebags over to a servant and went downstairs to the hall.

Deirdre was there, saying farewell to the guests as they left. He waited while she shook hands with one of the clay works owners and his wife and saw them out through the hall.

When Deirdre turned away from the others, he approached her somewhat uncertainly.

'Benjamin! Are you leaving so soon?' She pouted appealingly as she hurried towards him, arms outstretched to grasp both his hands. 'I was hoping you'd stay until after all the others had gone – although that will probably not be for quite a while. Lady Grove is with my grandmother and I suspect the general has returned to his room to lie down until she is ready to leave. They'll no doubt be here for much of the day, but that doesn't mean you can't stay too.'

'I've been hoping to speak to you while you are alone. About last night . . .'

'Are you having regrets about what we did, Benjamin? Is that it?'

'Not regrets, no. But I feel it was my fault. That I shouldn't . . .'

She was looking straight up into his face and he found it difficult to continue.

'It was nobody's *fault*, Benjamin. It just happened, that's all. I was very unhappy and turned to you. I needed comforting – and you did it wonderfully well. I'm really very grateful to you. Truly grateful.

Without your support I don't think I would have survived until this morning.'

Ben was confused. He was uncertain whether he was relieved or hurt by her words. 'Was there no more to it than that for you, Deirdre? Are you saying you merely needed *someone* to comfort you? That it might have been anyone?'

'Of course not. Dear Benjamin, you are being terribly sensitive. Nobody else could have comforted me – not as you did. And I would not have dreamed of going to the room of anyone else. All I am saying is that you must not feel guilty about anything. I certainly don't.'

Still confused by the almost matter-of-fact manner in which she was able to talk about what had happened in his bedroom during the night, he asked, 'Will I be seeing you again?'

'I most certainly hope so – and please make it soon. You are a wonderful source of comfort to me. Someone I can talk to. Someone I want to be with . . . but here come Mr and Mrs Collins. Goodbye, Benjamin.'

Standing on tiptoe, she kissed him on the cheek. 'And thank you – for *everything*.'

In another room of the great house, Lady Philomena Grove was looking out of the window of Lady Tresillian's room. She saw Ben riding from the house on his horse.

'I see that young Retallick lad is on his way home. I *am* surprised. I expected him to remain at the house for rather longer. Certainly until after all the other guests had left.'

'Why? Do you think he's taken with young Deirdre?'

'Of course he is! What young man wouldn't be? That young girl is far too attractive for her own good. Besides, with her family connections she'd be a fine catch for a young man with his ambitions.'

'Do I detect certain reservations about him, Philomena?'

'It's rather more than that. He talks a great deal about his wonderful family home in Rhodesia, but talk comes easily. It's very difficult to prove anyone a liar when he's telling you of something that's half a world away. Quite apart from the fact that it's so remote, it's doubtful whether anyone else has ever heard of it.'

'That's perfectly true, of course. Yet he has been given ownership of a clay works, and was travelling first-class on the ship from South Africa when we first met with him.'

Lady Grove snorted derisively. 'Years ago I employed a gardener who claimed once to have owned a China clay working. As Robert will tell you, many workings are virtually one-man concerns. Young Retallick's works is rather more substantial, I believe, but who knows what financial state it's in? As for travelling first-class . . . there *is* no other way to travel if you are hoping to meet someone who might

265

prove to be of help to you in the future.'

'You are surely not accusing young Retallick of deliberately setting out to cultivate my friendship because he hoped to capitalise upon it? I must refute that. It was I who spoke first.'

'I don't doubt that is so, but he certainly needs friends – respectable friends. I understand his grandfather was once found guilty of sedition and transported. He was later pardoned, but . . .' Lady Philomena Grove shrugged her shoulders expressively, highly satisfied with the expression of horror she saw on the face of her sick friend.

'This I did not know. Deirdre must be told she is to have nothing more to do with the young Retallick. Have her sent to me if you please, Philomena.'

'I think that would be a grave mistake. You know how stubborn young girls can be. I believe she's smitten with this young man, but perhaps not desperately so. By all means make him less welcome at Tresillian. That should not be difficult, your illness will provide all the excuse you need. In the meantime, I will have a word with Robert. I believe he has scant regard for young Retallick's business acumen. If things go badly for him in the clay industry he might be only too pleased to return to Africa and out of all our lives.'

Chapter 25

'I trust you enjoyed the weekend with your fine friends at Tresillian?'

'Not particularly.'

Ben replied to Lily's question as he sat down at the breakfast table in the house in the Gover Valley, the morning after his return from Tresillian.

He was up early this morning, before Ben or Miriam. This meal was a very different affair to breakfast in Tresillian House, but Ben felt much more at home here. However, the thought of what had occurred between himself and Deirdre still occupied a prominent place in his thoughts. He was embarrassed even to be thinking about it here, in the presence of Lily.

'Oh? Don't tell me the fine Deirdre and her friends didn't quite come up to your expectations?'

Trying to shake off his disturbing memories of Deirdre, Ben said, 'I didn't enjoy standing with a gun in my hands slaughtering birds just for the fun of it. Then, in the evening, there was a serious fire in the kitchen of Tresillian in which a young assistant cook was badly burned. Probably as a result of this, Lady Tresillian had a heart attack.'

'Well! Your weekend has been a barrel of laughs, and no mistake! Was it a fatal attack?'

'No, but I think Lady Tresillian is going to have to change her lifestyle a little.'

'Does this mean you'll be seeing more or less of her granddaughter?'

'I don't know yet. There wasn't time to have a discussion about it.'

Ben did not want to talk of Deirdre to Lily. He did not want to talk of her to *anyone* until he had settled in his own mind what he intended doing as a result of what had occurred. He was glad when the sounds of Josh coming down the stairs were heard and Lily returned to the kitchen to prepare his breakfast.

Over the meal, Ben told Josh of the discussion that had taken place at Tresillian among the owners of the clay works. Somewhat to his surprise, his grandfather was not immediately enthusiastic about the idea of an agreement to keep prices artificially high.

'If the buyers get wind of it, *they'll* probably form an Association to bring the prices down again. In the end they're the ones who hold the reins. You could find yourself selling clay at prices lower than before. If that happens you'll put every small working in the district out of business. Anyway, we've managed well enough up to now without any Association – or whatever you like to call it. We could manage now.'

'We might. But if we keep competing against each other, the only ones who'll show a profit at the end of the day will be the buyers. Ruddlemoor is running on too low a profit margin – and so are the other workings.'

'We've come through bad times before. They never last for too long.'

'They won't have to this time. If prices don't begin to rise it will prove disastrous for a great many of the owners in no time at all. I may know little about the China clay industry, but I can understand profit and loss ledgers. We're holding our own – but only just. The best way to push up profit is to work together. We've decided upon a joint policy, now we need to stick to it.'

Josh shrugged his shoulders. 'It's your company now, Ben. You must do what you think best – but don't put too much faith in others. China clay companies have always competed with each other. You can form as many Associations as you like, but you won't change the owners.'

As Ben was about to leave the house, Lily came from the direction of the kitchen. He had a feeling she had been waiting to catch him alone.

'Ben, will you have a word with Jo when you see her this morning, please? I spent some time at the house with her over the weekend. I couldn't get her on her own for long enough to have a good talk with her but I have the impression that she has something on her mind. See if she'll say anything to you about it.'

He promised he would speak to Jo, but there were a great many other matters on his mind on the ride to Ruddlemoor. Apart from Jo, there was the warning Josh had given to him about the other clay owners and their agreement. He wanted to dismiss it as nothing more than the caution of an elderly man, but he could not.

Ben could not help feeling that the other clay owners did not regard him as one of themselves just yet. They had included him in their discussions, it was true, but he could not shake off the feeling they looked upon him as a brash young newcomer. No more acceptable to them than was his grandfather.

He did not believe they would go back on their agreement, but he would need to keep his wits about him.

However, overshadowing all else was the memory of the night he had spent in the Tresillian bedroom with Deirdre. What course would their relationship take now? It was ridiculous to believe things between them could ever be the same again.

This thought led Ben to ponder on how he felt about *her*. He admitted to himself he was fond of her. Perhaps more than fond, but there had always been an element of pity too. When he first met her he had looked upon her as a young, innocent girl who was probably misunderstood and who lacked affection.

Perhaps much of this was true, but the night she had spent in his room at Tresillian had shaken his belief in her innocence at least. The Matabele girls he had known could have taught her nothing.

It came as a relief to arrive at Ruddlemoor and find work going on as though nothing had changed in the world. At least all seemed well with this part of his life.

As was usual on a Monday, Ben carried out a tour of inspection in the company of Captain Bray. As they talked, Ben wondered whether he should mention the agreement that had been reached between the China clay owners. He decided to say nothing. If Jim Bray was indiscreet and word reached the ears of the buyers they would be very unhappy.

When the inspection was almost over, Ben asked Jim Bray how Jo was coping with the loss of Darley.

'She's a poor lost soul,' said her father, sadly. 'It hasn't helped her peace of mind having her landlord tell her he's selling the house. It means she'll need to move back in with us. Not that I mind. I've always enjoyed having her in the house, but when you put Jo and her mother under the same roof they're like a couple of bantam cocks.'

'When was she told the house was being sold?' Ben thought this was probably the reason she had seemed so unhappy during the weekend, when Lily was with her.

'On Friday, but she never said anything to me until this morning. It must seem as though problems are being heaped upon her shoulders at a time when she's as low as I've ever seen her. Still, at least the landlord held off until poor Darley had passed on. Things would have been far worse had she been put out on the streets when she had a sick husband to care for.'

'Who owns her house? I somehow thought it belonged to Ruddlemoor.'

'No, it's been in Harry Lemon's family for as long as I can remember. Harry's a churchwarden in St Austell. He's been having a bad time lately. I've no doubt he needs the four hundred pounds he's asking for the house.'

Ben said nothing more about Jo and they completed the inspection of the works.

As they returned to the Ruddlemoor office, Ben announced he intended raising the price of clay for a while, saying only that he believed other workings would be doing the same.

Jim Bray felt that Ben should have spoken to him before reaching such an important decision, but kept his opinion to himself. He agreed that he would try to ascertain what prices were being charged by the other workings in the St Austell area.

Chapter 26

For a week, Ben continued to fret about the night he and Deirdre had spent together. He hoped he might hear from her, but there was nothing. Eventually he made a telephone call to Tresillian House.

The call was taken by a servant. After a lengthy pause, she told him that Deirdre was not available. What was more, the girl was unable to tell him when she *would* be at home. However, she was happy to tell him that Lady Tresillian was making a wonderful recovery. She was at that very moment sitting in an armchair in her room having a story read to her.

Something in the servant's voice caused Ben to believe that the story was probably being read by Deirdre. If that were so, it could only mean she had been told to say that Deirdre was not available.

Putting down the telephone, Ben wondered whether he was merely being over-imaginative. He doubted it. The servant had been far less communicative than was usual. But if Deirdre really *was* at home, then who had said his calls should not be put through? Not Deirdre, surely?

If it were not Deirdre, it had to be Lady Tresillian, but why should she suddenly make such a ruling? Ben paled. Could it be that she had found out about him and her granddaughter?

He dismissed the thought. He did not believe Lady Tresillian would confine her disapproval to disallowing his telephone calls. Ben decided he would need to ride to the house and find out for himself.

A few days later Ben arrived late at the Ruddlemoor works office. He had been hoping to catch Jo alone, but both Tessa and Eddie Long were there with her.

'Jo, will you walk down to the "dry" with me? Your father says we've been getting some poor quality coal delivered lately. I want to check on it and also discuss something else with you on the way.'

When Ben and Jo had left the office, Tessa said, 'I wonder what Ben Retallick needs to talk to Jo about that can't be said in front of us?'

'Perhaps he fancies her now she's a widow? After all, she knows what it's all about and there are no complications.'

'You've got a one track mind, Eddie Long, and it's dirt all the way.' She watched out of the window and saw Ben and Jo, their heads close together, deep in discussion. Suddenly, Ben reached across and gripped

271

Jo's arm. Seeing the gesture, Tessa added wistfully, 'Mind you, if I thought Ben Retallick was developing a taste for older women I'd put myself in line.'

As they walked away from the office, Jo suddenly blurted out, 'If it's my work you want to talk to me about, Ben, I can only apologise and promise to try harder. It's just . . . things have got on top of me a bit since Darley died . . .'

Ben reached out and squeezed her arm sympathetically. 'You've coped marvellously well, Jo. It's nothing to do with that. In fact, I hope you'll be pleased with what I have to tell you.'

As she looked up at him inquiringly, he said, 'I've just bought your house from Mr Lemon.'

Instead of displaying pleasure, she looked alarmed. 'You've . . . What does that mean? Are you going to move in there?'

'No, of course not. In fact, I've bought it and added it to the Ruddlemoor assets. It belongs to the works now. What it means is that no one can put you out. What's more, you can live there rent free for as long as you are working for Ruddlemoor.'

It took a few moments before Jo grasped the full import of what Ben was saying. When she spoke again, she asked quietly, 'Why are you doing this, Ben? You hardly know me . . .'

'I know you better than most of the people I've met since I came to England and I look on you as part of my Cornish family. I also liked Darley very much, and need someone I can trust working in the Ruddlemoor office. Do you need any more reasons? I'm sure I can think of one or two.'

After a long silence, Jo said, 'Has anyone asked you to do this for me? My pa . . . or Lily, perhaps?'

'No one's asked me to do anything, Jo. This is entirely my own idea. I thought you'd be pleased. If you don't like it . . .'

'I *do* like it, Ben. I think it's wonderful of you. If only you knew how much pressure it takes off me. I'm so relieved I . . . I could either cry or kiss you. I don't know which would cause the greater scandal.'

'I'll settle for the knowledge that it's made you happier, Jo. You've been a bit short on . . .'

He was interrupted by a sound that he thought at first was a rifle shot somewhere on the road. A few moments later there was another. This time it was accompanied by a painful grating sound. Then a strange machine came into view.

'What's that?' Jo was so startled, she immediately forgot the emotive subject of her house.

'It's a motor car,' said Ben. 'And it's turning into Ruddlemoor!'

The motor car with driver and woman passenger turned off the road and eased its way down the gentle slope towards the works office.

Without another word, Jo and Ben hurried back to the office to intercept the first motor vehicle either of them had seen in Cornwall.

It came to a juddering halt in the space in front of the office. Hitching up her skirts, the woman stepped to the ground, leaving the driver to push back the goggles he was wearing and remain seated behind the steering wheel.

'Can I help you?' Ben asked the woman who seemed intent on trying to pull various creases out of the coat she wore.

'I'm looking for Josh Retallick – and by the sound of your accent you must be a relative. Probably one of those he went to see in Rhodesia.'

Ben was taken aback by this woman's appearance and by her bold manner. He was no expert on women, but this one was dressy in a gaudy way that was as out of place here as it would have been at Tresillian House.

Wondering where her and Josh's paths had crossed, he said, 'Josh Retallick is my grandfather. He's retired now and I've taken his place. Is there anything I can do for you?'

'Yes, you can tell me where I can find him. He was once very kind to me. About ten years ago that would be now. He gave me money to help me out of serious trouble. Well, *I've* got money now. Lots of it. I'm here to pay him back and with interest too.'

After only a brief hesitation, Ben said, 'I'll take you to his home.' He welcomed this unexpected diversion in the routine of Ruddlemoor. He was also fascinated to learn more of Josh's association with this blowsy but very attractive woman.

'No, you won't. We'll take you. By the way, my name's Martha and this is my husband, Jannie.'

Jannie acknowledged the brief informal introduction with a quick nod of his head, but Martha was already talking to Ben again. 'Help me up. You'll ride in the back with me. It's great fun, although none of my family will ride in it. My father calls it a noisy contraption and says they'll never be allowed to travel regularly on the Cornish roads.'

As Ben followed Martha into the car, Jim Bray came to join the curious workers crowding around the vehicle.

Looking doubtful, he said to Ben, 'Surely you're not going to risk your life in that contraption?'

'There!' said Martha, triumphantly. 'What did I tell you? I'd forgotten how cautious the Cornish can be. There are bolder souls in Africa, I can tell you. Here, wrap this rug about your knees.' Wriggling closer to him, she said, 'Are you comfortable?'

As Ben assured her he was comfortably seated the silent, unsmiling driver got down from his seat and went to the front of the vehicle.

Reaching down, he gripped the handle affixed there and swung it three or four times before there was a sound like a series of rifle shots that sent the watching workers back a number of paces.

273

Suddenly the motor car began to judder alarmingly. The driver ran back to the driving seat and hastily adjusted one of the levers affixed to the steering wheel.

The engine took on a more even note now and the driver resumed his seat. He pulled down the goggles over his eyes once more and the motor car lurched forward.

He turned the vehicle in a slow, wide circle, scattering the clay workers. As it passed Jo, she called out, 'Thank you, Ben. I'll talk to you soon. But thank you very much.'

Clinging to the side of his seat, he released his hand only long enough to wave a brief acknowledgement. Then the vehicle was bumping up the uneven track to the road and Martha was clinging to him.

The driver called back for directions just before they left the Ruddlemoor track. Ben shouted them with some difficulty as the movement of the motor car rattled his teeth.

Then they were on the road and as Martha shrieked at her husband to: 'Slow down!' Ben looked back and saw the whole of the Ruddlemoor workforce gathered to watch their young owner make his first trip in a motor car.

Chapter 27

Josh was in the garden of his Gover Valley home when an unfamiliar sound brought him to the gate.

As the vehicle slowed, Martha saw him and gave a loud shriek of delight, ordering her husband to bring the motor car to a halt.

Jannie obeyed her with some difficulty, the vehicle seemingly intent on pursuing its course along the road towards the far end of the valley.

It eventually came to a halt some half-a-dozen car lengths past the gate, by which time Martha was cursing her husband in a most unladylike fashion.

Before Jannie succeeded in switching off the engine, she stood up, lifted her skirts above knee level with one hand and vaulted nimbly to the ground.

She ran along the road to Josh and before he could recover from his surprise, flung her arms about him and gave him a warm hug.

The greeting was watched in astonishment by Ben, Miriam and Lily. The two women had been brought to the door by the loud explosion emanating from the engine of the motor car after it had come to a reluctant halt.

Josh was still looking thoroughly bewildered, and Martha said, 'Don't you recognise me, Josh? It's Martha. Martha from Johannesburg.'

Taken aback both by the greeting and his recognition of the woman who was embracing him, Josh seemed to have lost his power of speech. All he could keep repeating was: 'Good Lord! Good Lord!'

Clinging to his arm, Martha dragged him from the garden to the car. Hauling him to a point where he could look closely at the driver, she said, 'Do you recognise Jannie? The owner of the Duchy Arms in Johannesburg? We were married six years ago. Since then we've both worked hard and made money. Lots of money. Despite that, you'd never believe how difficult it was to persuade him to come back home to Cornwall for a holiday. Unbelievable, isn't it? Well, I mean, what use is it making money if you don't get some enjoyment from it? Anyway, here we are, and we're staying in Cornwall for a month.'

'You need to keep on top of the competition in our line of work,' said Jannie, speaking for the first time since Ben had met him. 'If you don't then you go under.'

He added, unhappily, 'I dread to think what's happening back in

Jo'burg while we're here gallivanting around the countryside enjoying ourselves.'

Jabbing a finger at the motor car, he said scathingly, 'As for this! Not only has Martha persuaded me to buy it, but now she wants me to take it back to South Africa on the ship, then drive it home to Jo'burg from the Cape. Can you imagine breaking down on the veldt, surrounded by natives and wild animals? That's what'll likely happen. I've told her so a dozen times, but she takes no notice of what I say.'

As Jannie shook his head morosely, Martha said to Josh, 'He always looks on the worst side of everything. He'll enjoy the drive just as much as I will, really. Besides, you've been to Jo'burg, Josh. Can you imagine the effect a motor car will have on folk there? I wouldn't be surprised if we weren't able to sell it for enough money to cover the cost of our whole holiday!'

By now Josh had recovered from his surprise sufficiently to begin to enjoy the whole situation and to be amused by Jannie's determination to be glum.

'You'd better come inside – if only to satisfy the curiosity of Miriam and Lily. If we don't go in soon they look as though they might burst.'

At the doorway of the house Josh made the introductions. He tried to be discreet and not give everyone the full details of his earlier meetings with Martha, but he need not have bothered.

As they entered the house, she said in a loud voice, 'Josh and I met when we were both thrown into gaol in Pretoria, can you imagine that?'

Laughing raucously at the expressions she saw on the faces of Lily and Ben, she added, 'I might still be there now if Josh hadn't been so kind to me. I've never forgotten him, I haven't. Me and Jannie swore we'd find him again one day and repay him for what he did for me – and with interest too. Isn't that right, Jannie?'

The taciturn Jannie conceded with a nod of his head that it was indeed correct. Meanwhile, Miriam gave Josh a look that indicated she would later want to know more of his 'kindness' to Martha when she and he were alone.

Ben found the whole situation highly amusing. It would appear that Lily felt the same way.

Speaking to Martha, Ben said, 'I'd heard that grandfather got himself arrested on his way back from Insimo, but why were *you* in gaol?'

'It's a long story. No doubt Josh will tell you all about it sometime. Putting it briefly, I was arrested for breaking up a shop owned by my two-timing Cornish fiancé and the woman he married in South Africa instead of me.'

'The same shop mysteriously caught fire only hours after I'd had Martha released,' added Josh. 'I don't think they ever found out who did it.'

'It was no mystery,' said Martha, totally unrepentant. '*I* did it. He can consider himself lucky that he wasn't inside at the time.'

She shrugged. 'Still, it all worked out for the best in the end. If I hadn't gone back to Jo'burg and worked at the Duchy Arms I'd never have married Jannie. It was the best day's work I ever did – the best thing he did, too. Between us we've built up trade until it's the best tavern in the whole of South Africa – and with some of the best-looking girls too. We've become so well known that we have girls clamouring to come and work for us. We managed to keep going right through the war too, at a time when most of the bar owners were cutting and running and others were forcibly closed down.'

Martha smiled happily about the room at everyone, seemingly unaware of the impact her disclosures had made on everyone except Josh. 'But you don't want to hear me chatting on . . . Jannie, where's the money we've brought for Josh?'

Pulling a wad of money from his pocket, Jannie handed it to Martha who promptly thrust it at Josh. 'You'll find two hundred and ten pounds there.'

He looked startled. 'I can't take that. It's far more than I gave you.'

'It's the right amount, with the interest worked out all proper like by Jannie's accountant in Jo'burg. It's far less interest than Jannie charges on the loans he makes to prospectors, but if we'd applied *those* rates we'd have bankrupted ourselves! You take it, Josh. I've never ever been happier to give money to anyone. You did me a good turn at a time when there was no one else who would have done it. Not only that, you gave it without any thought of getting anything in return. I've never forgotten you for that, and I never will.'

'Would everyone like a cup of tea?' asked Miriam. Her initial reservations about this effervescent young woman had evaporated after listening to her chatter. Immoral she certainly was. Lacking in taste and discretion too, probably, but Miriam doubted whether there was a great deal of harm in the girl. On the contrary, she thought there was probably a wealth of generosity in her nature.

Miriam's observation was borne out by Martha's next words. 'I'd have something a little stronger if you have it. Mind you, I've no doubt I'll have more than enough to drink tonight. There's a girl coming to see me with her husband and we're planning to have a little celebration. She went out to South Africa, just like me, expecting to marry her young man when she got there. The only trouble was that he'd gone out there a few months before and hadn't liked it at all, especially with her being back home. So he turned around and caught a ship back to England, not knowing she was on her way to join him! Jannie would have had her working at the Duchy Arms until she'd earned enough money for her fare home – and Josh could tell you what sort of work *that* would be. Anyway, I remembered what Josh had done for me, so I gave her the money to come back again and she found her young man and married him. Well, I mean, if anyone has half a chance of happiness then you've got to help them grab it with both hands, haven't you? Not all of us are lucky enough to have the chance come round twice.'

Suddenly pointing a finger at Lily, Martha said, 'You remember those words, young lady. It's good advice. If the chance of happiness comes your way, then you grab it quick. Tie yourself to it so tightly it'll never get away from you.'

Martha and Jannie remained at the Gover Valley house for more than two hours. When they departed it seemed that everyone for miles around had gathered outside to see them go. There were squeaks of mock panic as the vehicle exploded into life. It set off along the narrow road accompanied by a series of explosions that sent a flock of sheep running panic-stricken to the end of a nearby field.

When the motor car and the energetically waving Martha had disappeared from view, Josh said, 'Well! That was a great surprise. I never ever expected to see young Martha again.'

'I'll bet you didn't, Josh Retallick!' said Miriam. 'The picture you've always given me of her is of some dowdy young girl who'd never been given a chance in life. You'd better come back inside the house and explain how it is she's turned into the girl who just went off in that motor car. She's the sort who'd turn any man's head when she walked into a room.'

The admonition was given with a smile that belied its note of warning.

As Ben and Lily followed them inside the house, Lily said suddenly, 'I sometimes wish I'd led an exciting life, like Martha. She's seen so many places. Done things I'll never do.'

'I think you should probably be grateful for *not* having done many of the things she has,' replied Ben. 'She's cheerful enough now, but I'd say she's led a very hard life.'

'Perhaps she has, but she's *done* something. Achieved things. I'll probably never go beyond St Austell. Never find out what the rest of the world is like.'

'Oh? What about Simon Kendall, your Trades Union man? He's ambitious enough. You settle for him and you'll go places and do things.'

'No, I won't. The girl who marries Simon will be expected to stay at home to take care of his needs and bring up his children. She'll be watching him do things, not doing them herself. That's the sort of man he is. Anyway, he's not talking to me at the moment. He still hasn't forgiven me for going off with you at Summercourt Fair.'

Somehow, Ben did not feel able to apologise for breaking up any romance there might have been between Lily and Simon Kendall.

Grinning at her, he said, 'Do you think it would satisfy your needs to do something if you were to go off and make me another cup of tea? I have an awful thirst. Must be all that African sunshine that Martha was talking about . . .'

Chapter 28

Simon Kendall was drinking with Eddie Long and some of his ex-army friends in St Austell's General Wolfe public house. This was where he gained most of his recruits to the cause of Trades Unionism, usually at a cost of no more than a pint or two.

Kendall had just bought a second round of drinks for the ex-army men and they were talking about the downturn in the China clay industry in recent months.

'Mind you,' said the Trades Union official, 'things are never as bad as the clay owners would have us all believe. They use it as an excuse to keep wages as low as they dare.'

'It shouldn't worry you too much, Eddie,' said one of the Boer War veterans. 'Josh Retallick has a reputation for being the best employer in the whole of the clay business.'

'That might have been so,' agreed Eddie, 'but he's no longer the Ruddlemoor owner. He's handed everything over to that grandson of his. Our new owner is hardly old enough to wipe his own nose. Not only that, he's South African. It's a strange world. I fought against the South Africans and lost a leg beating 'em. Then I return to my own country and the only way I can earn a living is to work for one of them! There's no way he's going to be the best of employers. Not for me, anyway.'

Taking a long swig from his glass, he added, 'Mind you, Ben Retallick can't do anything wrong as far as most of the women at Ruddlemoor are concerned.'

Eddie was feeling particularly aggrieved because a vitriolic Tessa had taken him to task for constantly complaining about Ben Retallick. In a moment of particularly bad humour, she told Eddie that although Ben Retallick might be young, he was twice the man that Eddie was now or had ever been.

'Is there anything particularly bad about him?' asked Simon Kendall. 'I mean, something that could be taken up on your behalf by a Trades Union?'

Eddie took another draught of beer, almost emptying his glass. 'He's just too young to be a clay owner, that's all. I don't think he's got what it takes to see us through the bad times.'

'You need to form a Union branch at Ruddlemoor. As you say,

young Retallick won't be able to handle things if the bad times continue, and it'll be you – the workers – who'll suffer, not the works owner. They'll cut wages and lay off men rather than lose a single penny profit. The trouble is, when times are good the men don't see any reason why they should have a Union. When things go wrong it's usually already too late for a Union to do anything about it. The time to have one is *now*. That way there'll be a strong Union in place to fight battles for the men when they're most needed.'

Finishing his drink, Eddie slid the glass across the table towards Simon Kendall. 'You're right, Simon. Too damned true, you're right . . . I'll have the same again, if you're buying.'

Remaining seated, Simon Kendall said, 'Then why don't you start up a Union at Ruddlemoor? Talk about it to the others and see if you can't persuade them to join. There's discontent in a great many of the clay works right now. Persuade other men to join and you'll have an organisation that's strong enough to face up to the owners and secure a good standard of living for all the clay workers in the St Austell area. If you could do that and you were the organiser you wouldn't need to feel beholden to Retallick, or to anyone else. You'd be an important man in your own right.'

The thought of heading a Trades Union branch at Ruddlemoor had never occurred to Eddie before. Now the idea had been fed to him it appealed greatly.

'You might be right. With you and the Ruddlemoor men behind me, Ben Retallick would need to listen to what I said to him. I like that idea.'

'Think about it – all of you – while I go and get some more beers.'

Standing at the bar waiting to be served, Simon Kendall looked back at the men sitting around the table he had just left. He was well satisfied with the seeds he had just sown. Now he needed to push the idea forward without sounding too eager.

He was in St Austell to help clay workers form a Union but his record of recruitment had been less than impressive so far. Even his courtship of the daughter of the most active Benefit Association organiser in the area had not brought him the success he had hoped for. He urgently needed to notch one up if he were not to be recalled to London and relegated to an obscure post somewhere in the depths of the building.

By the time he returned to the table, it was apparent that Eddie and his friends had arrived at a decision.

Taking up a glass of beer from the table, he said, 'All right, I'm willing to try to organise the Ruddlemoor workers. The others will do the same at the Varcoe works and try to recruit the men from their Benefit Association.'

'That's right,' said one of his companions. 'After all, the reason we fought in South Africa was so we could return to the sort of country we

281

wanted. You just tell us what we need to do and we'll get on and do it right away.'

On Sunday evening in the Retallicks' Gover Valley house, Ben sat in the lounge writing a letter to his mother. In the same room Miriam and Josh were enjoying an evening drink, including Ben in their conversation in a casual way.

There was the sound of the front door opening and shortly afterwards Lily entered the room. She had been to her parents' home for the weekend. Although she usually returned on Monday morning, it was not unknown for her to come back to the Gover Valley early and no one commented on her early return.

Josh invited her to sit down and poured a drink for her.

'Is it cold outdoors?' asked Miriam, conversationally.

'No, but there's quite a strong wind getting up.'

Lily looked to where Ben had completed his letter and was sealing it inside an envelope. 'Jo came to the house today.'

'She needs to get out more,' said Miriam. 'She's spent years caring for poor Darley, but she's still a young woman. It would be nice for her to get about a bit more.'

'She's much happier than when I last saw her – and it's all thanks to you, Ben.'

Looking from one to the other, Miriam asked, 'Oh? What's Ben done to make life easier for Jo?'

'I told him I thought Jo was very unhappy about something. He found out that she was having to get out of her house because it was being sold. Now Ben's bought it and told Jo she can live there rent-free. She's a changed person. Thank you, Ben.'

Embarrassed, he said to Josh, 'It's a good investment for Ruddlemoor. We can never have too many houses for our key workers. Besides, I like Jo.'

Miriam looked quizzically at him. 'That was a very generous thing to do, Ben.'

'I was worried about her.'

'We've all been worried,' said Josh. 'But none of us thought of buying the house for her. Miriam's right, that *was* generous, Ben.'

'I was happy to be able to give her peace of mind.' Sticking a stamp on the letter, he said, 'I think I'll go out and post this. It will be good to get a bit of fresh air before going to bed.'

The post box was about a quarter of a mile along the valley towards St Austell.

'I'll come with you,' said Lily, unexpectedly.

Ben was surprised, but he did not question her decision. He enjoyed her company but she had seemed to be avoiding him recently.

Once outside the house, she said, 'Josh was right, Ben. Buying Jo's house and letting her stay there rent free *is* generous. You've gained a very loyal friend. Jo thinks you're the most wonderful man in her life right now.'

Ben wondered whether there was an unspoken question in Lily's statement, but he decided to ignore it. 'That's very nice to know, but it's also a good business move for me. Ruddlemoor's gained an asset and we keep an efficient clerk.'

'Are you sure those are the only reasons for buying the house, Ben? Because it makes good business sense?' Lily persisted.

'No.' He decided to give her an honest reply. 'I'm very fond of Jo and I admire her for the devotion she showed Darley. Besides, she's family.'

'Does having family around mean a lot to you?'

'Yes. I miss everyone at Insimo sometimes and having you and the others means a lot to me. You're my *Cornish* family.'

Lily was not entirely certain she wanted to be thought of as part of Ben's family, but did not pursue this thought. Neither did she want to ask any more questions about his affection for Jo. Her sister-in-law was an attractive young woman . . .

'I also spoke to Tessa today.' Lily changed the subject abruptly. 'This is really why I wanted to speak to you tonight. Eddie Long is trying to organise a Union branch among the Ruddlemoor men.'

Ben knew very little about Trades Unions and said so to Lily.

'They are organisations that set out to protect the rights of workers. My pa has spent a lifetime fighting for his Association, which is quite similar really, so there's not much I don't know about them. Mind you, all it's ever done for Pa is to keep him out of work. Clay owners wouldn't employ him because of his views. A Trades Union is a good thing in many ways. It protects men from the worst employers, but we don't need one at Ruddlemoor. We especially don't want Eddie Long involved. He's got far too big a chip on his shoulder about you.'

Ben shrugged. 'I suppose I could always dismiss him. He doesn't do enough work to make any difference to Ruddlemoor.'

'That wouldn't be a very good idea at the moment, Ben. It might bring you into direct conflict with the Trades Unions – and they're gathering a lot of strength throughout the country. I'm sure that if you wait and watch for long enough Eddie will give you some other very good reason for getting rid of him. But I thought you ought to know what's going on. If Pa was still the man every one came to if they had a question about Trades Union matters he could have kept Eddie in check. Things are different now. Simon's been sent here from London on behalf of the Union – and he's ambitious. He wants to build a strong Union. When he does I think he'll try to do something to make a name for himself nationally. He'd like nothing better than to do so at *your* expense.'

Ben gave an exaggerated sigh. 'I seem to have acquired the uncomfortable knack of making enemies without really trying. I can understand Eddie Long, he's bitter at the loss of his leg and not bright enough to accept that I'm *not* South African, but what have I done to upset Simon Kendall?'

'He's jealous of you. You've come to England and been handed Ruddlemoor without having to work for it. He sees you as someone born into a rich family who gets everything you want.'

They had reached the post box now. Pushing the letter into the narrow slit, Ben turned around to walk back to the house and Lily turned with him.

The moon was dimly visible behind a veil of high, fast-moving cloud. Ben could see Lily's face, but not sufficiently to catch her expression when he asked, 'Is he jealous of me because of you too, Lily? Because we both live under the same roof and see more of each other than he would like?'

'Probably, but there's nothing flattering in that for me. He'd be the same if you'd come between him and anything else he wanted.'

'Does that upset you, Lily?'

They walked along in silence for a while before Lily replied, 'No. I thought it did once, but Simon Kendall isn't the man I believed him to be. I'd need to love him a great deal before I could accept his faults – and I don't.'

'I'm pleased about that.'

'Why should it matter to you?'

'Because he's not good enough for you.' Ben shrugged. 'I can't bring myself to like Simon Kendall, somehow. You deserve someone much better.'

'Is that because I'm family, the same as Jo?'

He would have liked to tell her that he was far fonder of her than he was of anyone else he knew. He almost did. But at that moment the unwanted thought of the night he had spent with Deirdre came back to haunt him.

'Perhaps.'

Lily told herself she had been foolish to hope for any other reply. She *was* 'family', albeit a poor relation. Ben Retallick could choose from any girl in the county. He was the guest of families like the Tresillians.

She was a working girl from a family in clay country. Had she not been related to Miriam Retallick he would never have even noticed her.

Putting all her foolish thoughts aside, she said, 'Let's walk faster. I'm beginning to find this wind chilly.'

Chapter 29

During the following week there was a worrying fall in sales of Ruddlemoor China clay. At the same time, Captain Bray reported that Eddie Long was having some success recruiting for the Union at the works.

More alarming was the situation at the neighbouring Varcoe clay works which shared a common railway line with Ruddlemoor. The works owner here had little interest in running the clay works efficiently and had refused to spend money on sorely needed machinery. It had been the cause of Jeremiah Rowe, the longtime captain of Varcoe, resigning in protest. Now a Union branch, organised by Eddie's drinking friends, was gaining a strong following there. It was rumoured the men might take strike action because of a threatened cut in wages.

During these crises Ben had tried twice more to telephone Deirdre at Tresillian. The calls had been taken by servants and the replies had been the same on each occasion. Deirdre was 'not at home'.

Ben was concerned that Lady Tresillian had somehow learned of what had occurred between Deirdre and himself during the eventful shooting party weekend, and feared she might have punished her granddaughter as a result.

After giving the matter a great deal of thought, he decided there was only one thing to be done. He would ride to Tresillian on Saturday and learn exactly what was happening.

He announced his intention of going to Tresillian that night over supper at the Gover Valley house.

'*This* Saturday?' The question came from Lily.

'Yes. Is there any reason I shouldn't go on that day?'

It was an unnecessarily sharp reply due entirely to the guilt he felt. The guilt was always strongest when the subject of Deirdre came up in conversation with Lily.

'What you do and who you see is entirely your business,' she retorted.

'Isn't Saturday Jo's birthday?' Miriam put the question hurriedly.

'That's right.' Lily rose from the table and began gathering plates. 'Ma and Pa are having a special tea for her. They think she deserves something nice after such a bad year. They are inviting all her friends and relatives.'

285

Glancing pointedly in Ben's direction, she added, 'Of course it will be a very simple affair and wouldn't suit everyone. I mean, we won't have servants to hand round the cakes or pour the tea, or anything like that. It will just be a *family* gathering.'

Ben thought of the family gathering for Jo's birthday as he rode towards Tresillian early on Saturday afternoon. He would have much preferred to be spending the evening with Lily and the others, but the visit to Tresillian was something he needed to do before he tackled the other problems that were looming ahead of Ruddlemoor.

When he first arrived at Tresillian House it seemed to Ben his visit would prove to be no more successful than his telephone calls.

The door was opened to him by a servant-girl. Leaving him seated in the outer hall, she went off and a few minutes later the Tresillian butler came out to speak to him.

'Hello, Mr Retallick, sir. Very nice to see you again. I'm pleased to tell you that Anna, the young cook you helped when she was burned in the fire, is making very good progress, sir. She hopes to return to light duties sometime in the next few weeks. The staff are most grateful to you.'

'I'm very pleased about that,' said Ben, with sincerity. 'I feared she might suffer permanent injury.'

'She probably would have, sir, had it not been for your presence of mind.'

'Please give the girl my best wishes when you see her again. Now, may I see either Miss Deirdre or Lady Tresillian, please?'

'I'm terribly sorry, sir. Lady Tresillian has suffered another, albeit mild, heart attack and is allowed no visitors at the moment.'

'And Miss Deirdre?'

'I regret she is not in the house at the moment, sir.'

'Can you tell me where she is, or where I may find her?'

'I'm very sorry, sir. I can't tell you her exact whereabouts and I have no idea when she is likely to be available.'

Now Ben knew for certain there was a conspiracy to keep him from seeing Deirdre. 'Is this what you've been told to tell me?'

A pained expression crossed the butler's face. 'I really am terribly sorry, Mr Retallick. All I can tell you is that neither Lady Tresillian nor Miss Deirdre is available at the moment.'

Ben knew he would get nowhere by standing here futilely questioning the Tresillian butler. 'I see. Well, as you and the staff are so grateful to me, will you at least ensure that Miss Deirdre knows I called to see her?'

For a moment Ben thought the butler's stiff manner was about to soften. Instead, he merely said, 'I can promise you that, sir.'

Ben left the house, quietly angry and also with considerable trepidation. He believed he was being barred from seeing Deirdre because Lady Tresillian had discovered what had happened between them. He did not believe it would end here.

Mounting his horse, he was riding slowly from the house when he heard someone calling his name. Turning, he saw Deirdre hurrying towards him.

As she drew closer, she called, 'I saw you from my window. I'm deeply hurt that you were leaving without speaking to me.'

'I was told that you were "unavailable" and that Lady Tresillian was not allowed to have visitors.'

Deirdre stopped a few paces from him. 'Oh! I didn't think Grandmother would do anything until she'd made a few more enquiries.'

'Enquiries about what, Deirdre?' Ben dismounted from his horse and stood facing her. 'Has she found out . . . about us?'

Her face coloured suddenly. 'No, of course not, and she never will unless it comes from you.'

Ben was puzzled. 'Then why have I been virtually barred from seeing you, and why am I no longer welcome at Tresillian?'

Deirdre looked unhappy. 'I told you Lady Grove would try to find out all about you and your background. It seems that she and my grandmother had a long conversation.'

'So? I had already told Lady Tresillian everything that Lady Grove learned.'

'I know, Benjamin.' Deirdre moved closer towards him until she was no more than an arm's length away. 'But Lady Grove thought you were not being truthful about your land in Rhodesia and about your mother's family.'

'And Lady Tresillian believed her? Why didn't she ask me? Everything I've said is the truth. In fact I've played down the size of Insimo because I didn't want it to be thought I was boasting.'

'*I* believe you, but how do we convince my grandmother? How do we persuade her that you are suitable to remain a friend of the Tresillian family?'

Ben could hardly believe what he was hearing. He and Deirdre had spent a night in bed together. They had made love. It was something that had occupied his thoughts for much of every day since then. He had thought it would be important to Deirdre too. Yet here she was talking only of persuading her grandmother that he would be a suitable friend of the Tresillian family! What had happened between them hardly seemed to matter to her.

'I really don't feel I want to persuade your grandmother that I'm suitable to be granted her family's friendship. I really don't give a damn for the Tresillians! All I wanted to hear is what *you* want.'

'Don't be silly, Benjamin. Life isn't as simple as that.'

'That's where we must disagree, Deirdre. For me life is *perfectly* straightforward.'

He had realised there was a huge gulf between the thinking of Deirdre and himself. He had worried about her unnecessarily. What had happened between them mattered far less to her than it did to him.

Suddenly, he felt the need to get away from here. Away from standards that were not those in which he had been brought up. He felt the need to be among the sort of people who were despised by Deirdre, Lady Tresillian and General Grove. People like Josh, Miriam, Jo – and Lily.

He was already on his horse and riding away from Tresillian when the 'sick' Lady Tresillian leaned from her window and ordered Deirdre to return to the house immediately.

Riding away from Tresillian, Ben felt a great weight had been lifted from his mind. The guilt and concern he had carried for Deirdre had never been necessary.

Thinking about all that had happened, he realised he had probably expected too much from Deirdre and her grandmother.

It was a salutary lesson. He now realised that, although they were from very different backgrounds, Deirdre and Tessa were two of a kind.

As he rode on his way, lost in thought, he suddenly remembered that today was Jo's birthday. The family were making a special effort to bring a little happiness to the recently widowed young woman. Suddenly, Ben felt the need to be with them.

Digging his heels into the flanks of his horse, he put the animal to a sharp canter. It was almost ten miles to St Austell and he would need to stop along the way and buy a present for Jo.

Chapter 30

'Well, look who we have here! And there's us thinking you was hobnobbing with the nobility, Mr Retallick . . . sir!'

The door of Jo Shovell's St Austell home was opened to Ben by Tessa. She held a half-empty glass containing sugared gin in one hand. Observing the high colour of her cheeks and the manner of her greeting, he decided that Tessa had already emptied many similar glasses.

'Ben!' Jo came from the kitchen and the delight on her face made him feel guilty that he had ever contemplated not coming to her home to help her celebrate her birthday.

'Lily told us you had to go to Tresillian. I never expected you to get back in time to come to my birthday party. It's a lovely surprise.'

She turned her cheek up to him. When he had kissed her, he said, 'I didn't stay long at Tresillian and put my horse to a canter all the way here. I left it at the stables just down the road.'

From behind his back he produced a small parcel and handed it to her. 'I bought this for you along the way. Happy birthday, Jo.'

From a shop in Probus, he had bought a mother-of-pearl and silver brush set for Jo's dressing-table. When she opened it, she gave a gasp of delight.

'It's beautiful, Ben! Thank you so very much.' She gave him a second, warmer kiss. 'And thank you too for coming. It's very special for me today, having my family and friends about me.'

There was a sudden tinge of sadness in her expression and Ben knew she was thinking of Darley. At that moment Tessa and a couple of the Ruddlemoor bal maidens claimed her and led her off to view something they had planned in the kitchen.

Lily had been watching from nearby and now she came across the room to speak to him. 'Is everything all right at Tresillian, Ben?'

'Yes. Lady Tresillian seems to be on the mend.'

'I wasn't thinking of Lady Tresillian so much as her granddaughter. I know you've been anxious to see her. Yet you've hardly had time to get there and back.'

'It was time enough to see her and have a chat. That's all I really wanted to do.'

It was evident to Lily that Ben did not want to talk about his visit to Tresillian. Well, that was his business. Lily gave a mental shrug and said, 'Jo's very happy you've been able to make it to her party. I know how disappointed she was when I told her you probably wouldn't be here.'

At that moment Jim Bray came across the room to Ben and handed him a glass of the punch that had been made especially for the occasion.

As Lily made her way to the kitchen in search of Jo, she thought about Ben's apparent reticence to talk about his visit to Tresillian. She had a strong feeling that all was not well between Ben and Lady Tresillian's granddaughter.

Shrewdly, Lily wondered whether the relationship between Ben and Deirdre had reached a point where Lady Tresillian had made enquiries about his family. If so, she would have learned of Josh's trial and subsequent transportation which would not have done Ben's cause very much good. Lady Tresillian might also have heard the rumour that Miriam was actually married to another man at the time she sailed into exile with Josh after his conviction . . .

Lily had little experience of Cornish society, but she believed that such a background might prove an insurmountable hurdle to any social ambitions Ben might have.

Behind her in the parlour, Jim Bray was talking to Ben.

'It's been good for Jo to have something like this to look forward to, especially now you've taken a lot of the uncertainty from her life by buying her house. I hope things will start looking up for her now.'

'I wish someone could do the same for us at Ruddlemoor,' said Ben. 'We've taken an alarming drop in sales this last week.'

'I wanted to talk to you about that,' said the Ruddlemoor captain. 'I mentioned it to a friend of mine who works on the dock down at Charlestown. He was surprised. It seems there's been no falling off in the amount of clay going out from there. On the contrary, he says the port's as busy as he's ever known it.'

Ben frowned. If all the China clay suppliers raised their prices he would have expected there to be a brief lull while the buyers checked to make quite sure they could not buy at the old price. *If all the suppliers had raised their prices . . .!*

As if reading his thoughts, Jim Bray said, 'I'd say we were wrong to raise our prices, Ben.'

'I discussed it with the other owners before doing it, Jim. They all said the existing price wasn't economical for first quality clay. We agreed we'd raise prices together.'

Jim Bray was startled. 'Since when have clay owners been able to agree on anything? I'd say someone's gone back on the agreement.'

Ben was thinking hard and shook his head. 'No, Jim. If there's as much clay still going out of Charlestown and Ruddlemoor's practically at a standstill then there's more than one works involved. I wouldn't be surprised to learn that we're the only works to have raised prices. I've probably been a fool to trust the others to do what was agreed, without checking they were doing it. Is there any way you can find out for me?'

The Ruddlemoor captain nodded. 'I'll make a start on it first thing Monday morning.' He hesitated, uncertainly. 'We have a lot of unsold clay stockpiled at the moment. This past week has seen it pile up at an alarming rate. Is all this likely to have an effect on the future of Ruddlemoor?'

'Not if I'm able to do anything about it – and I believe I am. But Jo and the others are coming back now. We'll forget about it for tonight. But I'd like those prices as early as you can get them for me on Monday morning.'

Jo's party came to an end at about ten o'clock that evening when it was discovered that Tessa had drunk herself into a state of unconsciousness. Unlike her earlier exuberance, she made very little fuss over it. One moment she was talking to one of the Ruddlemoor bal maidens, the next she slipped quietly to the floor to the cheers of the other girls.

'I'll take her home in the shay, if you like?' volunteered Ben as he helped Jim Bray lift her from the floor to an adjacent armchair.

'Oh no you won't!' said Miriam, firmly. 'Not if you want to have a shred of reputation left in the morning. Your grandfather and I will take her. You see that Lily gets home safely.'

The party broke up quickly after Tessa's collapse. As Ben walked away from the house accompanied by Lily, he thought Jo made a rather forlorn figure standing in the doorway of her home as the last of the revellers left. He made this observation to Lily.

'She's certainly very lonely, but she's had a wonderful day today. Probably the happiest since she was at the Summercourt Fair.'

Looking sideways at Ben, she added, 'You seem to have a happy knack of resolving Jo's problems.'

'How about you, Lily? Don't you have any problems I can try to fix?'

'No. My life is quite orderly at the moment, thank you.'

'How about Simon Kendall? Is romance in the past now?'

'It's been over for a long time.'

'I'm pleased. He's not the man for you, Lily.'

'Oh! So you're a matchmaker as well as Jo's knight in shining armour – and a successful China clay owner too?'

Ben smiled ruefully, although it was too dark for Lily to see his expression. 'At this moment I'm not terribly sure I qualify for any one of those descriptions, Lily.'

As they walked along, Ben told her of what Jim Bray had told him that evening.

'That's not good, Ben!' She sounded genuinely alarmed. 'Is it likely to prove serious for you – and for Ruddlemoor?'

'Not if I really am such a successful China clay owner as you seem to think. We should know for certain some time during this coming week.'

For the remainder of the walk along the Gover Valley they spoke of Ruddlemoor. Not until they opened the gate to the Retallick house did Ben suddenly say, 'There's just one other thing, Lily.'

'What's that?' She had turned and waited for him as he fastened the gate.

Without any warning, he stepped towards her and kissed her.

Pulling away from him less speedily than she might have, Lily demanded, 'What on earth do you think you're doing?'

'Just checking on something you said to me when I kissed you once before.'

'What? I don't understand.' For a moment curiosity stood in the way of indignation.

'You told me then I'd only kissed you because it was a moonlit night. There's no moon at the moment so I wanted to be certain that wasn't the reason I enjoyed it then.'

Lily could not decide whether to be angry or amused. Before she had made up her mind it was already too late.

Ben moved towards her once more, but this time Lily pushed him very firmly away from her.

'No, Ben. I told you just now I have no problems. That's perfectly true, so don't make any for me. Please.'

Chapter 31

'Have you heard what's happening at the Varcoe works?' Eddie Long entered the Ruddlemoor office so swiftly the crutch tucked beneath his arm struck one of the chairs and he almost fell to the floor.

It was almost the end of the lunch break on the Monday following Jo's birthday and Tessa was sprawled back in her chair with her eyes closed. She had been ill all day Sunday and for much of the night.

At the sound of Eddie's voice she winced and said, painfully, 'Do you have to come in here shouting like a lunatic, Eddie Long? Can't you at least *try* to behave like a civilised human being?'

'What *is* happening at the Varcoe works?' Jo was unsympathetic to the self-imposed suffering of her friend and curious to learn Eddie's news.

'They put in a pay demand this morning through their Association. When Mr Varcoe refused even to listen to them, most of the workers walked out in protest. They say they're not going back until he agrees to at least talk to them.'

'Then they're fools,' said Tessa. 'Everyone knows that Aloysius Varcoe has been talking of retiring from the clay business for years. He'll close the works down rather than give in to them. They're cutting their own throats by asking for more wages right now.'

'Nonsense, they're going to win,' said Eddie, enthusiastically. 'When they do, I think we should do the same at Ruddlemoor.'

'Now you *are* being stupid,' said Jo, contemptuously. 'You help with the books. You know just how little profit Ruddlemoor's making. Last week we didn't sell any clay at all.'

'That's only a temporary thing,' said Eddie, his enthusiasm undiminished by either of the women's scathing comments, 'Simon Kendall says . . .'

'Simon Kendall knows nothing at all about the clay industry,' interrupted Jo. 'If you want to speak to anyone about industrial relations, I suggest you talk to my father. He knows more about the clay industry than Simon Kendall ever will.'

'And what has all that knowledge ever done for your father except keep him out of work?' retorted Eddie, unkindly. 'Your pa is a man of the past. We need to look to men like Simon Kendall for our future. I'm going down to the dry to have a word with the men there.'

When Eddie had left the office, Jo said to Tessa, 'He's a fool – and so are the men at the Varcoe works. If they're not careful they'll have both the Varcoe and Ruddlemoor works closed down and a few hundred men will find themselves out of work. Their families certainly won't thank Eddie Long or Simon Kendall then.'

'Well, I never did claim I was attracted to Eddie for his brain,' said Tessa. 'But what can we do about it?'

'I suggest you try to use any influence you might have to prevent him from doing anything stupid this afternoon. Meanwhile I'm going to have a word with my pa. I think Ben Retallick should know about this.'

Jim Bray had been absent from Ruddlemoor for part of that morning and had only just returned. After listening to Jo he agreed that Ben should know what was going on. The problem was that he had not been seen that morning and the works captain declared he could not take time away from Ruddlemoor to go and find him.

'The best thing you can do is go to Gover Valley yourself. Tell him what you've just told me. Say that I also need to speak to him urgently – and make certain it's Ben you tell. Say nothing of this to Josh.'

Jo immediately demanded to know what was happening, but all her father would say was, 'This is between Ben and me. Something he'll want to sort out in his own way.'

When Jo arrived at the Retallicks' house she discovered that only Lily was at home. Josh and Miriam had gone to St Austell on a shopping expedition. Ben had said he was going to the telegraph office, after which he thought he might ride to Charlestown harbour before making his way to Ruddlemoor.

When Jo explained the reason for her visit, Lily said fiercely, 'Eddie Long's a fool! The whole future of Ruddlemoor and the men and women who work there is hanging in the balance, yet all he can think of is starting some stupid Union in order to cause more trouble!'

Realising she had probably sounded more passionate than she had intended, she said, 'I'll tell Ben about it if he comes here, but he'll probably be back at Ruddlemoor before you get there. Your pa will tell him everything that's going on. Stay and have a cup of tea with me before you return.'

'I hope Eddie won't already have stirred up any trouble before Ben gets there.'

Bustling about the kitchen making tea and putting out the cups, Lily said, 'You're very fond of Ben, aren't you, Jo?'

'Yes, he's been good news for me, and for Ruddlemoor too. How about you, Lily?'

'Me? Why should he be anything at all to me?'

'Why? Because he's a good-looking young man, you're an attractive young woman, and you're both living beneath the same roof, that's why.'

'He's family, Jo, as well you know. Besides, it's you he's done most for since arriving in England.'

'Don't use that as an excuse for not giving me a straight answer, young Lily. He's family, yes – but so distantly related it only makes him all the more interesting. Don't tell me he's not even noticed you, because I just don't believe it.'

'He's *noticed* me, but hardly more than that.'

Even as she spoke, memories of Saturday evening were intruding to make her out a liar.

'Anyway, Ben's sights are set a lot higher than the likes of me. He's been a guest at the home of Lady Tresillian, remember?'

'I don't think that counts for too much with Ben Retallick, but when you've made your mind up about how *you* feel then you let me know, you hear?'

'Why should you be interested in how I feel about him, Jo?'

She looked down into her cup of tea for a few moments before replying. 'We've known each other a long time, Lily. It was you who told me how Darley felt about me. You persuaded me I should tell him how *I* felt, do you remember?'

Lily nodded, she remembered very well. In those days she had been a young girl and jealous because she was aware how much her brother loved Jo. It had taken a great deal to swallow her own feelings and put the happiness of her brother before herself.

'I *did* tell him,' continued Jo. 'As a result he and I enjoyed some very happy years together, though they were all too few. Now he's gone and I miss him dreadfully, even though he'd not been able to be a husband to me in the full sense for a long time. Just having him in the house was always enough for me. Now he's gone and no amount of grieving's going to bring him back. It's left a huge hole in my life. But Ben's come along and he's been kinder to me than any man since I first met Darley.'

Observing Lily's expression of astonishment, Jo continued, 'Oh, I don't ever expect him to look at me with marriage in mind. I know full well it would never work even if he did, but I'm grateful to him, Lily – and I'm desperately lonely. For all that Ben's rich and has grand friends, I believe he's lonely too. Tessa has never tried to hide the fact that she's available, should he be lonely enough to want her. I'm just telling you that if ever he *is* then I'll step in and make sure he takes me instead of her.'

Lily looked at Jo in disbelief. 'I don't believe I'm hearing you saying all this, Jo! You mean you'd . . . ?'

'Yes, Lily, that's exactly what I mean.'

She stood up and placed the now empty cup on the table. 'So, you see, if you want him, you'd better do something about it before he realises I'm available too – and with no strings attached.'

As she walked from the Gover Valley, Jo knew she had taken a big gamble. She could lose Lily's friendship as a result of what she had just said. Nevertheless, she believed she had returned the favour Lily had once paid her. She believed Lily and Ben would make an ideal couple.

If Lily did *not* do anything about it . . .

Jo did not pursue this thought. She realised something of which she had not been aware before she carried out her supposed bluff. Too much of what she had said had been truth. If Tessa appeared to be making headway with Ben and Lily had done nothing, then Jo *would* step in ahead of her workmate!

Chapter 32

Unaware of the revelations taking place in the Gover Valley, Ben reached Ruddlemoor at about the time Jo walked out of the Retallicks' house leaving a disbelieving Lily behind her.

The Ruddlemoor captain's first question was, 'Did Jo find you?'

'No, has she gone looking for me?'

'She went off thinking she might find you in the Gover Valley, but where she's gone isn't important. We've got trouble here, Ben. The Varcoe men have walked out and Eddie Long's been trying to stir up the same sort of trouble here.'

'What's their grievance?'

'Money. The Varcoe men are picking up eighteen shillings a week, two shillings less than ours. They're asking for twenty-five. No doubt our men will do the same – but we'll all be lucky if we have a pay packet for very much longer. You were right. The other owners haven't raised their prices in line with ours. On the contrary, they've actually *lowered* them.'

Ben looked at his works captain sharply. 'Are you certain, Jim? Someone isn't trying to make trouble by telling you this?'

'It isn't just one clay working I'm talking about, Ben. A few of the smaller works are trying to hang on to the old prices, but all the bigger concerns have dropped theirs.'

He was deeply disturbed. This was no longer a question of other companies trying to make money at the expense of Ruddlemoor. This was a move to put his company out of business.

Times were bad. If some companies went out of business the chance that the others would survive would be greater. Most of them were struggling to break even by selling clay at the old prices. By lowering them for however long they could hold out themselves, they would expect Ruddlemoor to fail.

Few companies could survive if they sold no clay for a couple of weeks. They could certainly not then drop their prices to below the economical production level.

Ben felt anger surge within him. The 'agreement' he had reached with the other clay owners had been no more than a cheap trick calculated to drive him out of business. It must have been decided, even while he was a fellow-guest at Tresillian, that he was not 'one of them' and naive enough to be fair game for such an underhand trick.

'Are we in serious trouble, Ben?' The anxious Jim Bray was alarmed by his long silence.

'I'm not sure. I realised something unusual was happening and we may yet be able to turn the tables on the other owners. What's their selling price for top quality clay right now?'

'It's on the market at twenty-two shillings and sixpence a ton.'

'Right, get word to the buyers right away that *our* clay is on offer at twenty-two. No! Make it twenty-one shillings a ton – and we'll guarantee to undercut anyone who tries to go lower!'

Jim Bray's expression showed his concern. 'Can we afford to do that, Ben?'

'I can't answer that at the moment, but I can't afford to have over a thousand tons of clay sitting in the linhay with no buyers in view. As for the trouble with the men . . . Call a meeting in the "dry". I want to have a talk with them.'

Jo returned to Ruddlemoor as the men were gathering in the warmth of the China clay 'dry'.

'What's it all about?' She put the question to Tessa as they walked from the office.

'Eddie says it's because Ben Retallick's worried about the walk-out at the Varcoe works. Eddie says he'll announce a pay rise to try to stop the same thing from happening here. But, again according to Eddie, Ben will have to offer the full twenty-five shillings if he doesn't want to have a strike on his hands.'

'Has Ben said anything to make Eddie believe that's what he's going to do?'

'Not in my hearing. He came to the office a while ago and went through the production charts before going out again. While he was in the office he said nothing to anyone.'

'Well, we should soon know,' declared Jo, 'but don't be surprised if Eddie is proved wrong. He never has been a sound judge of Ben Retallick's character.'

The men and women of Ruddlemoor were kept waiting for almost half-an-hour before Ben put in an appearance, accompanied by Captain Jim Bray.

Ben appeared quite relaxed, although unsmiling. In sharp contrast, Captain Bray's face wore a grim expression.

When Ben climbed to the loading platform at one end of the 'dry', there was an outbreak of excited chatter.

He made no attempt to silence the workers. Instead, he remained standing in silence before them, until the hisses of 'Shh!' from among the waiting men and women grew in intensity and they fell silent.

'Thank you.' Ben faced his workforce, his expression giving them no hint of what he was about to say. 'I believe there's been a great deal of talk today of making a demand for extra pay?'

There was a murmur of assent from the workers, yet Ben noted it was not as loud as it might have been.

'Is this your idea, Eddie Long?' He had located the office worker among the crowd and looked towards him now.

Startled at being singled out for attention, Eddie appeared discomfited. 'All I've done is to pass on information about what's happened at the Varcoe works.'

'And no doubt you suggested that everyone at Ruddlemoor should follow their example?'

'If they get twenty-five shillings then I think we ought to get the same,' Eddie Long said, defiantly.

'I see. Did you also point out that the Varcoe works has been selling clay for the past week or so, while we have been stock-piling it because we haven't had a single buyer?'

'We've had bad weeks before. The buyers will come again. They need the clay.'

'All right, would you like me to agree that whatever Mr Varcoe does, I should follow suit at Ruddlemoor?'

Eddie Long felt he was being led to say something that would not be in the interest of either himself or of the Ruddlemoor workers. However, he had been assured by Simon Kendall that if all the men remained united their demands would be met. Kendall had said that no clay owner could afford to have his works idle for very long.

'Well . . . yes. Whatever Mr Varcoe agrees to do, you should do the same.'

The other workers had been fed the same story by Eddie and voiced their agreement in a crescendo of sound.

This died away uneasily when Ben remained silent. Finally he said, 'Very well, if that's what you really want . . .'

He was interrupted by an outbreak of cheering, but now held up a hand to silence the men.

'Before you become too enthusiastic about it, let me tell you that I've just come back from the Varcoe working. I spoke to the captain and asked what he was going to do. He told me that they can't afford to pay their workers a penny more than they're getting already.'

Sound erupted once more and this time it was jeers that prevailed. Once more Ben silenced them with a motion of his hand, but not before Eddie had called out: 'Varcoe can afford it – and he will when the strike starts hurting his pocket!'

'No.' Ben shook his head sadly. 'Those whose pockets will be hurt are the Varcoe workers . . . Mr Varcoe is far too old to become involved in a confrontation with the men to whom he's given employment for most of his life. He's shut down the pumps and padlocked the buildings. Even if the men offered to return at half-wages there would be no work for them. The Varcoe works has closed down.'

A stunned silence greeted Ben's news, but he had not finished with them yet.

'Is this what you want? To have Ruddlemoor follow the same path?'

There was a great deal of muttering and some shaking of heads. Encouraged, he added, 'It's not what *I* want – but it almost happened anyway, even before Eddie Long mentioned a pay rise.'

Ben had the attention of the workers once more. 'I've already told you that we've sold no clay for more than a week. Now I'll tell you why. The profit margin for china clay is so low that the clay owners decided they must bring the price up if all the works were to survive. I raised our prices – but the others did not. They cut their prices. By doing this they hoped to put Ruddlemoor out of business.'

Now the anger of the workers had taken another direction and Ben was quick to take advantage of this change of mood.

'I'm determined that they're not going to succeed. I shall drop the Ruddlemoor prices to *below* those on offer from the other works, but I'm going to need your help. You want twenty-five shillings a week and I'll give it to you – for a while.'

Before the puzzlement of the workers turned to cheers, Ben added quickly, 'But in order to get it, you'll need to work from daylight to dusk and beyond.'

The workers were uncertain now, but he said, 'If we resume normal working once the other clay owners have stopped trying to put us out of business, your wages will be twenty-two shillings a week. That's an increase of two shillings on the pound you're earning now.'

There was such an outburst of sound now that Ben could not make himself heard for many minutes. When order was restored, he said, 'Well, there you have it. I've been absolutely honest about the situation. The other clay owners are trying to put us out of business. I'm determined to fight them – and win! Are you with me? Are we going to keep Ruddlemoor alive?'

There was another babble of sound but it was difficult to know whether the men were in agreement or not. Then Captain Jim Bray stepped forward.

'You've all heard what Ben Retallick has said. He's willing to fight – and fight with his own money – to keep Ruddlemoor working. I'm with him. Now it's up to you. Those who'll work with us, show your hands now!'

There was a moment's hesitation and Ben thought his oratory had been in vain. Then, as though at a given order, almost every hand in the China clay 'dry' was raised in the air.

Among the very few who did not agree to Ben's terms was Eddie

Long, but it did not matter now. As the workers who only minutes before had been ready to strike set up a rousing cheer, Jim Bray clasped Ben's hand in a congratulatory handshake.

He had won the support of the workers. Now all he had to do was defeat the other clay owners.

Chapter 33

On his way to the Ruddlemoor office after speaking to his workers, Ben caught up with Jo. She smiled at him.

'I thought you handled the situation very well, Ben. You've got every man and woman in Ruddlemoor right behind you now.'

'Thank you, Jo. I sincerely hope you're right.' At that moment Eddie Long swung past them and entered the office, and Ben added, 'But I shouldn't have needed to work so hard to convince them that we're all on the same side.'

He saw Tessa coming towards them and said suddenly, 'Stay out of the office for five minutes, Jo, and keep Tessa with you.'

'What are you going to do?'

'I'm not quite clear yet.' He was formulating new plans just as fast as he could think. 'Ask your father to come to the Gover Valley to speak to me tonight.'

'Are you going to get rid of Eddie?'

'Probably – but just do as I ask for now. We'll speak again later.'

Entering the office, Ben said, 'I want to speak to you, Eddie.'

'If it's about what happened today . . . I was looking after the interests of the men. Unions are legal now, so there's nothing wrong with that.'

'*Everything's* wrong with it. You're employed by Ruddlemoor. *I* pay your wages, not the Union. In view of that I expect some loyalty from those who work here. Instead, you've come very close to sending Ruddlemoor along the same path as the Varcoe works. If you'd succeeded in bringing the men out on strike, Ruddlemoor would have had to close too.'

'You're exaggerating,' retorted Eddie. 'Things aren't as bad as that.'

'You know damned well they *are*! You've been working on the books for long enough to know there's a hair's breadth between profit and loss at the moment.'

Ben worked hard to control his anger at the other man's attitude, 'I don't need men like you working for me. You can take what's owing to you and go – right now.'

Eddie was startled. 'You can't do this! It's not me you're against, but the Union. They won't let you get away with it.'

302

'I've nothing against a Union – where it's needed. I'll be talking to Jethro Shovell about that this evening. If the men want to donate part of their pay to *his* Association, that's up to them. I'll offer to make a donation for every man who does, but it will be made clear to them that they are serving only one master – and that's me. Now, pack your things and go. I've work to do.'

Outside the office, Jo was standing with Tessa when Ben headed back towards them. 'Eddie is leaving Ruddlemoor this afternoon. I'm on my way to tell Captain Bray now. In the meantime, go inside and take over his books, Jo.'

Tessa showed dismay at Ben's words and hurried to the office to speak to Eddie. Jo said, 'I hope you know what you're doing, Ben? Eddie is likely to stir up trouble against you.'

'He's come closer today than anyone knows to having Ruddlemoor closed down. I don't need men like that , and I don't fear any Union. They exist to protect the interests of their members. Ruddlemoor has always taken care of its men and women and always will. All I ask in return is that they give me their loyalty and put in a full day's work for a fair wage.'

Ben returned to the Gover Valley later that afternoon. It seemed that Lily had been looking out for him. She came from the house and met him halfway along the path. 'Jo was here earlier today. Have you seen her?'

'Yes.'

'She said there was trouble at Ruddlemoor . . .'

'There could have been. Very serious trouble, but I've spoken to the men and dismissed Eddie Long. Hopefully, that will be the end of it. At least as far as the men are concerned.'

'You've sacked Eddie? How did he take it?'

'By threatening that the men would support him. They won't. He's been thoroughly disloyal and the men know I can't afford to ignore it. But I'll have to tell Grandfather about it over tea. When I do you'll hear about everything that's happened.'

As they walked to the door, Lily gave him a searching look. 'I don't think either Josh or Captain Bray would have found it so easy to dismiss Eddie as you did. There's a toughness in you that others don't immediately recognise, Ben Retallick. I think you're going to make a success of Ruddlemoor.'

'I *know* I am, Lily, but I'm glad to hear you say so.'

Josh agreed with the action Ben had taken over Eddie Long and the Ruddlemoor workers, but was alarmed to hear of everything else that seemed to be happening in the clay industry.

'I *told* you the other owners weren't to be trusted, Ben. They resented my coming into the industry after all my years in copper mining and have never forgiven me for making a success of Ruddlemoor and competing successfully with the best of them. They're gentry, Ben, and want to bring all clay production into their hands. I'm *not* gentry so I can never be one of them. When you were invited to Tresillian House, I hoped they'd accept you at least. It's obvious now they haven't. I hate to say this to you, but I believe that inviting you there was all part of some devious scheme they'd hatched up between them.'

'You don't think that Lady Tresillian was involved?' Ben found it difficult to believe.

'Most certainly. Many of the clay works around here are leased by the men we refer to as "owners". A great deal of the land itself is owned by the Tresillian family and they've grown rich on the dues. Years ago there was a dispute about the land worked by Ruddlemoor, Varcoe and a few other clay works. The Tresillian lawyers tried to prove it really belonged to them. Their case failed but whenever a substantial works or piece of clay land comes on the market, they're always in the forefront of the bidders.'

Josh's words made so much sense to Ben that it hurt. He had believed Lady Tresillian genuinely liked him, but should have realised the truth immediately he met the other house guests at the weekend shooting party. Apart from the ownership of a clay works he had little in common with any of them.

For a moment he wondered whether Deirdre had known what her grandmother and the others had in mind for him? Whether that night . . .? He dismissed the idea immediately. He was convinced that what had happened between himself and Deirdre had nothing to do with any plot against him. Had she known she would never have come to his room.

'I'm sorry if I've upset you by telling you about Lady Tresillian and the clay owners who are tied up with her, Ben, but in view of what's happened I felt you ought to know.'

'It doesn't matter. You're right, it's something I ought to know about.'

'I should have told you before. Then you might have checked on the selling prices of the other works before increasing yours. But I didn't think they would play such an underhanded trick as this.'

'Don't worry about it, Grandfather. Ruddlemoor will survive.'

'Are you certain, Ben? If you need any money, your grandmother and I aren't rich, but we're not poor either . . .'

'I don't need money – at least, I don't think I do. It will be a couple of days before I know for certain.'

'What are you going to do?'

'For now . . . nothing. But I do have some very serious thinking to do. If you don't mind I'll go to my room and work there.'

* * *

Ben had been in his room for an hour when there was a knock on the door.

'Come in.'

It opened and Lily entered the room carrying a cup of tea.

'We've made a pot for ourselves and I thought you might like some.'

Ben made space on the desk in front of him, pushing aside numerous sheets of paper, most of them covered with figures and calculations.

'You *have* been busy.'

He grimaced. 'Yes.'

'Then I won't interrupt you.' Lily hesitated for a moment but Ben did not suggest she should stay. She reached the door before she stopped and turned back to him.

'Ben?'

He frowned, the pencil in his hand poised over another line of figures. 'Yes?'

'Do you really believe that Ruddlemoor will survive everything that's happening at the moment?'

'I'm convinced of it – but I want to teach the other clay owners a lesson and make sure they never try anything like this again.'

Once again Lily felt there was a hard streak in Ben that others had not recognised. She also realised he had major problems on his mind, but there was one more question she needed to ask.

'How is this going to affect you and Deirdre?'

'It won't.'

'Oh!'

Lily was closing the door behind her when Ben spoke again. 'This won't affect Deirdre and me because there's never been anything between us. She made that perfectly clear when I went to see her, on Jo's birthday.'

'What are you smiling at, young lady? Not that I'm complaining, it's good to see someone in the house today who hasn't got a face as long as a shovel,' Miriam said as Lily entered the kitchen.

'I've just asked Ben whether things were going to be all right at Ruddlemoor. He said they were and I believe him.'

'Hm! I hope he finds some encouragement from your faith in him. He's got a great many more of us worried sick.'

Chapter 34

Ruddlemoor began shipping clay once more the day after Ben reduced the price dramatically. Suddenly, buyers were practically queuing, so eager were they to take advantage of the new low price.

Shortly before noon, Jim Bray brought word to the office that the major clay companies had dropped their price by a further sixpence a ton.

Seated in a chair in the office, Ben was aware that Tessa, Jo and Captain Bray were awaiting his reaction anxiously. He digested the information for some moments before saying, 'All right, we'll play their game. Bring our price down to a pound. They won't go lower than that.'

'But . . . we'll be losing money hand over fist, Ben!' Jim Bray was deeply concerned.

'True, but we've joined in the game. Now we've got to play it through to the bitter end.'

'It's going to worry the men when they hear about this latest price cut,' said Jo. 'They were talking about things when I went to the "dry" to check their shipping figures this morning. They're worried that there's no way we can win a battle with the other clay works.'

'Then we'll need to reassure them, won't we? Come on, Jim. Let's go round and talk to the men. After all, everything depends on their working as hard as they can. They won't do that if they don't believe in what they're doing.'

For the remainder of that day Ben and the Ruddlemoor captain walked around the Ruddlemoor workings, speaking to every man and woman from the quarry to the 'dries' informing them of what was happening. Doing their best to boost confidence, they assured the workers that Ruddlemoor would win through in the end.

The men and women responded as Ben hoped they might, working with a grim determination that the other owners would not put Ruddlemoor out of business.

However, when darkness fell and the men went home, they met others from local works in their homes and in the public houses, and doubt began to creep in that they would survive the crisis. The biggest question was whether Ben Retallick had the skill and experience to survive a price war when every other major works was lined up against him.

He went home that evening to find that Josh too was fearful of the consequences for the clay works he had so recently handed over to his grandson.

It was a gloomy supper at the Gover Valley house that evening as the crisis was discussed.

'I think the best thing you could do is to go and speak to one of the other owners, Ben,' said Josh. 'General Grove, for instance. He probably has more influence in the industry than any other owner. Ask him to call a halt to this ridiculous price war. The only winners in the end will be the buyers. It will be disastrous for the trade. If Ruddlemoor goes under then a great many of the smaller workings will probably collapse too. Even the larger companies will lose far more money than they can afford. Then there's the misery it will cause in countless homes if their men are laid off . . .'

When Ben made no reply, Josh said, 'I'll go and see him, if you'd prefer that?'

'*No one* will go and speak to him.' Ben spoke so firmly that the others looked at him in surprise. 'There's nothing General Grove would enjoy more than having a Retallick go to him, cap in hand, and beg his help.'

'So who cares what he thinks? Humility comes harder to a young man than to an old one. If it will help keep the men in work, and their families fed . . .'

'It won't.' Ben interrupted his grandfather for a second time and once again surprised all except Lily with his assertiveness. Fiercely, he continued, 'General Grove doesn't give a damn for those who'd lose their jobs. He certainly wouldn't do anything that might save Ruddlemoor – especially now Varcoe's closed down. He only needs to close down one or two more works and he and his friends will have control of all clay production in Cornwall and corner the market to the whole of Northern Europe. Once he has that, he and the others can raise prices as much as they like. Buyers will have to pay – or go without.'

Ben had the full attention of the others as he said, 'This isn't just an example of petty spite against Ruddlemoor. General Grove and the others are after a clay monopoly, no less. If they succeed they'll begin doing the same things among themselves, until one of them emerges on top – but knowing that is of no help to us. We've got to stop them now.'

Putting her knife and fork carefully on her plate, Miriam said, 'If what you say is true then Ruddlemoor doesn't stand a chance. You might just as well close down now, before too much money is lost. You can't fight against the combined strength of the other companies.'

'Ruddlemoor might not be able to, but *I* can – for a while, at least. Possibly for a lot longer than they think possible.'

'But if they drop prices still more?' asked Josh.

'They won't,' declared Ben, confidently. 'They know we're selling

307

at a considerable loss now. They'll stockpile their own clay believing that when our stocks have gone we must continue to work at a loss for as long as we're able if we're to meet our commitments. They'll let us go on in the belief, first of all, that we won't be able to produce enough to meet demand. When that happens they'll make up the shortfall – at a price.'

Looking around the table at the others, he continued, 'Secondly, they'll expect Ruddlemoor to lose so much money we'll be forced out of business within the month.'

'I'd say you've just given us a fair assessment of the situation,' said Josh, resignedly. 'Whether it's what they're thinking or not, we can't go on selling China clay for less than it's costing us to take it out of the ground.'

'As I said, I'm so confident of winning that I'm willing to put my own money on the line – but that's not all. I'm not just sitting back trying to ward off everything the other owners are throwing at me. That's never been the Retallick way. I have some ideas of my own that might make them sit up.'

The others waited for Ben to amplify his latest statement, but it was clear he intended saying no more on the subject right now.

Finishing his meal, he said, 'I think I'll go for a walk. It's a fine, clear night. Just right for clearing out thoughts of General Grove and the schemes of his fellow clay owners.'

'Do you want to walk on your own, Ben, or can I come with you?' Lily asked. 'I haven't been out of the house all day and I'd like a walk too. It won't take me a few minutes to clear the table . . .'

'I'd like your company,' said Ben. 'I'll help you clear.'

'No, you won't,' said Miriam. '*I'll* clear the supper things. Off you go, Lily, and see if you can talk some sense into this young man. We have a responsibility to the men and women who work at Ruddlemoor. Some of them came here from Bodmin Moor to work for us. Even so, they won't expect us to ruin ourselves on their behalf, fighting a hopeless battle that's not of our making.'

When Ben and Lily had left the room, Miriam made no immediate attempt to clear the supper things from the table. Instead, she sat back and looked at Josh, who was deep in thought.

'Well, you know the clay business better than any of us, how serious is this mess that Ruddlemoor is in?'

'More serious than anything I faced in my years in the business, Miriam. I feel sorry for the lad having this happen so soon after taking over. I feel I want to help, but he's right. I believe this might have happened whoever owned Ruddlemoor.'

'If he's right in that, do you think he can save Ruddlemoor?'

'I can't see how . . . but I've seen so much happen in my lifetime that

I'm probably over-cautious. There's one thing that makes me hopeful.'

'Oh! What's that?'

'He's a Retallick, through and through. When I listen to him sometimes I'm reminded very much of our Daniel. There's the same inner strength there. He's still a young man, but I think General Grove and his friends might have seriously under-estimated our grandson, Miriam.'

Chapter 35

The night was warm and cloudless and the almost-full moon dominating the western sky might have been held in place by an invisible thread.

Deep in thought, Ben looked up at the sky and said, 'Such nights remind me of Africa. I never realised England could be like this.'

'We've had a mild winter this year. You've been lucky. You wait until next winter. Some nights are really raw.'

'Raw?' Ben repeated. 'That's a very expressive word to describe extreme cold. It conjures up all sorts of images.'

'Do you wish you'd never come to England?' Lily asked the question abruptly and unexpectedly.

'Is it the weather that's prompted that question, or Ruddlemoor?'

'Everything – but especially Ruddlemoor.'

'I don't think so. No business ever runs smoothly. Problems are there to be overcome. We might even profit from this one.'

'How?' There was disbelief in the question.

'I can't answer that fully until I've had a reply to the telegram I sent off yesterday . . . That reminds me. I was going to ask a favour of you, Lily. If a telegram is delivered to the house for me tomorrow and I'm at Ruddlemoor, will you bring it to me right away? Time is a critical factor in everything I'm doing at the moment.'

'Of course. But what happens if things don't work out the way you want them to, Ben? What will you do?'

'I haven't given that possibility any thought. I suppose if the worst happened, I could always return to Insimo.'

It was not a serious reply, but Lily took it up immediately.

'You couldn't do that! For years Josh has talked of how he was one day going to pass Ruddlemoor on to you. Now he's done it. If Ruddlemoor fails and puts all his workers – his friends, as he calls them – out of work, that will be bad enough. If you left and went back to Africa it would break his heart. Both their hearts, because Miriam is just as committed as he is.'

'I could always take them back to Africa with me.'

'I doubt if either of them would go,' replied Lily, still taking him seriously. 'They'd both feel they ought to stay here and help everyone at Ruddlemoor.'

'How about you? Would you like to see Insimo?'

'It's something I've dreamed about for as long as I can remember. Even the name has a magical quality about it . . . But it couldn't happen, Ben. I'd stay here and take care of Josh and Miriam. They'd need me.'

Moved by her earnestness, he said, 'Well, Ruddlemoor isn't going to collapse, I can promise you that. But I want us to emerge from this so strong that the other owners will never again try to put Ruddlemoor out of business. The only doubt I have is how far I'm going to be able to go towards that end. The telegram should make that clear. That's why it's so important.'

'Will the telegram be coming from Insimo?' Lily had a sudden alarming thought. 'You're not going to borrow money to help Ruddlemoor?'

Sensing her genuine concern, Ben said, 'I don't need to borrow money, Lily. You see, before I left Rhodesia, the family agreed that Insimo should be taken over by Nat, as he's the eldest brother. Adam is happy with the farm in Transvaal that's come to him through his wife – and I was to have Ruddlemoor. But there's also gold on Insimo land. We've known about it since long before Pa died, but have never done anything about it before. When Nat decided he wanted to work it, we agreed that we should all take an equal share of the profits. The survey that was carried out shortly before I left suggested it was going to be a very rich mine indeed. I telegraphed Nat, outlining what was happening here and asking how much my share is worth. How much I can spend to save Ruddlemoor.'

They walked along the moonlit valley in silence for some minutes before Lily said, more quietly than before, 'You're really a very rich young man, aren't you, Ben?'

'I suppose I am. It was nothing I ever thought about before I came to England. Seeing all the men who work at Ruddlemoor who have very little has made me realise just how lucky I am.'

When Lily said nothing in reply and the silence had lasted too long, he asked, 'Does it worry you that I'm rich, Lily?'

'Why should it?'

'I don't know, but I've noticed that most people seem to behave differently when they learn I own a clay works. It seems they feel uncomfortable when speaking to someone whom they believe to have a lot of money. I don't want you to be one of them.'

'It shouldn't worry you. The people you'll be mixing with once you're fully settled in Cornwall will have money themselves. People like Lady Tresillian. It won't matter to them.'

'I don't think you're right there, Lily. I think having money matters even more to them than it does to anyone else. Anyway, if they all turn out to be like Lady Tresillian's friends, the clay works owners, I'm not very sure I want to mix with them.'

'You will,' declared Lily, positively. 'You've just had a bad

311

experience, that's all. They won't all be like that. Now, shall we turn back to the house? I have one or two things to do before I go to bed.'

They spoke very little for the remainder of the way back to the house and Ben realised he was disappointed with the outcome of their walk. On previous occasions when they had been alone, he had felt Lily warming towards him. He had wanted it to be the same tonight.

He would need to straighten things out between them – tell her that neither of them should allow his money to come between them. But first he needed to solve the problems faced by Ruddlemoor.

The telegram Ben was awaiting arrived at the Gover Valley house mid-afternoon the following day. With only the briefest of explanations to her employers, Lily threw on her coat and hurried from the house.

She ran for much of the way to Ruddlemoor and burst into the office, hot and out of breath.

'Where's Ben?' she asked a startled Jo.

'I don't know. He's somewhere about the workings, I'm not sure exactly where. Why? Has something happened?'

'Here's Ben now,' said Tessa. 'and he seems in an almighty hurry too. What's going on?'

Lily almost collided with Ben in the office doorway as he came in.

'I saw you arrive in a great hurry. Has the telegram come?'

Instead of replying, she held out the long envelope to him.

Feverishly, Bern tore it open and studied the contents as Lily watched apprehensively.

Suddenly letting out a whoop of glee, he grabbed her in an exuberant hug and swung her off her feet. When her lowered her to the ground once more he was still so excited he gave her a happy kiss that raised the eyebrows of the other two girls in the office.

'Can we take it you've just received some good news?' asked Tessa. 'Or do you intend behaving like this whenever you enter the office in future?'

'I might,' Ben said, happily. 'But you're right about one thing. The news couldn't be better!'

'Does it mean that no one at Ruddlemoor need worry about their jobs any more?' The question came from Jo.

'It means far more than that,' declared Ben happily. 'But I can't tell you any more at the moment.'

Suddenly he thrust the telegram at Lily, 'Do you remember what we were talking about last night, and the question I telegraphed to my brother? Here, look at the reply.'

The telegram was short, no more than two lines. But the message was all that Ben could have hoped. It said simply, 'Sky the limit. Insimo can cover all you spend. Good luck. Nat.'

Chapter 36

Ben wasted no time setting in motion the various plans he had formulated during the previous thirty-six hours. One of his first calls was upon the owner of Ruddlemoor's neighbouring clay works.

Aloysius Varcoe lived in a large house, Tregarrick, situated off the Pentewan Valley, on the far side of St Austell from all the clay workings.

Varcoe was a white-haired, stoop-shouldered man who walked slowly and stiffly, as though the joints of his legs required lubrication. He greeted Ben warmly, if not over-effusively, saying, 'It's good to meet you at last, my boy. I've known and admired your grandfather for a great many years. Envied him, too. I've always wished *I* had someone to whom I could hand over the clay holdings I've built up over a lifetime. Mind you, it wouldn't be doing a favour to anyone I cared for if I were to hand the works over to him at the present time. Speaking of which, I believe you're having your share of problems too? But come in! Come in, dear boy. Have a drink with me. It's one of the few pleasures I can enjoy now – although the damned doctor would take that away from me, if I let him.'

Following the stooped old man into a small but elegant entrance hall, Ben smiled. 'I'd like to have a talk with you but, if you don't mind, I'll leave the drink for some other time. I have a great deal to do this evening and I'm going to need a clear head.'

Awkwardly, Aloysius Varcoe turned to look at Ben. 'You're not closing down Ruddlemoor?'

'On the contrary, I'm fighting back – and I intend winning!'

'Good boy! Good boy! If only I were fifty or sixty years younger, I'd show 'em a thing or two as well . . . But I'm too old for fighting. Too tired to take on the world . . . and that's what it's seemed I've had against me this week. The whole damned world.'

They were in an airy, wood-panelled study now and the ageing clay works owner waved Ben to a leather-padded armchair before taking up a half-filled glass of scotch.

'You're quite certain you won't have a drink?'

'Quite certain, thank you.'

'You know best.' Varcoe sat down heavily in a chair similar to the one on which Ben was seated. 'Now, what can I do for you?'

'You've closed down the Varcoe works for the time being . . .' Ben began.

He was interrupted by the old man. 'No! It's closed down for good. It seems to me as though I've been fighting the other owners for most of my life. It had become second nature to me. I did it because I believed I owed it to my workers to keep the works open. Now they've shown their gratitude by turning on me and refusing to work unless I pay them more, it means I've no reason to fight any more. I can stay here, in comfort, and drink myself into an overdue grave . . . I'm sorry, I'm interrupting you. My apologies, dear boy. Please go on.'

'If the Varcoe works isn't going to reopen again then I wonder if I might make use of your "dry" – using my own men, of course? If I can keep producing clay, even if I'm losing on the selling price, I can beat the other owners. Not only that, they'll have burned their fingers so badly they'll think twice before playing underhand tricks again.'

'That's like saying you'll teach them to live without breathing, but I don't doubt you've thought out what you're doing. By all means, use the "dry", but you might have problems transferring wet clay from Ruddlemoor. There's plenty at the Varcoe ready to dry. Use that. Sell my own stock-piled clay too if it will help your scheme. Pay me back the price you get for it – less ten percent for yourself. I'm not out to make a profit any more than you are, it seems. If it defeats the others, I'll be happy.'

'That's very generous of you, sir. Now I know I can beat them.' Ben stood up. 'It's very rude of me to say I'm leaving after such a brief visit, having succeeded in what I came for, but I really do have a great many more things to do . . .'

'Don't apologise, dear boy – but I shall expect another visit from you when all this nasty business is over. Bring your grandfather with you. He and I can reminisce about days when clay owners were honest and honourable men.'

They were crossing the entrance hall, the old man ahead, when Ben said suddenly, 'Will you be selling your works?'

'Very soon. News of what's happened there has already reached the Tresillian lawyers. They were here this morning with an offer.'

Trying to contain his excitement, Ben said, 'I'll top any price they put on the Varcoe.'

'Will you, be damned.'

Aloysius Varcoe gave Ben another of his wry looks. 'Where is all this money you seem to have to play with coming from? Ruddlemoor hasn't made that much over the years.'

'I'm using my own money.'

'You're *that* confident you'll succeed?'

'I'm that *determined* to win.'

'I do believe you are. Well, if you're prepared to risk your own money, then I'll tell you what *I'll* do. The Tresillian lawyers made me a fair offer, I'll give them that. Trouble is, if the Varcoe workings get into their hands they'll go to the owners I've done battle with all these years. They'd be able to make things difficult for you too, especially as both Varcoe and Ruddlemoor are sharing the same railway line. If you're serious about wanting Varcoe you can have it for the price the Tresillian people have offered me. I don't *need* any more. When I die, everything I have will go to some great-nephew. I've never seen the brat and couldn't stand his father. Besides, it will be worth more than money to have the other owners eating humble pie at last. It's going to choke them! All right, young man, if you want the Varcoe it's yours. In the meantime, do as you will with it.'

'There's just one thing,' said Ben. 'I shall probably be re-employing a lot of Varcoe men. Is there anyone who can give me a list of the troublemakers? The ones I *won't* want back?'

'Go and see Captain Jeremiah Rowe. He lives at Bugle. He was my works captain until he and I fell out about six months ago. I dismissed him. It was the worst day's work I ever did. The argument was my fault and I should have apologised instead. If you need a good captain, the best in the business, you'll take him on again. Good luck to you, dear boy, and don't forget – I shall expect you to visit me soon.'

After leaving the home of Aloysius Varcoe, Ben changed his plans. Instead of returning to Ruddlemoor to speak with Jim Bray, he rode on to Bugle and enquired for the house of Jeremiah Rowe.

Ben liked the man immediately. Seated in the kitchen of his neat, small cottage, smoking his pipe in an armchair beside the fire, Jeremiah Rowe deliberated before he said anything. His manner gave the impression of a solid, reliable man, not given to making hasty decisions – about anything.

When Ben told Rowe the reason for his visit and that he had been recommended by the Varcoe works owner, Jeremiah sucked on his pipe for some moments before saying, 'Aloysius Varcoe was always a hasty man. A good boss for all that, most of the time.'

'Will you come back to the Varcoe and work for me?'

Rowe looked at Ben from serious, brown eyes and he had the uncomfortable feeling the older man was taking his youth into the decision he had been called upon to make.

'Well, now,' said Rowe, 'I quite enjoy being home to do all the things I never found time for before. I'm not at all certain I *want* to go back to working clay.'

'Don't you take any notice of him,' Jeremiah Rowe's wife interjected from the other side of the kitchen, speaking to Ben. 'He's been a lost man since he stopped working up at Varcoe. He's lived, talked and even dreamed clay, I suspect, for all his life.'

315

To her husband, she said, 'What do you think you're playing at, Jeremiah? Young Mr Retallick comes here with an offer for you to go back to what you enjoy doing most, and you're here "humming" and "ahing" as though he's asking you to put your head on a block. It would serve you right if he went away and took someone else on as the Varcoe captain!'

'I'm happy to offer you a rise of ten percent on what you were earning with Mr Varcoe,' said Ben. 'I intend giving a pay rise to the workers too. I want a good and loyal workforce at both Ruddlemoor and Varcoe.'

'That sounds sensible,' said Jeremiah Rowe, non-commitally. 'When do you want an answer?'

'I want the Varcoe working by the day after tomorrow. There are a lot of other things I have planned too. If you think you'd like to come and work for me, I'll see you at the Retallick house in the Gover Valley tomorrow morning at nine. If you come, I'd like you to bring a list of the men it might be better not to take on again. Those who caused the trouble that eventually forced Mr Varcoe to close down. Jim Bray will be there, and my grandfather too. I intend taking their advice on what I want to do.'

Jeremiah Rowe removed the pipe from his mouth and knocked it out in the fire before speaking. 'If you're prepared to listen to the advice of them as knows the business, like Josh Retallick and Jim Bray, then I reckon we might be able to get along. I'll think seriously about it, Mr Retallick.'

'He'll be there,' said Mrs Rowe in a no-nonsense voice that reminded Ben of his grandmother's. 'And you'll not find a better clay captain in the whole of Cornwall.'

Chapter 37

It was close to midnight when Ben returned to the Gover Valley. After speaking to Jeremiah Rowe he had intended going to Ruddlemoor, but along the way he had time to assess the momentous happenings of the day.

Things were moving far faster than he had planned and the unexpected availability of the Varcoe works had thrown his original plans into disarray. Now Ruddlemoor's near-neighbour had become essential to his new strategy.

If Varcoe fell into other hands it would be disastrous. The tramway linking Ruddlemoor with the main railway ran across Varcoe land. This was Ruddlemoor's lifeline. Were it to be closed to him, all Ben's schemes would be foiled and Ruddlemoor would be strangled to death.

The purchase of Varcoe had to be put beyond all risk immediately.

Returning to Aloysius Varcoe, Ben told him of the vital role his works would play in the scheme to defeat the other clay owners and the necessity to execute a sale immediately.

Aloysius Varcoe appreciated the importance of the deal to Ben and messengers were sent to the Varcoe and Ruddlemoor lawyers.

They worked through the evening and into the night. There were still a number of formalities to be completed, but when Ben went off to the Gover Valley he had a copy of a deed of sale in his pocket. He also rode in the knowledge he now owned both the Ruddlemoor and Varcoe works.

After stabling his horse, he walked quietly to the front door. Not a light was to be seen and he thought everyone must be in bed. However, as he reached the door, it opened and Lily was silhouetted in the doorway.

'I was waiting by the window,' she whispered. 'Come through to the kitchen. Josh and Miriam are in bed.'

Lily closed the door quietly behind him and Ben walked along the passageway to the kitchen, guided by a light shining past a partly opened door.

Entering the room behind him, she closed the door and scanned his face critically. 'You look exhausted. Sit down and I'll make you a cup of tea. The kettle's boiling already.'

'It's good of you, Lily, it's been a hard day. Since you brought the

317

telegram to me I seem to have ridden over half of Cornwall. But you shouldn't have waited up for me.'

He wondered how long she had been sitting in the darkened room watching for him through the window.

'It's been a worrying time for everyone who has anything to do with Ruddlemoor – but especially for you.' Lily poured him a cup of tea and handed it to him as he sat down heavily, close to the fire. 'Can I get something for you to eat?'

'I think I'm probably too tired to eat. After I've had my cup of tea, I'll go upstairs and collapse.'

'I've lit a fire in your room, so it should be nice and warm.'

'Lily, you're an angel. I've made a lot of extra work for you today, one way or another.'

'It will all be worthwhile if it means that Ruddlemoor has been saved. It *is* going to carry on working, isn't it?' she asked anxiously.

'More successfully than ever,' confirmed Ben. 'But I'll tell you everything in the morning. I've arranged a meeting here for nine o'clock. Jim Bray and Jeremiah Rowe will be coming and I want Grandfather to join in. His views will be important.'

Stifling a yawn, he said, 'I'll tell you all about it over breakfast. I hope you'll be as delighted about everything as I am.' Another yawn followed close on the first and Ben said, 'All this excitement has worn me out.'

Standing up, he walked slowly to the door, passing Lily. As he did so, he said, 'Thank you, Lily. Thank you for everything.'

It seemed a natural thing to do to kiss her and he did so, but it lasted too long for a 'thank you' and Lily broke away. 'No, Ben.'

'What's the matter?' He thought he had offended her but could not understand why. They had kissed before.

'It doesn't seem right. Not here in Josh and Miriam's house.'

'Would you feel better if we went outside and stood on the doorstep?'

The suggestion raised a smile and Lily shook her head, 'It's not that, Ben. I . . . I can't really explain it, but . . . it just doesn't feel right, that's all.'

'You're not angry with me?'

'Of course I'm not – but you're tired. Go on up to bed now. I want to clear up here before I go to bed.'

'All right. Good night, Lily. And I am truly grateful to you.'

When Ben had left the kitchen, she tried to analyse the feelings she had for him and the reason she had stopped him kissing her a few minutes earlier. She had wanted him to. Had hoped he would. Yet . . .

As she washed up the cups they had used and put them away, Lily realised she had spoken the truth to Ben. It did *not* seem right to carry on any sort of affair with him in the house where she was employed by his grandparents.

318

Whatever was said about her being 'family', she was an employee – and Ben was an extremely rich young man, with a future in the county. The best she could hope for was an affair with him, and pride would not allow her to contemplate this.

She was honest enough with herself to know she wanted Ben as she had never wanted anyone. If there were no reasons other than the differences in their station why they could not marry, she would probably not hold back from him.

Lily suddenly smiled as she thought of what those she knew would say if they realised she was assessing the situation in such a shameless manner. Her parents, Josh and Miriam, Jo – even Tessa – would all be deeply shocked.

But there *were* other reasons why there could be no romance between her and Ben. She was working for Josh and Miriam and was very fond of both of them. She believed it would hurt them deeply if she carried on an affair with their grandson beneath their own roof.

She could not, and would not, do this to them. Hard though it might be, she would need to keep Ben at arm's length and ensure that her feelings for him remained well hidden.

Chapter 38

'You look *awful*!'

The comment upon Ben's appearance came from Lily when he walked down the stairs the following morning. She was carrying breakfast plates from the kitchen to the dining-room from where he could hear his grandparents in conversation with each other.

'I'll survive,' he replied ungraciously. Aware that his reply had been less than polite, he added, 'I was tired last night, but my brain wasn't. I spent most of the night going over all that had happened during the day.'

Lily smiled at him. 'Go and join Josh and Miriam while I cook you some breakfast. They're both busting to know what's happening.'

'I'd like you to be there too, Lily. It's really very exciting news.'

'All right, you go and do your best to prevent them both exploding with curiosity until I've brought your breakfast in.'

As Lily had warned him, containing the curiosity of Josh and Miriam was not easy, but he managed to ward off most of their questions until Lily returned to the dining-room and sat down with them.

'Right,' said Miriam. 'Now we're all here, tell us what it was that kept you out for half the night and has left you looking as limp as a wrung-out dish-cloth?'

'I've bought the Varcoe works,' said Ben, matter-of-factly. 'Aloysius Varcoe and I had the lawyers working on it until late last night.'

The effect his announcement had upon the others was dramatic. Miriam and Lily looked at him with a mixture of amazement and disbelief. Josh dropped the fork he was holding to the floor.

'You've . . . what!'

'It wasn't part of my original plan,' admitted Ben, 'but when I went to ask Aloysius Varcoe for permission to use his "dry" for our clay, he told me he intended selling. He'd already had an offer from the Tresillian lawyers.'

Josh expelled air between his teeth in a near whistle. 'Had they got their hands on the Varcoe works it would have spelled the end for Ruddlemoor.'

'I came to the same conclusion,' agreed Ben. 'So I bought it – and I think Aloysius gave me a very fair price.'

'He's an honest man,' said Josh. 'But where is the money coming from? Ruddlemoor profits wouldn't cover that even in a good year – and this has been a long way from that!'

'I used my own money,' admitted Ben. 'As you say, we couldn't allow the Varcoe works to fall into the hands of the other owners – and that's what would have happened. Lady Tresillian would have bought the works and leased it out – and it certainly wouldn't have been offered to me!'

'I didn't bring you over here so you could pour your own money into the clay business.' Josh was apologetic. 'I wanted to give you something that would *make* money for you.'

'And so it will,' Ben assured him. 'A great deal of money. You'll see.'

Josh shook his head. 'It's lucky for Ruddlemoor you *have* taken it over. Had it still belonged to me, the other owners would have succeeded in what they're trying to do. I couldn't have raised enough money to buy the Varcoe works.'

A sudden thought came to him. 'But how are you going to run Varcoe? Jim Bray can't possibly manage that as well as Ruddlemoor.'

'I'm hoping the ex-Varcoe captain, Jeremiah Rowe, will come back to work for me. I went to see him last night and when I left his wife was telling him he ought to accept my offer. He and Jim Bray should be coming here to see me at nine o'clock this morning to discuss a few things I want to speak to them – and to you – about.'

'If you get Jeremiah Rowe to return to the Varcoe, then you'll be employing the two finest clay captains in the business,' said Josh.

He looked proudly at his grandson. 'To think that I was worried you might not be able to cope with running Ruddlemoor! Since taking over you've been faced with more problems in a week than I've had in ten years – and none of them of your own making.'

Ben tried not to let the others see how pleased he was with Josh's unstinted praise. 'I've not finished yet. Not by a long way. Everything I've done so far has been a fight for survival. Now I'm going to hit back at the other owners and put *them* on the defensive. That's why I've asked Captains Bray and Rowe to meet me here this morning.'

Turning to Miriam, he said, 'I hope you don't mind my inviting people here, but I do want Grandfather to be in on the talk I have with the captains?'

'You live here too,' said Miriam. 'You don't need to ask my permission to have people call.'

'What are the new ideas we're going to discuss?' asked Josh. 'Or would you rather leave the telling until the others are here?'

'No. I'd prefer you to have time to think about them. I intend putting both Ruddlemoor and Varcoe on shift working. I want both works to produce clay for a full twenty-four hours a day.'

The silence that greeted his announcement was an indication of the revolutionary nature of his plan.

'Well!' Josh shook his head in some bewilderment. 'I could probably give you a fistful of reasons why such a plan won't work. The main one is, how will the men in the pits see to wash out clay? You can have lamps in the buildings, but not up on the cliff face.'

'We can illuminate the whole thing,' replied Ben, leaning forward in his seat eagerly. 'With electricity. I've already spoken to the electricity company and they are going to begin work today. Three or four days are all they'll need to have it installed. They have promised to help me rig up the right sort of lamps for the cliff face in the pits. They'll also provide lights for the men who'll be building the huge new "dry" needed for the extra clay we'll be producing. I want the builders to work day and night too. The "dry" will be sited on land between the two present works so that clay from both can be dried there.'

Lily spoke for the first time. 'Where will you find all the extra men you're going to need if you're to work day and night?'

'There'll be no shortage. We'll take back all the Varcoe men – with the exception of a few trouble-makers – and there are plenty of others who've been laid off by the other owners. We've had them lining up at Ruddlemoor seeking work these past few weeks. I'll pay them Ruddlemoor rates which have always been better than any other works. They won't go back, even when the other owners realise the mistake they've made and begin producing more clay.'

Josh was still not entirely convinced that Ben's radical plans would prove successful. 'These grand schemes are all very well, Ben. But it's going to cost a great deal of money.'

'Not nearly as much as you'd think,' he replied eagerly. 'I've costed everything out carefully. All the machinery will be put to full use and I'm bringing in new and more powerful hoses to use on the pit-face – plus a brand new "dry" using all the most modern techniques. The production costs will possibly be slightly less than they are now. Both works will be turning in a regular profit when things are back to normal.'

Ben paused to look at his small audience one by one, his own expression still that of a man fired with enthusiasm. 'There's another bonus in all this too. Because we'll be taking on so many extra men, the other works will need to pay more money in order to attract workers. When they go into production again I intend holding my prices down for at least a month. By the end of that time the owners will be desperate to reach agreement with *us* – or go under. This time I'll make certain they honour their word. We'll be calling the tune and I'll make absolutely certain that's the way it stays.'

For a few moments after Ben had stopped talking there was silence in the room. It was broken by Miriam.

322

'Well! I'm impressed, young Benjamin. When your grandfather and I were in Africa we watched your father build up a trading business that stretched the breadth of the continent. He was only your age and I thought I would never see anyone to match his business sense and ability. Now I think I have. You're a true son of your father, Benjamin. I'm proud of you.'

It was the greatest compliment Miriam could possibly have paid to her grandson and Ben went to his room to dress for the day ahead glowing with pride.

Of the four people in the Retallick house that morning, only Lily did not share in the feeling that there was a rosy future ahead for all of them.

It had been brought home to her once again that Ben was an extremely wealthy young man. With his keen business sense and ambition, he would one day become the most important man in the whole of the Cornish China clay industry.

She shared the pride Josh and Miriam had in their grandson, but there was sadness in her too. Every step taken on the ladder of success by Ben Retallick took him farther away from her – and it was beginning to matter far too much.

Chapter 39

Events in clay country progressed as though they had been scripted by Ben. There was only one minor hiccough when Captain Rowe refused to re-employ two men. One was a proven troublemaker, the other too close a friend of his to keep on at the Varcoe works.

The men appealed to Simon Kendall, calling for Union support in their dispute with the Varcoe works management, claiming they were being victimised.

Ben chanced to enter the Varcoe office when the argument between Captain Rowe, Kendall and the two dismissed men was at its height.

As soon as the men seeking reinstatement saw Ben they made a dash for the door. While the works captain and the Union representative watched what was happening in total bewilderment, Ben kicked the door shut before they could make their escape.

Confronting the men, he demanded, 'What are you doing here?'

'I've refused to take them back on the Varcoe payroll and they've called in Kendall.' Jeremiah Rowe did not understand what was happening, but he replied to Ben's question. 'He's threatening to bring the weight of some damn fool Trades Union to bear on us.'

'I was making no threats,' said Kendall, heatedly. 'I was merely . . .'

'You'll do nothing,' said Ben, firmly. 'And if these two men don't get out of here immediately and promise that we'll hear nothing more of them, I'll have them charged with assault.'

He had recognised the two as those who had attacked him outside the Shovells' home soon after his arrival in Cornwall.

'Assault? I don't understand?' This sudden turn of events had Jeremiah Rowe baffled.

'They do,' said Ben, nodding his head in the direction of the two visibly shaken men. 'Well, what's it to be?'

'I wouldn't work here now if you were to double my pay,' said the bolder of the two. 'Come on, let's go.' He nudged his companion and both men hurried from the office, leaving an embarrassed Simon Kendall to cope with Ben and Captain Rowe.

'I'm sorry . . . I didn't know,' he stuttered, lamely.

'I don't believe you,' retorted Ben, bluntly. 'You were at Jethro Shovell's house when those two attacked me. In fact, you were one of those who ran from the house to help, although I seem to remember you were rather slower than the others.'

'Now look here, Retallick . . .'

Brushing aside Simon Kendall's protest, Ben said, 'I'll be writing a letter to your London headquarters. In the meantime, I don't want you coming near any Varcoe or Ruddlemoor men. I have no objection to their belonging to a Union, but they'll do it through Jethro, not you. Now, if you don't mind, I have business to discuss with Captain Rowe.'

Shaken and angry, Simon Kendall hurried from the office. When he had gone, Jeremiah Rowe looked at Ben with a new respect. 'You have a direct and very forceful way of dealing with problems, Mr Retallick. I'd say the other clay owners will regret the day they tangled with you.'

'I think they're worried right now. There have been crowds out every night to see our men working by electric light and we've had newspaper reporters talking to the men. I don't think it will be very long before a representative of the other owners pays a call on us to suggest a meeting to discuss the clay industry's "problems".'

'Will you meet them?'

'Eventually. We can afford to let them sweat a little first. I've just come from Ruddlemoor. Jim Bray tells me that, contrary to all expectations, we're almost breaking even at the moment. There's the electrical installation and the cost of the new "dry" to be taken into account, of course, but it looks as though we'll be able to pay for all the improvements much earlier than I thought. We've even had clay buyers offering us *more* than our selling price because they're worried about supplies while the other works are holding off to see what happens to Ruddlemoor. I'm in no hurry to put the other owners out of their misery.'

'I can see your point,' agreed Jeremiah Rowe. 'But those most affected by all the troubles are the families of the men who've been laid off.'

'I don't doubt it,' said Ben. 'But it's in their interest that things are settled once and for all. If they're not, we're likely to have this happen all over again one day.'

Jeremiah Rowe did not pursue the matter. Ben Retallick was riding high at the moment and in no mood to discuss the problems of others. The Varcoe works manager would bide his time.

In spite of the forecast he had made to Captain Rowe, Ben was taken by surprise when the clay owners' 'emissary' came to call.

Ben was at the Ruddlemoor works when a coach he recognised, pulled by a pair of matched grey horses, swayed down the steep incline that led to the works office.

The coach belonged to Lady Tresillian. As he opened the office door, he saw Deirdre waving vigorously from the open coach window.

'Benjamin!' Seemingly impatient with the driver who was still climbing from his seat, Deirdre opened the door and kicked the step into position. Raising her skirt above her ankles, she descended from the coach.

Ben leaped forward just in time to prevent her from falling as her foot caught momentarily on the step. A moment later he was holding her in his arms and she was gazing up at him.

'Thank you, Benjamin. That was very clumsy of me. What a good thing you were here to catch me!'

'What are you doing at Ruddlemoor?'

Deirdre pouted fetchingly. 'Could you not have asked that question *after* saying how nice it was to see me after all this time?'

'Very well, it's nice to see you – now what are you doing at Ruddlemoor?'

'I came to see *you*, of course, and to invite you to a weekend at Tresillian – but do we have to talk out here? Can't we go inside your office?'

'We can, but there are two girls and the works captain in there.'

'Send them away somewhere. It's been so long since I've had you to myself.'

Ben contrasted her behaviour with the coolness of their last meeting. 'I can't do that, they work in the office.'

'Oh, Benjamin! I've come all this way to see you. It's the *least* you can do.'

'Deirdre, I am a very busy man at the moment. In fact I need to go to St Austell to speak to my lawyer right now. If you like, I'll tie my horse behind your carriage and ride with you there.'

She pouted again and Ben had the distinct impression that it was an expression she used because she considered it to be attractive and appealing.

'Well, if that's the best you can do . . . but I must admit to being frightfully disappointed. I thought you might put yourself out a little more for me.'

'I'll help you into your carriage then go inside and tell Captain Bray what I'm doing. I'll only be a few minutes.'

Inside the office, Tessa and Jo were at the window, admiring the carriage and its occupant. Addressing Jim Bray, Ben said, 'I'm off to St Austell to speak to the lawyer, Jim. I'll go in the Tresillian carriage and tie my horse behind. I doubt if I'll be back today. I'll go straight home to Gover Valley.'

'You'll be riding in style,' commented Tessa. 'It must be as big as a bedroom inside there.'

Ben looked at her, suspecting an innuendo, but she was studiously looking out of the window.

'Don't I pay you to do some work here?' he asked pointedly.

'She's a pretty enough girl,' commented Jo, as Deirdre looked distastefully down at her dainty shoe which was smeared with wet China clay. 'But for all her fine clothes, she can't match young Lily for beauty.'

Jo's unexpected mention of Lily gave Ben an absurd feeling of guilt. He rounded on her far more sharply than was either necessary or wise.

'If you want to criticise people who come to see me, then do it when I've left the office. I don't want to hear it. Captain Bray, perhaps you can find something more for these two to do? They seem to have far too much idle time on their hands.'

As the door slammed behind him, Tessa said, 'Well! What was that all about?'

Jo smiled mischievously at her friend. 'I think I said something that touched a nerve. There's hope for young Lily yet!'

Chapter 40

'Aren't you going to kiss me as a reward for coming all this way just to see you? I thought you would at least be a *little* pleased to see me again.'

Deirdre made the complaint as the Tresillian carriage lurched up the final steep slope from Ruddlemoor and gained the relatively even surface of the road.

Ben gave her what was intended to be a perfunctory kiss, but she clung to him and made it last until he was forced to push her away in order to breathe.

Sulkily, Deirdre said, 'You've done better than that before today, Benjamin Retallick, or have you forgotten already?'

'I haven't forgotten anything,' he replied. 'The last time I saw you I seem to remember being told that Lady Tresillian didn't think I was a suitable companion for you.'

'You must forget all about that, Benjamin. My grandmother was still suffering from the effects of the heart attack. It's only now, when she's almost her old self again, that we all realise just how ill she was.'

Deirdre grasped Ben's hand and gazed at him with an expression he might have mistaken for adoration a few weeks earlier. He would like to have thought it the same now, but the word 'scheming' kept occurring to him instead.

'I think she's truly sorry because she realises her behaviour towards you has been unforgivable. When I mentioned that I hadn't seen you for a long time she suggested I come and invite you to Tresillian for next weekend. A few friends are going to be there, but she has arranged it especially for you. It's her way of apologising.'

'These "few friends", will they be the same as before?'

'Some of them, I expect. General Grove will be there, I know, but she's also suggested I invite a few younger people too. It will be fun, Benjamin. Please say you'll come.'

'I can't give you a reply right away, Deirdre,' he prevaricated. 'There's far too much happening in the clay industry at the moment. You must have heard what's going on?'

'I might have, but I certainly can't remember anything of what's been said. Anyway, don't you employ managers, or captains, whatever you call them? Surely they will be able to look after things just for a weekend? Nothing happens then anyway.'

'It's possible, but much depends upon what transpires between now and then. That's why I can't give you an answer right away.'

Deirdre released him and for a while sat looking down at her hands, clasped in her lap. It seemed she was sulking, but then she looked up and said softly, 'You'd have the same bedroom, Benjamin. I could make certain that everything would be the same as before for you – and us.'

He suddenly felt uncomfortably hot. 'I . . . I've told you, I can't promise anything right now, Deirdre. The future of my clay business is in the balance.'

'But you *will* try?'

'Of course.'

It was a blatant lie. He had no intention of spending another weekend at Tresillian House, especially if it was to be spent in the company of General Grove and the clay owners with whom he was currently in conflict.

Ben had no doubt at all that the weekend had been planned by Lady Tresillian. She would be concerned at the amount of revenue she was losing as a result of the present difficulties being encountered by the men who leased clay land from her.

He thought that using Deirdre in an attempt to tempt him to come to Tresillian was contemptible. He wondered how much she actually knew of what was happening and decided she probably knew very little.

They were at the outskirts of the town now and Deirdre suddenly asked, 'Where are you going in St Austell?'

'I think I should go to the Gover Valley first, to pick up some papers I left there, but you can drop me off anywhere. I can ride the rest of the way.'

'Nonsense! We'll take you to your grandparents' house. It means I can enjoy your company for a while longer.' Deirdre took his hand again as she called directions in answer to the coachman's enquiry.

Ben was not sorry when the carriage pulled up outside the house. He climbed from the coach, but before he was able to untie his horse, Deirdre called peevishly from the carriage, 'Benjamin!'

'What is it?'

'You haven't kissed me goodbye.'

Once more Ben was taken by surprise as the kiss he aimed at her cheek was deflected and turned into something that might have scandalised Lady Tresillian.

As the carriage drove away with Deirdre waving a handkerchief from the open window of the carriage, Ben led his horse to the gate of the house. It was then he saw Lily looking from the window. Suddenly he had the uncomfortable feeling that Deirdre's over-amorous farewell had been staged especially for her benefit.

* * *

It seemed Josh had also seen the parting between Ben and Deirdre.

'Am I right in thinking things are better between you and the Tresillian family?'

'I wouldn't say that,' replied Ben, doing his best to ignore the deprecating sniff which came from Lily. 'Deirdre came to invite me to Tresillian for the weekend though.'

'Oh! Then you'll not be interested in the invitation that's come in the post this morning. It clashes with Tresillian.'

'Who's it from?' Ben could not think of anyone else who knew him sufficiently well to issue an invitation to him.

'It's from Martha and her husband – the couple who are in Cornwall from Johannesburg. It seems they're returning to South Africa next week and are throwing a grand party first. We're all invited. Me and your grandmother, you and Lily.'

'Are you going?'

Josh shook his head. 'Your grandmother and I are too old for such things – especially when it would mean travelling all the way to Camborne.'

It was in tin-mining country, no more than twenty-five miles from St Austell.

'But I thought that you and Lily might like to go? Martha says that accommodation will be no problem.'

'What does Lily think of the idea?'

She ceased dusting a sideboard to say, 'I *can* answer for myself, you know. You don't have to ask your grandfather how *I* feel about something!' She fairly bristled with indignation.

'All right, what do you think of the idea?'

'What does that matter *now*?' she retorted contrarily. 'If no one else is going, I'm certainly not travelling to Camborne on my own.'

'You haven't answered my question,' said Ben, displaying a reasoned patience that Lily found quite infuriating. 'If I'd said I was going to the party at Camborne, would you have come with me?'

'I don't know. I might have . . .'

'Yes or no?'

'What does it matter? You're going to Tresillian, so why all these questions?'

Ben turned to Josh and spread his hands wide in exasperation. 'Perhaps you'd like to put the question to her. She might be more inclined to give you an answer.'

'There you go again, behaving as though I'm not here! All right, if you must know, I *would* have gone to Martha's party had it been possible. Does that satisfy you now?'

'Yes. Now I know what you want to do, I can make *my* decision. We'll go to Martha's party. If no one else wants to go, then we'll go on

330

our own. We can travel by train from St Austell to Camborne.'

'You said you were spending the weekend at Tresillian. With Deirdre and Lady Tresillian.'

'No, I didn't,' he corrected. 'I said I'd been invited to Tresillian. I don't think I said anything about actually accepting.'

'But – I've never travelled by train,' Lily stuttered inanely.

'That should make it all the more exciting. We'll sort out the details when I come home tonight. Now I have to fetch some papers from my room and attend a meeting in the solicitor's office in St Austell.'

When Ben had left the room, Josh smiled at Lily. 'There's no need to look so bemused. Ben has made it very plain that he prefers your company to that of Miss Tresillian. I don't think that's so terribly surprising. In fact, I think it shows a great deal of Retallick sense.'

'I'm sorry . . . I just don't understand. You saw him kissing the Tresillian girl when she went off in her grand coach?'

'No, Lily. *You* saw him kissing her. What I saw was *her* kissing *Ben*. It may be only a subtle difference, but it's enough for him to prefer taking you to a party rather than spend the weekend with Deirdre at her grand house in Tresillian.'

Chapter 41

Forty-eight hours before he was due to spend the weekend with Lady Tresillian and her friends, Ben telephoned a message that he was unable to accept the invitation. He did not ask to speak to either Deirdre or her grandmother. Instead, he left a cryptic message with the butler.

If he had needed further proof that the clay owners were acting in collusion with Lady Tresillian, it would have been dispelled that same afternoon.

Oliver Carter, one of the owners who had been at Tresillian during Ben's previous stay, called on him at Ruddlemoor. A slight, nervous, bespectacled man, Carter had been the worst shot at the weekend party.

Shaking hands almost apologetically, his manner belying his words, Carter said, 'It's very good to see you once more, Mr Retallick. I was hoping we might meet again socially this weekend, but I hear you won't be coming to Tresillian after all? It's a great pity. We were all looking forward to the opportunity for a chat with you.'

'I doubt if you've come to Ruddlemoor just to say how sorry you are that we won't be meeting this weekend, Mr Carter.' Ben did nothing to put the nervous clay owner at his ease.

'No. No, of course not. Er . . . is there somewhere we can speak privately?'

Jo and Tessa were in the office and taking a great interest in the conversation between the two men.

'I haven't got round to having my own office built yet, but we can walk around the works.'

'Yes, that will be quite satisfactory.'

The two men left the office, but it was quickly apparent that it was going to be difficult to find any place where men were not busily working. Those not engaged in producing clay were working on the nearly completed 'dry'. Wagons and men were everywhere. As the two passed the existing Ruddlemoor 'dry', a small locomotive steamed noisily out of the loading bay, towing a long line of clay-laden trucks.

'The activity here contrasts greatly with all the other works in the area, Mr Retallick. I had almost forgotten the bustle one would expect to find in a fully employed clay works. I still have a very small workforce producing clay, but the fruit of their labours is having to be stock-piled. I can't afford to sell at the present depressed price.'

'You and the others have only yourselves to blame for the present low price of clay, Mr Carter,' said Ben, unsympathetically.

'I regret that some wrong decisions have been made in the recent past, Mr Retallick. However, unless the price of clay rises to a sound economic level very soon, I for one will go out of business.'

'Yes – as would I, had I not been able to find money to support my business,' retorted Ben, bluntly. 'If you want to blame someone for your present predicament then I suggest you look elsewhere. On the other hand, if you decide to sell the lease I believe you hold from Lady Tresillian, I will be happy to make you a fair offer.'

'I sincerely hope such a situation will not arise, Mr Retallick.' Oliver Carter sounded genuinely alarmed. 'My clay holding was worked by my father, and his father before him. I trust we can arrive at an amicable understanding before things reach such a sorry state. Which brings me to the reason for my visit. As you are unable to join us for a weekend at Tresillian, General Grove suggested we might all meet up this evening, either at his home or at a venue of your choosing.'

Ben had suspected from the beginning that Oliver Carter was merely a messenger boy for General Sir Robert Grove.

'I regret that won't be possible. But if the general – or any other owner – cares to come to Josh Retallick's house in the Gover Valley at about seven o'clock next Monday evening, I'll be delighted to discuss your problems then.'

Oliver Carter knew that General Sir Robert Grove would be infuriated that this young man, hardly more than a boy, should have the power to dictate to him in such a manner. Carter himself found it a difficult pill to swallow. Nevertheless, Ben Retallick was holding all the cards in this game. The general would need to swallow his pride and acquiesce.

'I'll pass the message on. I'm quite certain Sir Robert and some of the other owners will be very happy to come to see you on Monday.'

That night someone attempted to set fire to the Ruddlemoor offices. A rag soaked in paraffin was pushed through the letter-box.

Fortunately, one of the men from the pit was on his way to post a list of the night-shift men through the same letter-box when the incident occurred.

The man approached the office in time to witness a sudden eruption of flame close to the office as a cloth dangling from the end of a stick was ignited. It momentarily illuminated the face of the would-be arsonist.

As the blazing rag was guided through the letter-box, the clay worker, belatedly aware of the intentions of the other man, shouted angrily.

Startled, the man at the office door looked up and saw the Ruddlemoor worker break into a run. He promptly took to his heels, leaving the blazing rag half in and half out of the letter-box.

333

There was no pursuit. The pit worker realised that his first priority was the office. Using the arsonist's stick, he removed the burning rag. However, part of the cloth had fallen inside the office and the doormat was burning.

When men from the nearby 'dry' reached the scene, alerted by the shouts of the pit worker, the door was promptly kicked down. The blazing mat was dragged outside and the flames stamped out by the heavy boots worn by men who worked in the hot-floored 'dry'.

A few minutes later the shift captain reached the scene and promptly sent one of the younger workers running to the Gover Valley to inform Ben of the incident.

Ben was thinking of following Josh and Miriam upstairs to bed when the Ruddlemoor worker arrived. He promptly sent him back to inform the shift captain that he would be there as quickly as possible.

'How will you get to Ruddlemoor?' asked Lily.

'I'll walk. I could be halfway there by the time I saddled my horse.'

'I'll come with you,' she said. 'If there's any clearing up to be done, I can do it.'

Ben did not argue. A few minutes later, after telling Josh what was happening, he and Lily were hurrying through the night, heading for Ruddlemoor.

At the works Ben was relieved to see that the damage to the office was not serious. The works carpenter was already at work replacing the hinges of the kicked-down door.

Lily began clearing up immediately and the pit-worker who had seen the incident was sent for to tell Ben what he had seen.

When he had described what had happened, Lily commented, 'That sounds like one of Eddie Long's friends.'

'I couldn't be certain of that,' said the pit-worker, cautiously. 'I have a feeling I've seen the man's face somewhere before, but I can't honestly remember where. I reckon I might have caught him had I chased after him, but I thought the office was more important.'

'You did the right thing,' agreed Ben. 'Had the office burned down we'd have been in serious trouble. All the orders and accounts are in there. I think you've earned yourself an extra month's pay for this night's work. See Captain Bray on pay day and tell him what I've said.'

'You've made one young man very happy,' commented Lily, as the delighted pit-worker returned to work. 'His name is Billy Kent. He has a new baby and a sick wife to take care of. The money will be a great help to him – and he certainly saved the office. Another five minutes or so and everything would have been well alight. As it is, you've got away with a ruined mat and a few charred floorboards.'

'I'll make sure we have someone guarding the offices here and at Varcoe from now on. We might not be so lucky another time.'

As they walked back to Gover Valley, Lily said, 'Do you think this is the work of Eddie Long and his friends?'

'It could be,' admitted Ben. 'They're all nursing a grievance. But it might just as easily be the work of the other clay owners.'

Sounding suddenly resigned, he said, 'When I think about it, the fire could have been started by any number of people. I seem to have made quite a few enemies since I came to England.'

'Does not having many friends bother you?' asked Lily.

'Not often,' he admitted. 'But I would like to reduce the numbers of my enemies. Especially among the clay owners. We ought to be working together to improve the industry for everyone, not stabbing each other in the back at every opportunity.'

'They'll never be fully at ease with you, Ben. You're far too ambitious. They'll always be looking for a way to bring you down.'

'Do you think I'm too ambitious, Lily?'

'It doesn't matter what I think – and I don't believe it really bothers you what the other clay owners think of you, either. You'll do what needs doing to ensure you're successful – and you probably will be.'

'It doesn't matter what the other owners think of me, Lily, but it *does* matter what *you* think.'

'Ben, please don't start that again. I've told you there can be nothing between us. If you can't accept that then it would be far more sensible if I didn't come to Martha's party with you. It will also make it increasingly difficult for me to stay working for Josh and Miriam.'

'I don't accept that we can't be more than friends, Lily. I never will accept it, but I won't do anything to drive you away from Josh and Miriam. They need you too.'

'If that's a firm promise then I'll let you hold my hand while we are walking home. It's a cold night and I forgot to wear my gloves . . .'

Chapter 42

'This is *fun*!'

Lily and Ben were on the train to Camborne. She sat in a corner seat of the carriage and watched the countryside flying past. It was occasionally obliterated by the pungent smoke from an asthmatic engine no more than a carriage's length ahead of them.

Ben smiled. The stark white spoil heaps of the clay workings, rising above the moors north of St Austell, had just passed from view. Now they were out of sight he began to relax.

'You'd enjoy travelling on a train in South Africa. There are dozens of different animals to be seen along the way. Elephant, giraffe, buffalo, lion . . . you'd love it.'

'Tell me more about your family and Africa, Ben?' Lily was also relaxed and happy to be travelling on a train for the first time in Ben's company.

He told her once again of Insimo, of his mother, the father and brother who had been killed by the Matabele, and of his two surviving brothers.

'The brother who has Insimo now – Nat – will he ever come to England?'

'He might. When he was scouting for the British during the war he became very friendly with the wife of one of the senior army officers who was killed in the fighting. She's married again but I know she writes often to try to persuade him to pay her a visit. I'm not at all certain his wife would want to come, though. When she first met Nat she could only speak Afrikaans and actually fought against the English herself. She was seriously wounded in a battle and Nat got her to hospital.'

'Your other brother fought for the Boers too, didn't he?'

'That's right. He knew Nat's wife at the time. Then he married an Afrikander girl and is now living on a farm in the Transvaal.'

'You have a very interesting family, Ben.'

'They've all gone their own way,' he conceded. 'Ma says it's the Retallick influence. Her family were much more conventional. Her father became the Governor of Mozambique soon after she and Pa were married. It was a very responsible post, the country being about six times the size of England.'

336

This information was difficult for Lily to comprehend. However, it only served to confirm her belief that Ben and his family possessed both wealth and influence, far beyond anything she had met before.

The knowledge detracted from the pleasure she felt at being on a train with him, but it was only a temporary depression. She decided she would enjoy his company while she could.

Ben told her of Nat's reluctance to become involved in the Boer War. However, when Insimo was raided by Boers from the Transvaal, he was unable to stay neutral any longer. For the remainder of the war years, while his brothers were away fighting, Ben was left to run Insimo.

'Don't you miss the life you led there?' asked Lily.

'Sometimes,' he admitted. 'But there's a lot I like here in Cornwall. How about you, Lily? What do you want from life?'

'Not much, really. I expect one day to marry and hope I'll be happy . . .' She hesitated before adding, rather wistfully, 'But I would like to travel a little first. To see something of the world beyond St Austell.'

'You mean you'd like to go to places like Camborne?' Ben mocked her gently, and Lily smiled.

'It's a start, yes.'

They continued the journey talking of places she would like to see and time passed pleasantly for both of them. Shortly before the train reached Camborne station, Lily looked at Ben as he gazed out of the window. She found it difficult to remember that he was potentially one of the most powerful men in the county.

This was the Ben she liked most and felt at home with.

Suddenly aware of her interest in him, he turned and smiled at her. 'I think we must be almost there. I hope it will be a good party.'

Ben and Lily arrived in a decrepit hansom cab at the house where Martha and Jannie were staying, this being the only vehicle plying for hire at the station.

It was mid-afternoon but the party was already in full-swing and some of the men appeared to have been drinking for a very long time.

Suddenly, Ben had misgivings about the wisdom of bringing Lily here. This was a rough crowd and not at all in keeping with the image Martha and her husband had projected when they had visited the Gover Valley.

Martha, who had also been drinking, introduced Ben – and Lily – as grandchildren of the man who had secured her release from a South African jail, even though he was imprisoned himself.

'I owe him a lot,' declared Martha. 'A whole damned lot. So does Jannie. If it wasn't for Josh Retallick he wouldn't have me now, would you, me old darling?'

337

She threw her arms about her red-faced husband, provoking cheers from those about them. It was at this stage that Ben decided he would drink very little for the duration of the party. It might be important to have his wits about him as it progressed.

It was evident that Lily had the same thought and she never moved far from Ben. During the course of the evening, more and more guests arrived until the house became so packed with people they spilled out on to the street outside where a brass band had put in an appearance.

The music attracted yet more men and women. Martha and Jannie were not known to most of them, but it made little difference. Beer was on offer from constantly replenished barrels, and shortly before dusk a wagon arrived with yet more.

This was a party which would be remembered in Camborne for generations.

For much of the evening Ben and Lily remained outside the stifling house, but when it began drizzling sometime before midnight, Lily said in Ben's ear, 'I don't think I'm really enjoying this.'

'I agree with you. What would you like to do now?'

'I feel like calling it a night and going to bed.'

Lily had been allocated a small attic bedroom in the house earlier in the day, when most of the occupants had been reasonably sober.

'I doubt if you'll get much sleep tonight.'

'I realise that, but it's becoming too rowdy here.'

'That's an understatement if ever I heard one!'

A number of fights had already broken out and the noise of the party and the brass band must be keeping most of Camborne awake. 'I'll come up with you and make quite certain you have a lock on the door at least.'

They climbed the dimly lit stairs, picking their way between seated miners and young men and women occupying the darker corners of the stairs and landings.

The last flight of stairs was relatively clear, but when they reached the room allocated to Lily, Ben discovered the door was locked. He rattled the handle and knocked and thought he heard a noise inside.

Ben continued knocking until the door was eventually opened. To his surprise, Martha stood before him, dishevelled and swaying in the doorway. Suddenly a young man slipped past her and hurried down the stairs. Ben had not seen him before, but it was certainly not Jannie.

'He didn't feel very well,' said Martha, her voice slurred. 'I brought him up here to get some air.'

Apparently considering the explanation to be sufficient, she pushed past them and made her own way with exaggerated caution down the stairs. When she reached the first landing, she called back over her shoulder, 'Have fun, you two.'

There was a lamp in the room and Lily lit it. By the yellow light she

338

could see the dressing-bag she had brought with her standing open on the floor. Some of the clothes were hanging half in, half out of it.

Dropping to her knees, Lily rapidly rummaged through her things.

'Is there anything missing?' asked Ben.

She nodded. 'My purse. I left it here because I thought it would be safer than carrying it around in the crowd.'

'Was there much in it?'

Again Lily nodded. 'About four pounds.'

Ben realised this represented about two month's wages. 'I think trying to report it to Martha or Jannie would be a complete waste of time. Don't worry about it, Lily. I'll make it up to you. I'll buy you a new purse too.'

'It isn't the money, Ben. It's just . . . Oh, I don't know! I've been so looking forward to today. It started off so well, with the train journey and us talking about things. But I'm not enjoying the party . . . I wish we could go home now.'

'I'm sorry, Lily, but there won't be a train until morning.'

Ben wished desperately he could do something to ease her unhappiness. 'At least you have a bolt on the inside of the door.'

'That's good.' She had a sudden thought. Nobody had suggested a room for Ben. 'What will you do now?'

'I'll find a corner downstairs and settle down there out of the way.'

'You won't get any sleep. This party is going to go on all night – and probably for much of tomorrow too.'

'I'll be all right.'

'No, you won't.' After only a moment's hesitation, Lily said, 'You can stay in here . . . if you like?'

Ben immediately thought of another night, in another place . . . at Tresillian House. The comparison evaporated when Lily added, 'But only if you promise to behave yourself, and sleep on the floor?'

'All right.'

'Here. You can have the eiderdown, and a pillow.'

Now the arrangement had been agreed, they both felt a little awkward. As Ben took off his shoes, Lily climbed into bed.

'Aren't you going to get undressed?'

'No. I think it's better if I stay like this.'

'Shall I blow out the lamp?'

'No, just turn it down a little.'

Ben turned down the lamp and looked at Lily. She had the bedclothes drawn up to her chin and her eyes seemed larger than usual in the poor light.

He leaned over to kiss her, but she suddenly turned her head away. Kissing her very gently on the cheek, he said softly, 'Good night, Lily. I'm sorry this hasn't been a great success. I really did want you to enjoy today.'

'It isn't your fault, and I have enjoyed being with you.'

It was perfectly true. She had enjoyed Ben's company even more than the novelty of travelling by train to Camborne with him. It could have been such a nice day. It *should* have been.

Lying there in the near-darkness, Lily doubted whether there would ever be another opportunity like today to be with Ben for a whole day – and for the night too. No doubt he would soon meet someone else. A girl like Deirdre Tresillian. They would marry and then she would probably never see him again.

The unhappiness of her thoughts coupled with the disappointment of the day and the events of the evening caused a tear to trickle down her cheek to the pillow. She felt miserable. Utterly miserable.

Suddenly and unexpectedly, a sob broke from her before she could stifle it.

'What's the matter?'

When Ben sat up he saw the tears glistening on the cheek closer to him before she turned her head away.

'You mustn't be so upset, Lily . . . It was only a purse, and I've said I'll give you the money that was lost.'

Another sob escaped her, unstifled this time, and he rose to his feet and crossed to the bed. 'Please don't cry, Lily.'

She looked up and suddenly her arms went out to him. Then he was lying on the bed, the bedclothes between them, holding her while she cried against him.

Chapter 43

Ben had no idea how long he lay on the bed holding Lily. He might even have dozed off. Suddenly he was aware of a loud noise on the other side of the door. Then someone banged against it. The next minute they were pounding on the door, demanding that it be opened.

Putting his feet to the floor, Ben realised he had no shoes on. Finding them, he slipped them on while the hammering on the door increased. Then a voice he thought sounded very like Jannie's called, 'Open this door! I know Martha's in there.'

'Martha's *not* in here.'

Ben called the information as he fastened the second of his shoes. He doubted whether Jannie heard him. There was a great deal of noise on the landing outside the attic room.

Suddenly there was a heavy crash against the door, as though someone had charged it with his shoulder. Someone heavier than the Johannesburg bar owner.

'Wait a minute, I'll open it. There's no need to break the door down!'

Another crash against the door was a clear indication that Ben's words had once again been lost.

Lily was swinging her feet to the ground now and Ben moved towards the door. He was no more than halfway there when there was another crash. The bolt parted company with the door jamb and, as the door flew open, two men fell inside the room. Neither of them was Jannie.

The larger of the two brushed a surprised Ben aside and lunged towards Lily, saying, 'Come out of here, you slut! Your husband wants you, 'though I'm damned if I know why!'

The stranger barely had time to take hold of her arm before Ben struck him on the side of the head, knocking him away from her. The second of the two men who had fallen inside the room had picked himself up now and launched himself at Ben. He suffered the same fate as his companion, but then more men were inside the room and Ben was involved in a desperate fight in the enclosed space of the attic.

Suddenly, he was aware that another man was assisting him. Between them they succeeded in driving the others outside. Not until now did Jannie put in a belated appearance. 'It's all right! Stop it! That's not Martha. I've found her. She was downstairs all the time . . .'

341

Gradually, the battle in the attic died away. Moments later the men who had burst into the room were clattering noisily down the stairs, chattering happily, unconcerned about the mayhem they had caused.

'Are you all right, Lily?' Ben asked her anxiously.

'I'm all right. And you?'

'Yes – thanks to you, sir.' Ben extended a hand to the man who had fought so valiantly on his behalf. 'I'm Ben Retallick and this is Lily. We're both very grateful to you.'

The man who had come to their rescue was aged about twenty-eight and possessed an infectious smile. 'Glad I was around. I'm Sam Doney, Martha's cousin – that's an apology, as well as an introduction. She was always a wild girl, but she's really excelled herself today. I feared something like this would happen. She's been leading Jannie a merry dance since arriving in Cornwall and he's had enough. It's a good thing they're both leaving tomorrow. Another week and Jannie would likely have gone back to South Africa alone.'

He looked about the room. 'But you can't stay here now. The door won't even close properly. You'd better come back to my place, it's just down the road. I've no doubt you'll still be able to hear the party, most of Camborne can, but it needn't bother you. Come on, let's get out of this mad house.'

Ben picked up Lily's dressing-bag and he and Lily followed Sam from the house, forcing their way through the huge crowd of hard-drinking guests.

As they walked away, the brass band struck up once more. They were noticeably more discordant than before they had enjoyed their most recent break for 'refreshments'.

Shouting to make himself heard above the music, Sam said, 'When you arrived, Martha introduced you as Josh Retallick's grandchildren. Are you brother and sister?'

Ben shook his head, 'We're distant cousins. I'm the grandchild. But we both live with Josh and Miriam.'

Ben saw Sam's sudden frown and realised he must have been aware Ben had been in the room with Lily when the door was broken down. He felt an explanation was called for.

'Lily was very unhappy at the party. Someone was in her room when she went up to bed and her purse and money had been stolen. The party was so rowdy that I feared someone else might try to get in. I decided I should stay with her. It was just as well I did. She'd have been terrified had she been on her own. We were both glad you were on hand to help us.'

His voice had not carried to Lily above the din. Sam looked at her before returning his attention to Ben. The grin reappeared and he said, 'I don't know, you seemed to be doing very well. You'd have probably laid them all out without my help.'

342

They had left the crowd and much of the noise behind when Sam turned in at the garden gate of a neat little cottage.

'Here we are, this is my place.' He opened the front door. There was no electricity in here, but lamps were lit in the hall and the room beyond, burning low.

Pushing the door of the room wide open, Sam said, 'Come in here and sit down for a while. When you feel a bit more relaxed we'll sort out where you can sleep.'

The room was a small sitting-cum-dining-room and Lily sank gratefully into an armchair. Suddenly a girl hardly older than herself entered the room dressed in night attire.

Seeing Ben, she gasped and turned to flee, but Sam called her back. 'Wait, Carrie . . . Here, take my coat. You can fetch a dressing-gown in a minute. This is Lily and Ben. They came from St Austell for Martha's party. There's been some trouble there. Lily's had her purse stolen and Ben and I had a bit of a fight with some of Jannie's miner friends from South Crofty. I've said they can sleep here. Lily can have my bed, Ben and I will sleep down here.'

Lily looked horrified. 'I couldn't possibly take your bed . . .'

'You can, and you will. Accept it as a totally inadequate apology on behalf of Martha.'

Lily was about to reiterate that she could not turn Sam and his wife out of their bed, when they heard a sound from the stairs. A moment later a very sleepy little girl of no more than three pattered into the room. Holding up her arms to Sam, she said, 'Daddy!' He picked her up and held her in his arms.

'What are you doing down here? You should be fast asleep now.'

To the others, he said, 'This is Pippa. She's a very lively little girl.'

'You woke me up and I heard you talking.'

'She'll be all right with me for a while,' said Sam to Carrie.

'Then I'll go up and get the room ready for Lily.'

Enchanted by the small child, she only became aware of Carrie's departure when the door closed behind her. Belatedly, she said, 'Is there something I can do to help your wife?'

Sam said sadly, 'She's not my wife, but my sister.'

'Oh, I'm sorry.' Lily wanted to ask more, but thought Sam might have lost his wife recently and be upset to think about it. However, he supplied the information without any prompting.

'It seems a long time ago, now.'

He hugged the small girl in his arms as she sleepily began sucking her thumb. 'Soon after Pippa was born the mine where I was working closed down. Most others around here were doing the same and there was little work to be had. Martha had been writing for years suggesting I should go to Johannesburg and make a fortune in the gold mines there.

Finally, in desperation, I decided to go. I left my wife and baby Pippa here.'

'Wasn't it a success?' Ben prompted, as Sam fell silent for a few moments.

'Oh, it was a success, all right. At least, financially it was. With Jannie's help I did well there. I was able to send money home regularly. Enough to buy this little house. Then, when I had been there just over a year, my wife caught pneumonia and died. I came home and bought a small shop. Carrie helps me to run it and also looks after Pippa. The shop will never make me a rich man, but we won't starve, either.'

By the time Sam had finished his story Pippa was asleep with the thumb still in her mouth. Smiling down at her fondly, Sam said, 'I'd better take this young lady back to bed. She'll sleep now she knows I'm home.'

Unexpectedly, Lily asked, 'Can I take her up?'

'Of course. While you're up there Carrie can show you your bedroom and Ben and I will see you in the morning.'

When Lily took Pippa from Sam there was an expression on her face that Ben had never seen there before. It was a gentle combination of tenderness and care.

When Lily and the child had left the room, Sam commented casually, 'She seems to be a very nice girl.'

'She is,' agreed Ben. 'Lily's looked after my grandparents for some years and very rarely has an opportunity to go anywhere – that's why I'm angry about all that happened tonight. She enjoyed her first train ride today and was really looking forward to the party.'

'Well, perhaps meeting up with Pippa might prove to be some small compensation to her.'

Soon afterwards, Carrie came downstairs with blankets for the two men, but it seemed they were not going to need them. They talked until the early hours of the morning about the clay industry, mining and South Africa.

It seemed to Ben he had slept for no more than a matter of minutes before he was woken up by Pippa's happy laughter. She was a bright little girl and chattered merrily to him and to Lily too when she came downstairs to help Carrie make breakfast.

Sam took Ben and Lily to the station in Jannie and Martha's car. He explained that it would be his when they returned to South Africa, a present from his cousin and her husband. They had decided against taking this particular car back with them. Instead, they would buy a newer model.

Carrie and Pippa came to the station with them. When the train pulled in, Lily gave Pippa a warm hug and received a kiss in return. Then Pippa kissed Ben too.

'I think she's absolutely lovely,' said Lily when she and Ben were inside their compartment and Sam held the little girl up to look inside the carriage.

'If you like I'll bring her in the motor car to see you when Martha and Jannie have gone back?' said Sam.

'Yes, please, I'd love that. You'll find us easily enough in the Gover Valley. If I'm not there I'll be at home in St Austell. Josh or Miriam will tell you how to get there.'

Ben was painfully aware that Lily had not included him in the arrangements she was making.

The guard blew his whistle and waved a green flag and the train pulled jerkily away from the platform. Leaning precariously out of the window, Lily waved until Pippa and the station had passed from view.

Much of the return journey was spent in talking of Pippa – and of her father too. It seemed the night's stay at the home of Sam Doney had driven away many of the bad memories of Martha and Jannie's party.

Ben was relieved, but at the same time felt a totally unreasonable jealousy seep over him.

Ben had money, Ruddlemoor and Varcoe, and he had growing prestige in the clay industry. Yet it seemed to him that in Pippa, Sam Doney had more to offer Lily than anything Ben possessed.

Chapter 44

The meeting of clay works owners at the Gover Valley house was attended by General Sir Robert Grove and eight others. Josh and Miriam were also present, the latter at Ben's insistence. She had considerable knowledge of the clay industry and would help to reduce the owners' advantage in numbers.

The meeting was held in the parlour. It was quite a large room, but Josh and Miriam did very little entertaining and it was discovered there was a shortage of chairs. A number had to be brought from other rooms.

No doubt the clay owners were more used to conducting business over port or brandy, but here in the Gover Valley they were offered tea, served by Lily.

Seated around the room, tea-cups and saucers in their hands, they looked decidedly ill-at-ease. Each seemed to be waiting for someone else to make an opening gambit.

Eventually, General Grove cleared his throat noisily before opening the debate in characteristic fashion. 'Hrrrm! Look here, Retallick. It's high time we stopped all this shilly-shallying and got down to business.'

'Which Retallick are you talking to, General? Me, my grandfather or my grandmother?'

'I'm talking to whoever can bring this damned silly price-cutting nonsense to an end!'

'Then you should direct your remarks to every man who owns a clayworks in the St Austell area, General – including yourself. I didn't start this "price-cutting nonsense", as you call it. I've merely proved that I'm better at it than you. If you recall, when we were all at Tresillian House I suggested we should all *raise* our prices. I thought we entered into an informal agreement on the matter. As a result I came back to Ruddlemoor and raised my prices to the agreed level – only to find everyone else had *dropped* theirs. Had I not been able to call up extra money, Ruddlemoor would have gone under. So don't complain to *me* about reducing prices, General Grove.'

'Hrrrm!' The general cleared his throat once more, this time to cover the embarrassment he felt. 'Very unfortunate, of course. Some misunderstanding, I expect, eh?'

'No, General, you and the others took advantage of my trust and inexperience.'

'Well, it's no use trying to apportion blame now. We're all in this together and each of us is trying to run a profitable business. We need to work together.'

'Co-operation depends upon trust if it's to work,' said Ben, bluntly. 'If I've learned anything at all since I took over Ruddlemoor, it's that not one of you is trustworthy.'

'I find that remark damned offensive, young man!' The general's fiery nature came to the fore and he rose to his feet.

'No,' said Ben, coolly. 'What you find offensive is honesty. Something I don't think you recognise.'

'I'll not stay here to be insulted by an arrogant young whippersnapper.' General Grove turned to leave and the other clay owners stood up uncertainly.

The general actually reached the door before he paused and turned back. 'Look here, young man. There have been faults, I admit that, but the rest of us have been in this business for a long time. Try to understand our point of view.'

'I'll willingly do that, General – as long as you remember that I intend being in this business for a long time, too. Not only that, I intend to be the owner of the biggest and best works in the whole industry.'

As Ben and General Grove glared at each other and the other men stood around, not certain what they should do, Miriam rose to her feet.

'If you men have met up merely to squabble then you're doing a good job of it – but I don't feel like staying and listening to you. I thought you'd come here to talk,. To discuss your problems – and there's no shortage of those in the China clay industry. There's a market out there for china clay and it's going to grow. So if the buyers can't get what they want in Cornwall, they'll look for it elsewhere – and they will find it, you can be assured of that. Now, as there seems to be nothing useful that might be done here, Lily and I will go out to the kitchen and do what needs doing there.'

As Lily followed Miriam from the room and the China clay owners stood around looking sheepish, Josh said, 'I think Miriam has said what needed saying. Now, gentlemen, shall we sit down and discuss what can be done for the good of the China clay industry?'

When the two women reached the kitchen, Lily went to the sink and suddenly Miriam heard her chuckling.

'What's amusing you, young lady?'

'You should have seen General Grove's face while you were talking. I don't suppose anyone's spoken to him in that manner since he was a boy at school.'

'Then they should have done. He needs to be reminded that he's not wearing a general's uniform now. He's not winning – or losing – battles with his red-uniformed soldiers. He's a clay owner, just the same as any

347

of the other men in there. The same as Ben and the same as Josh has been for this past ten years. He's no better and no worse than any other man.'

'One thing's certain: Ben isn't overawed by his being a general and a "Sir" as well.'

'True, and I'll give the boy a certain amount of credit for that. I admit that when he took over Ruddlemoor I was worried with him being so young, but he's more ruthless than Josh could ever be. Even so, he needs to learn tact, and perhaps to give just a little. There's no sense in making enemies when, with a little more thought, he could make a friend.'

Lily had begun washing up at the sink. 'Ben and I were talking about that the other day. He said he seems to have made far more enemies than friends since coming to Cornwall. I think it worries him.'

'Well, it's not entirely his fault. He arrived when the clay industry was going through a difficult time.'

Giving Lily an approving look, Miriam said, 'He's lucky to have you to talk to. The two of you get on well together.'

She was glad she had her back to Miriam. 'Well enough. But I'm not allowing myself to grow to like him *too* much.'

'Why on earth not? You're more attractive than any other young girl in these parts, and young Ben is handsome enough, surely?'

'You saw him just now in the other room. He's half the age of the youngest clay owner there, yet he's the one they've all come to talk to. Whatever they might *want* to do, it's Ben who'll make the final decision on what *will* be done. He's already the most influential of the clay owners. He's also the richest, and it comes natural to him to be entertained in the house of titled ladies. I'm Lily Shovell, daughter of an Association organiser who's been out of work for much of his life. If I wasn't working here for you I'd be a bal maiden – a woman labourer – because I don't know how to do anything else. Think about it, Miriam, I'd be a fool to let myself fall for Ben.'

Miriam gripped Lily firmly by the shoulders and turned her around. 'It seems it's not only the clay owners who need to be sorted out in this house today! Just you listen to me, my girl. Yes, Ben is all these things you say he is, but where do you think all that came from? How do you think it all began? I'll tell you. When I first met Josh, I was a barefoot girl who didn't even live in a proper house. My family lived in a place that was little more than a cave, up on the hill by Sharptor. If I ever worked at all it was as a bal maiden – and even there I was frowned upon by the others who didn't believe I was good enough to work with them. I looked up to Josh as though he was a god because, although he was the son of a miner, he was learning to read and write. I would have done anything for him – and did. Ben's father was conceived on the moor before Josh and I were married.'

348

Miriam saw she had shocked Lily, and smiled. 'I'm telling you this so you'll know exactly where Ben comes from, Lily. I don't want to hear any more of this, "He's far too good for me" nonsense from you. Ben comes from the same stock as you do.'

'All that happened a very long while ago. Ben has had all he wanted from the time he was born. He's never known what it is to be poor.'

'Is there any reason why he should?' demanded Miriam. 'Is being poor a virtue now? If it is then things certainly *have* changed since I was a girl. It never was then!'

When Lily did not reply, Miriam took hold of both her hands. 'Lily, I let Josh go once because I thought I could never marry him. It was only when I believed I'd lost him forever that I realised how much he meant to me.'

Lily believed that Miriam was talking about the time Josh was sentenced to be transported for life.

'That was different . . .'

'No, it wasn't, Lily! Don't you make the same mistake and let foolish ideas get in the way of what you want. Ben wouldn't. If you want him, go after him. I believe you're the right girl for him. Far better than that granddaughter of Lady Tresillian who came here.'

Lily remained silent and Miriam let go of her hands reluctantly. 'It has to be your decision. No one can point out the right man for you. Only you know if he *is* the one. All I will say is, if you do decide it's Ben then you'll have me – and Josh – on your side. Now I'll leave you to carry on with the washing up. There's nothing quite like having your hands in a bowl of suds to help you think . . .'

Chapter 45

A much higher level of agreement had been achieved at the Gover Valley meeting than Ben had dared to expect. The mutual antagonism still existed between himself and General Grove, but neither allowed it to stand in the way of their agreement.

It was decided a committee of six would meet on the first Monday of each month. The members would set a mutual price for the various grades of clay, and discuss any problems that might have arisen within the industry.

Ben would be a permanent member of the committee as the largest freehold owner of clay workings. The general would also be a member on account of his ownership of the largest leaseholding. Three other leaseholders would also sit on the committee, as would an owner, yet to be appointed, representing the numerous small workings scattered among the clay hills.

This latter inclusion had been Ben's idea. He felt it would give the owners of the smaller workings the opportunity to increase their profit as well as offering them a certain sense of security. It might, at the same time, remove the minor irritations caused by the small operators' readiness to undercut the prices of larger clay companies.

Josh approved of Ben's idea, but it was not accepted without resistance from the other owners. General Grove in particular.

'Dammit!' he said irritably. 'Some of these so called "clay workers" have no more than a father and a couple of sons working them. They probably don't even keep accounts, far less understand the costs involved in running businesses like ours.'

'Then it will be up to us to teach them what they need to know,' retorted Ben. 'To prove to them it's in their own interests to stay in line with us. Besides, the committee is being set up to help the business of each and every one of us. It's not intended to be yet another exclusive club for the benefit of a few country gentlemen.'

General Grove was still quietly fuming when he and the others left the house. Nevertheless, each owner had put his signature to a document which provided for the formation of a China Clay Owners' Association. The price of top quality clay for the forthcoming month had also been agreed and witnessed by all present.

'This time I think they'll keep their word,' said Ben with great satisfaction when he returned to the parlour where Miriam and Lily were now ensconced.

'I don't doubt it for one minute,' agreed Josh, heartily. 'They left here looking to me like men who'd learned a very hard lesson.'

The look he gave Ben was filled with admiration. 'I never thought General Grove would ever set foot in my house, far less leave it with a flea in his ear, put there by a grandson of mine! You'll be the top man in the clay industry before you're much older, young Ben, there's no doubt about that. None of the owners will dare do anything unless they've spoken to you about it first.'

Lily was watching Ben uncertainly as Josh made his statement.

Miriam tried to catch Josh's eye with a stern glance, but he did not look in her direction as he enthused, 'Yes, Ben. I wouldn't be surprised if one day you bought out all the other owners – including General Grove.'

Josh finally glanced in the direction of his wife and his smile was immediately replaced by a questioning frown. Before he could ask the question that sprang to his lips, Miriam shook her head discreetly.

Bewildered, Josh looked from Miriam to Ben, and then to Lily, but still did not understand.

Just then there was an unexpected knock at the front door and Lily left the room to see who was there.

When she had gone, Josh asked, 'What have I done wrong?'

'We'll talk about it later,' said Miriam, uncommunicatively, as Lily returned to the room. Behind her was James Smith, one of the clay owners who had just left the house with the general, but not one who had been chosen to serve on the committee.

Miriam thought the man had probably left something behind and her glance went round the room, but he was speaking to Ben. 'I've returned because I'd like to have a word with you, Mr Retallick.'

'Is it something you can say here?' asked Ben.

Suddenly seeming ill-at-ease, Smith said, 'I'm sorry to appear rude, but I would prefer it if I might speak with you in private.'

The clay owner looked apologetically at Miriam, but she said, 'That's quite all right. We have plenty to do elsewhere.'

Outside the room, Lily said, 'I'll go and finish clearing up in the kitchen.'

When she had gone, Miriam led Josh to the small room where she did her sewing, made up the household accounts and wrote her letters. Hardly large enough to warrant the title of 'study', it was more in the nature of a den, a place to which she could retreat when she wanted to be alone.

'What's this about?' asked Josh as Miriam closed the door behind them. 'I saw you looking at me earlier as though I'd said something wrong.'

'It's a pity you didn't understand what I was trying to tell you before you started talking about what a great man our Ben is going to be one day.'

'I'm sorry, Miriam. I don't understand?' Josh's expression showed his puzzlement.

'Tell me, Josh, if you could choose a good wife for Ben, who would it be?'

'Why, young Lily of course. We've spoken of it before. But. . .'

'But nothing!' retorted Miriam. 'The two of them might have been made for each other. But all this talk of money and power, of Ben going places in the county, is frightening the girl off.'

'Why should it? She's bright enough – and attractive too . . .'

'She's that and a whole lot more besides.'

Miriam agreed with Josh, but made the statement sound like an argument. 'The trouble is, she doesn't think she can compete with the likes of that Tresillian girl he met on the boat coming over from Africa.'

'I don't think Ben sees it that way.'

'I should hope not! Lily's worth ten of the likes of her – and Ben knows it too. Lily is the one we've got to convince.'

'How will we do that?'

'I'll work on it. All I want you to do is play down Ben's wealth and how he'll one day be the most influential clay owner in Cornwall.'

'Nevertheless, it's true, Miriam.'

'I know it is – but when he gets to where he's going, he'll need someone like Lily to keep his feet planted on the ground. We mustn't let her be frightened off.'

Josh smiled wryly at her. 'I doubt if we'd have looked upon having too much money as a problem when we were their age.'

'True. But I wouldn't wish them to have to face the problems we had, either.'

Ben saw James Smith to the door after their private talk. When he had gone, Ben came to the kitchen where Josh sat talking to Miriam and Lily.

'What did Smith want?' asked Josh. 'Was he asking you to give him a place on this committee you've just formed?'

'No, nothing like that,' replied Ben. 'He wants to give up the lease on his works and asked if I'd care to buy it from him.'

Taken completely by surprise, Josh forgot his recent conversation with Miriam. 'But . . . that would give you the biggest clay holding in the county. Larger than General Grove! You accepted, of course?'

'It isn't quite as straightforward as that,' said Ben, seriously. 'Smith holds the lease from Tresillian Estates – that means Lady Tresillian. She might not agree to my taking over the lease. In any case, I'm not

352

really sure I want it – unless she'll also lease me the land between the Smith works and Varcoe.'

The land leased by James Smith was the closest works to the Varcoe holdings, separated only by a piece of unworked land. If Ben could lease this too it would give him a line of clay pits that could work together. Without the intervening land, he would be working two separate entities and felt this would not work satisfactorily.

'Well, I'm certain Lady Tresillian will be willing to oblige – as it's you,' said Lily. 'If she doesn't, perhaps Miss Deirdre can persuade her grandmother on your behalf?'

'I'm hoping I won't need to deal with Lady Tresillian,' said Ben, seriously. 'With any luck it might all be arranged through the estate solicitors.'

Chapter 46

Despite all Ben's efforts, it seemed the transfer of James Smith's clay works could not be arranged through the Tresillian Estate solicitors. He waited patiently for more than three weeks for a decision, then learned that the lease of the works had been offered to the clay owners who owned adjacent works.

Ben sent an ultimatum to the solicitors. Either they negotiated with him within the next week, or his offer would be withdrawn.

Three days later, a messenger brought a letter for Ben from the solicitors. Lady Tresillian would like to meet him at Tresillian House to discuss terms for the lease of the Smith works. He was invited to lunch on the following Sunday. This was the only day on which Lady Tresillian could see him as she was leaving for a month in France on the following Tuesday.

'Then I suppose you'll have to go,' said Lily airily when he told her. 'After all, a summons from Lady Tresillian – and her granddaughter, no doubt – is the next best thing to a royal command!'

She was aggrieved because Ben had earlier accepted an invitation from her to have lunch at her parents' home in St Austell on the same day.

Lily had warmed considerably towards Ben since they had attended the Camborne party together – although Miriam was inclined to believe Lily had been influenced by the conversation she had with her on the day of the meeting of clay owners.

'I'm sorry, Lily, I really would much rather be coming to St Austell for lunch with you. I've been looking forward to it, but you can see for yourself what the letter says. If I don't meet Lady Tresillian this week, nothing can be done for more than a month.'

'Then there's nothing more to be said, is there? You'll have to go.'

Lily was particularly disappointed because she had tried hard to take Miriam's advice to heart. It had appeared to be working – until now. The summons from Lady Tresillian was a reminder to Lily once again that Ben's world and her own were far apart.

'Lily . . .' He reached out and took her arm, attempting to pull her gently towards him, but she shook him off.

'No! We agreed there should be no touching in the house.'

Despite the growing affection between them, the rule laid down by

Lily when she first became aware of her feelings for Ben, remained in force. There was to be no physical contact between them while they were in the house belonging to Josh and Miriam.

It was not the easiest of conditions to meet, for either of them, but Lily in particular knew how vital it was. Sometimes she would lie awake in the darkness of her room, aware that only a single wall separated her from Ben and his bed. He must never know how flimsy a barrier that wall really was.

Lady Tresillian had other guests staying at her great house. When Ben rode up to the house he saw Deirdre playing tennis with two girls and a young man, all of about her own age.

When she saw him, Deirdre put down her tennis racquet and hurried to meet him before he reached the house.

'Benjamin, how wonderful to see you again! I was beginning to believe you were deliberately avoiding me.' She pouted from force of habit. 'Had it not been for your wretched old clay pits, I don't suppose you'd be here today.'

'I'm not entirely to blame for staying away, Deirdre, as well you know. I wasn't exactly made to feel welcome when I last visited Tresillian House.'

'Oh, well, all that silliness is forgotten now.'

One of the young men with whom she had been playing tennis had left the others and was approaching them. Calling on him to hurry, Deirdre said, 'Come and meet my great friend, Benjamin Retallick. We were on the same ship together, coming back from South Africa.'

When the young man reached them, Deirdre said, 'Benjamin, this is Charles Congreve, a very dear friend.'

The young man reached up to grasp Ben's hand and at the same time gave him a friendly smile. 'I've heard a great deal about you, Benjamin. Both from Deirdre and from my uncle, General Grove.'

Hiding his surprise, Ben said, 'I fear your uncle will have little to say about me that's complimentary.'

'On the contrary, he has a great deal of respect for you – and so do I. Few men have managed to better my uncle in business – and more's the pity. I find his arrogance difficult to swallow most of the time.'

Ben decided his first opinion of this young man was correct. He *did* like him.

'I hope you are not both going to spend your time here discussing business? It will be very *boring* of you.'

'Talking of business . . . I have an appointment with Lady Tresillian.'

'Hurry up and get it over with, Benjamin. Then you can come and join us at tennis.'

Deirdre took the arm of Charles Congreve and they headed back towards the tennis court, leaving Ben to carry on to the house where he turned his horse over to a waiting groom.

Lady Tresillian was waiting for Ben in her private drawing-room. With her was the solicitor representing the Tresillian family trust.

'Good afternoon, Benjamin. How lovely to see you again.' Lady Tresillian smiled at him as though he had always been one of her favourite visitors.

'Good afternoon, Lady Tresillian. I'm very pleased to see you looking so well after your recent illness.' He decided he could play the hypocritical game too.

'This is Edward Couch, my solicitor.' She indicated the man who sat at a nearby writing desk.

The two men shook hands and Ben sat down in an armchair close to Lady Tresillian.

'I believe you wish to lease the land currently being worked by James Smith?'

'I understand he intends giving up the lease. He suggested I might like to take it over,' countered Ben. 'I am interested.'

'Did he tell you the terms of the lease he holds?'

'I don't want to know what he was paying. I *do* have an idea of what would be economical for me.' This was not strictly the truth. Ben had studied the Smith works ledgers very closely.

'Oh? Then perhaps you should tell me?'

Lady Tresillian was not used to doing business with someone quite so blunt as Ben. She had expected to offer him her terms and have him accept them. His manner was an uncomfortable reminder that he had played the other clay owners at their own game – and won.

'Two thousand pounds for a twenty-one year lease and dues of two shillings on a ton of best quality clay.'

'That is quite out of the question!'

Lady Tresillian's indignation was not feigned. Ben had offered exactly half of what James Smith had been paying. She had intended asking half as much again.

'Please inform Benjamin of the terms we were going to suggest, Mr Couch.'

Nervously, the solicitor adjusted his spectacles on the bridge of his nose. 'Er, Lady Tresillian was thinking more of *five* thousand pounds for the lease, and dues of *five* shillings per ton for the finest quality clay – reducing, of course, for lesser quality clay.'

Ben spread his hands in philosophical regret, then rose to his feet. 'I'm sorry, Lady Tresillian. We seem to have wasted each other's time. I'll see myself out.'

'Wait a minute, young man!' Lady Tresillian waved him to his seat once more. Turning to the solicitor, she shook her head in mock exasperation. 'The young people of today are so impatient! I despair

356

for the future of business and politics in this country. Sit down, Benjamin. A more mature man would argue his case with me, not walk out. Do you want to lease the Smith works, or don't you?'

Ben shrugged nonchalantly. 'At the right price it could add to my profit. But if I took it at your asking price – or anything close to it – and there was a slump in trade, I would stand to lose far too much. Smith knew this at first hand. Had his lease been more generous he would have been able to weather the recent problems. They weren't, and he couldn't. I have no intention of making the same mistake.'

Wondering how far she might push him, Lady Tresillian said, 'I might be prepared to come some way to meet you if you are prepared to take the land on a shorter lease . . .'

Ben was shaking his head before she had finished talking. 'If I am going to spend that much money, I need security of tenure.'

Angry now, Lady Tresillian said, sarcastically, 'You weren't afraid of losing money in order to score a victory over the other owners.'

'True,' agreed Ben, amiably. 'But that was in the short term only. I don't intend making a habit of losing money.'

Meeting Lady Tresillian's angry glare, he added, 'I would raise my offer for the lease to three thousand pounds, but not the dues on output. I intend working night and day, as I do in my other works. That means you would receive as much, or more, in dues as you are getting now. If you are not happy, then I withdraw my offer. You will be the loser, Lady Tresillian, not I . I know you have already offered the lease to the other owners – at considerably less than you are asking of me. They turned it down. I must do the same. I have no intention of adding a crippling burden to my holdings. I'm currently making a higher profit than any other owner and that's the way it's going to stay. I won't lose any sleep because I don't have a lease on the Smith works and I doubt if you will either. Perhaps we should leave things as they are.'

Edward Couch was shaking his head doubtfully when Lady Tresillian said unexpectedly, 'Very well, I agree.'

The solicitor was more startled than Ben. 'But . . .'

'There are no "buts", Mr Couch.'

To Ben she said, 'You have a very good business head, young man. You will make money for yourself and for me. I have no intention of falling out with you over petty details. Draw up a contract, Mr Couch. Now, Benjamin, off you go and find Deirdre. Have an enjoyable time with her friends. You may stay the night, if you wish. I understand some of the others are.'

As Ben turned to leave, she said, 'By the way, I was speaking to a friend of your family the other day. Lady Dudley.'

Ben frowned. 'I'm sorry, I can't remember her.'

'She was probably Lady Vincent then. Married to an army officer.'

'Thomasina?' His expression cleared. 'Yes, of course. She was a

357

great friend of my brother Nat. They met during the Boer War and she came to Insimo a couple of times. Her husband was killed during the war when Nat was scouting for him. Now you mention it, I remember Nat saying she was married again.'

'She was telling me about your family lands in Rhodesia. It seems you were unduly modest about them.'

'I don't remember being either boastful or modest. I was born at Insimo. It was always there for me and my brothers, and I told you about it exactly as it is.'

'Of course. I'll have Mr Couch draw up a provisional agreement for the Smith works. You can sign it before you go. Run along and find Deirdre now. The dear girl has been longing to see you again.'

Chapter 47

Ben had been hoping to return to the Gover Valley immediately after settling details of the lease with Lady Tresillian. However, he would have to wait until her solicitor had drawn up an agreement.

He had secured a very good deal – better than any other owner who leased clay land from her. No doubt the awareness that he was a very eligible prospective grandson-in-law had a great deal to do with the unexpected agreement.

A maid took Ben to the room where Deirdre was now playing cards with her friends. She made a great fuss of him and asked eagerly whether it meant that he had decided to stay. She seemed very disappointed when he explained he would be leaving when the solicitor had drawn up a provisional lease.

For more than two hours Ben played cards with the other four young people. He did not know the games they were playing and needed to be instructed. He made a great many mistakes which provoked shrieks of shrill laughter from one of the girls. Ben found it both jarring and irritating. He and they were much of an age, yet he felt much older than any of them.

It came as a great relief when a maid came to tell him that Lady Tresillian requested his presence in her room.

The document had been drawn up in duplicate and Ben read it through quickly. All seemed to be satisfactory. However, he said that if Lady Tresillian would sign both copies he would take them with him. After his own solicitor had inspected them, he would sign and return a copy to Edward Couch.

Before leaving the room, he politely wished Lady Tresillian a pleasant holiday in France then made his way downstairs.

Still trying to persuade him to change his mind about staying at the house for the night, Deirdre walked with him to his horse which had been brought to the front of the house.

Ben excused himself by pleading the extra work that had been caused by the other owners and a need to make arrangements for taking over the Smith works.

He thought his excuses sounded weak and was convinced Deirdre thought so too, but either she had decided to accept his reasons for not staying or else did not want to face the truth.

359

'You work far too hard, Ben. Is it really necessary?'

'At the moment, yes.'

'Well . . . do try to call again very soon after Grandmother and I return from France. I have been unhappy at not seeing you for so long. It gets terribly lonely here at Tresillian.'

'You have your friends here with you today, and I think Charles Congreve is very pleasant.'

'He's *too* pleasant – and boring. His brother is much more exciting. He races horses and does all manner of interesting things. He's also the Viscount Congreve.'

Ben gained the impression that the title possessed by Charles Congreve's elder brother mattered more to Deirdre than any of his other attributes.

At that moment Charles and the two girls came from the house and Ben said, 'Goodbye, Deirdre. I hope you have a wonderful holiday.'

Giving him a kiss that might have lingered had he allowed it to, she said wistfully, 'I *do* wish you were staying tonight . . .'

Ben rode off with considerable relief, feeling as though he had just escaped from something.

When he reached St Austell, Ben went to the home of his solicitor. There was business for him to attend to even though it was a Sunday. The solicitor read through the agreement and gave it his approval, saying he thought Ben had made a very good deal with Lady Tresillian. Ben signed the lease which would be formally agreed at a later date. There was no immediate hurry now. He had all the authority he needed to carry on work at his latest acquisition.

His business concluded, Ben thought he would go to the Shovell home in St Austell and share his success with Lily. He hoped she might be more relaxed with him in her own home than she seemed to be in the house belonging to Josh and Miriam.

Arriving at the house, he was greeted by an effusive Jethro.

'I'm very glad to have seen you, Ben. I've heard you might be taking over the Smith works? I hope the rumour is true? They've had one or two labour problems lately, but some very good men work there. If you show them you're going to look after them, they'll serve you loyally. You have my word for it.'

'I've only agreed the details of the lease with Lady Tresillian today, but yes, I will be taking on the Smith workings. We'll discuss it at length some other time . . . Where's Lily?'

'She's off having a very exciting day. Someone you and she met at Camborne called to see her today – driving one of these motor car things! He's taken her off for a ride. I believe he called in on Josh and Miriam first. When he found neither of you there he came on here. It caused quite a stir among the neighbours, I can tell you. They had half

360

the street outside to see them off. You'd have thought it was a visit from royalty!'

Ben was unable to share Jethro's enthusiasm. The exhilaration he had felt as a result of the deal struck with Lady Tresillian had suddenly evaporated. He remembered Lily's reaction when she had met Sam Doney's daughter after the eventful farewell party thrown for Martha and Jannie.

'Come on through to the lounge. Lottie will make a cup of tea for us and we can discuss the future of the Smith works. As I said, if you bring the wages in line with those at Ruddlemoor and Varcoe, I'll guarantee you a trouble-free workforce. It may seem as though you're spending more money than you need, but it will pay off in the long run.'

'Yes.' Ben was not really listening. 'Do you know where Sam Doney was taking Lily?'

'No, but he had the little girl with him and Lily said something about taking her to see the sea. Now, about the Smith works . . .'

'Come and see me tomorrow, Jethro. By then I should have spoken to all my works captains and know something of what I'm going to do.'

Ben left the Shovell house abruptly, without even speaking to Lottie. Behind him, Lily's parents stood in the doorway gazing after him, wondering what had been said to upset the youngest member of the Retallick family.

Chapter 48

The day after Ben's visit to Tresillian, Lily arrived at the Gover Valley house very early, as was usual on a Monday.

As Ben came downstairs he heard her humming a tune happily as she cooked breakfast in the kitchen. Looking in at the kitchen doorway, he said, 'You sound happy this morning?'

'And why shouldn't I be? The birds were singing as I walked here, I caught a glimpse of a badger – and it looks like being a fine day.'

'Is that all? It's nothing to do with the fact that Sam Doney called for you and gave you a ride in his motor car yesterday?' It was the question of a jealous man, although Ben hoped he had not exposed his feelings too blatantly.

Lily looked up at him quickly, then back down to the frying pan in which two eggs were spitting at the world. 'That's right. We took Pippa to the beach at Crinnis. She's only been in the sea once before. She had a wonderful time.'

Separating the eggs with a knife, she added, 'I hope your day went just as well at Tresillian? No doubt Deirdre was delighted to see you.'

'I stayed only long enough to secure a lease for the Smith works. Then I came back here.'

'Pa said you'd called in and told him you were taking over the new works. Is the lease on your terms, or hers?'

'Mine.' At this moment, Lily's outing with Sam Doney loomed larger in his mind than the lease for the Smith clay works.

'I'm impressed. Lady Tresillian has the reputation of being a shrewd and forceful businesswoman. She must have a very good reason for wanting to keep you sweet.'

Ben was reminded of his own thoughts on the subject. That he was probably regarded as being an eligible husband for Deirdre. Nevertheless, he said, 'It was a business decision. No more, no less. I happen to know she'd offered the lease to the other owners and they'd turned it down. If she hadn't leased it to me she'd have been left with it on her hands, possibly for years. My offer was the lesser of two evils.'

Lily glanced up briefly before adding the eggs she was cooking to a plate containing bacon and sausages. 'Do you always calculate everything so carefully before you do it, Ben?'

'When it's business I try to stay one step ahead of those I'm dealing

362

with. Among the Matabele it was what made the difference between a headman and one of his tribesmen.'

He grimaced ruefully. 'I don't seem to meet with the same success in my personal life.'

Choosing to ignore his statement, Lily said, 'I'll take your breakfast to the table for you. Don't let it get cold.'

When Ben arrived at Ruddlemoor that morning, Tessa and Jo were already working. Jeremiah Rowe, Captain of the Varcoe works, was also there.

'Hello, Jeremiah, I didn't expect to find you here at this time of the morning. I hope we don't have any trouble over at Varcoe?'

'It's not trouble exactly,' said the slow-speaking clay captain. 'But Aloysius Varcoe died over the weekend. His funeral is being held on Thursday. I know him and me didn't see eye-to-eye towards the end, but I was his captain for a great many years. Me and the shift captains would like to attend.'

'Of course. Anyone else who genuinely wants to go can have time off too. I'm very sorry to hear the news. I didn't know him well, but I liked what I saw of him. I'll probably be there.'

'Thanks. By the way, is there any truth in the rumour that you've leased Jim Smith's works?'

'Yes. I've also leased the piece of clay ground between Smith's and Varcoe. If we open that up we can have a single railway link running the length of all my workings. It will cut costs considerably.'

Turning to the two women, he said, 'By the way, I'd like one of you to go to the Smith works for a week or two. Go through all their ledgers and let me know the details of all income and expenditure for the last two years. I want to know everyone who's bought clay from them, and how much they've been paying their men. Would either of you like to volunteer? I'll get someone else in to help out here while you're gone. Come to that, we could do with extra help anyway.'

'I'll go,' said Tessa, before Jo had even thought about the matter.

'Good. Finish whatever you're doing here and begin at the Smith works this afternoon. I think we'll have to change its name too.'

Turning back to Captain Rowe, he said, 'Will you take Tessa across there this afternoon? The workings adjoin Varcoe and I'd like your opinion on what needs to be done.'

'I can tell you one thing before I even set foot in the place,' said Jeremiah Rowe. 'Get rid of Captain Mahler and his three shift captains. There's not one of 'em is worth so much as a sweeper's pay.'

A sweeper was usually a semi-retired employee, no longer capable of holding down any work involving strength or skill.

'You know them well?' Ben put the question to his works captain.

'I've had trouble with every one of 'em at some time or another.'

'Right, but I can't afford to have you getting involved in any more trouble on my behalf. When I first bought Varcoe, Lily told me about one of your men who helped her and Darley when someone tried to steal the Ruddlemoor pay. Is he still here?'

Jeremiah Rowe took the pipe from his mouth and grinned. 'Lanyon Sweet? Yes. He's a lot bigger around the girth than he was in those days, but there's no one in these parts would dare cross him.'

'Good. Take him with you and keep him alongside you wherever you go. Let me know what you think needs doing and I'll see that it gets done.'

When Ben and Captain Rowe had left the office, Tessa said, 'Now *that's* my sort of man.'

'Anyone's *your* sort of man,' retorted Jo, but not unkindly. 'Who were you talking about in particular? Ben, Cap'n Rowe, or Lanyon Sweet?'

'Ben Retallick. He knows his mind and sets out to do what's needed right away. I wish he'd look in my direction just once in a while.'

'You'd have to step over my dead body first,' said Jo. 'But why were you so eager to go to the Smith works? Who do you know there?'

'No one in particular,' said Tessa, evasively. 'I just want to go. I'd be starting afresh if I worked there. I always enjoy trying something new. Besides, I don't have a hope in hell of finding a man who might have serious intentions towards me at Ruddlemoor. The ones I can't abide spend all their time trying to persuade me to go up in the fern with them. Those I *do* like are scared I'm going to carry *them* off there.'

'I've never before known you to be fussy who took you in the fern, or anywhere else come to that. No, Tessa. I know you too well. There must be another reason. Perhaps I should go instead of you and find out?'

'All right,' said Tessa, reluctantly. 'If you must know, Frank Trudgeon's at the Smith works. He was once a friend of Eddie's and I think he's something special. He's been working there for a couple of weeks now.'

Jo looked at her friend in disbelief. 'Don't tell me you're carrying on with one of Eddie's friends? After the way they behaved?'

'Why not? Frank even hinted at marriage before things turned sour for him. Not only that, he's got two good legs. I was beginning to think that Eddie Long was as much of a man as I was ever likely to take to the altar.'

'Getting a man to the altar's only the *beginning* of married life. You're better off unmarried than being tied to a man you don't really like for the rest of your life. Think about things, Tessa. Remember the life you had when your pa was alive? How he treated your ma and you? Is that the sort of life you're looking for?'

'Frank's not like Eddie in that way. I can manage him,' Tessa insisted. Suddenly fearful, she said, 'You won't say anything to Ben? Please, Jo.'

'I won't say anything, but he'll find out soon enough that you're going out with someone he's already had dismissed. You must know that for yourself. In the meantime, you just remember what you're going to the Smith works to do — and don't forget who's paying your wages. It certainly isn't any of Eddie Long's friends!'

Chapter 49

Ben spent much of that Monday with his solicitors, helping in the preparation of a detailed lease in respect of his latest acquisition. At the end of the afternoon he went to the Varcoe works to discuss extending the quarrying operation beyond its present bounds.

He arrived back at the Gover Valley house late that evening to find Lily alone in the house. She explained that soon after Ben had left the house, a letter was delivered with the news that Malachi Sprittle, Josh's long-time mine captain at Sharptor, was seriously ill. Josh and Miriam had set off in the shay to visit him.

'That's a very long journey for them, at their age.' Ben was concerned. Sharptor was about twenty miles distant. 'Do they intend returning tonight?'

'They said they would – and I can't imagine Miriam forsaking her own bed, even for a single night.'

Ben found it a strange sensation being alone in the house with Lily. For much of the evening he seemed to be following her around, from lounge to dining-room to kitchen. Eventually, she rounded on him, saying it was like having a pup in the house, finding him underfoot whenever she turned around.

When the meal was ready and they sat eating together, Ben said, 'It's wonderfully cosy with just the two of us in the house.'

'So it might be, but don't let it give you any ideas, Ben Retallick.'

It was merely a jocular remark, but it reminded him of Sam Doney's recent visit and of the excursion Lily had made with him in the car. It took the edge off the pleasure he felt at being alone in the house with her.

Their conversation for the remainder of the meal was of the changes taking place in the clay industry, and Ben told Lily of the death of Aloysius Varcoe.

When the meal was over, she said, 'You go and sit down in the parlour. I'll clear away the things from the table then make a drink for us.'

'It's all right, I'll help you clear away.'

'You don't have to do that, Ben. You've had a very busy day. Mine has been easy without Josh and Miriam in the house.'

'I'd like to help. It's not often I have the chance to talk to you without someone else being around.'

Ben helped Lily to clear the table and carry things through to the kitchen. It was a simple thing to be doing, but it somehow brought them closer together. Both were aware of the feeling.

He had carried the last of the things from the table to the kitchen and was returning along the passageway when he met Lily at the entrance to the dining-room immediately after she had extinguished the lamp.

For a few moments they stood close together in the semi-darkness, as though each was waiting for something.

It seemed to Ben the most natural thing in the world to reach out for Lily and draw her to him. She came to him without any resistance and he kissed her, gently at first, then more demandingly. For a few moments, Lily responded with all the eagerness Ben could have wished. But suddenly she turned her head and pushed him away. 'No, Ben!'

'Why not, Lily? Why won't you just relax with me for once?'

'We've been through this before, Ben. I . . . I just can't, that's all. I feel I'd be betraying Miriam's trust in me . . .'

Even as she spoke, Lily remembered what Miriam had said to her about Ben. Perhaps she would not be as shocked as Lily was suggesting. All the same . . . it would not be wise.

Ben was still holding her, although not as close as before, or as close as he would have wished. He began to pull her to him once more when, suddenly, they both heard sounds from outside the front of the house.

Josh and Miriam had returned!

Miriam was first through the door and found Ben and Lily standing on opposite sides of the kitchen. He was manoeuvring the heavy iron kettle from the hob to the hot coals of the fire. Lily was at the sink, vigorously swabbing a dinner plate with a dishmop.

'Well, here's a busy scene, I must say. Had I known what you two were up to, I'd have stayed out longer. We might have got the whole house cleaned through!'

Ben was convinced he must look guilty. Lily's cheeks too were far ruddier than was natural.

Josh saved them from further embarrassment by entering the kitchen and speaking immediately to Ben.

'Ah, there you are. I thought you might already have gone to bed. I'm glad I've caught you. I've been wondering exactly what's gone on about the Smith works today? Have you got it all settled? Come on through and tell me all about it. I'd like a drink, Lily, when that kettle's boiled. It's not a cold night out there, but there's an edge to the wind. I need something to warm me up.'

When Ben and Josh had left the kitchen, Miriam said to Lily, 'I'll help you make the tea.'

'It'll be a while. Ben's only just topped the kettle up and put it on to boil.'

'That's all right. It'll give us time to talk. I'm afraid poor Malachi

367

isn't going to last very long. But at least he recognised us, so he knows we've been to see him. He has all his family about him. I think that's the way a man should end his days, surrounded by family.'

Lily made suitably sympathetic noises as she continued with the washing up.

Miriam had been watching her closely and now she said suddenly, 'What have you and Ben been up to while we've been away?'

'Nothing.'

The reply came too quickly. The denial too emphatic. Lily realised this and added quickly, 'Ben's had a very busy day working on the takeover of the Smith works. He didn't come in until late. Then I had supper with him and talked about his day. We'd only just finished clearing away when you came home.'

Miriam gave a sigh that expressed more exasperation than anything else. 'Had I thought it would have helped to leave you two together any longer, I would have kept Josh out, even if it meant driving around the countryside for half the night. I'm beginning to despair of you two. It must be that all those years spent in the sun have thinned the Retallick blood. I can't see how any young man could prevent himself from simply sweeping you off your feet.'

Lily smiled. 'I don't believe Ben's the type to sweep a girl off her feet, although I think he's probably quite keen on me.'

'You *think*?' Miriam echoed, indignantly. 'Why, in my young days . . .'

'All right, I *know* he's attracted to me.' Lily amended her statement before Miriam launched into one of her 'then-and-now' stories. 'But nothing has changed since I last spoke to you. In fact, the gulf between us has probably widened. He owns the Smith works now and is already selling more clay than any other owner. When Ben thinks of marriage he'll want a wife who knows something of the ways of his fine friends.'

'You're talking nonsense, girl.'

There was a loud hissing from the kitchen range and Lily left what she was doing to right the kettle which had slipped sideways and was spilling water on the hot coals.

When the kettle was upright once more, Miriam continued. 'If I've judged Ben correctly he'll choose the wife *he* wants, not one who's right for his so-called friends. But you've heartened me, girl. If he's let you know he's attracted to you then he'll do something about it. From what I've seen of him since he's been here, neither hell nor high-water will stop Ben from getting what he wants.'

Chapter 50

Miriam's reference to 'high water' proved to be a prophetic one. Four hours after the remark was made, the Gover Valley household was awakened by a frenzied banging on the front door.

Ben's room was almost immediately above. He looked out and called, 'Who is it? What's wrong?'

'It's Tom Carne, Mr Retallick. Tool boy over at Varcoe. There's been an accident. The shift captain sent me to run and fetch you.'

'What sort of an accident?' Ben did his best to shake off his sleepiness.

'In the pit. The men were washing-out clay and must have broken into an old flooded tin-mine tunnel. Water and waste gushed out over everything. Three men were buried. One's been pulled out alive. I don't fancy the chances of the others . . .'

'Go back and tell the shift captain to call in every available man – take them from Ruddlemoor and from the Smith works as well. I'll be there as soon as I'm dressed.'

As Ben struggled into shirt and trousers, there was a knock at the bedroom door and Josh came in. Behind him, on the landing, Ben caught a glimpse of Miriam and Lily in the doorway of Lily's bedroom.

'It was a young lad from Varcoe,' said Ben in answer to Josh's question. 'There's been some sort of an accident. Two men are missing.'

'I'll come with you,' said Josh.

'You make your way at your own speed. I'm going straight there on my horse.'

As Ben hurried down the stairs, there was a call from Lily for him to take care.

When Ben reached the Varcoe works, he found them in near-darkness. Water and rock had spewed from a man-made cavern in the sheer cliff face of the pit, carrying all before it. One of the first casualties had been the recently installed electric light system. This alone made rescue work more difficult than it would otherwise have been.

Another, more dangerous hazard in the darkness was the thick, milky lake which covered the floor of the pit to an indeterminate depth. It was a combination of waste and water released from the mine, together with rocks and china clay.

369

Normally, clay washed from the walls of the pit would have been allowed to remain only long enough for the sand carried with it to settle. The remaining milky liquid would have been drained off to an underground 'drift' and pumped away from the pit.

The sheer volume and consistency of the inundation had overwhelmed the pumping system and left a lake in its wake.

The shift captain was a young man appointed by Jeremiah Rowe and Ben did not even know his name.

'Have either of the missing men been located?' was Ben's first question.

'No. We believe they're probably under there.' The shift captain nodded to where parties of men, some carrying lanterns, probed the depths of the pool with long poles.

'Where did the water come in?'

'Up there.' The shift captain pointed upwards, to where the deeper black of a gaping hole could just be seen, some thirty or forty feet up the steeply sloping side of the pit.

Between the hole and the creamy lake was a trail of rubble containing rocks, rotting wooden pitwork, and even a length of rusty tramway.

'Get the men working on clearing that away. Begin at the top, closest to the tunnel, and work your way down, into the water. In the meantime, try to float someone out to the launder and clear the drain holes in it. When they're cleared set the pumps to working at double speed.'

The shift captain began to protest that the engine was not made to work at such a speed, but Ben cut him short.

'I don't care if we blow the engine up in the attempt. Clear this lot away. AND FIND THE MISSING MEN!'

Ben had considered having the workers dig a channel to carry off the waste water, but there was nowhere for it to go. This was the lowest point of the pit. It would have to be pumped away.

Josh had arrived and was standing with Ben, surveying the scene of devastation, when the men who had been set to clear away the wreckage between tunnel and pit floor suddenly set up a shout.

'We've found one of them – and he's alive!'

Ben scrambled up the slope, followed more slowly by Josh. Elbowing his way through the group who had been clearing the rubble, he was in time to see a man pulled from beneath the rubble.

His face was streaked with a combination of mud and clay and with a cut on the side. The man was in obvious pain, but was murmuring a fervent, 'Thank God! Thank God!'

'Take him to the office – gently with him, now. Is any man here a good rider?'

When one said he was, Ben ordered, 'Take my horse and fetch a doctor. Tell him it's urgent. The rest of you men clear off this rubble. The other man might be here as well.'

Finding one man alive had given the rescuers new heart. They dug at a rate that would have amazed the most critical works captain, urging each other on with the thought that the missing man might also be only feet away from them, and still alive.

Ben followed the group carrying the rescued man to the office. Electricity was still on here and when the man had been cleaned up, it was possible to make a rough assessment of his injuries. It was clear he had a broken arm, possibly a broken leg and ribs too, but he was conscious. After someone had produced a flask of brandy, he felt able to talk. He told them that he and a companion, Denis Tregunna, had been standing together when the torrent burst from the pit wall. The man rescued earlier had been standing some distance away. It meant that the missing man should be found not far away.

He was. However, unlike his companion, Denis Tregunna was dead, crushed by the weight of rocks which had bowled him over and buried him.

A doctor was at the clay works within half-an-hour and gave his opinion that the first man had been found only just in time. 'He's had a heavy weight lying on his chest,' he said. 'Probably some of those rocks I've seen out there. He's almost certainly got a couple of broken ribs, but I don't think anything has pierced his lungs. He's a lucky man.'

'Thank you, doctor.' The injured man had been given a sleeping draught and was beginning to feel drowsy.

'It's not me you have to thank,' he said, rising to his feet. 'From what the man who fetched me said on the ride here, it was Mr Retallick who told them to dig where they found you. He's the one who saved your life, there's no doubt about that.'

Ben had very little sleep that night, but first thing the following morning he told an equally weary Josh that he intended visiting the family of the man who had been killed at the Varcoe clay works.

'Can I come with you?' asked Lily, unexpectedly. The others were equally surprised and Lily explained, 'I know Denis Tregunna's wife. She used to live close to us in St Austell.'

'Then I'd appreciate your company,' said Ben. 'It's not going to be an easy visit for me.'

When they arrived at the Tregunna house, three small, unhappy and confused children were being led out by a neighbour.

She nodded to Ben respectfully and seemed to know Lily. 'I'm just taking these three mites along to my house for a while. They've brought their father home. He's laid out up in the bedroom. They've seen him, of course, but I think it's morbid for children to be in the house with their dead father. You know where I live, Lily, if you have need of me.'

'How's Kathleen taking it?' Lily put the question as the woman shepherded the three children past the visitors.

'She's got over much of the crying now,' said the woman. 'Someone's gone to fetch her mother, from Mevagissey. She'll no doubt be a help to her.'

Kathleen Tregunna looked far too young to be the mother of three children – and a widow. Her eyes were reddened from weeping and her face was puffy, but she acknowledged Ben's commiserations bravely.

'What will you do now?' asked Lily, gently.

'I don't know.' Kathleen Tregunna shook her head and her eyes misted despite her efforts to hold back the tears. 'We've got no money saved . . . I . . . I just don't know. I'll probably go to live with my mother. She's on her own in Mevagissey and I expect I'll find work there, probably in one of the fish cellars.'

'Don't hurry the decision,' said Ben. 'You can stay in this house for as long as it suits you. As for the money . . . I'll give you the equivalent of two years' wages. I know it's not going to bring your husband back, but it will help you over a difficult period. In the meantime, if there's any way in which I can help you, then please let Lily know.'

He was anxious to leave the house, but Lily said, 'I'll stay here for a while, if you don't mind, Ben?'

'Of course.'

She walked to the front door of the cottage with him and on the way said quietly, 'That was very generous of you, Ben.'

'Generous?' he said, fiercely. 'A woman's lost her husband and the children their father – and you say I'm being generous by giving her a pittance? That's not generosity, Lily.'

'You're a strange man, Ben Retallick. But there's not much wrong with you.'

Chapter 51

It had been a long day. Riding back to the Gover valley from Ruddlemoor that evening, Ben felt very weary. Nevertheless, he saw the figure standing in the shadow of some trees long before he reached the spot.

At first he took only a passing interest. This area was popular with courting couples. The man was probably waiting for his girl. Then, as Ben drew closer, he stepped from the trees and Ben suddenly tensed. He recognised the waiting man as one of those who had attacked him outside the Shovell house and who had later been dismissed from the Varcoe clay works.

However, there was nothing belligerent in the man's manner at this moment. Removing his cap, he fingered it nervously as he stood in the road awaiting Ben's arrival.

He pulled the horse to a halt a few lengths short of the man who said, 'I'd like to speak to you, Mr Retallick.'

When Ben made no reply, the man said, 'I'm Frank Trudgeon . . .'

'I know who you are. I also remember our previous dealings.'

A pained expression came over Trudgeon's face. 'I'm sorry about all that, Mr Retallick, I really am. When we stopped you outside the Shovell house, that time, I thought we were being clever. I realise now we were just behaving stupidly.'

'I wouldn't argue about that, but is there a point to this conversation? If there is I'd be grateful if you'd come to it. I'm tired and hungry and on my way home.' Ben was still wary of the man, but after looking all about him was convinced there was no one else in the vicinity.

'Yes. My father is Harry Trudgeon, the man whose life you saved at the Varcoe workings during the night. If it hadn't been for you he'd have died. He says that himself. Ma and me are in your debt – and I reckon I can pay some of it off right now.'

'Go on.'

'When you sacked us from Varcoe, me and Harry Ince got a job at the Smith works. Eddie Long's there too now, working in the office.'

The information came as a great surprise to Ben. He had not yet paid a visit to the Smith works but had given Captain Jeremiah Rowe the task of assessing what would need doing there. Rowe would not know that Eddie had been dismissed from Ruddlemoor.

'Thank you for telling me.'

'That's not all. Things haven't been too happy at the Smith works in recent months. The men have had a lot to put up with.'

'They'll find things will change quickly now I'm taking over. Captain Rowe should start a night shift tonight. As soon as it's working the pay of the men will be the same as those at Ruddlemoor and Varcoe. That's a lot more than they've been getting.'

'That's not going to stop trouble. You've got nigh on a hundred percent membership of Simon Kendall's Union there. They were strong for the Union before and Eddie Long has made every new man join before he would put them on the payroll. Kendall has spent a lot of time talking to the men. He says that twenty-two shillings isn't enough pay for doing shift-work. To back him up, Eddie has been giving the men figures to show that the works have been making a hefty profit under Mr Smith – and will be making twice as much for you.'

'I don't know where he's found such figures. The Smith works have been running at a loss for months. With the capital I intend spending there, I'm not likely to see any profit this year, at best.'

'I don't know anything about that. I'm just telling you what's being said.'

'I'm grateful to you, Trudgeon.'

Ben still sat his horse as the other man put his cap back on his head and began to walk away.

'Just a minute. Will you keep me informed of anything new that happens at the Smith works?'

Frank Trudgeon hesitated. 'I may be in your debt, Mr Retallick, but I'm still one of the workers. Not a boss's man.'

'If something isn't done about what you've already told me there will be *no* workers at the Smith works. I have no intention of paying the men any more than my own workers at Ruddlemoor are getting now. I haven't signed the full lease with Lady Tresillian yet and will relinquish it rather than give in. Far from being a boss's man, you'll be doing something that will profit the men far more than anything Eddie Long or Simon Kendall is suggesting for them. Remember that when you have something worth telling me.'

That evening, Ben told Josh of the conversation with Trudgeon.

'I can't believe it,' said Josh, sceptically. 'The men have more sense than to listen to anything Eddie Long has to tell them.'

'I would have thought so,' agreed Ben. 'But Kendall's the one doing the talking – and he's quite clever at that. Eddie is just supplying the figures for him, and making them prove whatever Kendall wants.'

'What are you going to do?' Josh was worried. He knew far better than Ben that once Cornish men got an idea in their heads, it would be very difficult to dislodge it.

'Right now I'm going to go to bed and catch up on some sleep. Then,

374

first thing in the morning, I'm going to the Smith works to dismiss Eddie Long.'

'You don't think that might precipitate trouble?' asked Josh, anxiously. 'If Kendall and Long between them have full Union membership at the works, it could mean that they'll all walk out.'

Ben was beginning to feel irritable. 'If I'm honest, I don't really care. I'm beginning to wish I'd never heard of the Smith works. Buying a lease and having to pay dues is expensive. It's never going to make the profit that Ruddlemoor and Varcoe are bringing in. If there's trouble, the men working there will learn that I don't make idle threats. I'll speak to them tomorrow and let them know exactly where we all stand.'

Ben went to bed and within minutes of laying his head on the pillow was asleep, the problems of the Smith works something to worry about in the morning.

Downstairs, Josh, Miriam and Lily discussed the latest problem that had arisen for him. Eventually, at Josh's suggestion, Lily put on her coat and left the house. She was going to see her father.

Jethro Shovell was an Association man with considerable knowledge of Trades Union affairs. It was time to see whether the men would listen to *his* reasoning rather than that of Simon Kendall.

Chapter 52

Josh and Miriam sat up until late discussing the problems facing the clay industry and the Retallick interests in particular.

Josh had a nagging suspicion that Ben's lack of years might have precipitated the present crisis at the Smith works,.

Miriam did not agree.

'Things are changing everywhere, Josh. Young men – men like Eddie Long and his friends – have been away from home and seen something of the world during the Boer War. They've learned how others live. Seen the things they are able to enjoy, things that the young men in Cornwall don't have. No doubt they'll also have realised what fools some of the men who lead them are. They're no longer ready to tug a forelock and do as they're told without question. Think about it. How would you have been had you needed to work for someone else when we returned from Africa? I'd say that it happens to be Ben's bad luck that he's coming into the business at such a time.'

Miriam smiled affectionately at Josh. 'All the same, I'm glad he has taken over from you. If he hadn't, it would be *you* trying to solve a problem that has no solution. The men want more than the owners will, or can, pay them, and they'll not be satisfied with excuses. They have Union backing now. As soon as it's able, the Union will be flexing its muscles. It's got to provide something to show the men that their money's not being wasted.'

Miriam rose to her feet and it took more effort than she would have wished Josh to witness. 'Now, forget about clay and Unions and our Ben for tonight. It's time for bed. We'll think about it in the morning. Things always seem a sight better in daylight.'

Lily too was discussing the ambitions of the Clay Workers' Union, but she was finding her father far less helpful than she had expected.

He agreed there was trouble brewing at the Smith works, but declared there was nothing he could do about it, adding, 'This is Simon Kendall's doing, not mine.'

'But you've worked with the Unions all your life. The men know you. They *trust* you. If you spoke to them, you could make them see sense.'

'They *did* trust me once, Lily. Now they feel I'm too tied in with the

376

employers. I'm married to Miriam Retallick's niece, you're working in their house, and Jo is in the Ruddlemoor office.'

'What's that got to do with anything?' Lily was angry. She had expected her father to support her. 'It's never stopped you from helping them before.'

'This is different. This dispute concerns a member of the family – however distantly related he might be. They'd say I'm biased.'

He shrugged apologetically. 'I know it's hard on young Ben, but I believe this is very important for the whole Trades Union movement. It's a chance to show what they can achieve if they stand firm.'

Lily looked at her father in disbelief. 'I don't believe I'm hearing this! Because of your knowledge of Ben, you should know better than anyone else exactly what it's going to achieve. He will simply close down the Smith works. All the men you profess to care so much about will be thrown out of work.'

'You're being over-dramatic, Lily. No clay owner's going to cut off his nose to spite his face. Ben will do everything to keep the works open for as long as it's making a healthy profit . . .'

'I don't think you've listened to a single word I've said. Ben will close down the Smith works because it *isn't* making a profit, and hasn't been for months. He intends putting money in to bring it up-to-date, so there's no likelihood of its coming into profit for months, perhaps years.'

'You're living with the Retallicks, Lily. You hear only their side of the story. I hear the workers' view of things . . .'

'What you've been listening to are the lies that Eddie Long's been spreading out of sheer spite. I'm surprised, and disappointed. I believed that you, of all people, would know better.'

'There's no sense in arguing about it, Lily, because it doesn't really matter what I believe. Simon Kendall is in charge of Union affairs at the Smith works. He's the one you need to convince, not me.'

Lily left the house frustrated and disappointed that she had failed to gain the support of her father. She had felt certain he would be able to do something to avoid a confrontation between the workers and Ben.

Her way back to the Gover Valley led her past the General Wolfe public house. It was late and the customers were turning out of the premises. Much to her surprise, Simon Kendall was among them, talking to a number of clay workers.

She had never intended broaching the troubles of the Smith works with him, in spite of what her father had said, but it was as though fate had put him in her path.

Pushing her way through the men about him, ignoring a number of crude remarks and an occasional whistle, she reached him and said, 'I'd like to speak to you, Simon.'

'Well, this *is* an honour. A relative of one of the clay owners waiting outside a public house for me!'

The remark was made for the amusement of his companions and they reacted accordingly.

'She must be keen, Simon . . .' 'You'll be all right there, tonight . . .'

'Is there somewhere we can speak, without the chorus?'

'She wants to be alone with me, so I'll say goodnight to you all – and see you at the Smith works tomorrow.'

Simon Kendall set off with Lily, followed by a ribald chorus from his drinking partners.

'Were your remarks really necessary?' Lily asked scathingly as they walked from the public house towards the edge of town.

'They didn't mean anything. Anyway, if you wait for me outside a public house you must expect it.'

'I wasn't waiting for you. I was on my way back from my home when I saw you. I suddenly thought it might be an opportunity to talk to you about the Smith works.'

'I'm disappointed now. I really thought you were interested in me. If you're not then you're wasting both our time. Where the Smith works is concerned there's nothing to talk about.'

'I think there's a great deal to be said. I've heard that you're stirring up trouble there. I've even heard talk of a strike. I thought the idea of a Union was to protect the interests of the members and their families? At least, that's what my pa used to say.'

'The best way to protect workers and their families is to pay them a fair wage for the work they do.'

'The men employed by Ben Retallick are paid more than any others in the clay industry.'

'They're the only ones working shifts. They should be paid even more.'

Lily glared at Simon. 'They were satisfied before someone stirred them up.'

'They needed stirring up.' Kendall was well rehearsed in such arguments. 'The working man has spent too long under the impression that his employer shares a platform with God. The Cornish more than most.'

'If you carry on the way you're going, they'll have no employers to look up to!' retorted Lily. 'I fail to see how that's going to make them better off.'

'It won't come to that,' said Simon, smugly. 'Retallick will see sense first.'

They had reached the end of the gas-lights. Ahead was the Gover Valley, and darkness. Lily stopped and turned to face him, 'It's *you* who needs to come to your senses. The Smith works hasn't been in profit for months and won't be for at least a year.'

378

'That isn't what Eddie tells me.'

Lily looked at Simon in pained disbelief. 'You'd put the livelihood of hundreds of men at risk on the say-so of Eddie Long?'

'He's the one who does the book-keeping at the Smith works.'

'Eddie Long is out to make trouble for Ben. If you really want to know the truth, I'll ask Ben to let you examine the books for yourself.'

'I've no doubt you could persuade Retallick to do anything for you, but I've no reason to doubt Eddie's word.'

'What you mean is, you don't *want* to doubt him. You're as bent on trouble as he is. I'll remember this conversation, Simon Kendall. One day you'll have cause to remember it too.'

Leaving this threat hanging on the air behind her, Lily turned her back on him and the gas-lit streets of St Austell.

She had not gone far when she heard footsteps hurrying to catch up with her. Falling in beside her, Simon Kendall said, 'I'll walk home with you, Lily. A young girl shouldn't be walking on her own away from the lighted streets.'

'I'll be safer in a dark lane than in town with the likes of your friends from the General Wolfe, no matter how many lights there are!'

'They didn't mean any harm. They thought you were waiting for me.'

'Well, I wasn't – and you did nothing to set them right.'

'Perhaps I didn't want to.'

'What's that supposed to mean? No . . . don't tell me. I don't want to know.'

'What's happened between us, Lily? There was a time when I wouldn't have been surprised to find you waiting for me outside a public house.'

'There's never been a time when I would do that for you, or for any other man, so let's set the record straight right now.'

'Not even for Ben Retallick?'

'Ben doesn't frequent such places – or mix with such company.'

'No, of course not. He hob-nobs with lords and ladies, doesn't he? Mind you, when he's bored with such company he can always come home to you. Living under the same roof, I've no doubt he finds you far more obliging than his society women. But you'll never be more than a bed-warmer for him, Lily. Do you realise that . . . or doesn't it matter to you?'

Her reply was to stop dead in her tracks. When Simon Kendall did the same, her right arm swung and her open hand met his face in a resounding slap.

Leaving him standing alone in the darkness, Lily strode off angrily.

She had not gone far before she heard footsteps once more, but this time they were running. She only half turned before Simon Kendall collided with her. His impetus knocked her from the pathway to the

379

grass bank nearby and he went with her.

'I'll teach you that it doesn't pay to hit me, you little bitch! You wouldn't have hit Ben Retallick like that, and you'll not do it to me again.'

'Get off!'

Lily struggled as Kendall sat astride her, his hands fumbling at her skirt.

'You'll go to prison for this . . .'

'Oh no I won't! I've too many witnesses who'll testify that you were waiting for me outside the General Wolfe when it turned out. It's later at night than any decent girl should have been out on the streets.'

Even as she struggled desperately to throw him off, Lily knew he was right. No magistrate in the land would believe that she had not led Simon Kendall on.

He was crouching with all his weight on her now, one of his hands between her legs. As he leaned over her she could smell the stale beer on his breath.

Suddenly, as she flailed around with renewed urgency, her hand came into contact with a stone. She snatched it up, only to drop it again almost immediately.

For a few seconds she thought it had gone. Then she found it again. Holding it more firmly this time, she brought the stone up and struck Simon Kendall with it on the side of the head.

He shouted in pain and she promptly hit him again.

This time he fell sideways and, pushing him from her, Lily rose to her feet and ran.

She did not stop running until she tumbled in through the doorway of the Retallick house, sobbing in relief. She was grateful that Josh and Miriam had gone to bed. It meant she would not have to explain why she was covered in dirt and shaking uncontrollably.

In that moment, Lily wished more than anything else that Ben was awake to comfort her as he had when she had suffered a similar experience at the Camborne party.

Chapter 53

'What have you done to your face?'

Ben put the question to Lily the next morning at breakfast.

She instinctively put up a hand to her cheek where there were a number of ugly scratches. She had tried to keep that side of her face turned away from everyone while she served their food, but it was impossible to hide it for very long.

'I went to visit Ma after you'd gone to bed last night and walked into a bush on my way home,' she lied. 'I'm not used to walking home in the dark, I suppose.'

'It must have been a very active bush,' said Miriam, with thin-lipped sarcasm. 'I've just looked at your coat hanging in the passage. It's torn and covered in mud.'

Ben looked from Miriam to Lily. 'What really happened last night?'

'I've already told you once.' Her temper flared angrily in self-defence. 'I'm not staying here to be cross-examined by you. If anyone wants me I'll be upstairs, in my room.'

As she hurried out, Ben rose from his chair to follow her, but Miriam put up a hand and stopped him. 'Leave her alone, Ben. I'll find out later. You've got enough on your mind right now.'

He sat down once more, but as soon as he finished his breakfast he went upstairs, ostensibly to his own room. Instead, he knocked at the door of Lily's.

'Are you all right?'

'Of course I'm all right! What's the matter with everyone? I walked into a bush and fell over, that's all.'

'If you're quite sure . . .'

While he was talking, Ben tried the door. It was secured from the inside.

'If you're quite certain there's nothing else wrong . . .'

There was no reply from inside the room. Reluctantly, Ben made his way downstairs again. After saying goodbye to Miriam and Josh, he set off for what he knew was going to be a very difficult day.

Ben went first to the Varcoe Works where Captain Jeremiah Rowe greeted him cheerfully. He cut his greeting short when he saw Ben's expression.

'Is something wrong?'

'There's a lot wrong – and most of it at the Smith works. I think you were right about the captain there. He seems to have let things get out of hand.'

Without disclosing the source of his information, Ben told the Varcoe captain what Frank Trudgeon had told him.

Captain Rowe frowned. 'I don't think I know this Eddie Long . . .'

'He lost a leg in the Boer War and blames the whole world for it.'

'Ah! Yes, he's there. An awkward young cuss who refused to let me examine the ledgers. I didn't make a big issue of it at the time, but I put him on my list of those who need to go if we're to have an efficient and happy workforce there.'

'It sounds to me as though the Smith works has become a breeding ground for trouble.'

Ben appeared to lose himself in thought for a few minutes. Then, as though suddenly making up his mind, he said, 'The best thing we can do is to go there and sort it out right away.'

As an apparent afterthought, he added, 'It might be as well to bring Lanyon Sweet along too.'

When Ben, Jeremiah Rowe and Lanyon Sweet reached the Smith works they found that all the men had stopped work to attend a meeting being held outside the works office.

Standing in the office doorway, addressing the assembled workers was Simon Kendall, with Eddie Long at his side.

The arrival of the three men from Varcoe caused some consternation as they pushed their way through the crowd to the office. Men who appeared slow to make way were lifted bodily out of the way by the giant Lanyon Sweet.

When they reached the office, Jeremiah Rowe was the first to speak. Addressing a small, bearded man wearing a suit who stood at the front of the crowd, he asked, 'What's going on here, Cap'n Roberts?'

'The Union has called a meeting of the men.'

'The Union called it? Is it paying the men's wages? The workers at the Smith works are paid to produce clay, not hold meetings.'

'This was an emergency,' Simon Kendall interrupted the Varcoe captain. 'I was called in to address them . . .'

'You're on private property, Kendall. If you want to speak to the men who work here, then you ask permission from me first.'

Ben spoke angrily to the Trades Union leader. At the same time he observed that Kendall had extensive grazes and bruising to the left side of his face.

'What is this "emergency"?' The question came from Jeremiah Rowe.

'The men are unhappy about the pay they're being offered for working shifts,' replied Simon Kendall. 'They want me to negotiate for more.'

382

'If there's any discontent about anything to do with the Smith works, they come to see me first,' said Ben. 'Not you.'

'*I* asked him to come and speak to the men,' said Eddie Long, belligerently, speaking for the first time since Ben's arrival at the works. 'I'm the men's Union representative . . .'

'You're nothing at all at the Smith works,' Ben cut across Eddie's statement. 'I dismissed you from Ruddlemoor for stirring up trouble and I'm doing the same here. I'll not have you working for me anywhere, in any capacity. You can go right away!'

An angry murmur rose from the men close enough to hear what had been said. It grew as word of Eddie Long's dismissal was passed to those farther back in the crowd.

'Trades Unions are perfectly legal, Retallick,' said Simon Kendall, arrogantly. 'You'll have serious unrest on your hands if you dismiss a man just because he's a Union representative.'

'Belonging to a Trades Union has nothing to do with it. Eddie Long is going because he's a troublemaker. I don't keep such men working for me. Now, I want you off my premises too and the men back where they belong – working at making clay.'

Eddie Long had been leaning on his single crutch, glowering. Now he said, 'This has got nothing to do with the Union, or work, Simon. Ben Retallick is getting his own back on you, same as he did me, because we've both been out with Lily Shovell. He must have found out she was waiting for you outside the General Wolfe last night.'

Ben rounded on Simon Kendall instantly. 'You saw Lily last night?'

Ben began putting things together. Kendall's bruised and battered face, Lily's injuries and torn clothes . . .

Simon Kendall suddenly appeared nervous. 'We met briefly last night when she was on her way back to the Gover Valley.'

Ben took a pace towards Kendall. Before anyone was aware of his intention, he swung his fist and hit the man hard in the face, knocking him among the crowd.

Kendall rose only to his knees. He shook his head and blood spattered from a cut lip over the clothes of those about him.

Another angry murmur went up from the crowd and Lanyon Sweet advanced to stand alongside Ben.

He stood facing the Smith workers defiantly. Raising his voice so that he could be heard by all except those at the very back of the crowd, he said, 'Lily Shovell went out late last night to visit her home. On her way back it seems she met up with Simon Kendall – your Trades Union organiser. She arrived home with a badly scratched face and her clothes torn. You've seen Kendall's face this morning. I'll leave you to guess what happened. If this is the sort of man you want to follow, then neither you nor the Smith works is for me.'

There was a stunned silence and for a few moments Ben thought he might have swayed the crowd. Then someone at the heart of it called, 'We only have your word for what happened. It sounds to me like just another trick to avoid paying us any extra money.'

The unknown speaker's words brought cheers from the crowd and Ben knew he had lost his bid to win over the men.

Shrugging his shoulders, he looked towards the office doorway where a pale-faced Tessa could be seen looking out.

'Bring the ledgers out to me, Tessa. All of them. We'll take them back to Ruddlemoor with us and work out what's owed to the men. I'll have words with you when we get there.'

To the small, bearded man in the front of the crowd, he said, 'Close down the engine and the pumps, Captain Roberts – and extinguish the fires in the "dry". When you've done that you can send all the men home and lock up the office and all the buildings. I'll have a team sent in to remove everything of value that might be stolen. If anyone else wishes to take up the lease, I'll return everything – but I think that's extremely unlikely. I doubt if the Smith works will ever open again.'

Chapter 54

Later that morning, when all the ledgers had been removed from the Smith works, Ben went to Ruddlemoor. He was not in the best of moods and his anger was directed against Tessa.

Confronting her in the office, he said, 'I sent you to the Smith works because I trusted you. Why didn't you tell me Eddie Long was working there too? Was it because you and he had been going out while he was here?'

'No, it wasn't!' Tessa was indignant. 'If you really want to know, the first thing I did when I went there was to go through the ledgers — and I found several things that were wrong. Very wrong. But I needed to be certain of my facts before telling you. In the meantime, I didn't want Eddie taking fright and running off somewhere.'

'What do you mean, there were several things wrong?' Ben asked suspiciously. He thought Tessa might be trying to justify her inaction in some way.

'There are two things, really. The first is that I added up the money being paid out for coal and it didn't tally with the price we were being charged. When I looked into it I found that the price Eddie was marking down in the ledger was higher than that actually being paid to the coal merchant. He must have been putting the difference in his own pocket.'

'Can we prove this?'

'Yes — but that isn't all he was doing. The names and addresses of all the Smith employees are entered in the wages book. When I looked through it I found one that I knew was false. One of the addresses was in a street in Bugle — but I know the numbers in that particular street don't go as high as this number. When I checked I found that at least half-a-dozen men on the payroll don't exist. Eddie Long's been making quite a bit of money for himself by falsifying the accounts.'

Ben looked at Tessa less suspiciously now. 'Can all this be proved from the ledgers?'

'No doubt about it.'

'It seems Eddie Long has overstepped the mark this time. I'll report this to the police and we'll take Eddie to court. In the meantime keep the ledgers locked away safely. This might just be enough to make the men at the Smith works see sense, but I doubt it. There's a hardcore of troublemakers there. They seem to view a strike as a personal crusade.

385

Mind you, it might be a different story when they have no money coming into their homes.'

Suddenly contrite, he said, 'I'm sorry I doubted you, Tessa. You've done very well.'

'Well enough to ask you a favour?' she said cheekily.

'What is it?' Ben's suspicions returned once more.

'Give Frank Trudgeon work again – not here, but at Varcoe.'

Sitting close to Tessa, Jo's face showed disbelief that Tessa should dare to ask such a question. She knew nothing of Trudgeon's part in the dramatic happenings at the Smith works.

After only a moment's hesitation, Ben nodded his head. 'Tell him to go and see Captain Rowe in the morning. Say I want him taken on – or we could take him on at Ruddlemoor if you'd rather?'

Tessa could not hide her delight. 'Thank you! Thank you very much – but I think it would be best at Varcoe. Too many people would say too much to him about me here. I . . . I think he's serious about me.'

'That's *wonderful* news,' said Jo, warmly. 'I hope this one works out all right.'

'So do I,' said Tessa, fervently. Returning her attention to Ben once more, she said, 'At the Smith works, after you hit Simon Kendall, you said that something happened between him and Lily last night. Is she all right?'

'I don't know. I'll go home as soon as I can and find out exactly *what* did happen. Right now I have things to do. I need to stop my solicitors from going any further with the lease of the Smith works before I do anything else.'

When Ben had left the Ruddlemoor office, Jo said, 'What's all this about Lily and Simon – and Ben hitting him?'

When Tessa had related all that Ben had said and done, Jo said, 'I hope nothing too serious happened to Lily, but one thing is certain – Ben has nailed his colours to the mast as far as she's concerned. By the end of the day there'll not be a man or woman in St Austell who won't know how he feels about her.'

Ben was not in the habit of returning to the Gover Valley at lunchtime and his arrival took Lily by surprise.

There seemed to be nobody else in the house and when he asked her, she said, 'Josh and Miriam have gone to my house. I was supposed to have gone with them, but I didn't feel like it.'

'I'm not surprised. I saw Simon Kendall today. His face is a lot worse than yours. What did you hit him with?'

Lily paled. 'He didn't tell you . . .'

'He didn't have to *tell* me anything. When I was told that you met him outside the General Wolfe late last night, I was quite capable of putting two and two together.'

386

'No doubt you made them come to five, the same as a great many others did? It wasn't a planned meeting. I was on my way home as the General Wolfe was turning out.'

'It was a very late visit home.'

'That's right.' Ben's scepticism stung her. 'I went there to talk to Pa. To see if he could do something to help you at the Smith works. I stopped to talk to Simon for the same reason.'

'You put yourself at risk for me. Why?'

'It wasn't only for you. I did it for all those who work at the Smith works, and for their families. Many of them are my friends.'

Ben felt a certain disappointment at her explanation, but he accepted it. However, there was still the question of her injuries to be explained.

When he asked Lily about them once more, she was as evasive as before. 'I ran into a bush and fell,' she said, repeating the story she had told that morning.

'Did Simon Kendall run into the same bush, at the same time?'

'I know nothing about that,' she lied.

'I think you do, Lily. I believe that your injuries and his are linked. I told him so this morning. He didn't deny it.'

Ben did not bother to explain that Simon Kendall had been in no condition to deny anything at the time. However, her next words gave him confirmation that his actions had been justified – or at least, he was able to justify them to himself.

'He thought I should find him more interesting than I do. He's not the first one to make that mistake.'

'I wish you had given me the full story this morning, Lily.'

'Why? There was nothing to tell. It would only have worried Miriam and Josh.' Shrugging off the topic, she said, 'Now, since you're home can I get you something to eat?'

'No. I have to see my solicitors again. I'm afraid all your efforts were wasted. I tried to avert trouble at the Smith works, but the men seemed hell-bent on a confrontation. I've closed the works and have told my solicitors not to proceed any farther with the lease. The Smith works is closed. I doubt if we'll see it reopen again during our time.'

'Oh!' Lily sounded bitterly disappointed. 'A lot of families really are going to suffer because of it, Ben.'

'I don't doubt it – but what can I do? If I pay the men what they're asking, others in every works in clay country will want the same. It will push prices sky high – and the industry's walking a tightrope right now. If the men had agreed to accept the pay I'm giving the Ruddlemoor and Varcoe men, there would have been employment for an extra hundred or hundred and fifty, with a reasonable wage going into their homes. Thanks to Eddie Long, Simon Kendall and the men themselves, not only has that opportunity gone, but some two hundred other families will

387

lose their income. I just don't understand it. They are the losers, not me.'

'I'll speak to my pa again. He might change his mind and try to persuade them to return to work.'

'It's too late for that, Lily. Once I tell the solicitors I'm not going to sign the lease, that will be the end of it. But thanks for wanting to try. Thank you too for what you tried to do last night. I'm sorry about the way it turned out.'

As Ben spoke he put out his hand and touched the scratches that marred Lily's cheek. Reaching up, she held his hand there.

A moment later he was kissing her – but not for long. She suddenly pulled away and, dropping his hands to his sides, Ben said resignedly, 'I know . . . "Not under Josh and Miriam's roof". Would it make any difference if we were to go out in the garden?'

Lily laughed self-consciously. 'I'm sorry, Ben. I know it can't make much sense to you, but that's the way I feel about it.'

'You make it very difficult for me to get to know you better, Lily.'

'Perhaps that's just as well.'

Before he had time to contemplate the meaning of this ambiguous statement, she said, 'If you're not eating and you have the time, perhaps you'd like to walk with me into St Austell? If I speak to Pa with Josh there he might see things differently and make a move before it's too late.'

Along the road to St Austell, Ben said very little. Lily believed him to be pondering on the prospects for the Smith works.

She would have been surprised to learn that his thoughts had nothing at all to do with the clay industry. Instead, he was wondering how he could best bridge the gulf that lay between them. It seemed no narrower now than it had been when he first arrived in England.

Chapter 55

For a few days the men of the Smith works picketed the gates of the closed workings in large numbers. Their spirits were kept boosted by occasional visits from Simon Kendall who assured them they were striking a blow for their fellow clay workers by holding out for a 'fair' wage.

The strikers were still feeling sufficiently confident of themselves to heckle the policemen who arrived to pluck Eddie Long from their ranks and take him into custody.

There was a half-hearted attempt to prevent the officers from carrying out their duty, but it was quickly dealt with. The sergeant in charge of the arresting party warned them off, calling each of the men by name. He was a local man. Asking after the families of several of the men, he suggested they might more usefully fill their time by returning home and tending their gardens.

The sergeant added, meaningfully, that any food they grew might form a significant part of their diets in the difficult months that lay ahead.

Gradually, the novelty of not working wore off. It was replaced by a suspicion that they were picketing a clay works that no one *wanted* to enter.

Then, a week after they had begun their action, a solicitor's clerk from the practice representing the Tresillian Estate arrived at the works and affixed a 'Lease For Sale' notice on the gates.

Only then did full realisation come to the Smith works' pickets that there would be no victory. Simon Kendall's promises of support from their colleagues in the industry meant nothing at all. Furthermore, there could be no dispute if there was no owner with whom to do battle.

All Simon Kendall had helped them do was talk themselves out of work.

A meeting of the Clay Owners' Association, as they now called themselves, took place that same week. In his presence, the owners declared unswerving support for Ben in his confrontation with the clay workers. Behind his back, he suspected they were delighted that his plans for further expansion had suffered a set-back.

Ben was immersed in thoughts of the meeting as he rode along the Gover Valley later that afternoon. Coming within view of the Retallick home, he suddenly pulled his horse to a halt.

Standing on the roadway outside the house was the motor car he had first seen being driven by Martha's husband, Jannie. It meant that Sam Doney was paying another visit to Lily.

A wave of unreasonable jealousy swept over Ben. Tugging unnecessarily hard on the reins, he turned his horse around and headed back towards St Austell.

He felt he could not face the Camborne man today. Neither did he want to be inside the house, watching Sam Doney making up to Lily.

Ben had no idea of where he would go, but rode in a desultory manner through St Austell before taking the Pentewan Road.

He reached the entrance to Tregarrick, the home of the late Aloysius Varcoe. Acting on a sudden whim, he turned the horse in through the gateway. The house would be empty, but he thought he would like to look around the outside. He remembered it as being a most attractive house. Looking at it again today, he was not disappointed, even though it was heavily shuttered.

Ben was sitting his horse looking at the house when the main entrance door opened and an elegantly dressed young woman stepped out of the house.

She was followed by an elderly man who blinked at the world through a pair of small, round-lensed spectacles that perched precariously on the bridge of a very large, hooked nose.

'Can I help you?' The woman's accent matched her appearance.

'No . . . Please pardon me for intruding. I didn't realise anyone would be here. I was riding past and knew Aloysius Varcoe had died. It was more idle curiosity than anything else . . .'

'You knew Aloysius?'

'We did some business together and I called here on a couple of occasions. I'm sorry, I should introduce myself. I'm Ben Retallick.'

'Ah! Now I can put a name to your accent. You're the young Rhodesian who purchased the Varcoe Clay Works and saved my husband and me the problem of disposing of it. I'm Clementine Varcoe – and this is Mr Button, Aloysius's personal solicitor for very many years. My husband heard only last week that he'd inherited this rather lovely old house. Unfortunately, we're in the process of emigrating to Canada. The last thing we want is to have a house in the heart of Cornwall on our hands. As my husband is terribly busy, I said I would come here and try to arrange for its sale.'

'It's a beautiful house,' said Mr Button, in a high, thin voice. 'One of the finest to come on the market in this area for very many years.'

'It *is* very handsome,' agreed Ben. An exciting idea was beginning to take shape in his mind as the solicitor extolled the virtues of the old house. 'But I've really only seen one or two rooms.'

Making a snap decision, he said, 'I wonder if you would show me around the house sometime, Mr Button?'

'Of course. Make an appointment with my office . . .'

'Why not have a look around now, Mr Retallick? I have a couple of hours to spare before my train leaves,' Clementine suggested.

'Why not? I'm doing nothing else.'

Ben remembered *why* he was at a loose end and it momentarily soured the moment. Then he was leading his horse to the small yard between the house and some outbuildings. Here the others had left a light carriage. Ben tied his horse beside it.

Along the way Mr Button launched himself into practised patter about the finer points of the house and its position. 'So convenient to the town.'

The house had no need of Mr Button's professionally enthusiastic salesmanship. By the time they were no more than halfway through the inspection of the interior, Ben was hardly listening to what the solicitor was saying. He was absolutely charmed by the ancient manor house.

It was small compared with Lady Tresillian's huge house, yet it was very much larger than Josh and Miriam's Gover Valley property.

By the time the small party returned to the front entrance hall, Ben knew he wanted to own the house – and for more than one reason.

'It is a lovely house,' declared Clementine Varcoe, echoing his thoughts. 'Had we intended remaining in England, I would certainly have kept it and probably spent a great deal of time here. As it is . . .' She shrugged.

'Have you decided how much you'll be asking for the house?'

Ben put the question to the solicitor, who looked quickly at Clementine Varcoe. He then named a price which was more than Ben had paid for the Varcoe works. Ben thought it very high.

Something of his thoughts must have showed in his expression because Mr Button added hurriedly, 'Of course, that includes three hundred acres of farmland and the farmhouse.'

This certainly made the price more realistic and it was clinched for Ben when Clementine Varcoe said, 'For only a thousand pounds more you can have it complete with contents.'

This was a generous offer indeed. It would have cost Ben very much more to furnish the house – and he would be gaining some splendid old furniture.

'I really don't think I can turn down such an offer,' he said, trying to hide the excitement he felt at having decided he wanted to own the wonderful old house. 'I'll be delighted to buy the house – and its contents.'

Later that evening, the deal clinched, Ben and the solicitor were seeing Clementine Varcoe off at St Austell railway station.

As she was about to enter her carriage, Clementine said to Ben, 'Do you have a young lady in mind to share the house with you?'

'I do,' he replied. 'But I haven't asked her yet.'

'I think she would be very foolish to refuse you,' smiled Clementine. 'I hope you will both be very, very happy there.'

With this, she leaned forward from the carriage step and kissed Ben on the cheek.

No one in the group saw the motor car which had stopped outside the station and the hiss of escaping steam from the train's engine drowned the sound of the vehicle's engine.

Inside the motor car, Pippa Doney waved gaily to the passengers who smiled in return from the carriage windows.

The smile was not reflected on Lily's face as she and Jo watched Ben being kissed by an elegant young lady whom he was seeing off on the London-bound train.

From where she sat, Lily thought the well-dressed young woman looked suspiciously like Deirdre Tresillian.

Chapter 56

The house was in darkness when Ben returned to the Gover Valley. He was bursting to tell someone of his purchase, but there was no one awake in the house for him to tell. He also wanted Lily to be the first to know – but he would need to choose his moment.

As he lay in bed in the darkness he decided that he would let her tell him about the visit of Sam Doney before he mentioned the house to her.

It took him a long time to go to sleep as he thought of the house and all its possible implications for his future with Lily.

He was annoyed when thoughts of Sam Doney returned – and even more upset that they should bother him so much.

Breakfast the following morning was a somewhat strained affair. After waiting in vain for Lily to say something of Sam's visit to the house, Ben decided to keep the news of his purchase of Tregarrick to himself for a while longer.

When he was about to leave the house, bound for Ruddlemoor, he tried to give Lily an opening to mention Sam Doney, saying, 'You've been very quiet this morning, Lily. Is something bothering you? Has anyone said anything to upset you?'

'No. Why should something be wrong?'

There was such aggression in her voice that Ben was taken aback. 'It was no more than a civil question, that was all.'

'I suggest you tend to *your* business and leave me to look after mine. *I'm* not responsible for leaving hundreds of men, women and children staring starvation in the face.'

She flounced off to the kitchen, leaving Ben staring after her, open-mouthed.

Miriam was following Lily into the hall and heard the exchange. Appealing to her, Ben said, 'What was all that about?'

'I'd say it has to do with the Smith works,' snapped Miriam, unsympathetically. 'A lot of people are going to face hardship as a result of what's been happening there.'

Ben was bewildered. 'I'm as sorry as anyone else about what's happened – but how can I possibly be held responsible? I offered the men who work there a higher wage than they've ever had before. What's more, I intended doubling the workforce. It meant that almost

393

single-handed I would have wiped out unemployment in the St Austell area. Instead of being delighted, the Smith workers turned around and kicked me in the teeth! What was I supposed to do?'

'I don't know. *You're* the great works owner. But closing a place down doesn't help anyone. You're playing a game with people's lives. Ordinary people with families to feed.'

Miriam followed Lily to the kitchen, leaving Ben staring after her, open-mouthed.

Josh had been listening in silence and now he grinned wryly at Ben. 'Don't look for sense in anything that your grandma feels strongly about, Ben – or Lily either, come to that. They're two of a kind. The Bible says that God made women from Adam's rib, but he didn't find their logic from the same source, I swear.'

It came as a relief to leave the house that morning, but the problem of the Smith works remained to haunt him. Ben found a delegation of half-a-dozen men waiting for him at the end of the Gover Valley road.

But these were not the jeering, jubilant men he had last seen outside the works gates. These were anxious family men, fearful for the future of their families.

They stood in the morning drizzle, heads uncovered respectfully. As he approached they called politely and asked if they might have a word with him.

When Ben reined in, they echoed Miriam's words, begging him to reconsider his decision to close the Smith works.

'I'm afraid that's impossible,' said Ben, firmly. He was trying hard not to allow himself to be influenced by a wide-eyed young girl who was looking up at him. Wearing holed long socks and boy's boots, she clung to the hand of one of the workers.

'I had signed only a provisional lease for the works when you men put in your demands. I was offering a fair wage, one accepted quite happily by my men at Ruddlemoor and Varcoe. Had I agreed to pay more it would have been years before the works came into profit – possibly never. I would have been spending money to buy trouble. I don't need that so I told my solicitors to break off the purchase. The Smith works is nothing at all to do with me now. The time for you to have made your pleas was when everyone else was clamouring for more money. I didn't hear your voices raised in protest against what was happening then.'

They looked sheepish and the man holding the hand of the small girl said, 'We were foolish, Mr Retallick. Too ready to listen to that Kendall man from London. But saying I'm sorry isn't going to put food in the belly of young Tamsin here – or the five others I've left at home with a sick wife.'

'I'm running a China clay business, not feeding Cornwall's needy.'

Ben's reply was harsher than he had intended it to be. The steady, wide-eyed stare of the young girl was beginning to get to him.

'Of course. We're sorry to have troubled you, Mr Retallick.'

He had intended riding on without looking back at the men. He told himself this was his right. He had given them an opportunity to work for a good wage and they had thrown the offer back in his face. What happened to them and their families now should be on their own conscience, not his.

He did look back. The men were talking in a defeated, subdued group – and the wide-eyed, heavy-booted girl was still staring at him.

'You there!'

The men all turned to look at Ben in response to his call.

'Go to Varcoe and speak to Captain Rowe. He's due to begin breaking new ground in the next few days. He'll need more men. Tell him you've spoken to me and I've said he's to take you on.'

The relief on the faces of the men touched him, but Ben was concerned they might interpret his change of heart as weakness. 'If any of the Smith trouble spreads to Varcoe, you men will be the first to go. Is that understood?'

'There'll be no trouble from any of us, Mr Retallick, I can promise you that – and thank you.'

It was Tamsin's father who called out the gratitude of the men as Ben rode away. When he turned around once more the small girl waved a hand to him. He returned the wave, then went on his way.

Chapter 57

'Will you be coming with Lily and me to Camborne for Pippa's birthday party?' Jo put the question to Ben when they were alone in the Ruddlemoor office later that morning. Tessa was in St Austell with an escort of men collecting the wages for both Varcoe and Ruddlemoor Works.

'I don't know anything about any birthday party,' he replied. 'If it's anything like the last party I went to there, I'd be quite happy to give it a miss.'

'I've heard all about that night.' Jo giggled. 'This will be very different. It's to be a very small party for a few of Pippa's little friends. Sam and Pippa drove to St Austell last night to ask us to be there.'

'Are you and Lily included among Pippa's "little" friends?'

'It seems like it.' Jo smiled enigmatically at Ben. 'But Sam included you in the invitation too. I'm sure he'd like you to come. So would Lily.'

'I doubt it.' Ben did not share Jo's good humour this morning. 'She never even bothered to mention Sam's visit this morning.'

'Perhaps she thought you had other things on your mind?' said Jo. Ben thought she was referring to the problems of the Smith works, as Lily herself had been, but Jo continued, 'We saw you last night with a very well-dressed young lady.'

'Where was this?' The revelation took him by surprise.

'At the railway station. Sam took us for a drive and as we passed by we saw you there with this young woman and an older man.'

'Oh, yes, I *was* there.' Ben knew Jo was waiting for an explanation, but it could not be given without revealing the secret he was keeping for the right moment.

When it became increasingly apparent that he was not going to enlighten her as to the identity of the young woman on the station, Jo said, 'Will you come to Camborne with Lily and me?'

'No,' he said, shortly. 'I have too much to do. I'm sure you'll both have a wonderful time without me.'

Ben was on his way home from Ruddlemoor to Varcoe when he passed the carriage that had been sent to St Austell to draw the wages for the men of both works.

From inside the wagon Tessa saw Ben and waved frantically to attract his attention. He turned his horse, but Tessa was out of the vehicle and hurrying to meet him long before he reached the carriage.

'The news is all around St Austell that Eddie Long has been released by the police.' Tessa was so excited by the news, she found it difficult to remain coherent.

'Why? There can be no doubting his guilt. The ledgers prove it.'

'I know, but he defrauded the money from Mr Smith – and he's out of the country. No one knows when he'll be back. Without him there's no case to answer. Eddie's been released by the police.'

Ben frowned. 'That's not good news. Eddie at large is trouble – and he's vindictive. Make certain that Captains Rowe and Bray know about this. Eddie Long is not to come anywhere near any of the works.'

'I'll tell them, but from what I hear he's already making trouble. He's going around saying he was released because the police realise he's an innocent man. He claims the only reason he was arrested is because he tried to get a fair wage for the men at the Smith works.'

'That's a load of nonsense! He's a thief.'

'You and I know that, but there are a great many men who are ready to listen to him. I'm worried. He must know it was me who told you he was stealing money from the Smith works . . .'

'Try not to worry, Tessa. If it looks as though there might be any trouble, I'll have you picked up from home in the mornings and taken back at night. You're safe enough at work and there are plenty of people near at hand when you're home. You'll be protected from him, I promise.'

'Thank you. But you'll need to be careful too. You're the one he's always had a grudge against.'

By Friday, Lily was feeling foolish. What had begun as a brief flare-up of temper aimed at Ben, had dragged on for the remainder of the week. She was also well aware that he had tried on more than one occasion to heal the breach between them.

She was honest enough with herself to admit that she was the one who was to blame for the widening gulf, but this awareness only brought out an irrational stubbornness that would not allow her to respond to his conciliatory moves.

The incident with the elegant young woman at St Austell railway station had – almost – been fully explained.

Mr Button had met the young lady from a London train the day before. While awaiting her arrival the solicitor had enjoyed the hospitality of the station master.

The two men had gossiped about the solicitor's reason for being at the station. As a result, the station master had later informed the ticket clerk that the young lady was a relative of the late Aloysius Varcoe who was visiting St Austell to wind up the late clay owner's estate.

The ticket clerk was a neighbour of the Shovell family's and this information was passed on over the garden wall when he and Jethro were working in their respective gardens.

When the news reached Lily, she thought she knew the reason for Ben's presence at the station. It had *not* been Deirdre Tresillian then, and she realised the other man she had seen must have been Mr Button, the late Mr Varcoe's solicitor. The meeting with the elegant woman must have had something to do with Ben's purchase of the Varcoe works.

True, there was the kiss to be explained away, but in a rational moment, Lily conceded to herself that the woman had kissed Ben, and not the other way round. It had also been no more than a perfunctory affair. Hardly more than a handshake, really.

There was another reason Lily would have liked the foolish differences between herself and Ben to come to an end. She really did want him to accompany Jo and herself to Camborne.

However, having dug the metaphorical hole in which she now found herself, Lily could think of no way of asking him to go with her. Not having told him of Sam Doney's visit to the Gover Valley did not make it any easier for her.

Lily was aware that Jo had spoken to him about the visit and hoped he might be the one to broach the subject and make the offer to accompany her and Jo to Pippa's birthday party.

When Friday arrived and nothing had been said between them, Lily had almost braced herself to apologise to Ben. Then, late in the morning, all her good intentions were shattered. The cause was a telephone call from Deirdre Tresillian.

The young lady spoke to Lily as though she were a servant. When told that Ben was at Ruddlemoor, Deirdre demanded that Lily get a message to him, *immediately*.

The message was that Deirdre would meet him at four o'clock that afternoon at Probus, a village on the road from Tresillian to St Austell.

Deirdre's autocratic manner made Lily want to utter a rude word and hang up the telephone. Instead, she frostily assured Deirdre Tresillian that she would send someone to Ruddlemoor with her message.

As it happened, the Retallicks' handyman was absent in St Austell, buying some supplies for Miriam. The only certain method of passing the message was to take it herself.

When she set off, Lily was quietly fuming about Deirdre's telephone manner. The anger became some form of defence mechanism at the thought of having to talk to Ben and built up along the way. By the time she reached the Ruddlemoor office she was in a furious mood.

Fortunately, perhaps, Ben was not there. Jo too was absent, being in St Austell buying stationery. It was a relief and Lily remained at

Ruddlemoor for half-an-hour, chatting with Tessa and calming down.

Eventually she set off for home, leaving Deirdre's message to be passed on if Ben returned in time.

The message took Ben by surprise. He had believed Deirdre and her grandmother to be still in France, enjoying their holiday.

It also caused him some concern.

He could understand Lady Tresillian wishing to see him, to discuss his withdrawal from the agreement they had reached over the Smith works. But Deirdre . . .?

Uneasily, his thoughts returned to the night they had spent together at Tresillian House. His fears of the possible consequences had only just begun to subside. Now they returned with renewed dread.

Chapter 58

Deirdre Tresillian *had* called the meeting with Ben at Probus to discuss the night she had slept with him – but it had nothing to do with the possible consequences he had feared.

In fact, Deirdre Tresillian was a very happy girl.

She rode there side-saddle in company with a groom whom she dismissed with orders to return to Tresillian as soon as Ben put in an appearance.

After Deirdre's effusive greeting, Ben said, 'I thought you and Lady Tresillian were on holiday in France? What went wrong?'

'Nothing at all is wrong, Benjamin. On the contrary, everything is wonderfully *right*.' She gave him one of her practised wide-eyed appealing looks. 'At least . . . it *is* if you behave like the gentleman I believe you to be.'

'I'm sorry, Deirdre. I still don't understand . . .'

'You remember Charles – Charles Congreve?'

Ben remembered the rather pleasant young man he had met on his last visit to Tresillian. 'Of course. I liked him.'

'I'm so glad, Benjamin. That makes everything so much easier. I didn't tell you when we last met, but Charles has asked me to marry him. In fact, he has asked me many times. I've always liked him too, of course. Liked him *lots*. All the same, I wasn't allowed to become *too* fond of him, even though there was a viscountcy in the family. Charles has always been a younger brother, with not too much money and very meagre prospects. Grandmother wouldn't have dreamt of there being anything between us. Charles was a suitable companion for me, no more.'

'I still don't understand . . . What is all this to do with me? Why have you asked to see me? I thought . . .'

'Be patient with me, please, Benjamin.' Deirdre reached across and rested a hand on his arm. At the same time she glared at a ragged young boy who had stopped to stare at her with innocent curiosity.

'Let's ride out of the village a short way. I find it impossible to talk here.'

She flicked her reins and the startled horse moved off rapidly, causing the small boy to jump out of its path.

Ben's horse soon caught up with her, but she said nothing until the cottages of the village had been left behind and they were riding along a narrow, tree-lined lane.

Reining in her horse to a slow walk, Deirdre said, 'Grandmother and I were in Calais. We remained there for a few days while she recovered from the effects of the crossing. We were still there when we heard of the death of Charles's brother, the Viscount Congreve. He was killed in a riding accident.'

'Oh, I'm sorry to hear about that. Please pass on my commiserations to Charles.'

'Thank you. We were saddened too, of course – but Charles was his brother's heir. It means that he is now the Eleventh Viscount Congreve.'

'Good Lord!' Ben had liked Charles Congreve but he was surprised that he had inherited a peerage. He had seemed a somewhat insignificant young man.

'Yes, it's taken us all by surprise. It has also made a tremendous difference to my grandmother's opinion of him. As well as the title, Charles has inherited the family house and a great deal of land. He has suddenly and unexpectedly become a wealthy man.'

'I see,' said Ben. 'He has also become a very eligible husband for you?'

'Yes.' Deirdre looked at him as though she was saying something that was going to leave him desolate. 'Would you be terribly hurt if I accepted him, Benjamin?'

Ben looked at her in astonishment, then looked away again quickly. He wondered what make-believe land she existed in.

'My greatest wish is that you and Charles should be very happy, Deirdre.'

'I hoped you would say that, Benjamin – and I believed you would. You are a wonderful man and I will always be very, very fond of you. I . . . I would hope we might still be able to see each other occasionally after I am married? You must come to stay with us at our home in Devon. I will also be returning to Cornwall to visit Grandmother occasionally, of course.'

Ben made vague murmurs which might have meant anything, but it did not matter. Deirdre was bubbling over with her own thoughts.

'You don't know what this will mean to me, Benjamin! All my life I have been living in the shadow of my grandmother and her title. It's been "My Lady this", and "My Lady that" from everyone, while I've just been "Miss Deirdre". But when I'm married I shall be Viscountess Congreve – and as a Viscountess I shall take precedence over Grandmother. Can you imagine that!'

Ben remained quiet. It was evident that being Viscountess Congreve meant far more to Deirdre than did being married to poor insignificant Charles.

'There's just one thing, Benjamin . . .'

He turned to look at her. She was once more appealing to him with one of her wide-eyed expressions. 'Promise me you will never tell anyone what we did that night you stayed at Tresillian?'

'Of course I won't.' His shock at her question was unfeigned, but he quickly realised this was not quite the reaction she wanted. He qualified it hurriedly. 'I'll never *forget* what happened. How could I? But it will always be a secret that only you and I share.'

'Thank you, Benjamin,' Deirdre said breathlessly. Moving her horse close to his, she said, 'You may kiss me, if you wish.'

It was not something he particularly wished to do but he obliged her, relieved by the knowledge that on this occasion it would lead to nothing more.

'You *are* a darling, Benjamin. Now I can marry Charles in the knowledge that I do not have a single care in the world.'

Assuming yet another of her wide-eyed looks, she said, 'I would like you to see me home now, Benjamin. As far as the lodge, at least.'

The ride did not take very long and along the way Deirdre chattered incessantly. She talked of the aborted holiday, about her tennis prowess – and of the forthcoming wedding.

When they reached the lodge gate she said farewell to Ben, wringing the maximum drama from the occasion. Reaching across from her horse, she gripped his arm, almost in tears. With a husky, 'Goodbye, dear, dear, Benjamin,' and a final squeeze of his arm, she rode in through the lodge gates and put her horse to a canter without another backward glance.

Feeling quite light-hearted, Ben was about to turn his horse towards St Austell when one of two young women hanging out clothes on a line in the lodge garden waved to him.

He knew he had seen the girl before – and then he remembered where and when. It was the girl who had been caught in the kitchen fire at Tresillian House.

Riding his horse closer to the lodge fence, he called, 'Hello, it's Anna, isn't it? How are you? Have your burns healed completely now?'

'Yes, thank you, sir.' The girl's face had turned pink with pleasure that Ben should have remembered her name. 'My legs are fine now.'

'That's good. Are you still working for Lady Tresillian?'

Much of the pleasure disappeared from the girl's expression. 'No, sir. I was off work for so long that Lady Tresillian said she couldn't afford to be without a second cook any longer. She found someone else. I'm staying here with my sister and her husband until I find another post.'

Looking at this healthy young girl, Ben had an idea. 'You were second cook at the house. How good are you at cooking?'

Anna's sister replied for her. 'She's good enough to have done most of the cooking herself when she was up at the house – and the new second cook better be able to do the same. Lady Tresillian's old cook uses a lot of wine when she's cooking – but there's more goes inside her than in the pot. If you ask me, it was her who caused the fire.'

'Would you consider coming to work for me as my cook?' Ben asked Anna.

The young girl's face lit up in delight. 'I would that, sir, – and you'd never have cause to regret taking me on, I can promise you that.'

'Good! How soon can you start?'

'Soon as you like, sir. I'll come back with you this minute if you so wish.'

Ben smiled. 'I've only just bought the house, but I plan to move in this weekend. Have your things ready and I'll collect you on Sunday afternoon. Will that suit you?'

'Thank you, sir. Thank you very much. I'll be ready and waiting for when you arrive, whatever time on Sunday you come.'

Riding away from Tresillian Lodge, Ben realised that now he had decided when he would be moving into Tregarrick it was a very exciting thing to be doing. He was about to move into his first house. One that belonged to him.

The only thing that gave him pause was how Josh and Miriam would react – and Lily too. But the decision had been taken now. He would tell them about it when he reached home that night.

Chapter 59

Ben reached the Gover Valley very late that evening. Now he had made the decision to move into his new home, he discovered there were many things to be done.

Mr Button had given him the name of the woman who had been Aloysius Varcoc's housekeeper for very many years. Doris Rodda, now elderly, had moved in with her sister to a small cottage in a nearby village and needed a great deal of persuading to come out of her brief state of retirement. However, she eventually agreed to resume her old post as housekeeper at Tregarrick, at least on a temporary basis. She would move back there the following day.

It was dark when Ben reached the house which had been his home since arriving in England. As he approached the door he wondered for the umpteenth time how everyone would take the news that he had purchased Tregarrick and would be moving out over the weekend.

He was particularly excited about what Lily would say. He wondered whether she would realise the implications of the purchase. It would remove the self-imposed barrier she had created between them by reason of them both being 'under the same roof'.

Unfortunately, he learned he would need to wait for Lily's reaction.

Trying hard to contain his excitement, he entered the room where Josh and Miriam were sitting and said, 'I have some news for you – but I'd like to tell everyone at the same time. Where's Lily?'

'She's gone to stay with Jo for the night. They're both catching an early train to Camborne in the morning. What's your news? You're not going to tell us you're getting married to that Tresillian girl?'

Despite his disappointment at the absence of Lily, Ben managed to grin at his grandmother's consternation. 'There's never been anything but friendship between me and Deirdre. No, my news is that I've bought a house. I'm going to live in Aloysius Varcoe's old home, Tregarrick.'

Miriam's response to the news was one of astonishment. 'But that's a *huge* house. You'll rattle around in there like a pea in a colander.'

'Not really. It looks more impressive from outside than it actually is. It's really very cosy. You must come along and see it tomorrow morning.'

Trying hard to disguise his disappointment, he added, 'I was hoping Lily would be there to see it too.'

Miriam was thoughtful for a long time before saying, 'When are you thinking of moving into Tregarrick?'

'I'll shift most of my things tomorrow and be in there for Sunday.'

'So soon!' Miriam was genuinely dismayed. 'Aren't you happy here with us?'

'I'm very happy being with you, but I can't stay here for always.'

'You can as far as your grandma and me are concerned,' said Josh. He too was taken aback by the announcement and the speed of Ben's anticipated move. 'We won't be here for ever and this house is yours when we die.'

'I hope that's not going to be for many years yet,' said Ben jocularly, hoping to shake his grandparents out of the melancholy which had descended upon them. 'Besides, there's another reason why I need to leave.'

'I knew it!' declared Miriam. 'There had to be something else. No young man's going to give up the comforts of a good home to go and live on his own unless there's a reason for it. No doubt there's a girl in this somewhere. Who is she, one of the well-bred young ladies you've met at Tresillian?'

'There is a girl in my thoughts, yes, but I met her right here, in this house.'

Miriam stared at him for a few moments as she gathered her composure. 'Not . . . our Lily?'

'That's right, Lily.'

'Are you telling us she's going to leave us too and come to Tregarrick with you?' This time it was Josh who expressed anxiety.

'I hope she will one day, but it will never happen if I stay here. Every time I try to show any affection she puts an immediate stop to it by saying it's betraying the trust you and Grandma have in her. The only way forward that I could see was to move out. Perhaps I'll stand a chance if I'm living somewhere else.'

Miriam relaxed in her chair with obvious relief. 'Well, now, this is making a bit more sense. If that's the way Lily's thinking then the sooner the two of you have different roofs over your heads the better.'

Ben smiled once more. 'Tregarrick really is a beautiful house. I'm hoping that might help influence her too.'

'It's more likely to scare the living daylights out of the girl,' said Miriam unhelpfully. 'But I don't doubt she can get over that. I wish now I'd stopped her from going off tonight. But it won't matter too much. The pair of you have a lifetime ahead of you. What's a couple of days? You can show your grandad and me the house tomorrow morning. Then I'll tell you what you're going to need there if you intend impressing young Lily . . .'

As the train carrying Lily and Jo pulled noisily out of St Austell station,

Lily drew her head in and closed the window of the carriage.

'Who were you hoping to see . . . as if I don't already know?'

Lily shrugged. 'I just thought Ben might change his mind and decide to come to Camborne with us after all.'

'Did you let him know you *wanted* him to come with us?'

When Lily made no reply, Jo answered her own question. 'No, you didn't. As far as I'm aware you didn't even tell him Sam Doney had come to St Austell. You certainly didn't tell Ben he was included in the invitation.'

'I don't suppose it would have made any difference. Sam Doney and Pippa aren't important enough for him to want to spend a weekend with them – or with *us*, come to that. He'd rather spend his time with rich friends like that arrogant, spoilt trollop from Tresillian.'

'Miaow!' said Jo, and Lily rounded on her immediately.

'What's that supposed to mean?'

'It means, my young sister-in-law, that you're jealous of Deirdre Tresillian.'

'I'm nothing of the sort!' retorted Lily, heatedly. 'But I feel sorry for Ben if he's going to end up with someone like her.'

'My impression has always been that he'll end up with someone like *you*,' said Jo. 'After all, there's no one better placed, is there? You're at home waiting at the end of each day when he comes home feeling tired and needing someone to talk to. Then, when you go to bed, there's only a wall dividing you – I presume you *have* kept that wall between you?'

'Of course I have!' Lily spoke indignantly. Then, after a brief reflection, she grimaced. 'Perhaps that's the trouble. I'm far too fond of Miriam and Josh to ever break their trust in me. Even so, I admit I've been tempted to, once or twice.'

'I think you've got the wrong idea about Miriam. From what I hear, she never let anything stand between her and Josh. In my opinion there's nothing she'd like more than for you and Ben to get together. I believe she'd lock you and him in a room together and throw away the key for a week if she thought it would work.'

'She probably would,' agreed Lily. 'She's said as much to me.'

'Well then! What's the problem? There's you eating your heart out for him and, from what I see, he feels the same way about you. The whole world is doing its best to help you, so what's going wrong?'

'We're from two different worlds, Jo. You've seen the sort of friends he has. He's rich and important. I'm . . . I'm nobody.'

'You're talking utter nonsense, our Lily! He was born and brought up in Africa. That must have been a totally different way of life from anything we know. But it will be just as strange to Deirdre Tresillian and her friends. It means too that Ben will find his own way and decide what *he* wants, without any of the prejudices held by Deirdre Tresillian – yes, and you too. You're doing him a great disservice by thinking

406

otherwise and putting yourself down for no good cause. If he marries you it will be because he loves and wants *you*. That's the best basis I know for any marriage. Of course, if you're not certain enough of how *you* feel about *him*, that's a different matter entirely.'

Lily was silent for so long that Jo thought she might have offended her. Then Lily said quietly, 'I *do* love him, Jo. I lie awake at night sometimes and my whole being cries out to be with him. When he goes off to Tresillian I have an almost physical pain just thinking about him being there – with *her*.'

Jo leaned forward and gripped both Lily's hands in her own. 'That's what I've been *waiting* to hear you say, Lily. Now, for heaven's sake, *do* something about it when you get back to the Gover Valley. Let him *know* how you feel about him – and to hell with all these foolish ideas you have about upsetting Miriam and Josh. You *won't*. Anyway, they've lived their life – and lived it to the full. You've got to think of your own life now.'

'All right. I will. Thank you, Jo . . . but how about you and Sam? Do you think you and he might make a go of things?'

'I don't know, Lily. I really believe that's what this weekend is about. I'd like to think so. No one will ever take Darley's place in my life, but I don't care to think that I'm going to spend the rest of my life on my own.'

She grimaced at Lily. 'So, you see, I had a selfish reason for wanting Ben to come along with us today. He'd have kept you occupied while I had a chance to get to know Sam better.'

Jo had a sudden thought and said, 'Ben does know of Sam's interest in me?'

'I doubt it. I haven't told him.'

'Then he probably thinks that Sam was in St Austell to see *you* and not me, when he came to give us the invitation. Oh, Lily, you are a fool! For someone who thinks so much of him you have a damned funny way of going about proving it.'

Chapter 60

'It's a beautiful house,' admitted Miriam, as she and Josh came to the end of the tour. 'But it definitely needs a woman's touch – and it will be the devil of a job to keep warm in winter.'

Ben smiled at her observations. He was also secretly relieved that she had not thrown up her hands in horror because the house was much larger than she was used to. He hoped Lily's reaction might be the same.

'With luck I'll be able to overcome both those problems. But sit down, and I'll pour us all a glass of Aloysius Varcoe's excellent brandy. We'll drink to the health of Tregarrick, and the future of the Retallicks who live here.'

Seated in a chair in the high-ceilinged study, Miriam looked about her. She took in the long, tasteful velvet curtains and the expensive carpets that covered most of the polished wood floor, but her next comment was not of these.

'I don't think I could take being stared at by all those pictures wherever I went in the house. There's not a smile on the face of a single one of them.'

Josh shook his head in amused apology at Ben. 'It's a wonderful house, Ben. I'm sure you're going to be very happy here.'

'I'd like to think Lily would want to share it and be happy here too,' he said. 'You don't think she'll be over-awed by everything?'

'She'll be scared to death,' declared Miriam, startling him. 'But it's the sort of fright any sensible young girl can get over very quickly if she puts her mind to it.'

Returning on the train to St Austell, Jo was radiant. Sam had said nothing about a future together for them, but they had found they had a great deal in common during the weekend in Camborne. She was convinced it would be only a matter of time before he broached the subject of marriage.

Jo also waxed lyrical about Pippa. 'She's a lovely little girl. If she ever is mine, I'll spoil her to pieces, I just won't be able to help it.'

Lily smiled. Jo had talked in this manner from the time she had woken that morning. Lily had gone to bed early the previous night, leaving her downstairs with Sam. It seemed that all had gone well for them. She hoped things might work out as successfully for Ben and herself.

Lily admitted to herself that she had made things extremely difficult for him during the months he had been in England. Much of this had been because she had been frightened of her own feelings for him, the strength of which had alarmed her. She would not allow such foolishness to stand in her way again.

'We're almost there. Look, there are the clay workings.' Jo pointed out of the window to the white conical hills of China clay waste to the north of the railway line. 'I shall miss them if I leave.'

'You will leave,' said Lily positively. 'And when you're married to Sam, you won't give them another thought.'

'It makes me very happy to know I'll have your approval if I do marry him, Lily. I've been very worried that you might think I'm being somehow disloyal to the memory of Darley. I'll never forget him, you know.'

'Of course you won't, but you can't spend your lifetime married to a memory. You made Darley very happy when he was alive, and I'll always love you for that.'

'Thank you, Lily. I hope things are going to work out as well for you.'

The train was slowing to enter the station now and both girls stood up and gathered their belongings.

'Are you going to your home, or will you come to my place for a while?'

'Neither. I'm going to the Gover Valley. I want to have an honest talk with Ben.'

Seated in the kitchen of the Gover Valley house, Lily was completely bemused. 'But . . . why did he leave so suddenly? Why didn't he say something to me about it before the weekend?'

'Only Ben can give you the answers to those questions,' said Miriam, 'but I had the impression that you two didn't have very much to say to each other during this last week.'

Lily was very upset. 'I know, and that was entirely my fault, but I didn't think it was serious enough for him to leave here and go off and live on his own!'

'Well, if you ignore a housekeeper and a number of servants, I suppose he *is* on his own, but I think there's more to the move than that. We spoke about it and his feeling was that he had no chance of getting anywhere with you while you were both living in the same house. Something to do with your misguided sense of propriety, I've no doubt?'

'So he *has* left because of me! Yes, I am to blame for giving him that impression. I haven't handled the whole situation very sensibly, have I? I came to that realisation while I was away with Jo. I came back today fully intending to make things up to Ben and to apologise for being so stupid.'

'Well, as far as I'm aware, nothing's happened to prevent you from doing that. You'll just need to walk a little farther in order to do it, that's all.'

'You're right, Miriam. I'd better do it before my courage fails me again.'

'You've got time to stop and have a cup of tea before you go. It will give you time to gather your thoughts together.'

'No, I'll go now.' Lily stood up and looked sheepishly at Miriam. 'Thanks for being understanding and for not telling me how stupid I've been.'

She had reached the doorway when Miriam called to her. When Lily turned, Miriam took her in her arms and kissed her. 'I wish you luck, girl. If you and Ben were to wed, it would be the happiest day of my life.'

Lily's resolution faltered a little when she approached Tregarrick and realised how large it was. She had always known the house was here, but had only glimpsed it through the trees, from a distance. She had never thought very much about it before now.

Bolstering her flagging courage, she reminded herself that Ben had told Miriam he was buying the house to improve his chances with her. All the same, the house looked extremely grand now she was closer.

She needed to pause once more and summon up more will-power to tug on the bell-pull. She did it hesitantly, believing that the sound must be echoing through the whole of the old house.

Lily seemed to wait on the doorstep for a very long time. She was contemplating whether or not to ring the bell a second time when she heard footsteps on the other side of the door.

There was the sound of a large bolt being drawn, then the door swung open. An elderly, thin-lipped woman stood before her.

Eyeing Lily up and down, she said, 'What do you want? If you're here after one of the servant's jobs the back door is the place – but not on a Sunday. There'll be no one employed for this house on a Sunday.'

Trying hard not to show the affront she felt, Lily said, 'I've not come here looking for work. I'm here to see Ben Retallick.'

'Are you now – and *Ben* Retallick, is it? Well, you're out of luck. He's not at home.'

'Oh!' Feeling thoroughly deflated, Lily said, 'Do you know where he's gone, and when he'll be home?'

Sniffing in a manner that was intended to show her disapproval of Lily, the housekeeper said, 'I'm not at all sure that it's any of your business, but he went to Tresillian House – that's the home of Lady Tresillian, I believe. He didn't tell me when I could expect him back.'

Chapter 61

Anna was ready and waiting for Ben when he arrived at the Tresillian House lodge. She stood outside the door, her possessions divided between a battered suitcase, secured with rope, and a bulging hessian flour sack, scrubbed spotlessly clean.

Her wide smile of greeting suggested she was both pleased and relieved to see him.

Ben had found a well-cared for pony-cart in the Tregarrick stables and the tenant farmer who occupied the manor farm had loaned him the horse.

'I hope you haven't been waiting outside for too long?' he said as he lifted her luggage inside the small vehicle.

'Not very long,' Anna lied. 'I was just too excited to sit about inside the house while I waited. This is the first time in my life I've ever been away from Tresillian. I was born here on the estate and went to work in the house when I was eleven.'

'I hope you'll enjoy the change, Anna. It's not a huge house if you compare it with Tresillian, and I haven't got around to entertaining yet, but I'll try to give you enough work to keep you happy.'

'Don't you worry none about me, sir. I'm not too proud to turn my hand to something outside the kitchen if there's work as needs doing.'

'Good! It sounds as though I've found myself a real treasure, Anna. You're exactly what Tregarrick needs.'

She was still blushing with the pleasure Ben's words had given her when her sister, brother-in-law and their children came from the lodge to bid her farewell.

On the road to St Austell Ben chatted amiably with Anna and she became increasingly relaxed. When they were still a few miles from their destination, she suddenly said, 'I hope you won't think I'm being impertinent, sir, but is there any chance that you'll be marrying Miss Deirdre and bringing her to Tregarrick?'

'No chance at all, Anna. In fact, I think she'll soon be announcing her engagement to Charles Congreve – or Viscount Congreve, as he is now.'

'Fancy! Miss Deirdre becoming a Viscountess! She'll like that, I've no doubt. So will Lady Tresillian.'

'Does it disappoint you that you won't be working for Miss Deirdre at Tregarrick?'

'Oh no, sir. Not at all. I'm very pleased . . .' There was a slight hesitation and then Anna said, rather more hesitantly, 'Not so much for me, sir – but for you.'

'Oh! And why is that?' Ben turned towards her, showing immediate interest.

Anna's cheeks had become scarlet and she said, 'I'm sorry, sir. I'm speaking very much out of turn. I shouldn't have said anything at all.'

'Now, Anna! You've said so much, you can't just leave me to *guess* what you might have said. Besides, I doubt if either of us will ever see Miss Deirdre again.'

Ben tried to look stern, but failed miserably and grinned instead. 'Oh, come on, Anna. If you've a nice juicy piece of gossip, don't keep it to yourself.'

Still hot-cheeked, she said hesitantly, 'Well, sir, there were a great many rumours about her and the husband of a tutor she had a year or so back. The servants would say that he taught her a lot more than his wife – and it wasn't how to read and write!'

After hesitating once more, the next words came out in a rush. 'There have been others too, sir. Too many for them all to be brushed aside as no more than servants' gossip. If you'll pardon me for saying so, I think you're well to be out of all that.'

'Yes, Anna, I think you're right. I *am* well to be out of all that.'

They rode on in silence for a while before she said, 'Excuse me for asking, sir, but am I likely to be cooking for a Mrs Retallick before too long?'

'That's a good question, Anna. The truth is, I don't know. I'd like to think so, but nothing has been said yet. Would you like to be cooking for a *Mrs* Retallick?'

'I don't mind, sir. I'll be happy doing whatever pleases you. If it wasn't for your quick thinking on the night of the fire I don't suppose I'd be working for anyone right now. I owe you more than I'll ever be able to repay and I won't ever forget it, you can be sure of that.'

Ben did not expect Lily to learn about his move to Tregarrick until she returned to work at Josh and Miriam's house on Monday morning. He went to Ruddlemoor, as was usual, hoping she might find some excuse to come and see him there. If not, he would call in to see her at the Gover Valley house that morning.

Jo was at her desk in the office, but hardly bothered to reply when he asked about the weekend she and Lily had spent at Camborne.

'It was fine.'

Ben waited for some amplification of the curt response, but none came. 'Did Lily have a good time?'

Jo shrugged, 'You'll need to ask her that yourself.'

'I will, but I don't know when I'll be seeing her. I'm not living in the

Gover Valley now. I moved out on Saturday. I've got my own place now – Tregarrick. You'll have to come and see it some time.'

'Yes.'

Ben was puzzled by her attitude. It was as though she was angry with him for some reason. Or perhaps it was because the weekend had not gone as well as she had been expecting. In a bid to find a reason for her coolness towards him, he asked, 'Was Pippa happy to see Lily?'

'Yes. She's very fond of Lily.'

'I expect Sam Doney was pleased to see Lily too?'

Jo glanced up at him briefly, but he could read nothing from her expression. 'He made us both very welcome.'

'He would. Well, I'm glad you both had such a good time.'

Ben left the office more convinced than ever that he had offended Jo in some way. He could not for the life of him think how. But he soon had something else to think about.

Captains Rowe and Bray were approaching the office, talking earnestly together.

'Is something wrong, Jeremiah, or are you just paying a social visit to Ruddlemoor?'

'I've come here hoping to see you. I think that Union man, Kendall, has been stirring up the men at Varcoe. I was told this morning that he's been at the works over the weekend. Last night some of the night-shift men broke off work to hold a meeting.'

'What was the night-shift captain doing to allow it to happen?' asked Ben, angrily.

'He's sick. He was admitted to hospital on Saturday morning. I'm convinced Kendall came to the works to speak to the men, even though no one wants to say anything about it. I don't know what he said, but the men are fired up about Eddie Long. They say he's being victimised for falling foul of you. They also want increased money for working at night and are demanding full recognition of their Union.'

'Isn't it enough for them that they all have work to go to, Jeremiah? What would they do if I stopped the night-shift?'

'That might be the best thing we could do. We brought in a lot of new men to work nights. They haven't the loyalty towards you and the Varcoe works that most of our day men have.'

Speaking for the first time, Captain Bray said, 'We're likely to have trouble with the night-shift at Ruddlemoor for the same reasons.'

'We'll have to try to nip this in the bud. In the meantime tell all the shift captains to keep Kendall out. He's trouble and we can do without that right now. Our men are being paid more than anyone else and I couldn't put wages up any more even if I wanted to. It would cause discontent throughout the industry – and that would mean pits closing. No owner can afford to run at a loss – and most are coming dangerously close to it. We've pushed prices up as far as we dare. It's already

413

caused demand to drop. It will stay low until the price rises work their way through.'

'That reminds me of another piece of news you could possibly do without,' said Captain Rowe. 'I think I've discovered where the cheap clay that's reaching Charlestown harbour is coming from. It's going through the Smith works and being sold off by the Tresillian Estate.'

Ben shrugged. 'They have quite a lot stock-piled there. Lady Tresillian's entitled to get what she can for it. It's annoying, but not disastrous. The stocks won't last for ever.'

'They might if what I've heard about it is true. I've heard that three out of every four loads supposed to be coming from Smith works are in fact from the stockpile in General Grove's works.'

'Do you believe that?'

Jeremiah Rowe nodded his head without saying a word.

'He must need money desperately to want to sell at a reduced price. All right, leave me to deal with that. Remember what I said about Kendall. Keep him out. I'm going to have a word with Jethro Shovell. We'll see if we can't get Kendall shifted from St Austell permanently.'

Chapter 62

Jethro was no more helpful than he had been when Ben had tried to enlist his support during the Smith works dispute.

Sitting in the front room of the Shovell house, he said, 'I'm sorry, Ben. As I told you before, Simon Kendall has signed up these men for his Union. I can't interfere in any way.'

'How would it constitute "interference"? I thought the whole concept of a Union was to take care of the interests of its members? How can it possibly be in their interests if they are persuaded to take action that will affect the livelihoods of hundreds of men? It doesn't make any sense at all.'

'I don't think things are quite as serious as that, Ben . . .'

'That's what you said before I closed down the Smith works. You've got to be realistic, Jethro. So has Simon Kendall. At the moment there isn't enough profit in the clay business to make it worthwhile coping with the problems of a dissatisfied workforce. If I were to raise my wages, the other owners simply couldn't afford to follow suit. Some would have to close and that would put men out of work. Most of my problems at the moment seem to be with my night-shift, so if they give trouble I shall simply cease operating shift working. That will mean the loss of another two or three hundred jobs. Are you telling me this is what the Union wants?'

'It's not the Union but the men who decide what they want,' replied Jethro, lamely.

'I don't believe that,' retorted Ben. 'It's my opinion that if the Union didn't interfere they would take any complaints they had to their captain. He'd speak to me and we'd sit down and talk things over. After airing our different views we'd reach a solution. But that's not the way Kendall's playing it.'

He stood up to leave, feeling he had wasted his time by coming here. 'You've disappointed me, Jethro. My grandfather has always sung your praises, saying you are a man who's been prepared to go through fire and water for the sake of the men you've represented in the past. He's admired you for that and, through him, so have I. Perhaps you've been doing it for too long. The water has finally put out the fire.'

With this parting shot, Ben left the house. He was at the gate when he met Lottie Shovell coming in.

She looked tired and drawn, but when she saw Ben, she said, 'You're just the man I want to speak to. Come inside while I put this basket down.'

'I've just had words with Jethro. I don't think I'll be particularly welcome in your house for a while.'

'Then we'll talk here.'

The tone of Lottie's voice puzzled Ben as much as had Jo's manner. Her next words did nothing to solve the mystery of their attitude towards him.

'What's been going on between you and our Lily?'

'I don't know what you're talking about. Nothing has been going on.'

'Don't lie to me. I've never seen our Lily as upset as she was last night. She didn't get that way all by herself. Besides, she said you were to blame.'

Thoroughly bewildered, he said, 'What's the matter with everyone today? I met Jo in the Ruddlemoor office and *she* behaved as though she wished I wasn't there. Now *you're* accusing me of something that's never happened. I haven't seen Lily since Friday morning. Ask Jo what happened when they were at Camborne this weekend. If Lily's upset then the cause probably lies there. Anyway, why don't you go to the Gover Valley and ask her what's wrong?'

'She's not at the Gover Valley. She's gone away.'

Ben looked at Lottie, not understanding. 'What do you mean, she's "gone away"? Where's she gone?'

'If she'd wanted you to know, she'd have told you.'

'But . . . I want to sort this out.' Ben was thoroughly confused. 'I bought Tregarrick because of Lily . . .'

'You're very good at buying things, Ben Retallick – but you certainly can't buy our Lily! She was a very unhappy girl last night. I can't believe you don't know the reason why. But, whatever the truth of it, she's gone away to get things sorted out in her own mind. If there's anything you ought to know when she's done that, I'm sure she'll tell you.'

Ben left the Shovell house feeling that troubles had been heaped on him that morning in unfair profusion. He wanted to find out more about Lily, but needed time to think and so returned to Tregarrick.

In the library, which was already his favourite room, he sat down in a bid to think things out. He had not been here long before Anna came in. Behind her was the housekeeper, showing tight-lipped disapproval of having a cook come through the house to find the master.

'I thought I'd come and tell you I've made a hot-pot 'specially for you, sir. I couldn't do very much more because we're going to need to get in a lot of stores. There's practically nothing in the larder.'

'That's all right, Anna. You go out and order whatever it is you need

416

and tell the tradesmen to deliver it. I suppose I'd better open accounts with them.'

'Very good, sir. Would you like me to serve up your lunch now? You look as though you could do with it?'

Ben's lunch was served up by Anna because they had not yet employed a maid capable of serving. It was a task that fell below the dignity of the housekeeper.

'That was an excellent meal,' he declared when he had finished. 'In fact, so far it's been the only bright spot in my day.'

The stern housekeeper had been standing in the doorway during this conversation. When Anna had left the room, she said to Ben, 'If you don't mind my saying so, sir, that young cook is far too familiar. I believe you saved her life in a fire when she was working at Tresillian House?'

'I helped her when her clothing caught fire. I'm not certain I saved her life.'

'All the same, it's not a healthy state of affairs when a young master shares his house with a servant who is over-grateful to him. If you're not careful you'll have folk talking about you. It's something of which dear Mr Varcoe was particularly careful.'

The housekeeper left Ben with the realisation that he still had much to learn about life in England.

After his meal, Ben decided he would call on Miriam and Josh. He found his grandfather working in the garden, weeding around a bed of flowers.

'Go inside, Ben. I'll be with you in a minute, I just want to finish this first. I daren't let the handyman loose in the flowerbed. He thinks that if a plant isn't a vegetable then it should be pulled up and tossed away – and these are your grandmother's prize blooms.'

Inside the house Miriam was at work stitching a cushion cover. She seemed pleased to have an excuse to put it aside and greeted Ben with, 'Hello, young Ben. How's that house of yours?'

He made a despondent gesture. 'Nothing seems to have gone right since I moved in there. I came here to see if you could tell me where Lily might have gone?'

It seemed to him that Miriam immediately went on the defensive. 'I haven't seen her since she returned from Camborne and went off to Tregarrick to see you.'

'She went to Tregarrick? I didn't see her there. What time was this?'

'I'm not certain. Half-past three? Four o'clock, perhaps.'

'I wasn't at home then, I'd gone off to fetch the girl I've taken on as cook. But the housekeeper never said anything about anyone calling. Mind you, she's getting on a bit and might well have forgotten.'

A sudden thought came to Ben. 'You don't think Lily was over-awed by the size of the house?'

'I wouldn't have thought so, but I wouldn't really know.'

417

Ben thought she was being particularly vague. 'You've no idea at all where Lily might have gone? Lottie hasn't said anything to you?'

'I've already told you, Lily never returned here after leaving to go to your house . . .'

At that moment there was the sound of someone stamping on the mat at the back door. Miriam called, 'Josh! Take off those muddy boots before coming in this house.'

They could hear him grumbling and Miriam said, 'That's the trouble when he's been gardening. We finish up with more earth in here than outside.'

'Will you let me know if you hear anything of Lily?' Ben persisted.

'I'll see.' Miriam was non-committal. 'If the girl doesn't want to see you then she probably has her reasons.'

'Unless I find out what they are then I can't possibly do anything about them,' Ben persisted, but at that moment Josh entered the room in his stockinged feet.

'It's a sorry state of affairs when a man's dictated to in his own home. I suppose I'll need to make my own cup of tea too, now that Lily's gone gallivanting off to the-Lord-only-knows-where?'

'You've never had to do it yet,' declared Miriam. 'And you're too old to make a start now. Sit down and I'll make tea for you – and for you too, Ben.'

As she left the room, Josh lowered himself slowly and stiffly into his chair, saying, 'It beats me why young Lily needed to rush off somewhere as she did. From what I heard, your grandma and Lottie are saying it's got something to do with you, but I don't suppose you know any more about it than I do?'

'I'm totally bewildered,' confessed Ben. 'But I'll find out – and I'll find her too.'

'Good! Now, I believe you've got other things on your mind?'

'That's right. Simon Kendall's been stirring up trouble again. The Varcoe works are his target this time. He's been talking to the night-shift. He might have spoken to some Ruddlemoor men too, but I don't think he's been inside the works there. It seems he's using Eddie Long's arrest as an excuse to make trouble for me.'

'Why? Eddie is hardly every man's idea of a hero.'

'Probably not, but he's a local man who was crippled fighting for his country. I'm the villain who's come from South Africa and bought control over the lives of a few hundred Cornishmen. It's only natural that their sympathies should lie with Eddie Long. I can accept that. What I can't understand is why they should blindly follow Simon Kendall when he's leading them straight over a sheer cliff.'

'It's always been that way here, Ben. There's a stubbornness in Cornishmen that won't let them listen to reason once they've made up their minds about something. Have you spoken about it to Jethro?'

'Yes, and I might as well have saved my breath.'

'Then there's not much I can do for you, Ben. The men who worked for me would listen to anything I said to them, but I can't influence the new men you've taken on. I'm afraid this is a problem that's beyond me. Do you have anything in mind?'

'If things go on the way they are, there's only one thing to do, however galling it will be for me personally. I'll return to day working only. It will reduce profits to a minimum, and output will fall so much I won't be able to dictate terms to the other owners. It will also put a great many men out of work – but it's their doing, not mine. If they want to follow Simon Kendall then he'll need to pay them. I'll not employ men who are more ready to do his bidding than mine.'

Chapter 63

The morning after his talk with Josh, Ben arrived at the Ruddlemoor office to find a grim-faced Captain Bray waiting for him.

'Have you heard the news? Eddie Long's been declared innocent by the courts.' The Ruddlemoor captain imparted the news before Ben had time to greet him. 'He appeared before the magistrates yesterday afternoon. They said there was no case to answer.'

Ben was shaken. 'But . . . he's as guilty as hell!'

'True. I don't doubt the magistrates knew that too – but who did he defraud?'

'James Smith, of course.'

'Exactly – but no one knows where James Smith has gone, so there's no complainant. It's not good news, Ben. Some of the men are saying it's proof that Eddie Long *has* been victimised. As you might guess, Simon Kendall has been making the most of it.'

'What do you think the men are likely to do?'

'I don't know. All my news is second-hand. It's the night-shift men who have been got at by Kendall. It seems to be spreading, though. At first it was only Varcoe, but I believe it's Ruddlemoor too now. Production wasn't what it should have been last night and it's been dropping at Varcoe for a few nights.'

'Very well,' said Ben. 'You and Jeremiah call in the captains of the night-shifts. They're more likely to talk to you than they would to me. Find out everything you can. I want to know where all this talk is taking place; where they're meeting; what the men are *really* thinking – and what it is they're hoping to gain from all this.'

Captain Bray nodded. 'There's one other thing. Tessa hasn't come to work this morning. I think Jo's quite concerned about her. She said Tessa was all right last night when she and Frank Trudgeon called to take her out for a drink before Frank went to Varcoe for the night-shift.'

'I'll go and speak to Jo.'

She was writing out a notice when Ben entered the office. She looked up, then quickly returned her attention to her work.

'Captain Bray says you're concerned for Tessa?'

'Yes, she hasn't come in this morning.'

'Is there any special reason why you should be concerned? It could just be that she isn't feeling well.'

Jo shook her head. 'I was with her last night. She was very worried about Eddie Long being freed by the magistrates. He's a very vindictive man and knows it was her who told you how he'd been altering the accounts and taking money.'

'I'll go and see her, make sure she's all right.'

Jo nodded. Ben was about to leave the office when he stopped and asked a question. 'Did something happen when you and Lily were at Camborne that might have upset her?'

'Nothing at all. She was perfectly happy until she got back to St Austell.'

'What happened then to upset her?'

'I would have thought you'd know the answer to that! She came to Tregarrick to see you.'

'So I've been told, but I wasn't there. I didn't see her.'

'No, you were with your fine friend at Tresillian.'

Now, at last, Ben thought he was getting to the heart of the mystery of Lily's disappearance.

'Who told you that?'

'Your housekeeper told Lily.'

'I doubt if she said I was with Deirdre. Lily probably jumped to that conclusion.'

'Are you saying you *weren't* with Lady Tresillian's grand-daughter?'

'That's right, and I doubt whether I'll ever see Deirdre again. She's getting married very soon. I wasn't even at Tresillian House. I'd gone to the lodge to collect the girl who was burned in the fire they had at the big house. She's come to work at Tregarrick as my cook.'

'Oh!'

Ben realised from Jo's expression of dismay that he had stumbled upon the truth. 'Did Lily believe I'd gone to see Deirdre?'

Jo nodded.

'And it mattered enough for her to decide to go away somewhere?'

'It mattered a great deal to her, Ben. You see . . .' Jo was anxious to make amends now the truth was out. 'Sam and I get along very well. The weekend at Camborne was really a sort of trial, I think. To see how I fitted in at his home. With Pippa, and his family. I believe . . . I hope, he'll ask me to marry him.'

Now it was Ben's turn to realise that he too had made a mistake. 'I thought Sam was keen on Lily!'

'I believe Lily wanted you to think that. At first, anyway, but she reached some sort of decision this weekend. That's what she went to tell you as soon as we got back.'

'And, instead, she was told I was at Tresillian with Deirdre?'

'Yes. It hit her very hard, Ben. I've known Lily since she was a small girl and I believe this affected her more than anything I've ever known before. She's a girl who doesn't make up her mind in a hurry. When she

421

does, it's because she's thought about it very carefully and deeply and knows it's what she really wants. That's what's happened here.'

'Do you know where she's gone? Where I can find her?'

Jo shook her head. 'I'm sorry, Ben.'

'I'll find her. But if she gets in touch with you first, then let her know the truth. You can also tell her I've bought Tregarrick for her – and because of her. She'll know why.'

Tessa opened the door to Ben's knocking, and he thought he had never seen a more frightened girl.

'I came to see you because Jo was worried about you. She thought there might be more wrong with you than just not feeling well.'

'There is.' Tessa put her head outside the door and looked both ways before saying, 'Come in. Ma is working cleaning someone's house and I'm on my own. I don't mind telling you, I'm scared.'

'Why?'

Ben asked the question as he entered the house and the door was closed behind him.

'I can answer that in two words. Eddie Long.'

'Why? Because he was cleared by the magistrates yesterday?'

'No, because he was waiting here for me when I returned home last night after being out with Jo and Frank Trudgeon.'

'He was here? What did he do?'

'He didn't *do* anything. Not then, he didn't, but he said he was going to because I'd pointed out to you what he'd done in the Smith works ledger. I told him I wasn't scared of him – that's when he pulled out the gun from underneath his coat.'

'A gun? What sort of gun?'

'One of those long-barrelled things. A shot-gun? He said he'd use it on me.'

Ben was seriously alarmed now. 'What did you do?'

'I kicked his crutch from under his arm and he fell down. Then I ran indoors.'

'Good for you. But I think we ought to tell the police in St Austell about this.'

'No! It was telling the police about him falsifying the ledger that started all this in the first place. I don't want anything more to do with them. All I want is to stay clear of Eddie Long until he starts behaving normally again.'

'Right. Well, I suggest you stay home for today. Tomorrow, Captain Bray will come here to take you to work. He'll bring you back here in the evenings too. I don't think Eddie will do anything as long as someone else is around.'

'I hope you're right – but there is one more thing.'

'What's that?'

'He threatened me and I believe he's serious, but that wasn't all. He said he'd get *you* too. That when he did you'd either scurry back to South Africa or be lying in a grave, here in Cornwall.'

Chapter 64

At two the next morning the Varcoe night-shift walked out. They made their way to Ruddlemoor and, after a noisy encounter with the men working there, half the Ruddlemoor night-shift joined their ranks.

Captains Bray and Rowe came to Tregarrick at six o'clock that morning to appraise Ben of the situation. Their insistent banging on the door woke Anna and the housekeeper.

Such emergencies did not fluster Anna. She immediately set to and cooked breakfast for Ben and his two works captains. As the men ate, they told Ben what had been happening.

'What is it the men are asking for?'

'The reinstatement of Eddie Long and an extra five shillings a week for the night men.'

'They have no chance of winning either demand,' said Ben scornfully. 'Where are the night men now?'

'Most of them are hanging around the gates of Varcoe,' said Captain Rowe. 'But there's probably a hundred or so outside Ruddlemoor. They obviously intend intimidating the day workers when they come on at seven o'clock.'

Ben looked up at the large grandfather clock standing in a corner of the breakfast room. It was now half-past six.

'We'll be there to stop them,' he said grimly. 'But we're going to need some help. Jeremiah, you go to St Austell police station and try to round up some constables. Jim and I will go to Ruddlemoor and see if we can get the day shift started.'

The howling of the men gathered outside the Ruddlemoor Works gate was a blood-curdling sound, but Ben was unperturbed. 'It almost makes me feel at home,' he said to the ashen-faced Ruddlemoor captain who walked beside Ben's horse. 'But the Matabele tribesmen could teach them a thing or two. Their enemies have been known to drop dead when they set up a shout like that.'

The workers bunched together to block the path of the works owner and captain as they approached. Ben brought his horse to a halt when it was still several lengths from the men.

'You men are out of order blocking the way to the works,' he said, evenly. 'You'd be well advised to move out of the way quietly and make no attempt to interfere with either the work, or with the Ruddlemoor workers. I've asked the police from St Austell to come here, but I would much prefer it if you were gone by the time they arrived.'

His reply was another howl, this time signalling derision.

Ben shrugged. If the men would not move in response to his appeal, he would need to play for time, pending the arrival of the St Austell police.

'What's all this nonsense about? You're already the highest paid clay workers in the district. What else do you want?'

'Take Eddie Long back,' someone called from the rear of the crowd. 'An extra five shillings a week for night men,' called another. Both shouts were greeted with enthusiastic agreement from their colleagues.

There were a number of other, less coherent demands and Ben said, 'Do you have a spokesman to set out the demands for you?'

His question was greeted with more derision and someone shouted, 'There are no spokesmen. We're all in this together.'

'Please yourself. I have no intention of staying here conducting a shouted conversation with a crowd of men who have no leader and no clear idea of their demands.'

'Eddie Long's job given back to him and an extra five shillings are good enough for a start,' called one of the men who had spoken before.

'I suggest you all go away and think of something else,' said Ben when the men's cheers had died away. 'Eddie Long will never work for me, and extra money is out of the question right now.'

His statement was greeted with renewed derision and Ben said, 'If you care to employ an accountant I'll be quite ready to give him access to my account books. There is no money to spare for any increase in pay.'

'An accountant would side with you,' called one of the men in the crowd. 'Simon Kendall says . . .'

'Simon Kendall knows no more about clay working than anyone else from London. I've made you an offer. I suggest you go back to work tonight and think about it. If there's no clay worked at Varcoe tonight then I'll stop shift working altogether. There'll be only day work in future at both Varcoe and Ruddlemoor.'

His words brought an angry response from the listening men, but Ben was already urging his horse forward. 'Make way there, please, I want to go in to Ruddlemoor.'

Most of the men moved from his path, but a few were reluctant to allow him through. It was one of these who, as he passed by, pulled a nail from his pocket and jabbed it viciously into the flanks of the horse.

The pain caused it to rear, throwing Ben from the saddle. As its hooves flailed, it downed two of the men. It was the signal for violence to erupt all around horse and fallen rider.

Ben and Captain Bray were kicked and punched to the ground,

although even as his senses were reeling, Ben was aware that as many men were trying to save him from the blows of their fellows, as were actually attacking him.

He had no idea how long the violence lasted before there were whistles blowing and half-a-dozen policemen waded into the tangled crowd. Batons flailing, they cleared a path to Ben and his works captain.

'Are you all right, sir?' It was the police sergeant who had attended the troubles at the Smith works and Ben nodded his head gratefully. Beside him, Jim Bray rose to his feet, brushing dirt from his clothes but otherwise unhurt.

'Let's get you inside, sir, and get someone to look at that forehead. It doesn't seem too serious, but it is bleeding rather a lot.'

Not until now did Ben realise that he had been cut just above his left eye and blood was running down and obscuring his vision.

Later, as Jo dressed Ben's cut eye, she recalled that she had once done the same for Darley, when he had been injured by men who had tried to rob him of the Ruddlemoor payroll.

'You must ask Lily about it,' she said, unthinkingly. 'She was there and did her share to save the money, as I remember.'

'I recall it well,' said the sergeant, unexpectedly. 'I was a young constable at the time. It was one of the most serious crimes we'd ever had to deal with in these parts, at that time.'

The policeman shook his head ruefully. 'But at least that was a fight for a purpose. I can't see no sense in this at all. Any man who has a living wage today should think himself lucky. There's a great many down Camborne and Redruth way who'd be pleased to be taking home any money at all.'

'What's going to happen now?' asked Jo.

'We've made one or two arrests outside the gates. They'll be charged with making an affray. Tonight I'll have a couple of my men here and at Ruddlemoor. There shouldn't be any trouble and they'll do their best to see that any men who want to work have the opportunity to do so. More than that I can't do. Will you be meeting the men and discussing their grievances with them, Mr Retallick?'

'I don't think there's anything to be gained by it, Sergeant. They have no spokesman and seem to think that they only have to shout loud enough to get what they want.

'They certainly won't succeed in having Eddie Long reinstated, no matter how loud they shout . . . Thank you, Jo.'

Ben stood up as she completed dressing the wound on his forehead.

'Ah! I'm glad you've brought Eddie Long up in conversation,' said the police sergeant. 'Perhaps you'd let me know if you see him anywhere? I want to question him about the theft of a shotgun and ammunition from the house of someone with whom he's acquainted. I don't think there's any doubt it was him who did it. Quite apart from the theft charge, I'll not rest easy thinking there might be a shotgun in the hands of a man as unstable as Eddie Long.'

Chapter 65

Ben went to the Ruddlemoor and Varcoe works that evening to ensure there were no more ugly scenes similar to the one in which he had been involved that morning.

The police had turned out in force for the same reason but there was no trouble. Only half of the night-shift at Ruddlemoor turned up for their duties. At Varcoe no one entered through the works gates.

As Ben silently sat his horse to one side of the men gathered outside the gates, a number of them came up to apologise for the violence of the morning. One of them was Frank Trudgeon.

'Only a few of the men are causing trouble, Mr Retallick. But once started it's not easy to bring it to an end. I know the men involved, and me and a few others think we'd be better off without them. If you want their names when this is over, I'd be happy to give them to you.'

'Thank you, Frank,' said Ben. 'But for now I'd like you to stay close to Tessa. Have you seen her today?'

'No. I waited for her to finish work this afternoon. She must have left early, or something.'

'She hasn't been in today.' Ben told Trudgeon of the threat made to her by Eddie Long.

The young man was alarmed. 'She needs to take it very seriously, Mr Retallick. You too. Once Eddie has a grudge against someone it becomes an obsession. Times like this I wonder whether or not he's normal. You take care, Mr Retallick. I'll go and find Tessa now and not let her out of my sight until all this is over. I might take her back to my home and let her stay with my ma. I doubt if Eddie will look for her there.'

'That's probably a very good idea. Well, it looks as though there are enough constables to deal with anything that might happen here. I think I'll go home. It's been a long, hard day.'

By the time Ben arrived at Tregarrick the aged housekeeper had been in bed for a couple of hours, but Anna was still up.

She was very concerned about the wound on his forehead and made him sit down while she examined it and put fresh ointment on it from the medicine kit she kept in her own room.

When it was done, she said, 'You go and pour yourself a drink now,

428

sir, while I cook you some nice steak I got special for you today. It won't take long and you look as though you could do with some sustenance in you.'

Ben would rather have gone straight to bed, but Anna was very concerned for him and he did not want to disappoint her. It was quite obvious this meal was important to her.

It took a little longer than half-an-hour to produce, but it was every bit as good as she had promised. When it was over, Ben sat back in his chair and said, 'Anna, I think one of the best things I've done since I came to England is to take you on as my cook. You're an absolute wonder.'

She glowed under his praise and said, 'Well, you go off and get to bed now, sir, while I clean these things away and wash up.'

'You can leave them until the morning if you like, Anna. I don't expect you to do all the work around here.'

'I don't mind sir. Mrs Rodda took on a young girl as a general maid today. She'll be starting towards the end of the week. Things will be easier then. Anyway, I need to get things ready in the kitchen for breakfast. It won't take me a few minutes to have everything cleared away.'

Ben was on his way up the wide staircase when he heard a sudden crash of plates and clatter of cutlery. He thought Anna must have dropped something and was about to call out to her that it didn't matter, when she began shouting. 'Sir . . . Mr Retallick, sir. Come down, quick!'

Appearing in the entrance to the passageway, she said, 'There's a fire in the stables, sir. The flames are already going up through the roof. I saw it through the window on my way to the kitchen.'

Ben bounded down the stairs as Anna drew the bolts on the outside door, her fingers trembling. It was partly excitement, yet Ben knew she must be remembering another fire . . . at Tresillian House.

In spite of this, Anna was first out through the doorway, with Ben immediately behind her. The stables were at the side of the house but the reflection of the fire flickered on the trees and bushes flanking the turning space in front of the house.

Suddenly there was a deafening report as a gun was fired from close range. Ben felt a number of sharp pains in his neck and shoulder, as though he had been stung. At the same time, Anna was knocked back against him, as though swiped by an unseen giant hand. Ben caught her but was knocked off balance and as she slumped to the ground he stumbled to his knees, still holding her.

The action undoubtedly saved his life. A second shot blasted into the door frame above his head, scattering splinters around him and inside the hallway.

Laying Anna down on the wide, flat step, Ben leaped to his feet and lunged into the bushes close to the door. He had seen the flash from the second shot only feet away from the doorway.

He cannoned into the man holding the gun and knocked him off balance. There was a curse from the gunman and Ben recognised the voice of Eddie Long. At the same time, something turned beneath his feet.

Thinking it was the gun, Ben reached down and snatched it up. It was Eddie's crutch, dispelling any doubt he might have had about the murderous gunman's identity.

There was just enough reflected light from the doorway and the stable fire to make out Eddie as he sat on the ground. Ben swung the crutch viciously and struck him in the face, knocking him backwards. Then he threw the crutch with as much force as he could muster into the nearby trees.

Something glistened on the ground. It was the blue-steel barrel of the shotgun. This followed the crutch.

There was a moan from Anna, lying in the doorway, and Ben hurried back to her. Kneeling beside her, he said, 'Let's get you inside . . .'

'No! I hurt too much. I'm sorry, sir . . . just leave me be.'

'I can't do that.' Ben lifted her head gently and cradled her in his arms. Suddenly there were men running up the driveway from the road and he called to them.

'Here! Come here, quickly!'

'Your stables are on fire!' gasped one of the unseen men.

'I know – but one of you run to town and fetch a doctor urgently.'

'Why?'

'Just do it! This girl's been shot. She's hurt very badly.'

The stranger wanted to ask more questions, but something in Ben's voice prevented him and he hurried away.

There were more people running to the house now. The flames had been seen in St Austell. Someone informed him that the fire service had already been alerted but Ben hardly heard.

He was cradling Anna in his arms and she moaned again.

'It's going to be all right, Anna. I've sent for a doctor. He'll be here in a minute. Just hold on until he arrives.'

It was a stupid remark to make, but he was speaking in desperation. He could feel her blood warm on his hands and arms. She had caught the full blast of the shotgun in her chest and upper abdomen and was bleeding profusely.

Anna raised her head weakly and looked up at him. 'You'll not . . . be able to save me . . . this time, sir.'

'I *will*, Anna. I promise you. I *will*.'

He never knew if she heard his rash promise. She did not speak again.

A couple of policemen arrived before the doctor. One was the sergeant whom Ben had met on a number of occasions before this.

Still holding Anna, Ben told them what had happened and directed them to where he had left Eddie Long.

They found him almost immediately. As the doctor arrived, one of the policemen called out to him, asking him to have a look at the one-legged man.

'You'll deal with Anna first,' said Ben, fiercely. 'Eddie Long can wait.'

Lamps had been brought from the house and placed nearby. The indifferent light they cast made the blood that glistened on the step and on the front of Anna's dress appear as a sinister black stain.

The doctor crouched beside her. After checking her pulse, he lifted one of her eyelids, then gently closed it again. 'I'm afraid nothing can be done for her, Mr Retallick. The poor girl is already dead.'

'Are you quite sure?' Ben almost pleaded with the doctor, his voice sounding strange.

'Quite certain,' replied the doctor, sympathetically. 'But I see you're bleeding too. Perhaps we could go inside the house. I can probably deal with you more efficiently there.'

'What about Anna? We can't just leave her lying here on the step. She saved my life. She took the shotgun blast that was meant for me.'

'You haven't got off scot free, Mr Retallick. I'd say you've been hit by a number of shotgun pellets yourself.'

'You go on inside, Mr Retallick,' said the police sergeant, his voice more gentle than Ben had heard it before. 'Send out a sheet or something and I'll see that the young lady is covered respectfully before she's removed to the mortuary. This is a murder case now and we've arrested young Eddie Long. I'd like you to look at him later, doctor. I fear he has a broken jaw – but he'll keep until you've dealt with Mr Retallick.'

The rest of the evening passed in great confusion for Ben. There were statements to the police, while firemen saved what they could of the stables and Ben had a number of shotgun pellets removed from his neck and shoulder.

The St Austell doctor told him he was very, very lucky. The pellets taken from him had probably hit Anna first.

During the whole of this confusion, Mrs Rodda, Ben's housekeeper, was very much in evidence. She provided the sheet to cover Anna's body, organised women among the curious bystanders to make and carry tea to the firefighters, and fussed about Ben. Later still, when Anna's body had been carried to the mortuary, she had the steps scrubbed clean by the same women.

Eventually, in the early hours of the morning, the last of the firefighters left and a constable moved the remaining few bystanders away from the house.

431

The housekeeper brought Ben a drink as he sat in the study, in near darkness, trying to come to terms with all that had happened during that eventful and tragic night.

'Here, sir. The doctor said you were to take this before going to bed.'

'Take it away, Mrs Rodda. I don't want it.'

'It doesn't matter whether you do or don't want it. The doctor said you were to have it and I'll just wait here and make certain you do.'

The tone of her voice reminded Ben of his grandmother and he reacted in the same way as he would have done for her. He drank the doctor's potion.

It was not very long before he realised the drink was some form of sleeping draught. He climbed the stairs wearily, undressed and got into bed. His neck was painful and whenever he closed his eyes he could see Anna as she had been while he was holding her in his arms. Her face pale in the lamplight and her blood everywhere. He especially remembered the blood . . .

Then he lapsed into a drug-induced sleep that was mercifully dreamless.

Chapter 66

When Ben awoke the sun was high enough to have painted a frame around the heavy curtains at the bedroom window. He turned over and looked at the clock on the mantelshelf and was shocked to see that it showed half-past nine.

The movement brought pain to his stiff shoulder and neck – and memories of the night flooded back to him. His face contorted with the agony of remembering and he swung himself out of bed.

He washed and dressed himself gingerly. As he did so he thought he could hear voices downstairs, but did not particularly care. His attitude probably had something to do with the doctor's draught he had drunk the night before. It could not have worn off completely.

He made his way downstairs, feeling as though he had just completed a long day of physical work.

Mrs Rodda was passing through the hall as he gingerly negotiated the stairs. She stopped to watch him with increasing concern.

'You ought to have stayed in bed for the day, Mr Retallick. You've had a very nasty experience and the doctor said . . .'

'I thought I heard voices, Mrs Rodda?'

'You did. Captain Rowe, Captain Bray and that Jethro Shovell are sitting in your study drinking tea. I told them I didn't expect to see you this side of noon, but they insisted upon waiting. If you ask me, it's most unthinking of them to have come here at all at such a time. There's nothing that couldn't have waited, I dare say . . .'

'It's all right, Mrs Rodda. I'll go and speak to them – and thank you very much for all you did last night. You were a tower of strength.'

Successfully hiding the pleasure she felt, Mrs Rodda said, 'That's what housekeepers are for, Mr Retallick, but you'll need to find a younger woman to take on the post as soon as you can. I'm getting far too old to have to cope with too many nights like that.'

Ben believed there could never be another night like it, but he said nothing and made his way slowly to the study.

The three men seated around the room rose to their feet hurriedly when he entered, but he waved them to their seats again. The movement caught him off-guard and he winced as he reopened one of the incisions made by the doctor.

'Are you feeling all right, Ben?' The anxious question came from

433

Jethro. 'You look awful. I'd have come to see you in the night, but I think Lottie and me must have been the only ones in St Austell who didn't hear 'til this morning what had been going on during the night.'

'I'm all right. But what are you all doing here?'

The two clay captains looked at each other and Jim Bray said, 'I think we ought to let Jethro tell you first what he's been doing. What we have to say follows on from that.'

Ben looked at Jethro who appeared vaguely uncomfortable. 'It has a lot to do with what you said to me the last time we met, Ben. About a Union being formed to *help* the men and not merely to unite them in confrontation with the employers.'

Ben was not at all sure he had voiced those exact words. However, as they were in accord with what he believed, he did not contradict the other man.

Jethro continued, 'As you may know – or perhaps you don't – I've spent the greater part of my life persuading working men to join together in Benefit Associations and the like. I've also acted as their spokesman whenever they've needed one. As a result, I've gained a certain reputation amongst Union men around the country. Despite this, I've never tied myself down to any particular Union, although I've been asked to on a great many occasions.'

Ben frowned irritably. 'Is this relevant to anything, Jethro? I'm not concentrating terribly well this morning . . .'

'I'm sorry, Ben. To cut a long story short, I took to heart what you said to me and realised you were right. I believed that any caring Union would feel the same too – so I went to London and spoke to the officials of the Union that sent Simon Kendall to Cornwall.'

Jethro looked for a reaction from Ben to this startling news, but he said nothing.

'I had a very long meeting with them, Ben. It went on until well into the night, but I got what I wanted. I returned to St Austell with a letter for Kendall, recalling him to London.'

Ben did not share Jethro's enthusiasm. 'There will be other Kendalls. Men whose personal ambition outweighs the principle they are supposed to be upholding.'

'Not for a very long while.' Jethro spoke triumphantly. 'The officials in London persuaded me that if I *really* had the men's interests at heart then the best thing I could do would be to represent them here. They've appointed me the Union's representative for the whole of the clay-working area – and there are a lot of members, Ben, especially on the night-shifts both at Varcoe and Ruddlemoor.'

When Ben still failed to react as Jethro had hoped he would, the new Union representative said, 'It means I can – and will – order the men to return to work, Ben. If they have any complaints they can come to me and I'll discuss them with you. Not that I expect there to be any now.

The men have realised they are better off there than at any other works in Cornwall. They'll return to work right away. In fact, I believe it will come as a relief to them to be told that's what they should do.'

'He's right, Mr Retallick,' said Jeremiah Rowe. 'I had a deputation of men in to see me this morning. They've asked me to convey their deepest sympathies to you over the happenings of last night and for the part Eddie Long took in them.'

'The men at Ruddlemoor feel very much the same,' said Jim Bray. 'They're all ready to resume normal working again. You'll have a full night-shift on duty tonight at both works.'

'I'm not interested in whether they're ready or not to go back to work,' said Ben, unexpectedly. 'Am I supposed to feel *happy* because they've changed their minds about everything? Will any of that bring poor Anna back to life?'

'Nothing can do that, Ben, but you can't blame the men for what Eddie Long did . . .'

'I *do* blame them. Every one of them. Anna would have been alive today had they not supported Eddie Long and treated him as some sort of hero, instead of the criminal he really is.'

Captains Rowe and Bray exchanged concerned glances as Jethro persisted, 'Let what's happened fade into the past, Ben. The men have learned their lesson. I doubt if you'll ever have any industrial trouble with them again. They're thoroughly ashamed of themselves.'

'Good. But it changes nothing. I don't care how sorry they are. As far as I'm concerned they can all go back home and spend the rest of their days talking of what might have been had they come to their senses sooner.'

Thoroughly alarmed by Ben's intransigence, Jeremiah Rowe said, 'Does this mean you have no intention of resuming shift working for the two works?'

'It means far more than that, Jeremiah. You can go back to the works and send everyone home. You too, Jim. Both works will close as a mark of respect to Anna.'

Once again the two men exchanged glances, but this time it was dismay and not merely concern that they both felt.

'How long do you intend keeping the works closed, Ben?' Jethro shared the shock that his words had caused to his companions.

'I don't know. Certainly until Eddie Long is convicted of murder by the courts and goes to the gallows. It might even be longer. The way I'm feeling right now, I've had enough of the clay business and everyone who works in it. What I'd really like to do is walk away from it all and return to Africa. To Insimo. I've had enough.'

Chapter 67

In the Gover Valley, Miriam and Josh were sufficiently removed from St Austell not to have learned of all that had happened at Tregarrick during the night.

When Jethro and Lottie brought the news to them and Jethro repeated the conversation between Ben and himself, Miriam's first reaction was to demand that she be taken to Tregarrick immediately.

'We'll go to him, certainly,' said Josh. 'But before we do, let's decide what we can do to help him.'

'We don't need to talk about *that*,' declared Miriam with conviction. 'He'll come back here with us.'

'I doubt that very much,' said Josh, patiently. 'I think I've learned enough about young Ben to know that having folk about him is probably the last thing he wants at this moment. He's taken some very hard knocks these past few days. It must seem to him that the whole world is against him.'

'The men at both the works have expressed their sympathy and admitted they were in the wrong. If Ben lets bygones be bygones he'll have as loyal a work force as any in the whole of the clay country.'

'If I were Ben I'd be doing exactly what he's doing,' retorted Miriam. 'They had their chance to be loyal when he was providing work for them and food for their families – as well as paying them good wages. *They* deserve everything they're getting, but I'm not going to allow them to drive *my* grandson out of the country.'

'It wouldn't be so bad if he had someone with whom he could talk things over,' said Josh. 'Someone of his own age. It's a pity Lily ran off the way she did. She was the one he would talk to, and he'd listen to what she had to say.'

Miriam and Lottie both looked at each other and Miriam said, 'That's the answer! You've heard the truth of where Ben had gone when Lily went to see him on Sunday, Lottie?'

She nodded. 'Yes, Jo told me. He'd gone to pick up that poor girl who was shot last night. She was going to cook for him. Eddie Long will swing for her, that's certain. But from what someone told me, she saved Ben's life by going out through the doorway first. If she hadn't, it would have been him lying dead on the doorstep.'

'I don't even want to think about that, Lottie, but now we know that

Ben wasn't seeing that Tresillian girl, what are we going to do about putting things right between him and Lily?'

Miriam and Josh arrived at Tregarrick House with Josh driving them in the shay, pulled by their energetic little pony.

Ben was seated in his study, his gaze seemingly fixed on the trees outside the window.

'Ben! My poor boy.' Miriam advanced on him and as he stood up to greet her, she gathered him in her arms and hugged him to her. When she released him she looked critically at his bandaged neck and the padding beneath his shirt where the doctor had dressed his other wounds.

'How are you feeling?'

'I'm all right.' His pinched face and dark-ringed eyes belied the statement.

'All right is something you certainly are *not*,' she declared. 'Can I persuade you to come back home to the Gover Valley until you're better?'

Ben shook his head. 'I'm not very good company right now. I'd prefer to be on my own. I need to think things out.'

'Of course you do,' agreed Miriam soothingly. 'But you'll not reach any rational decisions about the future while you're here with the dreadful happenings of last night fresh in your memory. Your grandfather and I are going to take you to somewhere where you'll not be troubled by others. A place where you'll be able to think more clearly than anywhere else in the world. Believe me, Ben, as your grandfather will tell you, it's the one place I know where you can escape from the world and find the peace I'm quite certain you need right now.'

'I don't need to go anywhere, Grandma. I'll be all right here.'

'Oh no you won't! Now, Josh, you keep Ben company while I go to his room and pack a few things for him to take with him.'

When Miriam had left the room, Ben protested feebly to Josh, although he knew he had already lost the battle with his grandmother. 'I really *am* all right. I just need a day or two on my own, that's all.'

'I know, Ben. But trust your grandmother. She really does know what she's talking about, I can assure you.'

'Where am I going?'

'To Sharptor. To the house we still own there. Miriam's sister pops up from the village to keep it cleaned and aired for us. You really will find it more peaceful there than anywhere else and there'll be no one from the works bothering you. Walk about on the moor and you'll find the wind blowing away all your confused thoughts. It'll leave you seeing things the way they ought to be.'

Ben was unconvinced, but it was not long before Miriam returned to the study. 'I've packed all the things you're likely to need. They're in

437

the passageway outside Ben's room, Josh. You can bring it down for
him. I've also told the housekeeper to keep things together here while
you're away, Ben, so you needn't waste time worrying about anything
here while you're gone.'

'I still don't think all this is necessary . . .'

His argument was futile, and he knew it. He was still protesting when
he was in the shay and Josh was whipping up the horse to a trot on the
road that led away from St Austell.

438

Chapter 68

It took some hours to reach Sharptor, but the weather was fine and sunny. As they drove the last couple of miles hugging the edge of the moor, Ben grudgingly conceded that Miriam might have been right. The view from here was absolutely incredible. He felt that in this place his mind might just be able to break out of the shell that had closed about it during the past few days.

'There! I told you so,' said Miriam, triumphantly, when he confessed to his change of heart. 'But the best is yet to come. You'll be in the house on Sharptor looking out at this view every time you gaze from a window. I defy anyone to harbour bad thoughts when the Good Lord has provided so much beauty to be enjoyed.'

The house was all that she had promised and it had been kept neat and tidy. Miriam fussed about the rooms, putting his clothes away and peering into cupboards and drawers, but even she could find little with which to find fault.

'Doesn't this take you back many years, Josh? To the time when we moved in here on our return from Africa? If this young man can find himself again, as we did then, I'll know the magic is still here.'

Clutching Ben's arm, she led him outside. Pointing to a rocky outcrop surrounded by gorse on the side of the hill well up the slope from the house, she said, 'There's a small hideout in there. It's where your grandfather and I used to meet when we were children – and later, too. He taught me to write my name there. The day I did that, I was the proudest person in the world. There was little else to be proud about in those days. I'd never worn a pair of shoes until I was twelve. Then I took a bad beating from my pa when your grandfather and his family bought me a pair. I remember the shoes went on the fire and that hurt me even more than the beating.'

'Ben doesn't want to hear about things that went on all those years ago. They were special for us, not for anyone else.' The arm that Josh put about Miriam's shoulders softened his words.

'You're right, Josh, but they are happy memories – at least, they are now.'

Suddenly she looked at Ben from dark, bright eyes and was back in the present. 'All the same, pay a visit up there, Ben. For me, and for your grandfather too. Our old legs will never take us back there again,

439

but I'd like to think that you'd visited it for us.'

Ben looked up the hill to where the wind-smooth granite rocks protruded from a surrounding screen of yellow-flowering gorse. 'It's a promise. I'll probably go up there when you've gone. I don't feel like sitting in a house at the moment.'

'Good. We're going to leave you now and call in on my sister Patience before we go home. She lives in the village and will send up an evening meal for you while you're here. We'll also have supplies sent up from the village so you can make breakfast for yourself, and have a midday meal if you feel like something.'

'Thanks – and thank you both even more for caring enough to do all this for me.'

Miriam kissed him and gave him a warm hug. 'You've had a bad time, but it's over. Things are going to improve from now on.'

Josh shook Ben's hand and with a faint air of embarrassment said, 'It sounds foolish when said out loud, Ben, but you can believe what your grandma's said. The moor *is* a magic place. I found all I ever wanted here. I hope you might too.'

He watched and waved until the shay rounded a bend in the narrow track that led from the house. Then, without bothering to re-enter the house, he set off up the hill.

Once he paused to regain his breath and looked back. Below him was the old Sharptor mine. The engine-house was now little more than a ruin and there were holes in the roofs of the other buildings. Dotted about the landscape were other mines, their buildings in a similar state of decay.

Mining in this area was over – and yet there was not a forlorn air hanging over the moor. It was rather one of a serene contentment. As though the moor itself had decided it was time to bring centuries of mining to a close. To return to the tranquillity it had known in a time before the memory of man.

When he reached the gorse surrounding the rocky den, Ben could not at first find a way through. Then he noticed a faint, overgrown path that was capable of being traversed only on hands and knees.

For a moment he hesitated. Then he remembered his promise to Miriam. Dropping to the ground, he crawled through the narrow gorse tunnel. Needles pricked the palms of his hands and he became painfully aware that his wounded shoulder would give him trouble for some time yet.

When Ben reached the rocks and was able to stand up once more, he was glad he had made the effort. Here was the shallow shelter where Miriam and Josh had met so many years before. Theirs had been an adventurous, albeit a happy, life together.

For a few moments he wondered how things might have worked out had he and Lily met up here, he the son of a miner, she a barefoot, ragged urchin.

Perching himself on a rock, Ben found he commanded a breathtaking view that extended for perhaps fifteen miles across the wide Tamar Valley. With his back resting against a sun-warmed granite boulder, he absorbed some of the peace that had been absent from his life in recent days.

After a while, he found he was able to untangle part of the web of intrigue and actual hatred that had been woven by those about him and had tainted his own thinking.

He had left St Austell despising those who by their actions, or inaction, had been in no small measure responsible for Anna's death. Now he was able to think of others he had met. Frank Trudgeon; Jo and Tessa; the small, wide-eyed girl whose father had come to him seeking work; Anna . . . he quickly passed over the images her name conjured up . . . and then he thought of Lily. Where was she? What was she doing?

Seated here, with only the cry of a circling buzzard impinging upon his senses, he thought that he and Lily might have been able to resolve all their misunderstandings had they been able to share such a place as this.

He had no idea how long he remained in this secret place unravelling his tangled thoughts. The sun had sunk below the rim of the high moor behind him, although it still shone on much of the wide, patchwork plain through which flowed the River Tamar and its tributaries.

He wondered whether Miriam's sister had already been to the house with his supper. It would probably be a pasty. This seemed to be the staple food of the Cornish worker. At the clay works the men would heat them in the 'dry' with the fireman playing the part of cook.

Suddenly, Ben realised he could think of the men without rancour now. He began to think that Josh and Miriam *were* right. The moor might well be a magic place. A healing place.

Suddenly Ben heard a sound. It was probably an animal. A fox or perhaps a badger. He remembered Josh saying they were plentiful here.

Ben had never seen a badger and kept very still and quiet as whatever it was made its way through the same tunnel he had used to enter the den.

But this was no animal. A head of dark hair suddenly came into view – then Lily rose to her feet to stand before him!

'Hello, Ben.'

She spoke quietly and uncertainly, as though half-afraid of the reception she would be given.

For a long time, it seemed, he was too astonished to speak. Then he held out his arms. Not until he was holding her to him was he absolutely certain that this was not an apparition, conjured up by the moor.

After he had held her close for many minutes, it was time for questions and answers. The answers to his more immediate questions were easily answered. When she had believed the worst of Ben, Lily had come to stay with Patience. In these few days she too had discovered for herself the therapeutic qualities of the moor.

Today, before leaving for St Austell with Josh, Miriam had told her what Ben had been doing at Tresillian and of the tragic happenings since.

Later, holding Lily as they watched the shadows advancing across the Tamar Valley, Ben found he could close his eyes without conjuring up a vision of the last girl he had held in his arms.

'You know, I was beginning to believe this would never happen,' he said, a long time later.

'Then you should have brought me here before,' replied Lily. 'This is all we needed. Stars instead of someone else's roof over our heads. Let's stay here all night, Ben.'

That night, in the very place where Ben's father had been conceived, and where Lily's mother had found solace in the unhappy days of her childhood, another generation forged a bond. The troubled and as yet unknown years of the twentieth century lay ahead. But Ben and Lily were happy tonight in the knowledge that they would face those challenging years together.